WILL STARLING

a novel

Also by Ian Weir

Daniel O'Thunder

Will Starling

a novel

The Reckoning of WM. STARLING, Esq.,
a Foundling, concerning Monstrous Crimes and
Infernal Aspirations, with Perpetrators Named and
Shrouded Infamies disclosed to Light of Day, as set
down by his Own Hand in this year 1816.

IAN WEIR

GOOSE LANE EDITIONS

Edited by Bethany Gibson.
Cover and page design by Julie Scriver.
Skyline illustration by Chris Tompkins.
Paper texture by www.bashcorpo.dk.
Printed in Canada.
10 9 8 7 6 5 4 3 2 1

Library and Archives Canada Cataloguing in Publication

Weir, Ian, author
Will Starling: a novel / Ian Weir.

Issued in print and electronic formats.
ISBN 978-0-86492-647-0 (bound)   ISBN 978-0-86492-571-8 (epub)

I. Title.

PS8595.E47D65 2014   C813'.54   C2013-908079-1
C2013-908080-5

Goose Lane Editions acknowledges the generous support of the Canada Council for the Arts,
the Government of Canada through the Canada Book Fund (CBF), and the Government of
New Brunswick through the Department of Tourism, Heritage, and Culture.

Goose Lane Editions
500 Beaverbrook Court, Suite 330
Fredericton, New Brunswick
CANADA E3B 5X4
www.gooselane.com

To Jude and Amy, always;

and

In memory of my father

Prologue

LONDON
1st May, 1816

A man standing straddle-legged, pelvis outthrust and one-eyed lad in hand, braced on the lip of merd-urinous Fleet Ditch in the blackness of a cool spring night with an *aaaahhhh.* That's where it all began to turn — assuming that anything can really be said to begin anywhere, and isn't one great tangle of consequence snarling all the way back to Adam's first rumpety-bump with Eve. But that was the moment — right there — when an irrevocable step was took, which led to the next and then to the one that followed after, faster and faster, slip-sliding down a mountainside of feverish intentions 'til all at once the bottom had fallen away and there we were, plunging headlong and confounded to Perdition.

And there at the turning stands Dick Whycher.

Dick was a clerk at a ship chandler's. He'd been out on a spree with a mate of his, a carpenter's apprentice called Toby Fegen. They'd visited various boozing-kens in the winding streets by the river, and now they were stumbling homewards. Toby led the way, the light from his bull's-eye lantern lurching in the murk like the beacon on a ship at sea. The streets were slippery with rain from an earlier storm and Toby splashed through puddles.

"Half a second," Dick had announced, drawn up short by nature's call.

"I wouldn't, Dick," Toby warned, as he saw what his friend was about. "I would not do this. I've told you before."

Dick belched in reply, and rootled in his breeches.

That had been nearly a minute ago, for Dick Whycher was a prodigious pisser. It was a source of considerable pride to him, along with his teeth, which were largely unrotted. His hair was thinning, alas; but no man was ever perfect, and in any case Dick Whycher wore a hat, a low sloping affair that perched at a rakish angle as he gazed up into the night, listening to the splashing from below. The night was surprisingly clear, for London. The storm had blown itself out an hour ago and now there were stars, by God, twinkling down upon Dick Whycher pissing. It filled him with a sudden wonderment, as if something immense was being hinted to him about the universe and his especial place within it, which he might if just slightly more sober have grasped in an instant of blinding transformation.

"I know you don't believe me, Dick," Toby Fegen was saying darkly. "I'm just saying it's a Fact."

Toby had come up beside him, breeches firmly buttoned. A sailor had told him once of a creature like a tiny eel, with teeth, that lived in the rivers of somewhere treacherous such as Africa or possibly Peru, which would swim up the stream of them as pissed in the water and straight through the solitary eye of the breeches-adder, with consequences too shocking for any man to contemplate. The sailor knew a man this happened to, who died after three days of shrieking. Besides, it was Science.

Toby Fegen was not a learned man, but he knew about Science. This was a bold new age of discovery and Science was everywhere on the march, overturning new rocks each day and exclaiming at what wriggled underneath. There were men with telescopes looking at the stars, and men in balloons rising up towards heaven. And if there were microscopic eels in Africa or Peru, then Toby was not about to piss in Fleet Ditch. It was foetid and reeking and clogged with refuse, dead dogs and cats and rodents and worse, and God only knew what teeth might exist on any microscopic eel as could live in that.

"Jesus," Toby said abruptly.

"Eh?" said Dick, still gazing skyward.

Toby raised the bull's-eye for a better look. "Down there."

"What?"

"*There.*"

Dick peered.

A bundle of rags, or so he first assumed. Dimly illuminated beneath the dwindling arc of his waters, which sparkled in the lantern light. But it wasn't rags.

"Jesus Aloysius Christ," said Toby. "On a stick."

The man lay on his back, half sunk in ooze. A little man in a weskit that had once been red, with spindly legs akimbo, eyes wide and staring blindly up at whoever was pissing down. One arm was outflung, as if to grope for his spectacles, which poked up from the mire just out of reach. A cracked round lens caught the light and glinted.

Dick Whycher saw at once what must be done.

"Guy's Hospital," he said. "Across the bridge. We'll dredge him out and take him there. We'll take him to the surgeons."

"The man is dead! And not just dead, but murdered. Look —someone's gone and slit 'is throat!" In the lantern light it gaped in a dreadful grin. "We'll clear off, Dick, is what we'll do. Before someone comes by and supposes we 'ad somethink to do with it."

But Dick was clambering down into the ditch and calling for Toby to do likewise.

"Dick!" wailed Toby. "'Ee's long past needing of a Nospital —there's no surgeon in the world could be of use to 'im!"

"But *he's* of use to the *surgeons*, Tobe—and they'll pay. Four quid is the value on this one. Which is four quid more than you're worth, squeaking and flapping your arms. We'll take him to the Porter at Guy's Hospital. There's a door for it round the back."

"'Ow do you—?"

"Because I know it, Tobe. I once met a man, all right? Now give us a hand!"

Dick Whycher always seemed to know. He knew a man, or one who knew another man, or lived just round the corner from his cousin, and was according-wise stuffed full of the most remarkable bits of information from London's underbelly, sifted like coins from the sludge of the sewers. Now he was knee-deep in the ooze, squelching down to hoist the little man and snapping for Toby Fegen to make himself less useless.

For another moment, Toby stood rooted. It was horribly wrong, in every conceivable way. The man had been murdered and surgeons were ghouls and one instant of wretched misfortune was all it would take—a bleary-eyed Charley sloping round a corner, with a bull's-eye and a snort of surprise—for this to end with two necks in a noose and the Newgate Hornpipe for Toby and Dick. And that wasn't even taking account of the eels.

Four pound, on the other hand, was four pound.

With a gargle of desperate misgiving, Toby set down his lantern and slid.

Thus the turning began.

The monstrous re-enactment of a birth—so it must have seemed, if you'd been there in the darkness watching. Peering from the mouth of an alley, perhaps, with the rotting hulks of the buildings hemming you in like creaking old ruffians of evil intent, though what you'd be doing in such a wretched neighbourhood at such a time of night I couldn't say, a decent soul such as yourself. Two midwives cursing in the moonlight, knee-deep in slime. The twisted infant hauled upwards, pale and dripping. Then out of the ditch and away down the cobbles, the newly-born braced between the two of them, head lolling and toes dragging. Bound for the Death House and the slab and the surgeons, and one of them in particular. A man named Mr Dionysus Atherton, whose deeds—both prodigious and unutterable—are at the heart of all that follows.

And here I am at the end of it, scribbling these words by the stub of a candle in a small stone room, with St Paul's bell nearby counting out the days and hours that remain to me. A man might be moved to take stock, at such a moment. Reckon up the tally of a lifetime: the good deeds entered in one paltry desperate column — Christ, can there really be so few? — offset against all the sprawling ledgers of the small and mean and ill, with sheets to come, whole folios, of Opportunities Frittered/Squandered/Lost. A man might turn to prayer at such a moment. Just in case — cos you never know, do you? Perhaps there really is something beyond, though Meg Nancarrow said no — nothing but the darkness, she said, Old Night plummeting with vast black falcon's wings — and Meg was someone who should know the truth, better than any soul now living on this earth. A man at such a moment could begin to wail aloud in pure panic rising up, and desolation.

I will write as swiftly as I can. There is so very much to say, and such little time left in which to say it. I need you to know what Dionysus Atherton did. You must have the facts, and judge for yourself. What he did to Your Wery Umble Narrator, but most of all to others. To Bob Eldritch, rising from that table with a peacock scream, and Meg Nancarrow, and my poor friend Isaac Bliss. The awful deeds committed and the worse deeds done in consequence. The breaking of the very bonds that make us human, in the quest for being something more.

But once you've finished, you'll know the truth. I'll have achieved that much, at least. And I made my choices and did what I did, and have no right to be blubbering now.

If they ask you, tell them I smiled.

Part One

1

8th April, 1816
(Twenty-three days earlier)

The day had begun splendidly for Dionysus Atherton, though not so well for Ronald Peake.

Peake had a go at dying game. He tottered unassisted up the steps, and reaching the scaffold he raised his head and cried in quavering defiance to the multitude: "Soon I shall know the Great Secret!" But his nerve broke on the last syllable, and after that it was dunghill all the way, which was as much as anyone expected. Peake was a weedy little man, a poisoner. He took to caterwauling as Mr Langley the hangman tied up the halter and put on the white hood, and with his last uninterrupted breath was heard to cry out for his mother—which was dunghill as it gets, considering as his Ma was the one he poisoned. Then all words were gone with a hempen thud, and a great roar went up from the twenty thousand who had gathered outside Newgate Prison on this clear bright April morning.

Dionysus Atherton consulted his timepiece, and made a note: the subject dropped at one minute past eight.

The subject was now jerking like a fish on a line, since Mr Langley had not dropped him far, just the customary six inches. The rate of strangulation would depend upon several factors, none of which favoured Ronald Peake, whose weight—so Atherton had estimated with his practised eye —was no more than eight stone. Worse, Peake had no friends to offer financial encouragement, without which Mr Langley would not have waxed the rope. In the death cell Peake had broken down and admitted poisoning his mother, an elderly widow with whom he had lived throughout his adult life, on the grounds that she fed him slop. This revelation was detailed in his Last Dying Confession. Such a document was a time-honoured tradition at hangings, hastily printed on broadsheet and hawked about for a penny. The Revd Dr Cotton, spiritual adviser to the inmates of Newgate, was widely believed to be the source of the information, for which printers would pay handsomely.

At 8.04 the jerking ceased momentarily, before resuming with greater vigour.

Atherton stood in the very thickest of the crush. Here in the shadow of the gallows he was wedged in on all sides, which made it awkward to negotiate pencil and notebook. He might have bought a place in a shop window opposite, or upon a nearby balcony, amongst the young swells and the well-fed family groupings. There he might have observed unmolested, with keen scientific detachment. But that wouldn't prime the vital juices like standing with the throng. And nothing stirred the blood quite like a hanging.

"There is such life in it."

He had spoken aloud.

"Well, not f'much longer, ducks. But ent 'ee 'avin' a go! Dancing all the way to the churchyard, that one — 'ats off, there, you in front!"

A slattern, wedged by his elbow. Arched on tiptoes for a better glimpse, and eyeing him slantways.

"One of them scribblers, are you? Penny-a-line feller?"

Atherton chuckled by way of reply.

"No, then? No, you don't look the sort. Grubby little buggers, most of 'em. Wotcher doing then, 'andsome?"

"I am extending the range of human possibility."

She would have been quite fetching in her prime, with all her teeth and the dew of her youth upon her. Even now — two-and-twenty, at the least — she retained a cheerful fuckability. Her name, Atherton decided, should be Blossom.

"I got a room," said Blossom. "Not far. Extend something else f'yez, if you like."

Peake gave a twitch after some moments of dangling like an empty sack, and resumed thrashing. He was given up for dead at 8.12, and again at 8.17 and 8.33. All movement finally ceased at 8.48, and death was pronounced at two minutes past nine. But when the moment had actually come — or whether indeed it had come yet at all, as they cut him down and loaded him onto the cart — could not be said with certainty. Death's mechanism remained a mystery, despite all the advancements of Science. Dionysus Atherton knew that as well as any man in London. It was almost as great as the Mystery of what might come after.

*

Blossom's room was in Seacoal Lane, but they stopped in an alley nearby. It stank of piss and worse, but it was relatively private, and Blossom was duly encouraged onto her knees. Morning sun beamed in a warm shaft through the buildings as she tugged Atherton's breeches down about his thighs. There was nothing like it, he thought: sunlight upon his face, and an April breeze playing gently about the nethers, as Blossom bobbed briskly. Spreading his arms, he imagined himself upon a balcony in Rome, blessing multitudes.

Afterwards he gave her half a guinea. Whatever else he may have been, he was never mean with his purse. It wanted four minutes of ten when he arrived at Bowell and Son, in the warren of streets behind St Bart's Hospital. The sign above the door showed a painted coffin.

Peake was in the cellar, he was informed, the cart from Newgate having arrived some minutes earlier.

"How many minutes?"

The undertaker consulted his own timepiece. "Seven."

At 9.49 the clatter of hooves had been heard in the yard without, and at 9.51 the Subject had been unloaded. Yes, Mr Bowell assured the surgeon, these times were exact, Mr Bowell's timepiece being an instrument of great precision. It had been passed down from his grandfather to his father, both highly punctilious men, as was the present Mr Bowell.

Atherton frowned. The corpse cut down at 9.02, and in the cart by 9.04. Then another forty-five minutes before its arrival here, not half a mile away?

"Teeming humanity, Mr Atherton. The welter of the living. The cart must negotiate the crowd as it leaves the Event."

The undertaker gave a sigh, expressive of the ultimate futility of all mortal endeavour. His was a gaunt face with a blunt jaw and high cheek-bones, curiously reminiscent of a coffin. One wondered if he was born that way, or whether this was related to the phenomenon—well-known, though not Scientifically authenticated—by which owners came to resemble their dogs.

"Does Mr Atherton wish to view the Subject?"

He did, though he misliked those forty-five minutes. The delay would make no difference in the present case, since he intended no procedure upon this particular corpse beyond dissection—the customary carving-up in the reeking, shrieking charnel house at St Thomas's Hospital. But there were other procedures—there was One, in particular—for which he was gathering data and laying his plans. And forty-five minutes could well pose an obstacle, should he attempt it upon a corpse from the Newgate gallows.

"I will send my man round this evening to collect it," he said. "Keep it here for me 'til then."

The undertaker inclined his coffin-shaped head. This was no trouble; and even if it were, trouble would be gladly taken on Mr Atherton's behalf. Mr Atherton had always been kind, very generous indeed. There was a twitching of the cheeks, followed by a painstaking elevation of the corners of the mouth, as though Mr Bowell's smile were an outcome achieved via levers and pulleys.

"And how is the boy?" asked Atherton.

The smile creaked into an expression of regret.

"The apprentice, you mean? Still amongst the living, Mr Atherton. Still with us in this vale of tears. But he declines."

The boy's name was Isaac Bliss. He was crouched over a work-bench as they came down the stairs, his back bowed like a barrel hoop.

The workshop was a cellar room, dank and smelling of sawdust, with planks of wood stacked against one wall and a coffin taking shape upon a trestle. Light struggled in from one small window opening onto the yard; on sunny days, dust-motes would dance before Isaac. Nothing danced behind him, for behind was the room where the Subjects were laid out for preparation. Isaac could feel them at his back, as he worked; just there, on the other side of the wall, staring sightless at the roof beams. Sometimes when old timbers creaked he imagined it the sound of necks rotating, as they turned their faces towards him. *Plink-plink* went pennies, falling from eyelids.

"You have a visitor, Bliss," said Mr Bowell.

Isaac turned, but didn't straighten. Isaac never straightened. Because of this he had come cheap from the Foundling Hospital in Lamb's Conduit Fields, bent foundlings being available at a discount.

"It's the medical gentleman. Come to visit you again, of the goodness of his heart."

"Hello, young Isaac," said Atherton. Smiling, for they were

chums. He had noticed the boy some weeks ago, and come back several times to visit.

Isaac recoiled—as best a boy may do, whose back is bowed like a barrel hoop.

"Get away," he said.

"Bliss!" exclaimed the undertaker.

"You lied to me, Mr Bowell. 'Ee's not a doctor—'ee's a *surgeon*!"

He said the word as if it might summon the Fiend.

Mr Bowell's mouth turned down dramatically. The expression came naturally, and did not require mechanical assistance. "Who told you such a thing?"

There was movement at the top of the stairs. Thos Bowell the Younger peered down: a spotty youth of sixteen, trying not to look like a young viper with nothing better to do than to torment defective apprentices.

His progenitor continued to glower. "This gentleman is your benefactor, Bliss. You have your Place because of this gentleman!"

True enough. Discovering that Isaac was even more defective than he had supposed, the undertaker had been set to send him back to the Foundling Hospital. But Atherton, upon noticing the boy, had intervened, offering to reimburse Mr Bowell for Isaac's keep, with a little bit extra to offset inconvenience. Now he dropped to one knee, regarding Isaac earnestly. "I want to help you," he said.

"I know what you want."

"Does the pain grow worse?"

"There ent no pain," swore Isaac, clenching himself against it.

"Is it harder to breathe?"

"Never."

The curvature of the spine had been more pronounced each time Atherton had come. Today there was a rattling in the lungs. Isaac's eyes were huge and hollow.

"I'm fine, sir. Right as rain. So please go an' 'elp someone else."

He was twelve years old. Isaac Bliss was the name he had been given at the Foundling Hospital, where they were famous for the whimsicality of their naming. Isaac's only friend there had been Augustus Rectitude; the two of them had been daily cowed by a girl called Janet Friendly.

"Let me listen to your lungs."

"No," said Isaac, shrinking further.

"I won't hurt you."

"You're not to put me there," the boy burst out. "Not on one of them shelves you 'ave!"

"What shelves?"

"The ones you've got in the locked room at that 'ouse of yours, full of 'orrors! The little lamb with two 'eads, and the baby crorkindill, and them other things without they even got names, all twisted in jars!"

Bowell the Younger still hovered atop the stairs. Atherton shot him a look that had pure murder in it. But his face was mild as he turned back to poor Isaac.

"There is no such room in my house, and no such shelf, and no such intention of mine," he said. "You have my word upon it, as your friend."

He spoke with earnest intensity, holding Isaac with his gaze. He had blue, blue eyes, did Dionysus Atherton. The bluest eyes that ever yet existed.

"I'll tell you something else," he said. "Nature is a most cunning physician. I've seen fellows sink much lower than you — many of them, Isaac, and they were given up for lost — who awoke one fine morning and rose to their feet and snapped their fingers at the doctor. I've seen it often and again — snapped their fingers at him, exclaiming 'A fig, sir, for your powders and your potions!'"

He leaned in close, and lowered his voice. Isaac's whole world was the blue of those eyes.

"It is my private opinion, young Isaac, that you may outlive the lot of us. And so I ask you for a favour, friend to friend. On the day of my funeral — and may it be many years from now — on the day of my funeral, you must pause for a little moment, as you hear the procession pass by. You must say, to whosoever might be close to hand: 'There passes a man whom I knew in my youth. He did his best, and helped where he could, and I pray God will pardon the rest.' And then, young Isaac — this is most important of all — you must raise your hand in my honour, and snap your fingers."

It would have warmed every cockle of your heart if you'd been there to see, cos a flicker of actual hope had kindled in Isaac's eyes. This was Atherton's gift, one of so very many. He could summon such powers of reassurance that you could not help but believe him. And for the span of a slow spreading smile — in the pure blue radiance of the moment — I swear that Dionysus Atherton believed himself.

He slipped the boy a sixpence.

"There," exclaimed Mr Bowell. "Now, Bliss — what do you say to your benefactor?"

Bent like a barrel hoop, Isaac twisted his head to look up at the surgeon. A tremulous smile tugged. He raised one spindly arm, and snapped his fingers.

Atherton clapped his hands in delight. "Well done, young Isaac!"

Outside, he paused for a private word with Bowell the Younger, explaining what he would do to vipers who tormented defectives — the description would wake Young Thos up six nights running, with the gibbering meemies — after which he gave an extra guinea to the undertaker.

"Treat Isaac well," he said quietly. "Do you understand me, Mr Bowell? The scoliosis is grievously advanced, and there is nothing to be done. But he is a human creature, and deserves your consideration. Do not work him over-hard. Make sure he has sufficient food, and a blanket at night. And send me word directly, when he fails."

*

And you may say to Your Umble Narrator: How do you know? Were you there on that day to witness? At the hanging, or at Bowell's, or in that alley near Seacoal Lane where Blossom bobbed and Dionysus Atherton imagined himself exalted? Were you inside the man's head, to hear his inmost thoughts and share the deepest intimations of his heart?

And the truth is: no, I was not. Not on the day I've just been describing, or on many others still to come. But I know what Atherton did, on each of them. I've ferreted out the pieces, one by one, and puzzled them together. Oh, he's a great one for puzzles, is Your Wery Umble Narrator. A great one for ferreting, as you'll come to understand once we've been properly introduced.

So yes, I know what Dionysus Atherton did. I know what he did next, and I know what he was thinking while he did it. And what I don't know, I can guess — because I *know* the man. I have come to know his heart as I know my own.

Look at him now, striding down Aldersgate Street.

The streets are still choked with crowds from the hanging. Carts clattering, coachmen bellowing, drunken louts lurching amongst the long-suffering respectable, who hold their wives close and their purses closer. Outside a gin-shop some Nymphs of the Pave exchange jeers with a clutch of passing Rainbows — gay young bucks, that is to say, on a roister. Around the corner a half-pay officer trembles one of their sisters against the wall, to the great disgust of all right-thinking passers-by, and the greater delight of a murder of apprentices, who commence pelting the amorous couple with clods of horse-shit. In other words, London is being London, in this year of 1816.

It is a year since Waterloo. Bonaparte is in exile on St Helena, and our Redcoats are back home. Many are missing bits, to be sure; an arm or a leg. Tom Lobster may be seen hopping himself along any street in London, or sitting on the corner, cap in hand, such being the fortune of war. There is a public house with this very name — the Fortune of War at Pye Corner, which will shortly come into this narrative — so named by one of its long-ago owners who had lost one arm and both legs in a battle at sea. But there is a new energy surging through the Metropolis, after a lean and anxious decade. A sense that much may be possible again — and very little may be forbidden. The topsy-turvy feeling that something has utterly fallen apart, though you can't be sure what it is, and that something throbbing and burgeoning has begun. There is a mood of seeking and striving and seizing, and Atherton is as one with the spirit of his Age. He glistens with it.

Amidst the throng, he is half a head taller than all but the tallest, and handsomer than any. He wears fawn-coloured breeches and a sky-blue coat, and his hair is long and golden. He would have a man come in to curl it for an hour each morning, except he'd never have the patience. So it is wild instead, which suits him all the better.

Crossing Cannon Street he makes towards the Thames, bound for Guy's Hospital, where he is the brightest rising star in the chirurgical firmament. Guy's is on the south side of the river; he will hire a lighter to ferry him across.

He redoubles his pace.

He is forever eager to arrive, wherever he is going. Once there, he is eager to be away. He was in motion well before dawn today, when he arose to supervise a dissection, and many times he is still in motion when dawn comes peeping again. At Guy's he will conduct his rounds in a whirlwind, with worshipful students flapping behind. He will scarcely slow down when he lectures — pacing back and forth, words cascading.

There is no one swifter in surgery, either. Not even his old schoolmate Alec Comrie, whose own speed is legendary. And there is certainly no one swifter to reach for the scalpel to begin with. No one even half as swift, not when patients must be held down shrieking, and surgeons themselves are chalk-white as they commence. The only exception occurs at the dissecting table. There in the Death House—with the rats and the stench and the horror and the sparrows (oh, I'll tell you of the sparrows) and the corpses carved and grinning—Atherton is stillness itself. He'll stand for hours in searing concentration, separating layers of tissue with tiny measured movements.

"Soon I shall know the Great Secret!"

Ronald Peake's last words upon the scaffold. And by now Peake knows it, doesn't he? At ten minutes past eleven on this Monday morning, as Atherton is borne across the Thames with the air of a man who might choose to part it instead, the poisoner has arrived upon another shore. He knows what the surgeon does not.

Not yet.

2

When Jemmy Cheese was very young, his brother Edward had warned him about the fireplace. It gaped like a maw in the middle of the room, and if Jemmy ventured too near, the Devil would come bursting from the chimbley with a shriek and a bang, to hale him away with all the other wicked boys who fiddled with their willies. Unless the gobbling witch in the jakes got him first, clutching with her talons from beneath him as he squatted. Jemmy had in consequence spent his boyhood with a dismal clammy squirming in his guts.

He feels that way again tonight.

He breaks stride as they cross Whitechapel Road, switching the sack from one shoulder to the other and casting a chary look skyward, cos he does not like the looks of that moon.

"'S nothing to fret about," mutters Little Hollis, skulking alongside.

But a moon is always bad. This one has slipped behind the clouds, plunging them back into darkness. It has been doing this for some time. It disappears, but then an edge will come sidling out again, dirty-white and deceitful, like an old whore leering from a window.

Jemmy follows, but the clamminess grows worse. Another man might put this down to the oysters, which slosh with his long clumping strides. Jemmy Cheese has partaken of two dozen, along with four quarts of porter; tonight's enterprise is not of a sort that a man can approach in the nakedness of sobriety, with nothing to stand between him and what he is up to. But it isn't the oysters. It is the old gobbling-witch-down-beneath sensation, coming on all sudden and sick. It dawns upon Jemmy that he is having a whatsit, a thingummy, when a man senses that something dreadful is about to happen.

He had met Little Hollis at the Fortune of War Tavern, which is where these nights customarily began. After a period of fortification they had set off, stopping briefly at the alley where Little Hollis had stashed the implements. Now they are on the Ratcliffe Highway, angling east towards St George-in-the-East churchyard.

A premonition. It occurs to Jemmy that he is having a premonition. It is strong enough to make him break his stride, and puts him on the cusp of turning round again and long-shanking it straight home to Meg. Except how would he explain this to his brother? Ned would fly into a rage and call him *obtusus* and sundry cruel words besides, many of them in Latin, for Edward Cheshire is a scholard. Ned is cleverer than the surgeons themselves. He owns a pawn-shop near Old Street, and is going to become a dentist.

The moon slides through the clouds again, illuminating Little Hollis looking back. He hisses — "'S this way" — and gestures.

There is a wall around the churchyard, with spikes on top and doubtless broken glass as well, this being the sort of low trick they are up to nowadays, to thwart the Doomsday Men. A wide gate in the front, and another along the side, much narrower. Unlocked, just as Ned had promised; he had fixed it with the Sexton. It creaks on rusty hinges, and the trees along the graveyard wall stir uneasily. Barren branches rattle.

"Wait," says Jemmy.

Something is wrong.

Jemmy Cheese is not well suited to this work, even at the best of times. He has too much imagination for it, to begin with. But something is doubly wrong about tonight.

Little Hollis is already scuttling ahead, however, and Ned's wrath would be unbearable. Worst of all his lovely Meg might shake her head in that way of hers and wonder—for the ten thousandth time—what the Devil she was to do with him.

So he follows.

There are scores of graveyards dotted about the Metropolis, unweeded gardens of death. St George-in-the-East is one of the largest: three acres of festering putrefaction, with headstones jumbling higgledy like an old woman's teeth. This graveyard serves a parish of forty thousand souls, and Londoners die at a relentless pace, bless their hearts. They must be buried, and lie in peace 'til Gabriel's Horn sounds the dreadful Day of Judgement—or 'til the likes of Little Hollis and Jemmy Cheese emerge from the sable of the night, with shovels and sacks. Little Hollis hazards a wink of his bull's-eye lantern, sliding the gate open an inch. By the yellow gleam they find the grave they're seeking: fresh dirt piled on from this morning's burial, and a plain white cross.

There are pebbles as well, strewn apparently at random, and small white shells. These must be carefully moved, and meticulously replaced after the exhumation, for there is in fact nothing random about them at all. Friends of the departed with guile in their hearts will arrange such items directly after the burial, returning to see if they've been disturbed. If so, there will be exclamations of dismay, and the fetching of shovels, and louder exclamations if the grave turns out to be empty, and the swearing of terrible oaths. Often this will excite wider suspicion; neighbouring graves will be dug up, leading frequently to the discovery that these are equally vacant. In extreme cases it will be discovered that an entire graveyard has been honeycombed, as if it had been filled with corpses so saintly that the Almighty had been moved to rapture them directly skyward, snatching them from the very mouths of indignant maggots.

Such discoveries are always bad for the Doomsday trade. There is furious denunciation in the news-sheets and heightened vigilance, with Watchmen poking their snouts about. Worse yet, friends of the newly departed come into the churchyards at night. They lurk in places of concealment, with cudgels.

Little Hollis sets the lantern down, and they begin.

It is Necessary, this act they are about to perform; every Doomsday Man in England would tell you that, and so would every surgeon. There are hundreds of surgeons and medical students in London alone — never mind the rest of England — working at the hospitals and at the private anatomy schools, of which there are dozens; and each one of them needs cadavers to carve. How else are they to learn and experiment, save on living patients, pinned down and squalling? And there lies the foundation of the Doomsday trade. The Law entitles the College of Surgeons to take possession of four murderers hanged at Newgate each year — but only four, and thousands are required. For all the rest, the surgeons and anatomists must rely on the Doomsday Men — Resurrectionists — grave-robbers.

Dig a narrow slanting shaft down to the head of the coffin: this is the knack of it. The shovels are wooden, for these make less noise. It can take an hour or more, if the dirt is packed down and the coffin lies deep. But a proper planting costs money, and tonight's subject is only a coachman. The poor aren't dug so diligently. Often they'll be stacked atop of others, two or even three in the same grave, the topmost scarcely deeper than a potato.

Sure enough, they are barely two feet down when Jemmy's shovel thuds. They clear enough dirt away to expose the very end of the coffin, and Jemmy reaches for a crowbar to prise the lid — gently, now, to minimize the noise — snapping the cheap wood against the weight of the earth above. Little Hollis fixes a grappling hook to the burial shroud and then stands back as Jemmy sets his heels and hauls on the rope, like a fisherman raising his net.

Wind agitates the trees. They creak their consternation,

as if appalled that such wickedness exists in the world. As the body flops onto the ground, the coachman's face peeps out of the shroud, a bruised pupa unpeeled in its grim cocoon. It is the faces that haunt Jemmy: blue-veined and slack-jawed and ghastly white. It seems to him there is something he ought to do or say, if only he could think what it is.

He had confessed this once to Meg. She'd been drinking gin that day, and laughed at him. "Tell them to rise up and walk," she had said. Meg would get that way on the blue ruin. She is angry, Meg—the angriest person he has ever known. She keeps the anger stoppered up, but down deep she is seething and blue ruin uncorks the bottle.

Jemmy loads the coachman into the sack, and they shovel the dirt back into the grave. There is something special about this one, it seems. One of the surgeons, Mr Atherton, is particularly keen to have this one upon his dissecting table, and is paying extra for the privilege—six pounds, half again the going rate. Jemmy hasn't asked why, though he guesses the surgeon once performed some procedure on the subject, and wants to analyze the results. Surgeons are known to keep track of former patients for years, awaiting their chance.

Four pounds for a Large—that is the normal price. Things come in three other sizes besides: Large Small, Small, and Foetus. By definition a Small is less than three foot long, and such items are priced out by the inch. Jemmy Cheese hates harvesting a Small; these haunt him worst of all. Dead children come to him in the night. Spectral waifs with empty eyes, scrabbling with their fingers at his window. He will wake up in a panic, crying out. Sometimes Meg is angry at this, but other times she is soft. "There's nothing to fear," she will say. "It's all right, Jemmy. You're safe with Meg."

Not long ago she had thought she might be having a child of her own. Jemmy's heart had soared with this, and he begged her not to go to the Old Woman two streets over, who took care of such matters.

"How could we have a child, the likes of us?" she had said to him. She said it savage, being on the blue ruin that day.

"I'd look after you both," he said.

"You?" she said. "Look after a child? And what makes you so sure it's yours to begin with?"

That had dished him, a little. He'd had to go out for a walk, to consider. But he came back thinking it would be all right.

"I'd look after it anyways," he told her. "It might be happier, being someone else's. Prob'ly be smarter."

She swore at him for saying so, but her eyes went soft and afterwards she held him close. A few weeks later, when she bled and lost it, Meg was just as sad as he was. She has been sad ever since.

Meg is near as clever as Jemmy's brother Ned. It makes Jemmy marvel, to think how someone so clever would stay with him. She reads books, and from time to time has tried fitfully to teach Jemmy to read too, but she lacks the patience for teaching, and he can never seem to grasp the knack. The letters won't stay put, the way they do for clever people. Just when he has a few of them pinned down, they'll slide away and reverse themselves.

But Jemmy has other qualities. He's loyal to a fault — that's what Meg says — and remarkably strong. Meg loves the strength of him. At night she'll nestle against it, as if she were a child herself.

There is no bully to protect her, not since she left Mother Peachum's night-house, where she had lodged 'til taking up with Jemmy, and where the bruisingest bully in the Seven Dials kept watch over the girls. But once when a man treated her badly, Jemmy found out who it was, and went round to set him straight. Jemmy is a gentle soul, and dislikes the other job that he does for his brother, collecting money that Ned has loaned out to shirkers. But he is sixteen stone and a half, and once on a wager he lay on his back while a cart was rolled across his chest. You would need to stand on an apple-crate to look Jemmy in the eye, which you would not want to do when he is roused. He was roused the day he went round to see that man, whom he set exceedingly straight indeed. Word got round, and since then men in general have been very much nicer to Meg.

"'S go," hisses Little Hollis. They've been here too long already, and cannot afford to be seen.

A Resurrectionist had been lynched in Dublin, just two months previous. Battered unrecognizable and strung from a lamppost. That's what a mob will do, if they once lay hands — and it's all because of Judgement Day. On Judgement Day you will rise up to meet your Maker, and you're supposed to meet Him intact. But you can't do that, can you, if you've been dug up and dissected? You can't be resurrected whole. The Trumpet will sound and there you'll be, stripped down like the leftover carcass of a Christmas goose. That's why there exists such horror of grave-robbing, and such loathing of the Doomsday Men.

Jemmy's premonition has become a knot of dread. Something is amiss — he is sure of it, now — but what? The grave itself? Perhaps the pebbles are not quite right. He hesitates to look, and starts at the sight of his own shadow. The old whore moon is out again, behind him.

Little Hollis is on his way, scuttling swift and hunched. His arse is hiked high as if raised by frequent kickings, and it is broader than his shoulders. This gives him a frankly verminous air, as Jemmy might remark were he given to making hurtful observations about his friends, which he is not. Hollis is halfway to the gate, now; Noddy Sprockett will be waiting for them just outside, with his cart. Ten minutes earlier they had heard the clip-clop of Old Jeroboam's hooves arriving.

There are flowers on a nearby grave, a sprig of them tied with ribbon. On an impulse Jemmy stoops; he will take these home to Meg. She'll receive them carelessly, but secretly she'll be pleased.

In turning, Jemmy sees them. Two spectral figures, rising in the moonlight.

The dead. He knows it at once, with an icy clutching certainty; he has always known it must come to this. The dead are rising from their graves to take revenge. They will seize him and drag him down, with the Privy Witch and the Chimbley Fiend.

Little Hollis, hearing his cry, looks back. "Christ!" exclaims Hollis. "'S the Watch!"

But it isn't, nor revenants neither, issuing from the tomb. Much worse: these are cousins of the deceased coachman.

This will come out later, at the trial. They'd been delegated to keep watch in the graveyard, against precisely such depredations. A third had been with them when the grave-robbers arrived, who after a swift exchange of urgent whispers—gripping their cudgels and weighing the odds, but misliking their chances against the big one—had slipped away to alert the coachman's other friends, who were gathered at a wake just down the road.

Wrathful shouts beyond the wall. A whinny and a clatter of hooves, receding. Old Jeroboam has stirred himself to desperate exertion, and is bearing Noddy Sprockett off to safety. Little Hollis flees the other way, flinging his shovel aside. He moves at astonishing speed for one so elevated of arse.

That leaves Jemmy, standing frozen in the moonlight with a corpse upon his shoulder, as the coachman's friends pour through the gate. Four of them at first, then more, and more.

He wants to say: "I'll put your friend back in the ground —I swear, upon my davy. I'll dig up someone else."

"Kill him!"

He wants to say: "No, wait. Just—please. I need to take these flowers home to Meg."

"Kill the bastard!"

He drops the corpse and raises his fists. But they're on top of him now, and they cudgel him down.

3

Let me tell you about surgeons.

It was different in the high Georgian days, when the great John Hunter was setting out on his career. Half a century ago, physicians might stake some claim to respectability, with their gold-topped canes and formal education. But surgeons? Jumped-up barbers, who couldn't aspire beyond a shop in an alleyway, and a red rag wrapped around a pole. Hackers and dolts who had never been near a university. They learned by apprenticing themselves to older hackers and longer-established dolts; advanced the cause of doltishness by learning nothing new; were good for little but pulling teeth and setting bones, and oftentimes not even that.

But by the time John Hunter's heart failed him in 1793, and the great man discovered the Great Secret, much had changed. Surgery was becoming a Science, with all that follows from such a transformation: social standing, and coin of the realm, and patients — God bless 'em — who survived. Hunter was renowned across Europe for his anatomical learning; he owned a fine house in Earls Court and leased another in Leicester Square. Now, just a few years later, a surgeon might set his sights higher still, Mr Astley Cooper being the pole-star by which all brilliant and ambitious young men — such as Dionysus Atherton — set their course. Astley Cooper, who was rumoured to be verging upon a peerage, with an income exceeding twenty thousand pounds a year, and a country estate in Gadebridge, and a large house in Conduit Street, and a servant who earned six hundred a year in bribes alone, from patients seeking an appointment.

Alec Comrie was better than all of them.

Comrie lived over a gin-shop in Cripplegate. He had two rooms, a sitting room and a surgery, let from a woman named Missus Maggs who kept the gin-shop and attended as well to housekeeping necessities, when the spirit moved. He also had a boy who assisted him. This boy slept in an attic storage room and never made a sixpence in bribes, as he would tell you quite cheerfully. "Not a sixpence, your worship, nor threepence neither. Not so much in fact as a single fucking ha'penny, if you'll pardon my plain speaking. But I'm thankful, cos I'd sooner be an honest man. Now, are you a gen'lman as fancies from time to time a friendly game of hazard, to while away an afternoon?"

You'd do best to decline the offer.

He cut a fine little figure, the surgeon's boy, particularly if you saw him at a distance. A Rainbow, in fact, togged out in the latest fashion, or nearabouts. But the togs grew more threadbare the closer you came, and he himself drew nearer without ever growing much taller, the whole of him topping out two inches shy of five foot. He had a curious dark face, all triangles, and a silk snotter swiped from a stall just this morning, and a winning smile that he shone at you like sunrise. He also had three cups, and a pea that was assuredly in one of them, and you only had to watch his nimble fingers keenly to be sure — "oh, bad luck, sir!" — which one.

His name was Will Starling, and he is Your Wery Umble Narrator.

So here we are at last, you and I: face to face. Honoured to make your acquaintance, I am sure. You will picture my bow, and accept my heartfelt hope that I do not disappoint.

Mr Comrie had taken the rooms when he and I returned from Europe. He'd been a military surgeon — seven years on the Peninsula with Wellington, who esteemed him greatly. There was a story, indeed, that the Duke had a nickname for him — the Scotch Dreadnought — bestowed after Comrie had performed with brilliant competence a highly delicate operation upon the ducal tackle, which (just between the two of us) was mighty in dimension.

You'd want to take that particular story with a grain of salt, since I was the one who'd made it up. Still, Mr Comrie's prowess had been the stuff of legend — after the Battle of Salamanca he had performed nearly two hundred amputations in twenty-four hours. That is the truth; I speak upon my davy. One hundred and eighty seven it was, to be exact, and I know this cos I counted. He could have your leg off in two minutes flat, and your arm in half that time, speed being the only mercy with no way to dull the pain. Orderlies would stack the limbs on either side: trotters on one pile, flappers on another. When Mr Comrie needed both hands free he'd clamp the knife bechuxt his teeth.

I recollect a young Lieutenant on the morning after Badajoz, propped against the wall of a barn that was serving as a field hospital, staring in bleak bemusement at his right leg. It started out well enough, the trotter, before veering off at an extravagant angle. The break was above the knee, which would mean a disarticulation at the hip; Mr Comrie told him so, blunt as a slaughterman knocking mutton on the head.

"Will I die?" asked the young Lieutenant.

"Unless I operate directly."

There was no other way, with a break as bad as this one. With any break at all, really. You had to take the limb.

"I am at the Gate," said the Lieutenant. It seemed he had a poetic cast. "I lie at the Black Gate of Death itself."

"But I am on my way," said Mr Comrie.

He had gone to university in Edinburgh, although he had been brought up somewhere farther north — I've a notion it was Dunfermline, not that I could tell you much about it, having never been north of Lichfield myself. In moments of urgency he grew especially Scotch.

"Oilskin," he said to the Orderlies.

We were outside, and a foul grey rain was pissing down. In such conditions they'd hold an oilskin over the surgeon's head, and rain would drum paradiddles as he cut.

"Knife," he said to Your Wery Umble.

The young Lieutenant had begun to weep.

"Here I come," said Mr Comrie. "I come wi' steel and shrieking. But I'll bring you back."

He did it, too. Five minutes to take the leg, cos a disarticulation was always more difficult. The Lieutenant swooned halfway through, but woke up afterwards. Two weeks later he was sitting up on a bed of straw, losing money to Wm Starling. Last I heard he was back in London, reciting ballads on street-corners.

That is the truth. So — in case you wondered — is what I said about the size of Wellington's tackle. But as it doesn't concern the story I'm telling you now, you're free to forget I mentioned it.

After Waterloo, Mr Comrie resolved to build a civilian practice in London. "A matter of time," he was saying, on this particular day in April of 1816. "That's all it is."

He wasn't normally a man for the syllables. But he had a way of repeating things to himself, as if saying them doggedly enough would make them come about.

"Patients will come."

"'Course they will," I agreed, gamely.

"Just a question of time."

"It is."

"And they'll be walking up those stairs."

He was in his surgery, with Your Wery Umble on the landing, looking in. The surgery was Spartan, and clean — he was a stickler for cleanliness, believing that patients did better in such conditions. It was just a notion of his, unsupported by Science, but when Mr Comrie took a conviction it set like mortar. There were two wooden chairs and a wooden examining bench, with a box of sawdust kept underneath to soak up blood, which might otherwise seep through the floorboards and drip onto the head of Missus Maggs in the gin-shop below. Against one wall was a table with surgical instruments, laid out on a green baize cloth. Your

Wery Umble would clean these at the end of every day, and frequently after each individual procedure; Alec Comrie was a workman, and a workman respects his tools. Above the table was a cabinet, containing bottles and vials — ointments and liniments, some alcohol, and a small supply of laudanum, though Mr Comrie did not set much stock by it, laudanum being of limited efficacy against substantial pain. He took the view that pain was the patient's concern, to be coped with on a private basis.

On the walls were anatomical drawings: a cross-section of the brain, and human figures with skin stripped away to reveal the inner organs. Mr Comrie was in the process of supplementing this collection as I watched from the doorway, hanging a framed drawing in a prominent position: a black-lead sketch by the surgical artist Charles Bell, depicting a gunshot wound of the scrotum sustained at the Battle of Corunna. Mr Comrie had treated several such scrotums himself. The injury was more common than you'd like to think, being normally sustained when Tom Lobster knelt with bits a-dangle to fire. He had found the drawing yesterday at a street stall in Holborn, and had exclaimed with heartfelt admiration.

It was in truth superb. Bell's artistry was like Mr Comrie's own: detailed, meticulous, and appalling. The sketch was a close-up view, just thighs and abdomen, with the horribly swollen scrotum in the middle. Very much, indeed, like an immense fig in a still-life painting, except a fig will not normally have an entry wound on one side and an exit wound on the other, with a tail of fig-guts protruding. It had its own weird beauty; the question was whether it should be hanging on the wall.

I asked this question gingerly. You were careful when you questioned Alec Comrie.

He bristled. "What's wrong with it?"

Nothing, I assured him. Just—the wall of his surgery. Where patients would come, in a state of trepidation to begin with.

Other surgeons had skeletons, he objected. Atherton had a skull.

"Still," I said. "A scrotum."

At length he gave a grudging nod. "Fair enough," he conceded. "The ladies."

I had actually been thinking about the gentlemen. One look at that particular scrotum was enough to send you fleeing down the stairs to the gin-shop. But I didn't push the point, and after a moment he took the drawing down again, setting it reluctantly on one of the chairs.

"They will come," he said again.

"They will."

"A question of time."

"That's all it is."

"I will learn the trick of it."

He meant the skill that men such as Astley Cooper had. Atherton too. Both of them could radiate such empathy that patients breathed deep and unclenched their sphincters, at least until the instruments came out. When you went to Atherton's surgery in Crutched Friars, you met with earnest reassurance. Here above the gin-shop was a growling Scotchman with a bonesaw.

"I know my shortcomings, William," he muttered. With a shame-faced look towards Your Wery Umble—as if he was letting me down. Which he'd never done, not once, in all the years we'd been together. And never would do, neither, in everything that was to follow.

"I know my shortcomings, and I can change."

But of course he couldn't. We never can, can we?

That's when we heard raised voices, down below. Missus Maggs, demanding the business of some newcomer, and a woman insisting that she must see the surgeon.

"'Ere, you can't just barge..."

"Let go of me!"

A hammering of footsteps, and the woman came round the corner of the stair. Wiry and slight, her hair hanging wild. Great dark eyes in a narrow face. Too sharp-featured to be pretty, but almost beautiful nonetheless, in the way that a small fierce thing can have beauty. She was ragged from running, and her breath came in tearing gulps.

"They've done for him—they've stove in his head! God rot them in Hell—God rot you too—it's all your doing!"

"My doing?" Mr Comrie stepped out of the surgery, perplexed.

"Your fault—his—the other one—Atherton! The bastard lot of you!"

"If you won't make sense, I can't help you. Who are you, woman, and what has happened?"

"Foul filthy murder has happened! They've killed my Jemmy!"

Meg Nancarrow cursed wildly, and burst into tears.

4

They'd lugged Jemmy Cheese to the Giltspur Street Compter. It had taken Meg all morning to find that out, after learning from Little Hollis what had happened at the graveyard. Rushing to Giltspur Street she had found him alive but very bad indeed, so bad it could hardly be worse. She'd dashed to St Bart's to fetch a surgeon, but none seemed inclined to come running, just to save the life of a Resurrection Man. Somebody gave her Mr Comrie's name, and his address at Cripplegate.

"Aye," he grunted. "I'll come."

"Then hurry, damn you!"

He reached for his jacket — the one he wore for going out, with fewer stains. I followed with the pocket set of instruments, wrapped in leather, that we took with us on calls.

Giltspur Street Compter is at the east end of St Sepulchre's, just north of Newgate and no more than a stone's throw from the Fortune of War, where Jemmy's tribulations had begun. The Compter mainly held wretches arrested for Debt, but night charges were often brought in as well, since the Watch-houses were not permitted to retain prisoners. It was the Watch as had brought Jemmy here.

They'd been drawn by the hullabaloo in the graveyard—so Meg Nancarrow had pieced together. The coachman's friends had been set to hang him, as was done to that Resurrectionist in Dublin, except they thought they'd beaten him to death already. "Hang him anyway!" someone cried. But others weren't so certain, and two or three began to ask themselves whether killing a man was precisely what they'd had in mind, and whether the Law might not have something to say on the subject. Such was the state of affairs when two elderly Charleys creaked up with their bull's-eyes and their long staves, exclaiming "here-now-here-now" and "God's teeth!" As the pack began to scatter, the Watchmen commandeered the donkey-cart of an early-rising costermonger, and trundled Jemmy Cheese to Giltspur Street.

"They reckoned he'd be dead, the bastards." Meg spoke in ragged bursts as we hastened. "Dead and cold by the time they arrived, and they could take him to St Bart's and sell him to the surgeons." A look of incandescent accusation. "Sell him to the likes of you."

Mr Comrie took this sort of thing in stride, having been cursed by shrieking Lobsters halfway across Southern Europe. By 187 of them in a single day, after Salamanca. But I tended to take things more personal, on his behalf.

"The likes of him," I said, "is haring across the Metropolis to help you."

"I know that!"

She was so full of distress that she had to put it somewhere, so she'd grown furious instead. Here was my golden opportunity to leave well enough alone, and naturally I passed it up.

"Haring across the Metropolis," I repeated, deciding I liked the sound. I have a weakness for the mellifluous syllable, and a magpie's eye for shiny words such as *mellifluous*, which I'd found just the other night in Sam Johnson's dictionary. "And what's he likely to be paid for all his trouble?"

"Payment!" cried Meg. "Now we come to it, do we?"

"No one's consairned with payment," said Mr Comrie.

But he was beginning to fluster, cos she'd stopped right there in front of him. In the middle of Long Lane, with cows bawling in Smithfield Market beyond, and passers-by slowing to snicker and stare at the picture we made. A soiled dove shouting at a discomfited Scotch surgeon, and young Wm Starling, Esq., standing by, wishing he'd put a stocking in it.

"Here and now? On my knees in a pile of horse-shit? Then let's be getting on with it!"

Another man would have reacted differently. Dionysus Atherton would have pointed out which pile. But Mr Comrie just turned beetroot-red.

"Here, now," he said. "Your fellow needs me."

He hurried on, and I fell in behind him. Meg Nancarrow followed after, with a last look round at the faces snickering back at her. Defying them to find her filthy and ridiculous. As if she'd commit them to memory, every one, and come back at her leisure to slit each throat.

"God's swinging bollocks," Mr Comrie said to me, under his breath. He had the expression that soldiers in battle will wear, when they see a leg cartwheeling past six foot above the ground. "This one's a going consairn."

*

They were holding Jemmy Cheese in a small stone cell, with a cot and a wooden bucket. It was the anteroom to a larger chamber, where half a dozen others were lodged. Jemmy lay on his back, bloated with bruising and caked in blood; one side of his head was swollen grotesquely and his eyes were sightless slits. Some tragic troll, I thought, fallen headlong from a mountaintop.

"Is there hope?" asked Meg Nancarrow.

She hovered in the doorway, clutching her shawl. Her voice was low and husky, when she wasn't using it to hit you with.

Mr Comrie did not reply. Having scanned the long bones for obvious breaks, he probed the skull beneath the matted hair. His fingers were long and dextrous — remarkable fingers to serve at the extremity of such stubby arms, for the surgeon was otherwise a man of bulges and bandy legs. A man for the wrestling competition at a country fair, or just for digging stones out of fields.

"No broken limbs," he said at length. "But. Depressed fracture of the skull."

"What will you do?" Meg asked.

"Come back tomorrow. See if he survives the night."

"And then?"

"See what may be done."

"What can I do for him?"

"Wash him."

"Like a corpse?"

"He's breathing. Keep him warm."

"Is there hope?" she asked again.

He looked at her squarely. "A little. How much do you need?"

She looked back at him for the longest moment. Then she nodded.

In the morning, Jemmy Cheese lay pale as death. But he was breathing.

"He's strong," said Meg. She'd sat at his side all night; so the Turnkey told us as we arrived. "He's stronger than you could believe."

Someone else was here as well. A spindly man of one- or two-and-thirty, bespectacled and balding, with pursed little lips and womanly hands, scarce taller than Your Wery Umble himself. Filthy and fastidious in an old brown coat and a bright red weskit.

"*Ecce homo*," said Edward Cheshire, also known as Uncle Cheese. "Behold my brother, Mr Comrie. Brought low, and sinking steadily. Oh dear, oh dear, and vhat am I to do?"

He shook his head and looked away, like a sorrowful species of robin. The perfect round lenses of his spectacles caught the light from the one small window, and flashed.

"Go dig your own cadavers, Ned," said Meg. "Collect your own outstanding debts, from them you bleeds white."

He pretended he hadn't heard. "*Media vita in mortus sumus*," he said. "In the midst of our lives we die."

So it meant indeed, as I was later to discover when I looked it up. Or so at least it almost meant, allowing for certain imperfections in the syntax. And who would twist a man upon the rack of his declensions, at such a time?

I knew of Uncle Cheese, of course, as did Mr Comrie. Every surgeon in London knew of Edward Cheshire. He kept a pawn-shop in a lane behind Old Street, where he had been at work at the counter an hour previous when Little Hollis arrived with the dire news about his brother. He had come directly, locking the shop and cursing in Latin at a brandy-soaked man who was arriving with his children's warm jackets to pawn, now that spring had come. Most of Cheese's customers were of this ilk, although his most lucrative traffic was in goods as never graced a window: Things. Large, Small, and Foetus. He did a brisk sideline in teeth, as did others in the Resurrection trade, harvesting them for sale to dentists. Many of the dentures in London owed their provenance to Edward Cheshire, who was an unfailing source of fine fresh teeth at a reasonable price, often with bits of gum still sticking. He had another line of business as well, lending money to those as found themselves caught short. Medical students at the Borough Hospitals would turn to him in times of need, as did any number of others—gamblers and indigents, widows and wastrels, honest mechanics down on their luck—including one or two imprisoned here at Giltspur Street, for debt. Uncle Cheese would meet their needs, at interest compounded weekly. If they failed in their payments, he would send his brother to speak to them.

His brother, who lay stretched out before him. You could see the thought writ clear in Edward Cheshire's face:

a Metropolis full of chisellers, and here lay Jemmy Cheese in ruins.

"Oh, dear," he said. "Oh dear, oh dear, oh dear."

Mr Comrie had decided. "I will operate to relieve pressure on the brain."

He was already rolling up his sleeves. I had lugged the full kit of instruments this morning, against such an eventuality. Mr Comrie kept these in a metal box from Army days.

"A half-crown," he said to Edward Cheshire. "Before I begin. Without it I can't help your brother."

Words will not describe Ned Cheshire's grievance: that a surgeon would extort so brazenly.

"A man's *life*—" he began.

"Give the man," said Meg, "his coin."

Uncle Cheese drew himself to his full height, such as it was.

"Can you guarantee the operation will succeed?"

"Of course not," Mr Comrie said.

"And if he lives, that he will ever be the same?"

"No."

"Vell, then."

Uncle Cheese was a man of business, and grew brisk as he laid out his terms. A sixpence in advance, and a further sixpence should Jemmy survive the procedure. A third sixpence on such a day as Jemmy should sit up and point both eyes in the same direction, without drooling. And the final six pennies should Jemmy recover completely, able to perform all the functions necessary to a full and happy life. "Such as speaking in full sentences," said Uncle Cheese, "and controlling his bowels, and collecting outstanding sums from—"

"Give the man," said Meg, "his fucking coin."

Her voice was choked, but not with distress. Anger, so intense that it needed all her strength to hold it in. It was remarkable to see, that anger. Smouldering right down in the marrow, like a fire banked low. If she breathed too deeply, it would kindle. If she gave it oxygen it would surge, lighting her great dark eyes from within. She would rage into conflagration, blistering the stone walls and igniting the beams. She would burst from the Giltspur Street Compter and shriek across the rooftops of London, dancing them into flame.

Ned Cheshire fished out a half-crown. He gave it to Mr Comrie, who handed it to me.

"Find a blacksmith. Run."

When I returned the one side of Jemmy's head had been shaved, and his cot had been moved to the larger cell, where the light was better. Mr Comrie reached for his trephine, which was of sturdy Belgian make. Jemmy remained mercifully unconscious, and partway through the proceedings the Turnkey joined him, turning pale and dropping with a thud. Guards and prisoners had gathered like geese in the doorway to watch, for a chirurgical procedure was a rare treat, almost as good as a hanging—even better, in a way, considering as the conclusion wasn't so foregone.

The drilling took several minutes. A T-shaped handle was turned clockwise, once the drill-blade was placed against the skull. The blade was conical, the width of a shilling at the top, with depth-guards to stop it from delving too deep and damaging the brain. It was tricky, though—skulls come in varying thicknesses, and it's ever so easy to drill just that fraction too far. Once the hole had been drilled, relieving the pressure, Mr Comrie raised the depressed edges of the fracture, fishing out with his forceps stray slivers of bone, shockingly white against a brain as pink as blossoms. Then he screwed into place the coin—hammered wafer-flat by a blacksmith I'd found in Paternoster Lane—and sewed the flaps of scalp back over. A wonder with needle and thread, was Mr Comrie; he sewed like a seamstress.

Finally the wound was dressed and wrapped. Jemmy Cheese lay in waxen pallor.

"If he awakens, he'll want water," Mr Comrie said, straightening. "Don't give him too much."

"A half-a-crown," said Edward Cheshire. "In his *head*."

I swear he was mentally marking the spot, with an eye to retrieving it should his brother hop the twig. But of course the coin had been ruined. With a muttered execration, he left the room.

Mr Comrie left as well, and the spectators dispersed, leaving me alone with Meg and Jemmy Cheese. She sat still and silent by the cot, in slanting light from the window. Shadows haggarded her face, and I realized that she was younger than I had been supposing. She was not much older than I was myself: nineteen years. I can tell you that with certainty, since they kept records at the Foundling Hospital—though I couldn't tell you who my father might have been, or where my mother went after she bundled me up and left, or what name I had been born with.

"I'll come back this evening," I said, gathering up the instruments. "I'll bring a healing essence—you can use it when you change his dressing."

My organ of compassion had been stirred. I am also a shameless little show pony, as you have surely begun to guess, and I proceeded to trot out my knowledge of physick.

"It is rectified spirits of wine, with tincture of lavender and oil of origanum. Very efficacious"—another word magpied from Sam Johnson—"and stimulatorious of the healing processes. I will mix it for you beforehand, missus, having a modest expertise in the pothecary line, picked up along the way."

Meg Nancarrow had forgotten I ever existed. Her dark hair had fallen forward, curtaining her face.

I tried again. "He'll awaken. You'll see. I've seen men brought back who were ten times further gone—seen it often and again, on the Peninsula with Wellington. We saved men with musket balls in their brainpan. 'We' meaning Mr Comrie," I added, "myself being strictly speaking only his assistant. However valuable I may have proved, as he kindly said on several occasions. Being kind, Mr Comrie. Very kind indeed, despite appearances."

I once saw a hot-air balloon rising up from Vauxhall Gardens, as a breathless crowd looked on. It began with great promise, but sprang a leak as it cleared the trees and commenced losing altitude almost immediately. After sagging onward for a bit, it gave up and subsided into a gorse thicket, where it ended up sideways and tangled, with aeronauts limping and plucking out thistles. I had that feeling now.

Meg was speaking. "I won't let the surgeons have you, Jemmy." She spoke very low, dabbing his forehead with a bit of rag she'd moistened in rainwater. "They won't have you, if you die. I'll carry you on my back to the sea, if that's what it takes. I'll build a fire on the shore, and burn you. That's my promise to you, my love. And dogs can piss on the ashes, if you won't come back to me. I'll piss on them myself, I swear to Christ. I'll hike my skirts and straddle what's left, if you go and die on me, you bastard. Please Jemmy, God damn you, don't you go away."

5

The London Foundling Hospital was built by a philanthropical sea-captain named Thomas Coram, on the site of
an old cricket ground at Lamb's Conduit Fields. It squatted
— and still squats today — at the end of a sweeping drive
on the north side of Guilford Street, where the jumble of
the Metropolis begins to peter into fields and open spaces.
Behind a sweeping semicircular wall with iron gates are kept
the little wages of sin, for such is the governing notion of the
place. The foundlings gathered into Thomas Coram's arms
are the offspring of virtuous women who have Fallen. There
are two plain brick buildings and a chapel, fronting onto an
open courtyard; the west wing houses the little male wages,
and the east is for wages of the female persuasion.

Before accepting an infant, the Governors required evidence that the mother had previously been of good character,
to which she might — God willing — be expected to return,
once her little burden had been lifted. They also required
evidence of the father's desertion. If there was satisfaction on
both counts, then the fortunate mother could trudge away,
leaving her infant to the permanent guardianship of the

institution, in token of which the Governors would choose a new name to bestow. Inspiration had long since failed by the time Your Wery Umble arrived at the iron gates — or else it flared up in spurts of perverse whimsicality — the upshot being that the companions of Will Starling's childhood included Admirall Bembow and Richard Shovel, not to mention Edward Plantagenet and a gamine named Female Child, whom I loved to distraction for several years without the slightest glimmer of hope or acknowledgement.

Foundlings did not actually spend their earliest years at the hospital. Once accepted, they were farmed out to wet-nurses in Kent, where I lived 'til I was four. I have snippets of recollection from those days, but nothing adding up to a whole: a white cloud in a blue sky, the chill of a hard-packed dirt floor against my naked arse, the baleful ogle of a monstrous chicken. Most of all I recollect — or think I do — a red hand hoisting a vast white blue-veined breast. I couldn't tell you much about its owner, except that she must have been kind enough to the nippers in her care. After all, here I am today.

At length I was trundled to London on a wagon, and deposited at the Foundling Hospital, where I remained for the next ten years. They dressed us in uniforms and taught us to read from the Bible — taught the boys, at any rate. They taught odds and ends of skills as well, though nothing very ambitious. The girls would aspire to domestic service, it was supposed, while the lads would mainly end in the Infantry or Navy. A foundling might serve for fodder just as well as the next young man.

At fourteen years, the foundlings were apprenticed out to employers. I caught the eye of a chimbley sweep, as you might expect.

"Is he honest and reliable?" the sweep demanded of the warders who flanked me, one on either side.

Oh yes, they assured him, lying through their ivories. Yes, this was the very lad for slithering up his flues.

"I will do my utmost, sir," I vowed, my smile as earnest as God's promise of salvation. "I will not let you down."

I went off with him that same afternoon. The following morning he turned his back for a moment, and looked round again to see a scarecrow receding at speed: small, and growing smaller by the second.

I joined the Army some months later. I'd been making my way towards Kent, with notions of finding my old wet-nurse — I had it in mind that she might know something of my mother, who had never turned up at Lamb's Conduit Fields to reclaim me, as mothers sometimes did. How exactly I thought I might find my old nurse remains a mystery to me, considering as I had nothing to offer up but a description of one epic breast. That plus the chicken, which was assuredly dead by now. In any event I got myself off course, and ended up in Southampton instead, where I smiled my way into employment as a pot-boy at the Spyglass Tavern.

It was a boozing-ken near the docks, catering to sailors and sailors' whores. One night a recruiting party from the

Ninety-Fifth Rifles came in, and as I cleared tables the Sergeant took to me remarkable: a red-faced man with a roaring laugh and magnificent sidewhiskers. They were sailing to Spain with the morning tide, and he was damned if he could see why Your Wery Umble should not come with them. He stood me drinks, and clapped me on the back, and exclaimed what a dashing figure I should cut in a bright red coat. One of his fellows stripped his off and put it on me to prove the point. The sleeves were half again as long as my arms, and the hem trailed down below my knees, but Recruiting Sergeant Sidewhiskers swore that this was no obstacle; we'd find a tailor and have it taken in, and requisition a half-sized musket. Until it arrived I should serve as a drummer, leading Tom Lobster into battle. Men would cry huzzah, he predicted, and girls would fall right over backwards with their skirts up over their heads.

In fact they were not a recruiting party at all. My new friend was mere Infantryman Sidewhiskers, who found the notion of Your Wery Umble in uniform wondrous comical —and I was such a flat that I did not see it. Still, how much could you expect from a boy who would set off from London to Kent in quest of a gigantic titty, and end up in Southampton instead? So I found myself lurching awake on a troop-ship in the middle of the Channel, with a pounding nob and last night's libations on my shirt. I spent the rest of the journey spewing into a bucket, and I have never seen a gratefuller sight than the Spanish coast as it loomed through a bank of fog.

The ship dropped anchor and they rowed us ashore, and I was staggering onto the sanctuary of solid ground when behind me I heard the sounds of consternation. A sodger had taken a fall while disembarking—so I discovered in the hubbub that grew as they ferried him ashore. His fellows clustered round and shouts went up for assistance. Finding a stretcher they carried him into a dockside tavern, sweeping pots from a long wooden table, after which the press parted and voices exclaimed that the surgeon had arrived.

He came through them like a man striding into a howling wind. Bent forward, arms pistoning, head outthrust like a snapping turtle's. Expression like a snapping turtle's too, and a first glance told him that the leg was badly broken.

"You, there," he barked. "Take your thumb from out your arse, and be useful."

I had wormed my way through for a closer look—a bad habit of mine. Cats, and curiosity. But surely he wasn't barking at me?

"Yes, you! Run and fetch my tools. Tell them Mr Comrie commands it."

The instruments were still aboard ship, he said. That meant commandeering a boat—"Surgeon's orders, from Mr Comrie!"—and being rowed back out, to be hoisted aboard like a rat that had unsuccessfully deserted. But I liked saying "Surgeon's orders." It's a phrase, I discovered, as will puff a lad's chest. So I did as I'd been bid, making my way back to the ship and following a grumbling subaltern down a ladder.

Mr Comrie had shared a small cabin with three field officers. His kit was stowed underneath a berth, along with a flat rectangular metal box, considerably scuffed and dented.

I opened it, just to be sure, and there they were—gleaming back at me.

With luck, you've never seen a surgeon's tools. Ranks of them, laid out each in its place, with military precision. Most of them I could scarcely guess at, though I was to find out soon enough what each one did. There were needles and bone-handled amputation knives, two smaller ones and one long wickedly curving blade such as an Arabian pirate might clench in his teeth as he boarded your ship in a penny-blood tale. Forceps and tweezers and surgical hooks, and a long slender probe for musket balls, and a cranial drill and a sleek finger-saw. There were three separate bonesaws besides, the largest like a hacksaw with a detachable blade. You knew they were bonesaws just by looking; wedged amongst them was a sharpening stone. Sharpness of the blade was a constant issue in battlefield surgery—so I was soon to learn. If you're going to have a limb removed, try to be first up. After an hour or two, blades will start to bind as a saw will do in green wood.

I swear that they really did gleam, in the dim light that filtered through a porthole. I looked up to find the subaltern eyeing me slantways. You could see what he was thinking, of course. A box of precision-made tools, in the clutches of a shifty little chancer like Your Wery Umble.

"Got any idea what them things is worth?" he asked narrowly.

And yes, it had crossed my mind: close the box, flash the smile, and hotfoot straight to the nearest pawn-shop. But curiosity won out that afternoon—I won't call it virtue—and I did as I'd been commissioned. Clutching the box under my arm, I carried it back like a catamite bearing ritual knives to the priest who waited, bare-armed, at the sacrificial altar. Or no, not a catamite—wrong word—I looked it up just now, in Sam Johnson's dictionary. I believe I intended *acolyte* instead.

The crowd at the tavern had grown even larger, and in the midst of it Mr Comrie waited impatiently. "Thaire you are! Put them on the bench—beside me, close to hand."

The stricken man lay on the table, raising himself on one elbow and clamouring for another dram of pale before they set the bone. I saw with a start that it was Sidewhiskers. Mr Comrie ignored him.

"You, you, you, and you," he said, jabbing a finger at four strapping sodgers. "Hold him down."

They exchanged looks of alarm, but did as they were bid.

"Knife," he said to me.

"Knife?" cried Sidewhiskers, as realization dawned.

"Best to do it now," the surgeon told him. "Straightaway, while you're still in mettle. More chance of survival. The agony is diminished."

"You're not going to have my leg off—just set the thing!"

"Won't heal. Fester and rot, gangrene next. Dead inside a week, shrieking."

"Look here," someone was saying. "It's his damned trotter. His decision."

Apparently it wasn't. "Knife," Mr Comrie barked to me, again. "No, the other—with the curving blade."

The Arabian pirate's knife. It was used—I was about to discover—to slice through skin and muscle. Many surgeons still employed a technique known as the Master's Round: one sweeping circular cut. Mr Comrie insisted on carving a "V" instead, leaving longer skin flaps to suture together afterwards, over the stump. Much less pain, and a better chance of healing without rot.

"Hold him fast," he said to the four strapping sodgers, who now looked as chalky as Sidewhiskers.

"No!" wailed the stricken man.

"Two minutes, that's all. Two minutes out of a lifetime."

So it was. He sliced through to the bone, clean as carving the Sunday joint, and barked for the largest bonesaw. Two minutes later was calling for needle and thread. And Your Wery Umble, who had spewed all the way from Southampton, held his stomach down quite remarkable, handing over each instrument as it was barked for, and watching with fascination and something very close to awe. Truth told, I was a bit appalled with myself. You'd like to think you'd be more distressed by the suffering. But I was mainly exhilarated instead—by Mr Comrie's dreadful skill, and the notion that I had acquitted myself admirably. Afterwards, I groped for some words of reassurance to offer to poor Sidewhiskers, who groaned horribly as they carried him off.

"Well done," was the best I could come up with. "You'll see—right as rain. Back on your feet before you know it." I winced. "That is, back on your *foot*..."

Mr Comrie was wiping blood from his hands with a rag. It had soaked his shirt as well, though he didn't seem to notice. I cleared my throat, and waited for him to offer some gruff compliment.

"You can clean the instruments," he muttered. Forgetting, apparently, that I was not his servant.

"And what if he dies anyway?" I asked after a moment. "Holding him down like that, while he's screaming for you to stop."

"Then I'll have given him a chance. That's all a man can ask for, up against Old Bones."

Old Bones?

"The rattling fellow. With the scythe. When they're clean, you wrap them in cloth," he added, "before putting them back in the box."

I hesitated, and couldn't resist asking the question: "So what are these worth?"

A wintry look. "The skin right off your back."

"Right you are," I said, and commenced wiping the blood from the tools.

Mr Comrie continued to eye me. "I saw you on the ship," he said. "Running away from home? Or just haven't got one?"

"I expect that would be my business."

I said it with a careless shrug, the sort that marks out a London lad, tough as nails—and not at all the other sort of lad. The sort who'd find himself sobbing on the road to Southampton, with a sense that the world was much too large, with no one in it who'd care if he expired in the nearest ditch.

"I'm here for a sodger," I said to him.

He honked one abrupt syllable. Apparently this was a laugh. "Sodger, eh? You'd do better to tag after me."

"Not likely," I snorted, deciding to take against him strongly.

"How old are you?"

"Eighteen."

"And I'm the King of Portugal."

"Sixteen, then."

"Fourteen. At the outside."

He reached for his jacket, which he'd draped over a chair. Two wide-eyed Spanish pot-boys had arrived with sawdust, to sop up the blood on the floor. They were going to need more sawdust.

"I was fourteen when my father died," he said then, unexpectedly. "My mother died years airlier."

He said it like that: *airlier*. I shrugged.

"Bring the leg," he said.

"The what?"

He pointed. Sidewhiskers's severed trotter was lying on a bench nearby, attracting flies.

"We bury those."

"I don't take orders from you."

But it seems I did—and it turns out a leg is heavier than you might expect. I picked it up and followed him out the door.

And I followed Alec Comrie for the next five years, through the field hospitals of the Peninsula. Just a dogsbody at first, but by and by I was helping during procedures, even learning to tie off the arteries after an amputation, since it turned out I have a knack for this sort of thing—keen eyes and nimble fingers. Then I followed him back across the Channel, spewing every nautical foot of the way. Followed him to London, where I discovered a city a-swagger with the Spirit of the Age, and did my best to swagger along with it. And so we might have continued for many years, Your Wery Umble prancing in his show-pony way while Alec Comrie lanced boils in Cripplegate. Jemmy Cheese might have died — or lived — and faded from our memories, and Meg Nancarrow with him. Dionysus Atherton might have continued on his long and dark descent, with no further consequence for Wm Starling, and the great globe itself gone on turning, turning, turning through the heavens, just exactly as old Copernicus had predicted.

Then came the night of Bob Eldritch and the Wolves.

6

Bob Eldritch had fallen in with Dionysus Atherton and a dozen other members of the Wolves Club at a chop-house in Russell Street. I have this on the authority of witnesses. A barrister named Tom Sheldrake was with him, along with two or three cronies from the Inns of Court and several theatre men. The names of these others are not important, although I have them in my notes. They were given to me by one of the serving girls when I went to the chop-house some days later, intent on puzzling together the steps that Atherton had taken en route to the catastrophe that awaited at the culmination of the night.

Atherton had arrived at six o'clock. Seeing him, Tom Sheldrake exclaimed in dread.

"No!" he cried. "No, not yet — for Bob Eldritch is still alive!"

Bob summoned a pained smile, and a small obliging chuckle. He was a solicitor, a round mild man of two- or three-and-thirty, with a widow's peak and a twisted leg that caused him to walk with an awkward hirple.

"Back, thou implacable Nemesis!" cried Tom Sheldrake to Atherton.

He had flung himself dramatically in front of his friend, as a hero might do upon the stage, being convinced — or so he affected to be — that the surgeon stalked Bob relentlessly, covetous of studying his deformity. Tom was a witty fellow. "Back, I say, for Bob Eldritch ain't for pickling yet!"

Bob supplied another pained chuckle. By and large he accepted the terms of his friendship with Sheldrake, which involved a willingness to roll over at regular intervals with his tail wagging feebly and his legs in the air, and the tacit concession that Tom's life was writ in dramatic letters whilst his was confined to parentheses. "Hullo, Atherton," he added, his game smile not quite masking a secret concern that he was indeed being eyed with professional interest.

The surgeon returned the greeting, with a wink that stopped just short of reassurance. "Is there wine in London?" he asked, turning to the others. "Then fetch it forth!"

A cheer went up. Cheers often did when Atherton was present. His smile gleamed through the pall of smoke.

The chop-house was low-ceilinged and dingy, with dark stalls along one wall and greasy tabletops, and the composition of the meat pies was a subject of fierce debate. Tom Sheldrake held that the absence of rats would be an optimistic sign, except that there were no cats either. But Tom was ever the drollest of fellows — a sad dog, as his friends would put it. Besides, the dinginess suited the Wolves, for they were all rough dangerous fellows when gathered together, as wild as a band of highwaymen, however meek most of them might seem in everyday life. And the chop-house was just round the corner from Drury Lane, where Mr Edmund Kean was first tragedian. This evening he was to perform Sir Giles Overreach in Massinger's play *A New Way to Pay Old Debts*. It was the role he had been performing two nights earlier, when he had come within a whisker of killing Lord Byron dead.

Just as Atherton arrived, one of the Wolves had been re-enacting the poet's collapse.

"Lord Byron himself," exclaimed Bob Eldritch, now. "Two nights ago, Atherton—you've heard?"

Atherton had, along with half of London.

"A convulsive fit," said Bob, "and it was Kean's performance did it to him. The final act, as Overreach goes mad and rages..."

"Women dissolve into hysterics," interrupted Tom Sheldrake, to make sure the story was properly told. "They shriek aloud, Atherton, and swoon. The other players upon the stage turn pale; Mrs Glover must support herself upon a chair; and then suddenly down goes Byron. Drops in his private box—down, sir, like a poleaxed ox—clutching his throat and foaming."

"Perhaps not technically foaming," ventured Bob Eldritch, stung into a small display of independent spirit, "as a medical man might understand the term..."

"Foaming, sir, at the mouth."

"And whether strictly speaking a poleaxed ox could clutch its throat..."

"Go and find an anatomist's shelf, Bob, and perch yourself upon it."

"Yes, all right, but—"

"A peer of the realm, precipitated into convulsions by the

player's art. By the greatest display of passion, sir, ever seen upon an English stage. Upon any stage, to state my personal opinion, in the world — *that* is what we observed, those of us who were privileged to be at Drury Lane two nights ago."

"Although in strictest factuality" — a quiver of actual mutiny in Bob's mutter — "I don't recall your being there at all."

"Gentlemen — and I include my friend Bob Eldritch in this category, despite any quibbles that he himself might advance, upon technical grounds..."

"Indeed, Tom, I am the one who described to you how — "

"Gentlemen, and ladies too, for I note a few of the fair sex here present amongst us — and despite whether 'ladies' is the term that my friend Bob Eldritch would use, in his customary insistence upon strict speaking — for God's sake shut your cake-hole, Bob, and raise your glass — ladies and gentlemen, luminaries and Bob, I salute Mr Edmund Kean!"

A howl of approval shook the rafters. Atherton howled along with the others, for this was of course the very *raison d'être* of the Wolves Club. It had been formed at the instigation of Mr Edmund Kean, and existed to howl approval of him, as the greatest actor of his generation. On nights when Kean was not performing, it went to howl opprobrium at rival tragedians, many of whom as arrogant upstart pretenders deserved to be howled right off the stage. There were thirty or forty Wolves in total — men of the theatre, in one capacity or another, along with professional men — including those such as Atherton whose participation was occasional. When fully assembled, they howled very loudly indeed.

More Wolves had drifted in after Atherton's arrival, though they still numbered fewer than a score. But more would be waiting at the theatre, and the whole pack would descend upon Fountain Court afterwards, for tonight was to be one of *those* nights, on which wine would flow like the rivers of Babylon and maidens would bolt their doors in holy dread—or not, depending upon the maiden. In the meantime, those assembled throats howled so lustily that you could imagine the sound reaching the ears of Edmund Kean himself, who was currently in his dressing room, girding his loins for the evening's performance. This would involve quantities of wine and a second set of loins, belonging to a Cyprian. A third and even a fourth set of loins might be later called into play, at the intervals between the acts. Edmund Kean was the very Avatar of the Age.

He would certainly be at Fountain Court afterwards, along with Tom Sheldrake and Bob Eldritch and Dionysus Atherton. As fate would have it, Your Wery Umble would be there too.

*

I'd been to the Giltspur Street Compter that afternoon. It had been three days since the operation, and Jemmy was still alive. He was even awake, or partly so, lying in some twilight Limbo with his eyes half open. But he was ominously warm to the touch, and his breath came in shallow rasps.

"Fever's coming on," said Meg.

"I'll tell Mr Comrie."

"Fuck all he can do."

She was right, of course.

She had pinned her hair up and wore a different dress, a drab wool skirt of penitential grey, so presumably she had gone home at some point. But she was sitting where I had left her, at Jemmy's side. She had dipped a bit of rag in cool water and was dabbing at his face and neck, crooning as she did something soft and tuneless and unutterably sad. She seemed to me in that moment not a lover at all, but a haggard young mother, tending to a monstrous child.

I had come to change the dressing on Jemmy's wound. Meg stood to let me do so, and after a moment I felt the touch of a hand on my shoulder.

"You have a good heart," she said awkwardly. "I didn't like the looks of you one bit. But you been kind to us."

Hardly older than I was — and younger than my own mother had been, the last time she'd laid eyes on me. That was the notion that occurred to me, looking up at her, and what a curious one it was. I'd never seen my mother beyond my infancy, nor seen a likeness of her neither, though a Warder at the Founding Hospital told me once that she'd been slim and dark. "Like you," he confided, "except normal. Small and quite pretty, as I recollect, instead of pointy and stunted." I wondered now what expression had been on my Ma's face as she looked down one last time on her Changeling — a frail unlovely thing, staring back — and whether she'd looked as Meg Nancarrow did at this moment, a curtain of dark hair falling across pure desolation.

"I'll be back tomorrow morning," I said, and found that my voice was husky.

I returned to Cripplegate to find Mr Comrie sitting alone in his surgery, climbing down into a bottle of pale. He received the news about Jemmy as I'd expected. "The Devil am I expected to do?" he demanded. "If he's going to live, he'll do it. But he won't." Then he stood and reached scowling for his jacket.

"Will you want me to come with you?" I asked.

"Gah," he said, swatting one hand as if dispersing flies.

So while Mr Comrie stumped towards Giltspur Street, I hurried west to Drury Lane. I had it in mind to attend the play, but mainly I was hoping to see Miss Annie Smollet.

Miss Smollet was the most bewitching actress in London. This was my personal view, and in truth it was a minority opinion, which helped explain why she currently sold flowers on the street outside the theatre. But I had been intensely in love with her for several weeks, since seeing her upon the stage at the Thespis, a ramshackle gaff in Whitechapel.

I did this, from time to time: fell in love with an actress. But this was different.

She aspired to act at one of the patent theatres—that is to say, at Drury Lane or Covent Garden. This led to her current station outside the great playhouse; she was hoping to meet someone—a leading actor, or a theatre manager—who might be stopped in his tracks by the loveliness of the flower girl and exclaim: "There stands my Desdemona!" No luck yet, but she remained hopeful. This, I was coming to understand, was her particular gift. Some actors have a gift for tragedy, others for comedy; Annie Smollet's great talent was for hopefulness. Often she would pay three pennies to go in and watch the play, since much may be learned by studying. Once or twice she may also have accompanied a gentleman into a private box for twenty minutes, as young women of a certain sort were notorious for doing at the theatre, cos I fear Annie Smollet was no better than she should be. But then, how many of us are?

She was on the corner of Russell Street as I arrived: a slender figure amidst the milling crowd, with roses in a wicker basket. A bright green dress—it set off her eyes—and red-blonde ringlets tumbling from a straw bonnet. I don't know that you'd call her beautiful, exactly. Perhaps more pretty than beautiful; the girl who lived just down the road. But she had a way of carrying herself—as she would, wouldn't she? An actress. And that spirit of hopefulness, shining.

"H'lo, Miss Smollet," I said.

She looked over my head at first, as people did. Finding me, she was blank for just a moment, before warming into a smile of recognition.

"You again," she said, most amiable.

I'd seen her here last night. On eight of the ten nights previous, in fact. I'd bought a flower each time.

"A rose, sir?"

"By any other name."

"'Scuze me?"

"Would smell as sweet."

I'd been rehearsing that in my head, assuming she'd recognize the reference. She looked at me oddly.

"Yes," I said hastily. "A rose."

It had been wilted at eight o'clock this morning when she bought a bucket-full from a stall at Covent Garden, and the intervening hours had not improved its prospects. But it was a rose nonetheless, from Miss Annie Smollet. She shook it free from the basket, and was already scanning the crowd as I handed her a penny—looking for the next customer, or better yet for a theatre manager heaving into view with arms flung wide. She smelled of oranges.

"Did I tell you that I saw you act, at the Thespis Theatre?"

I'd told her so on eight of the past ten evenings. But I had at least half of her attention back.

"I'm grateful you'd remember me, sir."

"Remember you? Miss Smollet, you are *seared*."

The odd look. "'Scuze me?"

"Into my recollection. When I close my eyes, Miss Smollet, you are there."

She had to weigh this for a moment, deciding. Then she dimpled in a smile.

"I don't s'pose I was *that* good, was I?"

"Miss Smollet, you were a radiance, glowing like the dawn."

Let's be honest: it was laughable. The likes of Your Wery Umble, aspiring to Miss Smollet? She wasn't much taller than I—this wasn't the problem. But look at her, and then look at me: a counterfeit Rainbow with a wilted rose, and a dark phizog that was all sharp points and triangles. Still. It wasn't completely unhandsome, that phiz. There were girls who had thought so, and a few who had even said it. And I had my smile, and I always had words, and—look at this—I'd made Miss Smollet beam.

Her play had been a burletta of *Antony and Cleopatra*, which is to say Mr Shakespeare's drama with songs and rhymes instead of spoken lines. Like the rest of the minor theatres, the Thespis was not licensed for dialogue. This was reserved by law for the two patent theatres, the fear being that spoken dialogue would incite sedition and inflame the weak-minded, and send the Pit rampaging into the night to burn down the Houses of Parliament. Annie Smollet had appeared as an Egyptian handmaiden, and had done so thrillingly, in a black wig and a dizzying gossamer gown. She wore a look of such plaintive distress when the asp clamped onto Cleopatra that the queen was entirely redundant to the drama.

I believed that Miss Smollet should be on the stage at Drury Lane tonight, and said so. Or at Covent Garden, playing Juliet and Rosalind.

"Both of 'em at once?" she exclaimed, feigning to misunderstand.

"And Cleopatra as well, all in the same play. I believe you are the one actress in London who could pull it off."

"Pull *'im* off, more like, is wot 'ee's angling for," sniggered a voice beside us. "Dirty little devil."

Two of Miss Smollet's friends had joined us, in paint and plumage. They were actresses as well, more or less, but in the meantime they were more reconciled than she to Cyprian endeavour. The one who'd just spoke so wittily—an arch individual with eyes like a badger's—was actually an acquaintance of Mr Edmund Kean. So I later discovered. She had in fact known him very well for almost ten minutes during the second interval of *Richard III* the previous November. Right now she stood snorting with drollery.

Miss Smollet blushed most fetchingly, and raised one hand to hide it. I expect her aim was to cover her mouth, cos I fear Miss Smollet's teeth were not quite everything you'd hope, seen up close. But I only loved her more for her imperfections.

The Badger and her chum were already moving away. Miss Smollet went with them, and never looked back.

Tucking the rose into my buttonhole, I wormed my way into the crowd outside the entrance to the Pit, where they'd been lining up to see Mr Edmund Kean — by the hundreds, and then the thousands — since four o'clock.

The theatre was an enchanted palace, blazing with light, with room for three thousand, all crammed together in the smoke from the oil lights and the candelabras. The din was prodigious and remained so right through the pantomime and the musical interlude, cos it was always that way at the theatre. A cracking good play — or a dunghill play, for that matter, or even a play that was middling putrid — provided much to talk about. Besides, half the audience never came for the play at all. They were much more interested in seeing friends, or being seen, or securing a bottle of claret and transacting a brisk encounter at the back of a box with one of the scores of Cyprians who attended each night, drawn from the dozens of brothels in the district.

For my threepenny admission, I managed to struggle my way to the back of the passage that surrounds the Pit, where I was wedged in so tight that I could lift my stampers right off the floor. For an extra three-and-sixpence I could have gone up to the boxes—providing I had such blunt in my pocket, which I didn't, and assuming I could have extricated myself from the crush, which was impossible. So I tried my best to breathe, and glimpsed from time to time through the wall of reeking humanity a flicker of movement upon the stage.

To watch Kean act was like reading Shakespeare by flashes of lightning. That's what someone had said—Coleridge, I think—and I wish I could tell you whether I agreed. I'd seen Kean twice before, and it was always the same: I had an impression of a diminutive dark figure, much smaller than you'd expect, flinging himself herk-a-jerk about the stage. Over the din I heard a voice unexpectedly hoarse, not at all like the sonorous instrument that Philip Kemble possessed, and all tragedians were expected to emulate. But that is all I can relate. No fits amongst the audience. No poets clutching at their throats like poleaxed oxen, or otherwise. I suppose you can't have everything in a play.

I stayed for the comic afterpiece, after which I should by rights have gone home to Cripplegate. But I'd overheard something the Badger said earlier, as she'd swept Annie Smollet away.

"We're invited," she had said. "All of us, after the play."

"Invited where?" asked Annie.

"The Coal Hole, my dove. Where else would they go?"

"You mean, the Wolves?"

"Of course!"

The Coal Hole was a song-and-supper room, the likes of which had begun to sprout like mushrooms about London. This one lay below the Strand in Fountain Court, at the foot of a narrow passage that reeked equally of yeast and urine. A cellar, low-ceilinged and heavy-beamed, with a horseshoe bar looming yonder through a haze of smoke and a raised platform where several nights a week entertainments were offered up. There was also a private room upstairs, where a number of the Wolves had assembled already, for this was where their feast was to be held. Lupine voices rose in raucous laughter.

I found myself a perch against the wall downstairs, not far from the door, where I sat with a jar of the Genuine Stunning. A trio of rough flash-talking men in a nook nearby spoke in dark mutters of a mate who'd done the out-and-out upon a lagger by the docks, and who now awaited crapping in the Start. They broke off briefly as the entertainment resumed, in the form of a florid tenor in a battered hat who warbled most piteously of a Ratcatcher's Daughter who yearned to wed her sweetheart and — as these things go — drowned in the Thames on the morning of the nuptials. There was no sign of Miss Smollet or the Badger — and now that I was here, what precisely had I been thinking? They'd go upstairs to the private room, if they came at all. And imagine the likes of Your Wery Umble, with sinking heart and wilted rose in buttonhole, being asked to join them.

As the Ratcatcher's Daughter was being fished out of the river, I toyed with proposing a game of chance to my flash-talking neighbours—the ones whose friend had murdered a sailor, and now waited in Newgate Prison to be hanged. But on the whole, I thought not. I had all but decided to give it up and leave, when a commotion began outside. Shouts in the passageway, and a squawk of protest, then billowing shrieks of laughter. The door burst open and a knot of revellers spilled in—rudely interrupting the heartbroken beau of the poor drowned Ratcatcher's Daughter, who was just about to cut his throat for grief.

In their midst was a dark puny man, dishevelled by drink, with a cawing Cyprian on either arm. He gave a lurch and steadied. Heads swivelled, and as they did he gained a foot in height. I do not make this up. He grew before our very eyes. His own were black and—I swear to God—they flashed. The molecules about him began to dance.

"*Humani nihil a me alienum puto*," he exclaimed, quoting Terence—yes, I looked it up. "Nothing human is alien to me!"

He lurched again, and grew pale. Turned regally towards me. Bent over, with an acrobat's grace. And shot the cat upon my boots.

Mr Edmund Kean, in the flesh.

Upon the great man's either arm were the Badger and her friend; Tom Sheldrake and Bob Eldritch trailed. Tom was in conniptions of laughter, as Bob clung to the rictus of a smile and contemplated one urine-soggy leg.

It seemed they had stopped at several public houses en route from Drury Lane, and Kean had just finished pissing in the passageway outside. In this he'd been assisted by the Badger, who held the pizzle. She had in fact been practising penmanship by writing her name on the wall, when her hand had inexplicably slipped, directing the stream at Bob Eldritch instead. Now here stood Bob on his good leg, shaking the other like a cat that has stepped in something. And now the final member of this merry band came through the door.

Mr Dionysus Atherton. And on his arm was Annie Smollet, laughing most prettily at something he'd said, and remembering an instant too late to cover her mouth. She didn't even see me as they swept past — stooped down as I was, even shorter than usual, wiping the vomit from my boots with straw from the floor. Hessian boots, they were, quite stylish. I was singularly proud of those boots.

Atherton saw me, though, and recognized me at once. A swift spasming of visceral disgust, the look that crossed his face whenever he saw Your Wery Umble. Ever since the first shock of seeing me on his doorstep, one autumn evening more than half a year previous. Then he continued on his way, mounting the stairs with Miss Annie Smollet clinging to his arm.

The room above the Coal Hole was long and rectangular, with tapestries upon the walls. On nights when the Wolves Club gathered, it blazed with light from smoking lamps like Aladdin's Cave. There might be sixty men, or even more, all packed round a table that groaned with serving plates and glittered with bottles and decanters. There were women too, of course, sitting upon laps to be finger-fed sweetmeats, or coaxed beneath the groaning board, or in fact taken right there on top of it, to do some groaning of their own amidst loud huzzahs and joyful cries of manly exhortation. The Wolves were in addition to their theatre-going a philanthropical organization; they took up subscriptions for the deserving poor, and distributed geese at Christmas. But God's great swinging bollocks — as Mr Comrie would say — they did know how to howl.

An hour had passed, and I remained below in the tavern. Entertainment was now provided by a man who juggled while singing bawdy songs. I had meanwhile in the corner produced my three little cups — done so in a spirit of reckless dejection, and never mind the dictates of sense and logic, cos Your Wery Umble was exactly that sort of fool. "That's it, sir; try again, and sure you'll smoke it this time; oh, bad luck!" But above, a clamour of revelry had been building, hoots and chanting. And before I quite had time to get myself killed, I heard Miss Annie Smollet scream.

I was on my feet and running up the stairs. As I burst into the room, there were Wolves and women milling and exclaiming. Through the rout of bodies I glimpsed the table-top, strewn with food and shards of pottery, and there in the midst of it — slender and sobbing and clutching her torn green dress — was the object of my adoration.

Afterwards, I was able to piece it all together.

It had begun with the arrival of two serving men, bearing a suckling pig upon a vast pewter serving-platter. The pig was received indifferently, but the platter brought inspiration forking down upon Tom Sheldrake, who saw at once that they had the raw materials to re-create the Birth of Venus as a tableau. The platter would serve as the clam-shell, a wall-hanging as the billowing main. They required only the goddess herself, to share her charms and set loose tumbling auburn locks.

And there was Annie Smollet, with her strawberry ringlets.

Oh no, she said quickly. No, really. She was happy right where she was: upon the knee of Dionysus Atherton, eating sweetmeats.

Hoots of raucous encouragement. Venus shrank back. Atherton laughed, and heaved her to her feet.

Huzzahs. Tom Sheldrake reached to take her hand.

"Please, no. No, really, sir — I couldn't."

There was panic on her pretty face. Her tresses had tumbled, but she would not remove her clothes, no not on any account, not even with Tom Sheldrake's cheerful assistance. Indeed, sir, no; she would not stand naked upon that platter, with countenance demure. When Sheldrake persisted, she struck at him, to the merriment of all.

"Stop it!"

Venus had started to cry. In another moment, Tom Sheldrake might have paused to reconsider. One of the other women might have risen to her assistance, wrapping a protective arm about her and glaring remonstrance round the room. Possibly even the Badger, who was after all Miss Smollet's best friend.

But in that instant, Bob Eldritch rose up.

Over the course of the past few hours, he had been jeered at, interrupted, shouted down and pissed upon. It had been that sort of evening for Bob Eldritch; it had been that sort of life. Bob had had a bellyful, of ignominy and of claret. Now, with his keen legal mind, he had pierced to the heart of the matter and understood that Miss Smollet was being coy. Thus he lunged drunkenly at décolletage, and clutched.

Miss Smollet gasped. Breasts spilled out in a rending of cloth — milk-white orbs, b'God, exactly as described in plain-bound tomes that Bob Eldritch had furtively purchased from certain booksellers in backstreets near Paternoster Square. She cried out — "Oh, sir, fie!" — exactly as over-dramatic virgins were wont to do within such pages, thus confirming Bob in his conviction: play-acting.

Tom Sheldrake could scarce believe his twinklers. "Have at her, Bob, you shrivelled stallion!"

Miss Smollet screamed as she crashed down upon the tabletop with Bob Eldritch upon her. Amidst a great bray from his fellows, he wrenched at his breeches to free that Terrible Engine with which Lord Rutalot in plain-bound pages laid siege to the Temple of Hymen.

There was a problem, however. The breeches had bound up maliciously, to thwart the Amorous Knight. He hunched — he reared up on his knees — he uttered strangled oaths. But the treacherous breeches held fast, in such a manner as never afflicted Lord Rutalot, while the Ravishing Instrument raged within, bent in slantingdicular distress. Bob's face turned crimson — not at all unlike the suckling pig's. His eyes bulged, big as onions. He flapped feebly with one arm, like a gosling attempting flight, and clutched with his other hand at his throat. As the Wolves fell about themselves in mirth, Bob Eldritch uttered a soundless howl and toppled sideways.

This was the very moment I burst in. And the tableau before me was not at all what Tom Sheldrake had intended, when he had set all of this in motion. The milling revellers; the ruins of the meal; the suckling pig on its back upon the floor, trotters to the moon, like a battlefield casualty. And Miss Smollet crouching wretchedly on the table, clutching the tatters of her dress. Squirming through the press, I wrenched my coat off and wrapped it as best I could around her shoulders.

"What did they do?" I cried, ready to kill them all.

The laughter was beginning to turn. Not that I even noticed, at first, with my heart so full of rage and Annie Smollet. But the hoots were giving way to consternation.

"Christ, look at him," the Badger was saying.

Bob Eldritch lay on his back. His face was now a deep rich purple, and his legs were juddering.

"Come now, Bob!" exclaimed Tom Sheldrake. "A joke is a joke, sir, but you begin to go too far."

But Bob had gone too far already. He had gone a considerable journey down a long dark road, and if not hallooed in desperate haste he was not coming back. I saw this clearly, despite the tumult, and the distraction of Annie Smollet weeping against me.

Atherton saw it too. Shouting for the Wolves to stand aside, he shoved forward and knelt.

"Bestir yourself, Bob Eldritch," ordered Sheldrake, growing stern. "In a moment we shall lose all patience."

Bob Eldritch no longer moved at all. Atherton plunged his fingers down the gullet, but they would not reach. He called for a knife.

A candied plum: this was discovered subsequently. Some wag had thrown it in a moment of inspiration, as Bob had reared with mouth agape, wrenching at his breeches.

Atherton had the knife in his hand and cut down with the sharp point, notching a cross at the base of Bob Eldritch's windpipe. Blood brimmed, but did not bubble. If air were passing through, there would be froth.

"Christ A'mighty," said the Badger. "Is he dead?"

"No one is dead!" cried Tom Sheldrake, colour draining from his phiz. Tom was the one—of course it was—who'd thrown the candied plum. "Bob Eldritch, stir your stumps!"

Atherton was wrapping Bob in his own coat, and shouting for more. He needed blankets. And a bellows—yes, a fireplace bellows—quickly.

"Is he dead?" the Badger asked again.

Atherton seized the bellows. Thrusting the tip into the notch he had cut in the windpipe, he commenced to pump, as if Bob Eldritch could be inflated like a balloon and thus lifted clear of his dreadful predicament. As if he might burgeon and swell, and then—most remarkably, and with the deft insertion of a cork—rise like Lazarus. His chest rose and fell, and rose again with Atherton's exertions, causing the onlookers to exclaim in hopefulness. But when the bellows was removed, the wind whistled feebly from Bob Eldritch's lungs, like a toothless man attempting a tune. He deflated very slowly, and did not move again.

Tom Sheldrake was now as pale as a corpse himself. He shook like a linden leaf. "You are a wretch, Bob Eldritch," he cried, "if you suppose that you can die like this! Be manful, sir, and stand up!"

"Summon a carriage," Atherton commanded. "Quickly!"

A grimness had come upon the surgeon, and a gleam.

"A carriage?" cried Tom Sheldrake. "Where are you taking him?"

"To my house."

Tom Sheldrake howled. "No, sir—it is monstrous—you will not! I say you will not have Bob Eldritch upon your shelf!"

But such was not Dionysus Atherton's intent. Oh, no indeed. Such was not his intention at all.

7

Atherton had a house in Crutched Friars, near Trinity Square. Not a fashionable district — most certainly not Mayfair — but in the heart of the City, and not far from Guy's Hospital across the river. The house itself was a good one, large and detached, with stables in the back, as befitted a Rising Man.

Miss Phyllida Deakins lived in mortal trembling in that house.

Phyllida Deakins was a clergyman's daughter, and her father's own dear darling girl. She had been a governess in her last position, a decent Christian governess in a decent Christian house, with a window that opened upon the Devonshire sunrise, and two bright angels in her care. Now she was condemned to Crutched Friars.

To live under a surgeon's roof was distressing enough at the best of times. Patients creeping in for consultations, and sudden shrieks from behind closed doors. Besides, dissections took place in all such houses; everyone in London knew it. And Flitty Deakins had a mortal horror of dissection. To be stretched in your nakedness upon a table for anatomists to leer at; to be splayed and carved and severed, until you could never be Resurrected whole, and must face Eternity with missing limbs and your ribcage gaping wide. Since coming to this terrible house she had been haunted by unspeakable dreams, in which she awakened on Christmas Day to find herself laid out in place of the goose, with carollers gathered about the table and Mr Atherton standing golden and gleaming with a great silver fork in one hand and a carving knife in the other, exclaiming in ghastly bonhomie: "Now, who is for white meat, and who is for dark? And which of the children will have the Pope's Nose!"

Did she deserve this? Perhaps she did. Flitty Deakins admitted the possibility, as a Christian; perhaps she deserved such torment, and much more besides. Which one of us after all could claim to merit any reward, beyond God's Judgement upon our iniquities? And Miss Deakins had sinned in such a manner as must make the seraphim cry out in despair for her poor tatter of a soul—but still she could not think that she deserved to suffer so much.

The horror began as you stepped through the front door, where awaiting you in the entrance foyer was the articulated skeleton of a tiger. Upon the stair-post coiled the snarling skeleton of a stoat, and there was infinitely worse to come, for down the hall was Mr Atherton's Collection Room. A human skeleton stood beside the bookcase in this room, and organs and limbs and unholy deformities floated in sealed glass jars on shelves along the wall. Amongst these were jars containing *foeti*: three of them, human *foeti*, in ascending size. These gazed with empty hopeless eyes upon Miss Deakins as she scrubbed the floor, for this was one of her duties, to get down upon her knees in this unholy place and scrub, as if any water in the world could wash it clean.

Often in her toils she was watched by Odenkirk, Mr Atherton's man. A creature of angles and corners, was Odenkirk; he sloped suddenly around them, coming upon you all unexpected and demanding what you'd been up to. He'd be smiling, as often as not, but it wasn't the smile of a Christian at all, just a crooked slash across his face. He'd sprawl down onto a stool for an hour at a time, smoking his short clay pipe and staring at you while you laboured. His legs outthrust, for they were very long and thin, as was all the rest of Odenkirk, excepting his feet and his hands. They were huge, those hands; they were pig-sticking hands, for such was how Odenkirk had started off in life. He had begun by killing pigs, and he had done much worse than that since. Oh yes he had, for Flitty Deakins had made enquiries. Flitty Deakins had acquired certain Facts that would curl your hair.

Odenkirk would like to grip you with those pig-sticking hands. Imagining this, his smile through a haze of smoke was lupine. His hair was entirely grey, which was not natural, for Odenkirk was still a young man. Abruptly he would suck on his teeth and say, out of nothing at all: "You don't fool me, Miss Phyllida Deakins." He would chuckle down low in his throat. "I *know* you. I guessed what you was the instant I laid eyes. Maybe the Man Himself don't know, and most prob'ly he wouldn't care if he did. But I make it my business to establish what I'm dealing with, and I'd smoked you out within a week."

At the end of each harrowing day, Flitty Deakins would creep by candlelight up the stairs to the bed she shared with Cook. Past the tiger and the stoat, all the way to the second landing, where a turbaned Hindoo with emerald eyes awaited. Some nights he would let her pass, but other times he would leap and sink his fangs into her shoulder. Miss Deakins was much addicted to laudanum, which encouraged hallucinations.

But the Collection Room was real enough. So were the tiger and the stoat, and Odenkirk. And so was Flitty Deakins's distress.

"Two nights ago, Mr Starling. I have not slept one second since; I swear I may never sleep again. For every time I close my eyes, I see that chalk-white face rise up, and hear that dreadful shriek."

It was late morning as she described this to me. The two of us were huddled together at a table in the Duck and Dolphin in Leadenhall Street, in a shadowy corner furthest from the door. Miss Deakins did not set foot in such low places; she had never tasted gin. But on this one occasion she found she must accept a dram of pale— "a very small dram, Mr Starling; the very smallest they will serve, and not more than one; or two, at the uttermost limit" — on account of her nerves being shattered.

We'd met by chance a few minutes earlier, on the street. We knew one another already, more or less; I'd seen her several times at Atherton's house as I'd arrived on some errand or other from Mr Comrie. I had been on my way there that morning, when Miss Deakins had emerged suddenly from a pothecary's shop: tall and spare and dressed in black, her dress hanging slack and shapeless as a cassock. Miss Deakins always dressed in black, as if in permanent mourning for her own lost happiness. She gasped as I came round the corner at her, then calmed a little in recognition.

"Mr Starling, is it? Yes, of course—it is only my friend Mr Starling, Mr Comrie's man. You gave me such a start."

Something was clearly amiss, even by Miss Deakins's customarily agitated standards, so I lingered. Besides, a question had been gnawing ever since that terrible night above the Coal Hole, and after a moment of fragmented this-and-that, I asked it.

"A man was taken to Crutched Friars the other night. I don't suppose you heard what happened?"

She went rigid. "Man?"

"Two nights ago, a man called Eldritch. Atherton brought him in a coach, sometime after midnight. He died—leastways he must have done, cos his funeral's set for Saturday. But I couldn't help wondering... Miss Deakins? Are you quite well?"

She had begun to quiver uncontrollably. "Oh, Mr Starling," she said in a whisper. "Oh, that dreadful night!"

She had heard the coach arrive outside, she said, in a clattering of hooves. Odenkirk had hurried to meet it. Miss Deakins recognized his voice, and moments later she glimpsed him through the window, holding up a lantern and gesturing as he led the way across the stableyard behind the house. In the shaft of light there were three men, lugging something limp and heavy. Mr Atherton was with them; Miss Deakins heard his voice, exhorting them to be quick. It had been close to forty minutes, she heard him saying.

"Forty minutes?" Odenkirk's voice, uncertain what Atherton meant.

"Since the man has been dead. So there may yet be time."

"Time for...?"

"Hurry!"

The stable bulked in the darkness beyond.

Flitty Deakins lived in mortal trembling of that stable. No doubt it had once been used as Nature intended, for the keeping of horses. But Mr Atherton kept other creatures instead, outlandish beasts: peacocks and sloths and cassowaries, and some whose identities she could not even guess at. She could hear them, at all hours. They haunted her nightmares, and once in the creeping light of dawn she had awakened in her bed to see the face of Belial staring at her through the window. Her screams had petrified Cook, and brought Mr Atherton himself at a half-run. He had barked at her until she was able to stammer a description, at which he left again in a choler, calling to Odenkirk that the baboon had escaped. It was a serious matter, Odenkirk had later told her with a chuckle; the creature was dangerous.

"*Dangerous*? I told him, Mr Starling, I said to him: 'The creature is not *dangerous*. The creature is one of the four princes of Hell itself, Mr Odenkirk, drawn here by the wickedness of this house!' Oh, Mr Starling — dear young Mr Starling — you can have no idea what that house is like."

In fact I knew very well what went on in surgeons' houses, living as I did in one myself. Mr Comrie had no stable to fill with creatures for anatomical study, and he was never as active as was Atherton in transactions with the Resurrectionists. But from time to time there were the same night-time doings in Cripplegate as haunted Miss Deakins. Thumps and muffled curses on the stair; rough men in moleskins arriving in darkness, with burdens tied up in sacks, to be hidden 'til the donkey-cart should arrive to transport them to the Death House for dissection. Miss Deakins must surely have known this, but perhaps her need for a friend was so very great—any friend at all, even if it be a surgeon's boy she'd seen no more than five times in her life—that she invented in her head quite a different Will Starling, and poured out to him her poor heart.

She wasn't old. Not yet thirty, was my guess, though her hair was streaked with silver and her face was already gaunt with the habit of laudanum. But there at the Duck and Dolphin, in the writhing shadows cast by firelight, she might have been a beldame in a cave.

"The stable," she whispered. "I saw them take him—it—the corpse, for that's what it was. I knew this at once, Mr Starling, as surely as I'm sitting here before you. They carried the mortal remains of a human creature."

There was a loft in the stable, at the top of a wooden ladder, accessible by a trapdoor that was kept padlocked and bolted. Flitty Deakins had not seen this with her eyes, as she would not set foot in that stable. But others had; there were whispers. And there was a small cracked window in the loft, behind which Miss Deakins had from time to time glimpsed movement. Now she saw dark figures moving in the light of Odenkirk's lantern; they were laying something out upon a table.

"I stood as one astonished, Mr Starling. *A-stonied*—turned to stone—in the true original meaning of that word." She knew such things, for she had been a governess, with two bright angels in her care.

"And where were you, Miss Deakins?"

The question took her off balance. "In Devonshire, Mr Starling, as I have said before."

"I meant, where were you standing? Two nights ago, as you watched?"

Cos I wanted to be clear in my head. Even there at the Duck and Dolphin, so near the start of it all, I had the sense that I must be clear in my head.

"I was standing in my bedchamber, of course. I'd been wakened by the voices, and went to the window."

But I had a notion that the servants' quarters at Crutched Friars faced south and east—such was my quick calculation, based on the very few times I'd been inside—and not north, towards the stable. Atherton's surgery was at the back of the house, however, on the second floor. His surgery, where laudanum would be kept.

I looked at her closely. She didn't seem opium-addled just now, though of course you could never tell for certain with those long sunk in the habit. She clutched her glass of pale in both hands, gazing down in such fixed distress that you'd think she could see the events of that night, reflected in the surface like the portents in a Gypsy's crystal.

So: she'd crept down the corridor, to prig a stoppered brown bottle from Atherton's surgery. I pictured her reaching towards the cabinet, in the twisting light of her candle. Then the sound of the carriage — Miss Deakins freezes — voices from outside draw her in fearful fascination to the window.

"And what did you see?"

Miss Deakins closed her eyes. She drew a quavering breath, to steady herself.

"Miss Deakins?"

"I saw an arm."

"An arm?"

"Rising up."

"I don't understand what you mean."

But I had begun to guess. The first cold intimations commenced to spider up my spine.

They'd been busy about the body, she said. The corpse in the loft, upon the table. They'd been doing...things. Odenkirk, and Mr Atherton.

"What things?"

She could not say; she did not choose to imagine. Then they stepped back. There was a sudden flash of light; it lit the loft for a flickering instant, and she saw them revealed like players upon a stage. Then the arm rose up.

"The dead man's arm?"

"Yes."

"They raised the dead man's arm?"

"Oh, no. The dead man raised it himself."

It should have been midnight as she told me this. We should have been wreathed in yellow fog. She leaned closer, her eyes fever-bright.

"He lifted his arm, Mr Starling. He reached out. Like a lost soul reaching from the grave."

"And then?"

"It fell."

The arm fell back down. But there was another flash, and it rose again. The fingers moving this time, clenching. Miss Deakins saw commotion from the others, in that flash. Dark figures herk-a-jerk.

"And then?"

"There was another flash."

"The arm rose up again?"

"No, Mr Starling. Oh, no. Poor dear Mr Starling." If that were all, an arm, then Miss Deakins might yet hope to sleep again. "The third time, *he* rose up."

The man who was lying on the table: he lurched perpendicular. Sat there in the flash of light, and then turned his head. With hair on end and eyes like eggs, he stared across the night at Phyllida Deakins.

"And then he shrieked. Oh, Mr Starling. Oh, that cry...!"

Such a shriek of desolation as would haunt her the rest of her life, through all the nights that lay ahead; it would pursue her through all the winding byways of this world, and hound her gibbering at last — she swore it would — through the gates of Bedlam Hospital. Such a shriek as would not be heard again until the dead rose up at the end of days to face the Awful Reckoning. As she clutched my wrist with both her hands, it grew clear enough to me now, if ever I'd doubted it to begin with: Flitty Deakins was mad. Deranged, and an opium addict into the bargain—a woman beset by green-eyed Hindoos on the landing.

But what if what she said was true? The question whispered itself with a scrotum-tightening intensity.

"What happened afterwards? The man sat up, you say—the corpse. You say he looked at you. But then...?

I trailed away. Miss Deakins was shrinking as she gazed past my shoulder.

I turned to see a man lounging against a wooden post behind us. A long grey man with a smile slashed across his face. "Why, ent this just the prettiest pair?" drawled Odenkirk.

Mr Comrie was in his surgery that night, jotting in his case-book. He stopped as he realized what I was telling him, and closed the book slowly.

"And you are—what—*amused* by this?" he demanded.

I suppose I'd been chuckling a bit as I related the tale. The way you do when you're not at all certain about what you've heard, and even less about how it will be received.

"No," I said lamely.

"Then extinguish that smirk, and say what you came to say."

So I did. He stared at me fixedly 'til I'd finished. A clock ticked louder than any clock had done before, since the invention of Time.

They'd lodged together as chirurgical students at Edinburgh University years previous—the two of them, Atherton and Mr Comrie. They'd been friends of a sort, even good friends, difficult as it was to imagine, and friends of a sort they remained to this day, though I don't suppose that ever made them equals, certainly not in Atherton's eyes.

There was silence when I finished. Hammer blows from the clock.

"An attempt to revive a corpse," he said at last.

"Yes."

"According to the Deakins woman."

"Assuming we can believe..."

"Exactly. Laudanum, and green-eyed Hindoos."

"True."

"And one of the rising surgeons of London." His mouth pursed sourly. "Anything else to tell me, William?"

I felt a fool, by now. But in fact there *was* more.

"Threats were implied," I told him.

"Excuse me?"

"His man came in on us—Odenkirk. Warnings were intimated."

"Threats upon yourself?"

"And Miss Deakins."

"In so many words?"

Not exactly. Odenkirk had in fact waited 'til Flitty Deakins had fled the Duck and Dolphin, then pulled up a stool beside me. "What's she been telling you—eh, friend Starling?" he had asked. "The Deakins, with the red rag flapping in her gob." His head cocked in a just-between-us way, his smile a slash of comradeship. "Well, here's a word to the wise, as between two friends. Whatever she thinks she seen and heard — she didn't. She's an opium-fiend. A slave to it and a thief, poor soul, and a lying bitch besides, though it grieves me to say so. So whatever it was she said to you just now, you'll keep it to yourself. Yes? You'll forget you heard it in the first place, friend. Cos I have a fondness for the filthy lying slut, just as I have an amiable regard for you, and how distressed I would be to see you come to harm."

I gave Mr Comrie the gist. His eyes narrowed like clam-shells as he listened, and when I was done he grunted.

"One would see his point, consairning the source of your information."

"So . . . we do nothing?"

"Of course we do something, William. You will fetch my bollocking supper, if you'd be so good — a meat pie from the Black Swan, and a half-pint of brandy. And I in my turn will consume it."

Reopening his case-book, he turned his back and sat as he had done when I came in: straddling his stool, scritching with his quill and scratching with his free hand at an armpit, as elegant as a stone shed in a knacker's yard. And there behind him stood Wm Starling, Esq., squelched and smarting.

*

The first question is simply: what is life?

This was currently the subject of much debate amongst medical men, and broadly speaking there were two camps. In the first were the Hunterians. John Hunter had over his long and illustrious career come to believe in a Life-Force, carried in the blood, which was the source and spark of existence. It was not clearly defined, but very obviously this Life-Force must be something akin to a Soul. Hunter had advanced the theory late in his own life, when even the most rigorous men of Science may develop Mystical Leanings. But it continued to exert great influence, this theory, and over the past winter the surgeon John Abernethy — a disciple of Hunter's, and a fellow Scot — had delivered an acclaimed series of public lectures upon the topic, at the Royal College of Surgeons at Lincoln's Inn Fields.

In the other camp were the Materialists, disciples of a Frenchman named Bichat, who held that the Life-Force is just as actual as the faeries in the wood, and that life itself is neither less nor more than the sum of the physiological functions by which death is resisted, full stop. The Materialist view had most recently been trumpeted by William Lawrence, a former student of Abernethy's now risen to the post of Demonstrator in Anatomy at St Bart's. This spring he had delivered his own series of public lectures, gibbeting Mysticism and his old teacher with it.

This leads to the second question: when is a man actually dead? It is a question far more vexed than you might suppose.

Oh, there are signs that anyone may observe. A man is dead when he commences stinking, and his widow puts on her weeds. He is dead when his friends exaggerate his virtues, and the maggots go about their business. But what constitutes the very moment in time when a man passes from one side to the other?

The absence of respiration? Surely not, else many had returned from the dead. Not six weeks earlier, I'd watched Alec Comrie resurrect a child who had drowned in a rain-swollen ditch. She'd been dead fifteen minutes at least — a little girl, lying cold and blue on a tavern table as Comrie, fetched from his dinner, came bandy-legging in. He chafed her limbs and wrapped her in blankets, for the first thing was to warm her. Then he lifted her from behind and squeezed his fist hard into her stomach, just below the breastbone, at which she dribbled brown sludge and then spewed out ditchwater, retching and opening her eyes. Amidst wonderment and jubilation she wept and called for her sister, who was subsequently discovered at a gin-shop two streets over, batting her glims at a sodger.

Or was death the stoppage of the heart? But hearts had been restarted. Hanged men's hearts had done so on their own — men pronounced dead by the attending surgeon and cut down, only to splutter back to life at the foot of the gallows. I could tell you of another man, two days deceased, who sat up on the dissecting table in the Death House at Guy's Hospital, croaking in consternation at the anatomist who was just about to cut.

All of which led to a third, and darker question. Once a man is truly dead and carried pale and cold across the Styx — once Old Bones has put an arm about his shoulders and walked him through the Gate into Darkness — might Science yet summon him back?

Attempts had been made. An Italian named Aldini had tried just a few years previous, right here in London. His uncle Luigi Galvani had experimented upon dead frogs, hooking them with wires to voltaic piles and running electrical current through them, and Aldini went one better. He tried to galvanize a human corpse, a wretch named George Forster who had drowned his wife and baby in a canal and was crapped for it at Newgate. Aldini took possession of the body — one of the four hanged felons granted by Law each year to the Royal College of Surgeons for scientific examination — and conveyed it to a nearby house, where preparations had been laid.

Three troughs, each containing forty copper discs and forty more of zinc. Incisions were made in the cadaver, and metal rods connected. With members of the Royal College looking on and a crowd thronging round the house, swelling by the minute as word spread, Signor Aldini applied the electricity. The first surge caused Forster's jaw to quiver, as if he should groan aloud and blurt some dreadful message from the Undiscovered Bourne; he opened up one ghastly eye and stared. A second application caused him to raise his hand and clench it, while moving his legs and thighs, like a man who would be on his way directly if he could just get his stampers beneath him. Nothing more dramatic could be achieved, though many in the room had turned quite pale as the subject's phizog gurned. Aldini could still provoke movement three hours later by applying current to the ear and rectum.

"But of course," said Dionysus Atherton equably, "it was nothing but scientific enquiry."

"Or so Aldini maintained."

"You read his paper, Alec, just as I did. It was an exercise in stimulating the muscles. Aldini never dreamed of bringing back the dead."

"Did he not?" Mr Comrie cocked his head. The declining sun was directly behind Atherton, irradiating him in its golden glow, and his friend was forced to squint looking up at him. "I know what he said, Dionysus. But I can't say for a sairtainty what any man dreams. Can you?"

Atherton laughed a little. "Perhaps not. No, not for a 'sairtainty,' as you say. And it is true enough that men have dreams."

"Some of which would frighten the Devil in Hell."

"The Devil in Hell? Poor Alec — there's your Northern boyhood, rising up to clutch you by the ankles. All those Sundays in Kirk, hemmed in by Calvinist aunts."

"And yet."

"And yet what? Why are we standing here, debating Signor Aldini's dreams?"

"You made the attempt yourself. Two nights ago."

Atherton had been about to start away, towards a carriage that had just been hailed by Odenkirk. Now he stopped, and for just an instant stood quite still — almost as still as Your Wery Umble, whose jaw had commenced dropping with Mr Comrie's first words, and who now stood clutched by the queerest commingling of glee and foreboding. I had assumed the subject was definitively closed after my attempt to broach it two nights earlier. Evidently not.

"Who's been telling you such tales?" asked Atherton after a moment. Addressing his friend, but staring out of the sun at Wm Starling.

"Do you deny it, then?" said Mr Comrie.

We were in the quadrangle in front of Guy's Hospital, in the dying sunlight of an April afternoon. It was — is — a wide pleasant space, with the hospital on three sides and the clatter of St Thomas's Street outside the gate, and a statue of Thomas Guy the founder standing in the middle, wearing an expression of furrowed benevolence. Students streamed past, some of them bound for Guy's sister hospital St Thomas's down the road, or else — more likely — for one of the many taverns hereabouts. Above us all, in one or two of the windows on the wards, a wan face might be glimpsed gazing out upon light and life.

Atherton had been lecturing that afternoon. The lecture concluded, students had flocked to him like sparrows to a feeder. I worked my way through and managed to slip him a note scrawled in my employer's hand: Mr Comrie's compliments, and could Mr Atherton spare a moment? He never acknowledged my presence as he took it, but after a minute or two I saw him glance at the contents, and in due course he excused himself from the sparrows.

Mr Comrie was waiting by the statue in the courtyard. "No word yet, I'm afraid," Atherton had announced without preamble. "But I expect to hear directly." He was assuming the Scotchman had come regarding a possible position for him here at Guy's, as a demonstrator in anatomy, one afternoon a week. Comrie had asked Atherton to speak a word on his behalf—a favour it had wrung his pride to beg.

"Never fear," Atherton continued, cheerfully. "We'll have this resolved soon. And the very next morning, we will take you to a tailor—a real one, Alec, with two good eyes and opposing thumbs and four fingers on either hand, instead of the blind amputee you would appear to patronize. By God, that coat of yours would humiliate a dustman."

Mr Comrie had muttered a stiff appreciation. Then, as Atherton prepared to depart, he had bluntly and without warning changed the topic. Now he stood awaiting Atherton's reply, squinting into the sunlight, and looking scarcely less stony than Thomas Guy himself.

"Eldritch. That was the man's name?"

"It was."

"And did you do it?"

"Of course," said Atherton, almost carelessly.

"Attempted to resurrect a corpse?"

"If that's what you want to call it."

"What would *you* call it?"

"My duty."

"And you believed him to be dead?"

"I knew that he was in a desperate strait."

And it occurred to me: what else had I been expecting him to say? Here in the quadrangle at Guy's Hospital in the last light of an April afternoon, with laughter and voices all around us, and London churning about its business, and Odenkirk sloping up behind us gaunt and grey — what had Your Wery Umble Narrator been thinking? That a surgeon should deny having tried to save a life?

"But did you think him dead?" Mr Comrie demanded again. Clearly this had disturbed him considerably more than he'd let me glimpse, and he was not a dog to let go if once he set his grip. "Fountain Court — that's where it happened? All the way to Crutched Friars. Must have taken half an hour. More? I've brought back souls who were all but drowned, but that was a matter of minutes. Half an hour — an hour? — that's something else. That's trying to resurrect the dead."

"And what exactly *have* you heard?"

Again, looking straight at me. As was Odenkirk, from a little distance away. His eye had pig-sticking in it.

So I answered.

"I heard an experiment took place," I said. "In the stable, behind your house. I heard electrical current was employed."

Mr Comrie looked back to Atherton. "Is this so?"

"I tried to stimulate a choking victim's heart and respiration," he replied.

"After he'd been dead for — what — an hour?"

"Fifty-three minutes, by my chronometer."

"And of course you failed."

"I have made arrangements for the funeral," said Atherton. "Is that sufficient reply?"

"D'you intend to try again?"

"On Bob Eldritch, do you mean? No, I think not. He's lying in Bowell's back room, Alec, with his jaw swaddled shut and pennies on his eyes. I suspect poor Bob is beyond the reach of Science. I suspect the time has come to let him rest."

"You know what I'm asking."

"He leaves a widow and two young children. We're taking up a subscription for their support. Perhaps you'll want to contribute."

"D'you intend to try again on someone else?"

"Of course. At the very next opportunity."

Mr Comrie's mouth had tightened to a thin white line. Atherton laughed out loud.

"Look at you," he said. "As dour as one of your Calvinist aunts."

"Be careful, Dionysus."

"I am always careful."

"There are limits to Science. This experimentation with the dead—it does not do. Nor does the utterance of threats." He had turned to Odenkirk, glowering up at him with a look so black that it made the much bigger man blink. "This boy is under my pairsonal protection. D'you understand? Touch him and you answer to me."

Odenkirk seemed about to sneer a reply, and then found himself shuffling his feet instead, and scowling abashed into the middle-distance. And Wm Starling? He felt his heart rising in proud fierce happiness, and proceeded to spoil it by opening his gob.

"He sat up on the table," I blurted, "and turned his head."

All three of them swivelled.

"The dead man — Bob Eldritch. He turned his face and looked out of the window."

Atherton stared down from out of the sun. He had seen me amongst the confusion at the Coal Hole two nights earlier, enfolding a sobbing Miss Smollet in my arms as he disputed with Old Bones for possession of Bob Eldritch. Now he took my measure.

"Miss Deakins said that, did she?"

"Leave Miss Deakins out of it."

But of course I had dragged her in by this point, hadn't I? Dragged her quaking and weeping into the very midst of it.

"Poor Miss Deakins," said Atherton. "To see such sights — and at twenty paces on a moonless night."

"Then he screamed."

"Excuse me?"

"Bob Eldritch. He opened his mouth and shrieked."

There was stillness for a moment then. Atherton had shifted half a step to one side, enough to place himself directly in front of the sun. Half blinded by it, I seemed to see him as dazzling as Phoebus, and as terrible. I raised one arm to shield against the glare, and he smiled at me.

"Never form the habit of laudanum, boy. God knows what phantasms will haunt your nights." His smile was thin and gleaming as a bonesaw. "And if you come to visit us at Crutched Friars, you will almost certainly hear the peacock. It shrieks like a soul in torment."

*

That night the horse came to me again, on a twilit battle-field. Always the same horse, lurching out of the darkness and the mist, where I am lost on a vast plain of dead and dying men. It is a fine grey horse, and as it turns towards me I see that the bottom half of its head is gone, carried away by a cannonball. The eyes remain, huge and wild and beseeching, and as they fix upon me I understand that the poor creature is seeing in me its last hope of salvation. I cry out at this in pure despair.

"William?"

A shadow bulked above me. Mr Comrie stood in the doorway, holding a candle.

"A dream, lad. You've had a dream. That's all."

I was on the pallet in my attic room at Cripplegate. Clutching the blanket, sitting drenched and rigid and fight-ing to claw a breath into my lungs. I discovered to my shame that I was weeping.

"Oh, now," Mr Comrie muttered. "No, no. No call for it."

A wooden scrape as he reached for the chair. Drawing it towards him, he sat himself awkwardly beside me, knobbly and lumpen in his nightshirt. After a moment, there was the weight of a hand upon my shoulder.

"Not your fault," he said. "You've been to the wars."

As had half the men in London, or so it sometimes seemed. You'd see them every day: old sodgers, sitting hollow-eyed in public houses, staring ten miles off and starting at shadows.

Mr Comrie shifted uncomfortably. Emotion never failed to make him squirm—he had no notion what to do with it, being the sort who expressed himself best in rigorous action. If I'd required to have a limb sawed off instead, he'd have been the very man. And now he had commenced blaming himself, as he did every time the horse came upon me and my cries in the night brought him trudging up the stairs.

"Five years. A lad your age? God's bollocks, I should never have taken you along."

"It wasn't your choice."

"I should have sent you home."

"Home?"

"England. Kent. That house with the great flopping titty. Wherever the Devil home is." He shifted again. A mist of brandy and old sweat. "It is here, I suppose," he added, looking round. "Ah, well. We do all right, William, between us."

I forced myself to breathe more steady.

"There," he said. "Better?"

The blackness outside the one small window was beginning to leaven with the dawn.

"I'm sorry," I said.

"Gah."

"I woke you up."

"Sleep, now. Brandy helps."

"I had some."

"Have more."

He chuckled a little and stood, reaching down with his hand to ruffle my hair. In the doorway, he paused.

"It is not our affair, William. This business at Crutched Friars—whatever it was. Not my affair, and not yours. What Dionysus Atherton does, or does not do. And it makes no difference what he is to you, or isn't. Eh? No matter what exists between you, or ought to. A threat to you—now, *that's* my affair. But not the rest of it."

And he was gone. I heard his footsteps stumping down the stairs. His door creaked open and closed, below, and the house subsided back into unquiet stillness.

The horse had been real enough, as it happens. An artillery horse, wounded in a skirmish on the road, not far from Waterloo. They'd cut it free from the harness and tried to drive it away, but it kept wandering back to join the other horses. The gunners couldn't bring themselves to deal with it and someone seized at a notion to send for a surgeon instead; somehow—God knows—the errand fell to me. When I arrived the poor beast was trying to press itself up against its fellows, as though fearful of being left behind. And of course I knew what I must do, cos the creature was mortally hurt and suffering. But I couldn't do it. It was—I don't know—it was five years of death, I suppose. Five years of men maimed and shrieking, and horses as well—the horses suffered as horribly as anyone, and they'd never even had the chance to choose. And there was something that had happened to a particular mate of mine, Danny Littlejohn—something that had happened two nights earlier, which was preying most cruelly on my mind.

However it was, there was the poor ruined horse, eyes white and wild and no jaw beneath, and I just stood. There was a thin keening sound, going on and on, and it turned out that this was William Starling, weeping uncontrollable.

Mr Comrie showed up that time too. Someone sent for

him, or else he'd followed me on his own — I never did know for a certainty — and of course he knew what to do. Taking a sabre from a cavalry captain he thrust it swift and kind into the poor horse's heart. Then he put a heavy arm around my shoulders and led me away.

The horse came for the first time that very night, and continued to come every two or three nights thereafter. Sometimes Danny Littlejohn was on its back. His own face pinched and white, gazing at me with such reproach that I thought I could scarce survive it.

8

Bob Eldritch was buried on a Monday afternoon, in a cold April rain in St Mary-le-Bow churchyard. There was a hearse drawn by four black horses with black feathers trembling on their heads, and six mutes in tall black hats to follow after, all supplied by Mr Bowell and paid for by Dionysus Atherton. The turnout was quite good—as many as three dozen—which was something to be glad of, I suppose. You don't like to see a man slip from this earth without leaving so much as a stain, no matter what he's done. The Wolves were out in force, looking grave and guilty. Edmund Kean turned up, arriving late and leaving early, but in the meantime standing in such sable gloom that you'd swear the Melancholy Dane himself had come to St Mary-le-Bow.

Atherton held up a black umbrella under which the widow sheltered, clutching his arm for support. A poor half-risen dumpling of a woman, stunned into doughy stupefaction by the tragedy: exactly the sort of woman who would marry Bob Eldritch, and bear him little dumple-bairns. She gave a sad cry as the coffin was lowered, but held on to a pathetic dignity. No howls and swoonings from poor Mrs Eldritch, nor hysterical precipitations.

Tom Sheldrake supplied those.

I had been keeping half an eye on Sheldrake, from my vantage by the gate. He had been pacing on the periphery, just outside the cluster of mourners round the grave, clenching his hands and working the muscles of his face, and with the muffled thud of the first sod falling he burst out in anguish: "Bob Eldritch, you will cease this charade! Rise up this instant, sir, or you and I are no longer friends!" Then with a desolate wail he leapt headlong into the grave, like Hamlet flinging himself after drowned Ophelia.

They fished him out, Atherton and several of the others, pinioning his flailing limbs and urging him to manliness. At length he was carried off sobbing, while Atherton helped the widow to a carriage. I waited in the churchyard until the grave had been filled, then left to bear my report to Annie Smollet.

She lived with the Badger in a room they rented in Holborn. It had mildewed walls and a low sloping ceiling and a soot-streaked window with a prospect onto the privy behind the house. There was one bed for the two of them to share, with a wooden box for an *escritoire* and a shelf with knick-knacks of chipped *chinoiserie*, and clothes strewn with such abandon that you'd have thought a trunk had exploded.

"They've buried him," I said.

Miss Smollet was still considerably shaken by events; she sat pale and frayed on the side of the bed. The Badger sat protectively beside her, one arm about her waist. A scent of lavender and sour linen.

"You were there?" the Badger demanded.

"I watched them shovel the dirt on top."

I had thought Miss Smollet would want to hear this—to know that it was over and done. But her eyes, red with lack of sleep, began to brim.

"I did not wish him dead," she said.

The Badger did, and said so, fiercely. She hoped Bob Eldritch was howling this very minute, with all the coals of Hell banked high about him.

Miss Smollet's bottom lip had begun to quiver. "I did not ask for any of this," she said. "They have no right to blame me for it."

"No one blames you, my dove!" exclaimed the Badger.

But Miss Smollet believed they did, even though we both assured her otherwise. She was convinced that the mourners had gathered for an hour at the graveside, doleful in countenance but vengeful in thought, specifically to condemn her in their hearts. I began to have the curious sense that she saw Bob Eldritch's funeral as an event that had primarily happened to Miss Annie Smollet—though I could hardly blame her, considering what she'd been through at Fountain Court. Standing there in the open door, I could hardly imagine blaming Miss Smollet for anything, ever.

She had me describe the event in detail, beginning to end. She grew paler than ever, and consequently more lovely, as I told how the coffin was lowered by ropes. Her colour flared just once, when I described how Atherton had held the umbrella for the widow.

"I hate him!" she exclaimed. "Mr Dionysus Atherton is hateful."

I did not contradict her.

"But I never hated Bob Eldritch," she said. "Not even considering what he done to me."

She was standing now. She moved to the window, and turning back she seemed wan but somehow ennobled, as people do who have been purified by long suffering. "I hate no man in this world," she said, "and no woman in it, neither, nor no child. I pray for all their souls, each one of them, and I ask them in their turn to pray for me."

Her chin was lifted in a way that seemed both humble and defiant. It was as if she had been trying on roles like hats in a milliner's shop, and had suddenly settled on one that fitted. An odd hat for the occasion: you'd almost think she was a woman wronged and doomed, going bravely to her own execution. But oh dear God in heaven, she was lovely.

"Come back and see us, Mr Starling," she said. Her smile was Tragic but Enduring. "Come back another time, and bring your cheerful heart with you."

The Badger rolled her eyes.

*

They sentenced Jemmy Cheese the selfsame day.

I had counted him lost that night when the fever took hold—cos hadn't I seen it a thousand times? That's how it was, with Old Bones. Drive him out the door with steel and shrieking, and he'd slip back through the window under cover of darkness, achieving through guile and gangrene what he couldn't carry off by main force. And there was next to nothing a surgeon could do to stop him. How could you cure a corrupting wound, after all, or halt the creeping black rot, except by sawing off more chunks? It would set Mr Comrie to grinding his teeth; it would send him climbing down into another bottle.

But Alec Comrie was never one to give up a fight, even one that was lost. So he went twice each day to Giltspur Street, morning and evening. He bled and blistered the patient, and bid Meg Nancarrow wrap his head in water-soaked rags to cool the brain. She didn't leave Jemmy's side — not once, through all of this. When the chaplain came on the second night she drove him away with a curse, and on the morning of the third day — *mirabile dictu* — the fever broke. Jemmy lay limp and pallid, but by mid-afternoon he took a few spoonsful of beef broth with rice. By next morning he was able to sit on a chair beneath the single barred window of the cell, slump-shouldered and wrapped in a shawl, half his hair shaved away and the rest sticking up in clumps, like some mute lump of a grandmother troll.

Mr Comrie blinked at the sight, and came remarkably close to a smile.

"You done it," I said, standing at his shoulder. "Saved his life."

"I plugged a hole in his head. Soon enough we'll see how much leaked out."

Jemmy stared into nothing.

Meg stood. "I'll pay you," she said.

Mr Comrie made a Scotch noise. "Gah." Brushing aside invisible flies, he stooped to inspect how the incision was healing.

"I don't take charity," said Meg. "When I have the money, I'll pay what I owe."

He eyed her with a scowling respect, being proud beyond all sense himself. It still galled him that he had asked Atherton to help him find a demonstrator's position—which Atherton, by the by, had still not done. When he was finished, he muttered something that may have been satisfaction, and turned to leave.

"Mr Comrie."

He looked back.

"God bless you," said Meg. "Assuming there's a God, which there ent—and if there is, then fuck him for the bastard world he created. But you know what I'm saying."

Mr Comrie smiled at that. A wintry, unmistakable smile.

"Take care of him, now," he said.

"Oh, don't you fear."

The next day Meg ventured back out into the world, blinking in the dirty London sunlight. She went first to the room by Fleet Ditch that she and Jemmy shared, and after she had changed her frock and wrenched the tangles from her hair, she went down Ludgate Hill to the Three Jolly Cocks, the ale-house where she sometimes worked, to ask them to take her back. The Ale-Draper dismissed her irritably at first, but in the end she brought him round in the inevitable way, on her knees in a cellar store room. Alf, his name was. A red waddling man with a belly like a sack, and she thought how the guts would come coiling out, with a slither and then a whoosh, if you slipped your knife in at the pelvis and drew it smartly *lickety-snick* up to the breastbone. But by the time he'd helped her to her feet with a hand considerately extended—Alf was a pig of a man, with a heavy fist and a fondness for raising it, but he believed in the chivalric gesture—she had her position back. So she resumed working nights at the ale-house, and after two or three hours' sleep would arrive at Giltspur Street by late morning. Thus she was absent when the Bailiffs came on Monday at nine o'clock sharp, and bore Jemmy Cheese to Bow Street Magistrates' Court to answer the charge against him.

He sat in the dock as in some mountain fastness, his eyes dead and drifting; it was increasingly clear that they'd broken something inside his brainpan, the mainspring of something undefined but crucial, when they'd cudgelled him down in the graveyard. But this was ruled no obstacle by the court. After all, what would Jemmy have said in his own defence, even if he could have spoken? He'd been taken *in flagrante* with a cadaver in a sack. Not a criminal offence in itself, since a corpse was not a possession and as such could not be stolen. But it had been wrapped in the burial shroud, and there they had him. Theft: one shroud, near new. Six months' incarceration. The Beak brought down his gavel and adjusted his attention to the next item on the docket, a counterfeiter who wanted hanging.

Finally Meg arrived. Learning too late what had happened, she had run all the way from Giltspur Street, pelting through

Whitechapel and along the Mile End Road, and arriving in Bow Street just as the Bailiffs were hauling the prisoner to his feet. "Jemmy!" she cried.

A dim spark flickered in his eyes, like a candle in the depths of a cave. He swayed from side to side and made a low plangent sound in his throat. Meg cried out to the Magistrate, begging him to let her speak.

"Please," she said. "For the love of God, show some pity — no, stop it! Let me go!"

Under-Sheriffs held her back, while Bailiffs dragged Jemmy out the side door. He struggled against them, but he was shackled and still very weak.

"You bastards!" cried Meg.

They lodged Jemmy in Clerkenwell first, that being the usual gaol for grave-robbers. Subsequently they would take him out again and put him in a boat upon the Thames. Slowly down the river, to serve out the rest of his sentence in the bowels of HMS *Edgar*, a 74-gun third-rate converted to a prison hulk in the year '13 and renamed *Retribution*, lying at anchor in Woolwich Harbour.

On the evening of the trial, Atherton went back to St Mary-le-Bow churchyard. So I was told some days subsequent, by the Sexton. He arrived at twilight, and stood by Bob Eldritch's grave for a long while in silent contemplation, as a man might do who possessed a heart and had been touched in a place near the bottom of it. At last he would walk away into the deepening darkness; it would wrap itself around him like a cloak.

*

The following afternoon he was lecturing again at Guy's, this time on surgical practice. Guy's is a great teaching hospital, the first in London with a lecture theatre constructed especially for the purpose. A cockpit, horseshoe-shaped, with students — at least seventy of them on this particular day — crammed standing into semicircular tiers. Atherton was ever a great favourite and was today in prime twig, prowling the platform and holding forth with great vivacity. He was an artist of the lecture theatre, as great in his way as was Edmund Kean upon the stage. Above his head an articulated skeleton hung grinning from the ceiling on a chain, illuminated by a glow from the skylight as if this were the bones of some desiccated saint ascending. Possibly the exact same notion had occurred to him, for he stopped, breaking off in the middle of a tangent he'd spun onto, concerning the mysterious process by which the living body passes over into death. "And yet another one," he said, looking up at the blessed remains, "has slipped beyond our healing grasp. But what might bring him back to us, I wonder?"

Laughter from the students. Mr Atherton was being droll.

"An organ or two, for a start," some wag ventured. "P'raps a heart?"

"And a brain," called someone else, "assuming he wasn't Irish."

Except Atherton hadn't quite been joking.

"Is death such a cause for laughter? You might seek poor Pocock's opinion on that."

The merriment faltered awkwardly, and died.

Pocock was a surgical student here at Guy's, or leastways had been until the early hours of last Thursday morning. He had fallen deathly ill following a dissection the day previous, during which he had carelessly nicked his finger on a jagged sliver of bone. Dissections can be perilous if the corpse has begun to putrefy, as this one had. Within a few hours, terrible headaches began. Delirium followed and then haemorrhage, as the blood lost its capacity to clot. A little after midnight, he rallied sufficiently to ask for an *aegrotat* upon his forthcoming examinations, but just at dawn on the turn of the tide a silent bark set forth into the west, bearing poor Pocock away to an Examination far more rigorous than any the College of Surgeons could ever set. By nine o'clock that morning his devastated family had arrived to claim the mortal remains, before some swine had a chance to dissect them.

It was possible I suppose that Atherton had felt a fondness for poor Pocock, or more probably some memory connected to Bob Eldritch still haunted. One way or another, he had grown uncharacteristically pensive as he stood there in the glow of the skylight beneath the desiccated saint, with seventy rapt uncertain faces ringed around him. Seventy-one if you count Your Wery Umble, wedged into a corner in the uppermost row, perched like a raven on the battlements and looking down in beady fixity.

I came quite frequently to Atherton's lectures, when my schedule as Mr Comrie's assistant permitted — as it usually did, the Scotchman's services being in such little demand. I was never a student at Guy's, and had no right to be here. And yet I did, in my way — I had every right. I had more claim upon Dionysus Atherton than any man present, much as he would deny it. And I had already commenced my study—had been doing so for some months. Magpieing bits and pieces of the man and puzzling him together, for reasons that were not yet entirely clear even to myself. Had I already intuited something profoundly Wrong, in my heart or in my waters or wherever in the human organism such instinct may reside? I'd like to say this was the case—*Oh yes indeed, I was onto him from the start*—though in truth I doubt it. More likely it was just my personal sense of grievance, writhing and gnawing as grievance does, and leading to this—what, obsession?—why, yes indeed, let's call it what it was—that had clutched me so tightly in those days and weeks and months since my return to London.

"What is death?" he was asking now. "Obviously our friend here"—a glance to the desiccated saint—"is well departed. But what about those who are poised at the point of death? And there'll be scores of those in London—hundreds—even as I stand here speaking. What about those who have slipped just an inch beyond? Or six inches beyond that—or a foot? What about poor Pocock, as he drifted away? Might Science somehow have reached out to him? For we're nothing but children, in our understanding. We are infants, groping blind. But what lies beyond, for us to discover? And how far might our reach extend?"

He was looking round at them, but speaking as if to himself. They'd never seen him quite like this before. Neither had I.

"I was called once, to attend a dying girl. Or not called, precisely—I'd been seeking her. This was years ago, before

I became a surgeon. I was not much more than a boy — the same age as many of you." The glow from the skylight was dying in late afternoon; with it, a shadow had fallen across his face. "They'd laid her on a bed — a lovely thing, eighteen years old — and her eyes were open as I came through the door. I called her name, but she didn't stir. She was reed-thin and pale as chalk, but I could swear she would in the very next half-second blink, and turn her head, and light slowly in a smile. But she never did. I'd come half a minute too late, you see. She was already gone. Whilst I was hurrying up the stairs, she'd slipped away."

Amongst a multitude he was utterly alone, as solitary as a man may be in this world. And in that instant those infinitely blue eyes sought mine.

"I have never felt more helpless."

He spoke directly to me — I swear, as if it were one heart to another. Cos I alone knew who he meant, the doomed young woman he was mourning.

"Never more helpless," he repeated, "in all my life."

His face was almost haggard, and in that instant it seemed to me that I could understand exactly how he felt. The ache of his loss was my own as well, bringing with it such soft sorrow that I could weep. Then he turned his eyes away from mine, expanding his gaze to include all the others instead.

"And if there was an instant," he said, "a single moment that set me on the life's course I have followed ever since — then that was assuredly the one."

There were muted exclamations, and the rumble of rising applause. Oh, they loved him more than ever for this show of vulnerability. Atherton turned and drew a breath, as if he must steady himself against the welling of unmanly emotion. Then he shook the mood away, and like some splendid beast arising from torpor he resumed his leonine pacing, his voice ringing out in its wonted manner, and upon the hour he concluded the lecture—as he always did—by exhorting his students to tear up all the notes that they had been so diligently scribbling. "For Science marches relentlessly. What I have shared with you represents the summit of anatomical knowledge in this moment. But by tomorrow morning, I shall already have left it behind!" They applauded him thunderously, as they always did, and he gleamed in their adulation. You all but expected him to bow and blow a kiss, while roses rained down from the gallery and women went to liquid in the knees. He hadn't looked at me again, not once.

A performance.

There had been a moment. A moment of grief and loss and actual human connection, and he had offered it to me. Then he had reduced it to an actor's flourish. That may have been the instant I began to understand: I could come to hate Dionysus Atherton enough to desire him dead.

9

Uncle Cheese had been at his shop on the morning of his brother Jemmy's trial.

This I know for a fact, although admittedly much else of what I am about to tell you — about that day and the night that followed — remains conjecture. Events that transpired at the shop, and subsequently at Crutched Friars and later still at the Three Jolly Cocks. But I ask you now to trust me — or rather, I ask you again. I have researched these events, drawing wherever possible upon eye-witness reports. I have ferreted out such Facts as may be found, for that's how you must begin, as any Man of Science knows — marshalling your Facts and then constructing upon them a scaffolding of Theory. Assembling it with exquisite care, timber by timber, joist by joist, until you have an edifice that will stand — and thus you have Truth, or as close to Truth as we may glimpse through the boiling fog of this world. Thus old Copernicus placed the Sun at the very centre, and arranged all the Planets and their Moons about it; and if Copernicus might by this method puzzle together the whole universe in all its infinite clockwork, then surely Your Wery Umble Narrator may explain the movements of half a dozen Londoners during one single day and night.

And lately I have had much leisure as well, to think it through ten thousand times again, and view it from every conceivable angle. Oh, the long nights Your Wery Umble has had—you can surely take my word on this, even if you choose to question everything else I say—with nothing else to do but pace and ponder. Three steps forwards, turn, and back again. Given a choice I would study instead how to fly like a bird, straight out that narrow window and over the rooftops of London, darting like a swallow. There's little chance of that, of course—or of anything else at all, beyond these next few weeks.

But I have such a mighty deal to tell you yet, beginning with that day in late April when Edward Cheshire heard the news of his brother. Heard it, and made a series of decisions, each more ill-judged than the last.

*

The shop was in a lane behind Old Street, wedged between a tavern and a low lodging-house, with the three brass balls of the pawnbroker above the door. It was narrow and dim as a brigand's cave, smelling of Time and cat's piss and crammed with the flotsam of London: chronometers and snuff-boxes and silver spoons; boots and handkerchees and jackets; trinkets and books and lamps and children's toys, and pewter mugs and tea services. There were dresses hanging and Turkey rugs rolled up, and a fine set of plate that had strayed somehow from a house in Mayfair, and made its way through endless winding streets to Edward Cheshire's door. There were bars on the window and a dusty sill within, on which a vast ginger feline sprawled twitching its tail and contemplating with murderous equanimity the songbirds in cages hanging from the rafters. In the back was a counter, where Uncle Cheese examined the treasures that were brought to him and invariably found — alas — that they were not worth nearly what you'd hoped.

Just few minutes ago he had completed a very different transaction with a dentist's apprentice from Marble Arch, who had left with a leather pouch that gave a clicking like miniature dice when it was shook. Ned Cheshire conducted such transactions on a confidential basis in the shadowy reaches of the shop, though there was nothing at all to be ashamed of. He sold quality teeth, fine fresh ivories that might be fashioned into first-class dentures, or else implanted straight into sockets; and never mind the bits of gum still sticking. What else would be sticking to a tooth?

Once the apprentice was gone, he was able to devote his attention to a second customer, who had brought him a silver bracelet. After brief inspection he offered a shilling.

"A *shilling*?"

The customer laughed out loud. Mister Cheshire was clearly having his little joke.

"Yes, indeed," said this customer, chortling. "A shilling, Mister Cheshire says — and with a straight face — *very* good. A guinea, Mister Cheshire, and we'll call it square."

"A shilling, Master Buttons."

Master Buttons was a pear-shaped man of seven- or eight-and-twenty, with thinning golden ringlets and scarlet spiderwebbing on his cheeks. He looked like a derelict cherub, down on his luck, and now he reared up in dismay and indignation. No, he exclaimed, he would not credit it, for this bracelet had belonged to his mother. His voice swooped into a tragic register. "My Sainted Ma, God rest her soul. The only keepsake I possess, and you say to me a *shilling*?"

Master Buttons had been upon the London stage. He had in fact been celebrated in his prime, which had been round about the age of twelve. There had been at the time a brief vogue for Infant Prodigies, and Master Buttons had been prominent amongst them. He played one memorable season at Drury Lane, essaying with remarkable success several of the great roles of Shakespeare, being slender and lovely in those days, with a clear treble voice for which he cultivated the hint of a lisp. As Henry V he would bring the house down with his ringing declamation: "Cwy God for Hawwy, England and Thaint George!" There had been prints in shop windows, and a carriage to bear him to the theatre, and nothing in this world that could hold him back from greater glories yet to come—excepting only the fatal blunder of maturing, which against all sensible advice he committed. Two years later he was playing Harlequin for ten shillings a week on a fourth-rate circuit based in Blackpool.

Now he stood in Edward Cheshire's pawn-shop, breathing out gusts of gin and grievance. "My mother's bracelet for a shilling, Mister Cheshire? I should sooner hang myself. I should sooner open a razor and slit my throat!"

Uncle Cheese tilted his head to consider. The perfect round lenses of his spectacles caught the light and flashed. A razor? Yes, of course he had a razor. "Prime vorkmanship, Master

Buttons, wery sharp and clean. Or else — here's a thought — a bit of twine, which I could trade you for your bracelet, even up. A lovely bit of twine, six foot long. All you'd need's a rafter and a chair."

Master Buttons drew himself up, spluttering. Edward Cheshire was a vampire! He was a monster of unfeeling. Linwood Buttons would not relinquish his mother's bracelet for anything less than half a crown!

Uncle Cheese had been musing for some moments about how much he would like to put holes in Master Buttons's teeth. He possessed a new device for this, acquired from a dentist who had run up ruinous losses at Old Crocky's gaming house in Piccadilly. It was the most beautiful object Ned Cheshire had ever possessed: a dental engine, adapted from a foot-powered spinning wheel, with a tall thin stand like a fishing-rod and a drill hanging from a cross-arm. It inspired in him a reverence for human aspiration; he caught his breath just to look at it. With such a device he could excavate each tooth in Master Buttons's head, one by one, after which he could pull them out with his dental key — a device like a wooden-handled corkscrew with a tiger claw on the end, fashioned by a man in Leiden. A much more modest contrivance, but effective.

Within the year, Uncle Cheese intended to have saved enough money to set up as a dental professional, with a painting of a tooth hanging over his door, after which he would employ both devices on a daily basis for the rest of his life. He would move to a provincial town to do so, possibly Bristol.

Grow affluent and sleek and marry a merchant's fat stupid daughter who would bear him sons. He could practically shiver with anticipation, just thinking of it.

"Take the shilling," he said now, "or else go somewheres else, and take that trinket with you. Put it back on the coster-barrow where you prigged it, you sack of wapours. Your mother? Pah! I'll varrant your mother's alive to this day—down by the dockside, looking for sailors. A gleam in her eye and three rotten teeth in her head."

Master Buttons had gone quite pale. For an instant, there was a wild look on his phizog: the look of a man you might not wish to cross so cavalierly. But at that moment Meg Nancarrow came through the door, with a suddenness that brought the vast ginger feline arching to his feet.

"They've bunged him up, the bastards."

"My brother, you mean?"

"They come for him this morning. Six months!"

Uncle Cheese exclaimed, for this was dreadful news. His brother, scarce able to stand, condemned to Durance Vile—six months, with no one to care for him, and Edward Cheshire's half-crown in his head. And what of Nedward C. himself, with money loaned to half the shirkers in London, and no one to collect it? But Meg had come to him, for succour. Dark-eyed Meg, all alone in the world, and of course Uncle Cheese was precisely the man who could help her. He was more than a match for so many of those who held themselves above him. Oh, yes indeed. Edward was much wilier than they realized.

And Edward knew Secrets.

He placed his hands upon Meg's shoulders. She shuddered, putting him in mind of a bird he once found as a child, fallen from its nest. A sparrow, its heart frantic between his palms, quivering with the sheer distress of being a tiny bird in such a world.

"Leave it to Brother Ned," he said.

And all this while Master Buttons had stood forgotten —exactly as he had stood for the past fifteen years. Watching Ned Cheshire from the cat's-piss-scented shadows, his grievance bansheeing inside him. Keep one glim upon Master Buttons; that is my advice to you. Master Buttons had never in his brief half-hour of glory played Iago or Richard III, had never essayed one of the truly malignant villains.

But he could certainly start now.

*

In St Michael's Chapel at Westminster Abbey there is a monument to Lady Elizabeth Nightingale, who died in childbirth *aetat.* twenty-seven. In the statue, Lady Elizabeth swoons against Joseph, her husband, as Death slithers from his subterranean cell beneath them, aiming his deadly dart and reaching out his bony claw to seize her by the ankle. The Rattling Fellow is serpentine and stark; frozen in marble he moves with a clatter and a terrible swift coiling, and poor Joseph raises one arm in a desperate bid to ward him off.

This image rose to Atherton's mind as the coach bore him back to Crutched Friars. The night was foul. Rain slanted in torrents, lashing the coachman and volleying like musket-fire against the sides, while Atherton sat brooding within. He had been this evening to attend a woman in Mayfair who was afflicted by a painful swelling behind one knee—the wife of a baronet, no less, with extensive holdings in Buckinghamshire and five thousand a year. It was an aneurysm of the popliteal artery; Atherton had no doubt of this as he probed and smiled and radiated blue-eyed reassurance, keeping his thoughts very much to himself. Without surgery the artery would assuredly burst, with fatal consequences. And the surgery was certainly possible. He could tie the artery off, leaving the circulation to reroute itself. The procedure had been known for upwards of three decades; Atherton had performed it a dozen times himself, his successes including a coachman who had recovered and lived on for nearly six years, before expiring just the other day of unrelated causes, upon which he had been duly buried in St George-in-the-East churchyard—the selfsame coachman whose resurrection had been bungled by Little Hollis and Jemmy Cheese. Atherton had been keeping track of his former patient's whereabouts through a loose network of informers, as surgeons often did. He had intended to cut open the leg and investigate *post mortem* the results of that operation—to identify exactly how the healing had proceeded, and which veins and arteries had grafted themselves into service—a valuable scientific opportunity now squandered, with the coachman lying deep again and putrefying apace.

So yes, Atherton could perform the surgery. The question was: should he? A terrible, bowel-voiding procedure with no way to dull the pain, and the chance of success perhaps one in four—at best. And a baronet's wife was not a coachman. If surgery was a coachman's only hope, then of course any surgeon would perform it. Simple human compassion demanded no less. And if—alas—the procedure failed, then nothing really was lost, and nothing left behind but a coachman's widow and a snivel of coachman's children. But the wife of a man with five thousand a year—there would be blame, however unfair. There would be censure, and pursed aristocratic lips, and Society doors closed firmly in his face. Mr Astley Cooper had not risen to the verge of a peerage by attempting heroic surgery upon baronets' wives.

The coach rattled up Ludgate Hill and past St Paul's Cathedral, whose bell was striking ten. The rain continued in sheets. Atherton huddled deeper into his cloak.

Poor Joseph Nightingale in the statue is a monument to human futility: one arm outflung against Death—he might as well be holding back the sea—and on his face both horror and abjection. In one more instant the Rattling Fellow will have Lady Elizabeth's ankle; he will drag her shrieking down with him, and bolt his iron door against the light, and there is nothing that poor Joseph—or any man living—can do.

And yet.

And yet what if there were? A means to wrench open that door, and usher the dead back to life again. What *is* death, after all? And imagine being the man who could cast light upon the answer—or even the barest portion of it. That would be worth a lifetime of study—any number of mornings outside Newgate, observing and charting the process of strangulation. It would justify any number of experiments on animals, who were after all not capable of experiencing pain as we do. And perhaps—who could say?—it might even justify other forms of experimentation as well.

His sister Emily had believed him capable of extraordinary achievement. "I am in my soul half Gypsy," she had said to him one day, "and I glimpse you working wonders." Fourteen years old she'd have been, or thereabouts; three years younger than her golden brother. Her hands in his, eyes sparkling, and O!—his heart had burgeoned. He had been her hero and her protector, right up 'til the moment when she had actually needed him.

As the coach pulled up before his house, Atherton made a decision. He could not in conscience abandon the baronet's wife. He would cast about for some colleague willing to attempt the surgery in his stead.

And now a cloaked figure was hurrying to meet him, hunched against the squall: Odenkirk, extending an umbrella. He was saying something, seeming to think it important, as Atherton pushed past him. Entering the house, he shook off the rain. It occurred to him that he hadn't eaten, and he called for the housekeeper to fetch him bread and cold meats. Finally he heard what Odenkirk was saying.

"I believe it were the Deakins let him in."

"Who?"

"The upstairs maid, sir—the one as hears peacocks shrieking. The man is waiting for you now."

"What man?

"Our friend with the broken-headed brother, sir — and could have one himself to make a family pairing, if someone was to wish it. Nosing about the Collection, as we speak, sir. Cheese."

"A marvel, sir, is what it is. A vonder of the modern vorld. The foetuses and such — the *foeti*, I should say, as speaking to a man as has his Latin, like myself — the *foeti* in their jars, and all the rest."

He stood hat in hand, gazing. The three bottled foetuses gazed blindly back, like wizened miniatures of Ned Cheshire himself.

"What are you doing here?" Atherton demanded, arriving in the doorway.

"I do believe I am vorshipping, sir," said Uncle Cheese. "At an altar of natural philosophy."

The room was a library, in its way: lined floor-to-ceiling with shelves, with a ladder to reach the uppermost. Oil lamps cast a muted glow, and footfalls were smothered in a rug of deepest green. You lowered your voice in a room like this, immediately and instinctively. Words had a way of dying in the throat, for the books in this library were confined to a single squat bookcase in one corner, with a skull on top and a skeleton standing alongside. The shelves were for specimens instead. Scores of them — hundreds, even — row upon row. Some dried, and the rest in jars, lined up like the pickled preserves of some demented cook. Human and animal both: Atherton was an avid student of comparative anatomy, with an especial fascination with defects and deformities. Here were human shinbones with osteomyelitis, and the distinctive mal-union of a tibia and fibula; bones with bulging non-gummatous lesions indicative of syphilis, and a hydrocephalic skull as bloated as a bladder. A two-tailed lizard, and the beak of a squid, and a vast array of teeth from every creature you could imagine, as if Noah had awakened one night with a demented dental obsession and a pair of pliers close to hand. The larynx of a child who died with croup, and the penis of an elephant, and a kidney with tapeworm cysts. Stomachs of herons and pelicans and camels, and the femoral artery from a gangrenous leg; human eyeballs bobbing in alcohol, the heart of an ox and the skull of a monkey, and a baby crocodile forever lunging.

Ned Cheshire gazed in reverence at all of it.

"I ask again," said Atherton. "What the Devil are you doing here?"

He had guessed the answer to that already. The man was after money — though whatever imp of presumption had possessed him to come here, to Atherton's house, was another question.

"The Devil, Mr Atherton? Does he come into the matter? I suppose he does, sir, if it's considered in a certain light."

Uncle Cheese had turned to face him. He smiled a little, half in apology. "My brother, sir. Poor Jemmy..."

"...Is none of my concern."

Not true, and Atherton knew it. Despite his mood, he forced himself to listen.

The news was hopeful, on the one hand. Jemmy Cheese had survived his ordeal, and was recovering at this moment. Unfortunately — "and here is the fly in the ointment, sir, the *musca*, as one might say, in the *unguentum*" — he was recovering in prison, where he would languish for half a year, unless set free by gaol-fever, or the murderous inclinations of his fellows, or just the cracking of a noble heart from grief. And who was left to bear this loss but Jemmy's family? Ned Cheshire himself, deprived of both his brother and his half-crown — a cost that could be precisely rendered as one sibling, two shillings and sixpence — and of course poor Jemmy's woman, Meg. Weeping in her desolation, sir — for herself and all her babbies yet unborn — unless the surgeon upon whose business poor Jemmy had been engaged should be mindful of his responsibilities.

"But I told her wery earnest, sir. *Nil desperandum*, I said, and translated it for her benefit: never despair. For Mr Atherton is a man to recollect his duty, and honour the principle of the *douceur*."

Uncle Cheese held his hat in his hands. Rainwater dripped from his sodden clothes and puddled humbly at his feet. A little man in a red weskit, cocking his head like an obsequious robin, and gauging Atherton's reaction with slantways calculation.

Lounging by the door, Odenkirk caught Atherton's glance and arched one eyebrow in lupine query: *Shall I?* And God knows how sorely Atherton was tempted — on a night like this, no less, soaked to the skin and irritable with hunger, gnawed by misgivings about his patient the baronet's wife in Mayfair, and haunted by Shadows from the past. But like any anatomist he needed subjects for dissection, which meant he needed Edward Cheshire, who operated one of the most reliable networks of Resurrectionists in London. And the man was within his rights to demand a *douceur*.

This principle governed the relationship between the anatomist and his necessary associate. An anatomist made a private arrangement with a Doomsday Man at the beginning of each season—normally in October, just prior to the teaching term at the hospitals and private schools—at which point a fee was offered. This was a token of goodwill, ten guineas' worth perhaps, designed to foster the spirit of Christian co-operation and stimulate an uninterrupted supply of corpses right through to the end of the term in April. A finishing fee was normally paid at this juncture, to ensure that the milk of goodwill did not curdle over the summer months, during which the graveyard soil lay largely fallow, owing to short moon-bright nights and the rate at which Things ripened in warm weather. Behind it all lay an unspoken agreement: a grave-robber's family would be supported in the event of his being taken up. And Jemmy lay this night in shackles, with despair in his heart and Ned's half-crown in his head.

With a muttered execration, Atherton produced a banknote. Uncle Cheese took it, fastidious as a lady's spaniel accepting a sweetmeat.

"Ten pound," he said, folding the note into quarters and tucking it into his hat. "Thank you, sir; a good start."

"A *start?*"

"But of course, Mr Atherton, I should like to go many steps vurther. As perhaps the little fellow in the corner was thinking, as he arrived here at your house."

He meant the skeleton by the bookcase. A stunted thing with crooked legs and a clubbed foot on one side. The bones were a dull brown colour.

The silence was left to hang for just a moment. If bottled *foeti* could blink in non-comprehension, they might have done so now. When Edward Cheshire spoke again, his voice was silken.

"I am a man, Mr Atherton, as hears tales."

"And what tales are those?"

Ned Cheshire cocked his head. Lamplight flashed on his spectacles.

"Ah," he said.

Atherton began to laugh. "That skeleton cost me a guinea. I found it in a curiosity shop in the Gray's Inn Road, where it had been standing since God knows when, collecting dust. It's decades old, man—look at it. The bones are brown with age."

"Vith boiling, Mr Atherton. Boiling causes that discoloration, as any man of Science knows. That fellow might have been alive just yesterday."

Atherton's laughter had trailed away. A smile remained, but it was brittle as glass.

"What are you implying, Cheshire?"

"I, sir? Nothing at all."

"Then perhaps you should take care."

Odenkirk by the door commenced quietly flexing his hands.

If Uncle Cheese were to be truthful — as he would be on occasion, when there was no other option — he would admit to feeling a certain icy liquefaction in the bowels. A creeping sense that he might have overplayed his hand. But there was nothing for it now but to carry on.

"I propose," said Uncle Cheese, "that Mr Odenkirk should step to the casement, and look out, so as to see the man standing by the lamppost on the corner, getting rained on. The little fellow with the werminous air — yes, there he is, right there — and the elewated arse. He's soaked and shivering and cursing under his breath, no doubt. But he's holding fast to his instruction, vhich is to run directly for the Vatch if Nedward C don't emerge from this house in five more minutes. So what you'll do, Mr Atherton, you'll give me another ten-pound note to keep the first one company, and fifty guineas besides for the keeping of my brother's poor Meg, and her babbies yet unborn. And then Nedward's lips are sealed, Mr Atherton. It is done. All is resolved. Fast friends hereafter, *absit inwidia*."

*

And there I've done it, haven't I? Your Wery Umble has performed wonders of his own, entering the heart of another man and intuiting his innermost thoughts and secrets — down to the hunger he was feeling, and the conversation he had shared with his late sister three years before I was born.

But it is the truth. I am certain of that.

And now I'll tell you something else. I'll tell you about Flitty Deakins.

Her room overlooked the street. She often knelt at the window late at night in prayer, with the house in slumber below and Cook snoring in the bed they shared. Her shawl wrapped tightly against the chill, leaning her forehead against the cold glass.

She had been kneeling there that night, but found she could not compose her thoughts to pray. The agitation was too great — the mortal trembling and the green-eyed Hindoo on the landing, and the secret conviction that her own wickedness had placed her beyond all hope of forgiveness, in this world or the next. For her wickedness was grievous. She knew it, as did God, who Judges. He Judges each one of us, and he Judged the Revd Deakins's own dear darling girl, weighing her in the balance and finding her horribly wanting.

Raising her head, she found herself staring wretchedly down as a man emerged from the house: Uncle Cheese. Despite her dolour, Flitty Deakins recognized him in the spill of light from within. He was swallowed by the darkness, to reappear a moment later in the lamplight on the corner, where another man awaited. They exchanged brief words and then disappeared into the night, Uncle Cheese leading and his companion scuttling after, arse upwards.

Flitty Deakins could hardly have heard what they said, of course — no more than she could hear the voices in the Collection Room, two floors below. She couldn't tell you what Atherton and Odenkirk were discussing at that minute.

But I can guess — Your Wery Umble Narrator, who is telling you this story, from evidence puzzled together and long pondered. If you or I were at the door of the Collection Room, scarce daring to breathe with ear pressed against the keyhole, I wager we would hear Dionysus Atherton's voice, suffused with fury: "Who the Devil has been telling tales?" And Odenkirk's ominous reply: "P'raps I should speak with the Deakins, sir. P'raps I should do so directly."

I can tell you for a certainty what poor Flitty heard next — because she told me. In the darkness thereafter, as rain lashed down and wind shook the house until its timbers groaned, she heard heavy boots coming up the stairs. One flight, and then the second, as inexorable as Old Bones himself, ascending with his summons. The measured *tramp-tramp* of Odenkirk, sticker of pigs.

10

Uncle Cheese found Meg at the Three Jolly Cocks. She had come in storm-drenched some while previous and now sat barefoot on a stool by the fire, her shawl and her woollen stockings draped on the hearth, giving off a waft of drowned mutton that mingled with the blue haze of smoke and the familiar reek of malt and humanity.

The ceiling sloped lower here at the back of the room; Edward Cheshire was required to stoop as he drew near. "I feared I might have missed you," he said, "it being so late."

He had told her to meet him at midnight, which had come and gone an hour ago. But it was good for Meg to wait for him; it would encourage her to recollect where favours were owed. Pulling off his sodden coat he rubbed his hands, blinking through misted spectacles and flinching to see that Meg was drinking gin. Meg Nancarrow on the blue ruin could be a dickey proposition; it had a queer effect on her. Instead of reeling with it, she'd grow steadily more intense, each drink adding to a cold unnerving clarity. Just now she was staring round at the men in the room, as if measuring each one in turn. These were such riff-raff as you would expect to find at such a time of night: swindlers and rogues and petty villains; a trio of house-breakers huddled in terse conference; some watermen who had wandered up from the Thames. Just inside the door a blind beggar sat with a mongrel that someone had shaved to look like a poodle. One of them had growled as Uncle Cheese passed by. The dog, presumably.

"Looking for an honest man?" he asked Meg, hoping to jolly her.

"I'm deciding how they'll die."

He tilted back his head, to peer underneath fogged lenses. This was dark, even for Meg.

"*Stipendium peccati*—eh, my girl? The vages of sin. But surely, Meg, you won't be killing all of 'em."

"Oh, no. I won't need to do it myself."

She lifted her chin, pointing with it to a red-faced rogue with bulging eyes. That one, she had decided, would die of a choking apoplexy. The one next to him would have his guts spilled out by his best friend's knife. Over there was a man marked out for gaol-fever, and there was one destined to die at the end of a rope.

"But not at Newgate. By his own hand, drunk and despairing. Fouling his breeches, underneath a bridge." She spoke with cool satisfaction, which gave Uncle Cheese the willies, truth be told. It put him in mind of a witch. Not the sort that lurked in the privy, to the torment of younger brothers—the other sort. A witch that dances naked with the Devil.

"Stand us a drink, Cheese."

Ned complied, being in an expansive mood. He was in fact halfways giddy with sheer pleasure at himself: two of Atherton's ten-pound notes folded carefully into his hat, and the prospect of fifty guineas still to come. A dangerous game, but Ned was a bold and clever fellow, and had played it to perfection.

There had been a stab of qualm a few minutes ago, when he and Little Hollis had gone their separate ways just north of St Paul's Cathedral. Hurrying on through the squall, he'd had a sudden sense of someone following: heavy footsteps—*tramp, tramp, tramp*—that went silent when he stopped. The feeling had crept upon him again as he reached the head of Black Friars Lane, but when he turned round quick and sudden there was no one behind him—or no one that he could see. Ahead, the light from the Three Jolly Cocks glowed with the promise of warmth, and banishing his misgivings he had hurried towards it.

"Have you seen him?" Meg demanded.

"Atherton? Oh, yes."

"Will he pay?"

"He will."

"How much?"

"Five pound."

"That's *all*? For the breaking of Jemmy's head? For six months, rotting in gaol?"

"The man is cold, Meg. There is vinter at the wery heart of Mr Dionysus Atherton. But the five pound is yours, whole and entire. *Ipso facto*, Meg, and *totus tuus*—I make no claim."

He fished from his weskit pocket a tattered note, and slipped it into her hand. Discreetly, of course—you didn't flash five-pound notes in a place like this. Their fingers brushed together, skin against naked skin.

He discovered it pleased him to have given her so much; it brought on a feeling of varmth and wirtue. Whatever else was said about Edward Cheshire, he was a man who stood by his family. He would be happier still to stand Meg against the wall outside, and hike her skirts, cos he had often imagined Meg Nancarrow dancing naked in the moonlight, and imagined as well a devil dancing with her, who looked most remarkable like Nedward Cheshire. But this of course was another proposition entirely, and must needs be negotiated with care.

"Five pounds," she repeated, incredulous. "And nothing more?"

"Upon my davy."

"Go back to the bastard. *Threaten* him."

"I have done, Meg, what there is to be done. Five pounds is all he vill give us."

He raised his narrow shoulders in an eloquent shrug, expressive of the essential futility of being human. As befitted a man with Latin, Uncle Cheese was capable of great Stoicism, especially in the face of others' misfortune. You could imagine him in a toga, masticating grapes.

Meg's eyes narrowed like a cat's.

"You wouldn't be lying to me, Cheese?"

"No, Meg."

"You wouldn't be chousing me, and holding back?"

The very notion cut him to the quick; he said so. He was her true friend — truer than ever, now that she was alone in the world, with poor Jemmy sent away, and scant odds besides that he would ever be his old self again.

"And what if he isn't?" Meg cried. "I'll have to look after him somehow. I'll need money for that."

For a moment there was the catch of despair in her voice. Behind them, by the door, the blind man lifted his head. The mongrel dog at his feet had drifted into a doze and made tiny whiffling sounds, expressive of the pursuit of rabbits.

Uncle Cheese grew more Roman than ever. "These are the facts of the matter," he said, "as ve must face up to. Oh dear, oh dear, oh dear. *Sunt lacrimae*, Meg, *sunt lacrimae* — there are tears for such things. But I make a pledge to you."

His heart brimmed with earnest intention. He placed his hand on her knee.

"Vhatever you need, Meg, in this time of desolation. Turn to Nedward, and Nedward is there."

"You will do three things for me," she said.

"Name them, my girl."

"Remove that hand, before I mistake it for a spider. Stand up. And fuck off into the night."

Ned Cheshire's solicitude curdled.

"You vant to think, my girl," he said. "Think on how you make your living, vhen you're not serving ale. Vith men, Meg — and don't think Edward Cheshire doesn't know it. Men far less presentable than Edward C. himself. Think on that — then think some more. Poor Jemmy in his current plight, and Nedward offering friendship. Brother Ned, as owns a shop, and changes his linen by the week. Edward Cheshire, as is nigh upon the estate of dentistry. And you think yourself too fine? The likes of you, Meg? Miss Nobuddy from Nowhere — the draggle-tail descendant of common sluts and criminals—a father hung for house-breaking and two brothers both transported, and you yourself upon your knees for any man with a silver coin. You might vell think again."

Meg regarded him with the bitter juniper clarity of gin. "You'll have your weasand slit," she said. "That is how it ends for you, Cheese. It comes to me—I can see it."

Despite himself, he felt a chill. "Don't you threaten me."

"No threat. Just a certainty I'm having."

"*Nemo me impune*, my girl. Nobody."

"Slit from ear to ear. Lying like a dead cat in a ditch. Pray God it's many good years off."

11

This had taken place on a Wednesday — so I firmly believe. Edward Cheshire's visit to Crutched Friars, and his subsequent meeting with Meg at the Three Jolly Cocks. I hadn't gone outside on Wednesday myself, having experienced a day of the Black Dog's visitation, when the world was very bleak and rising did not seem possible. On such days I quite often thought of my friend Danny Littlejohn.

Danny Littlejohn was a Londoner, like myself. He had taken the shilling and sailed to join the fighting in the Spring of '13, not long before the Battle of Vitoria. In due course he arrived at a field hospital to seek attention for a shrapnel wound — deep enough to need sewing up, but too shallow to send him safely home — and we hit it off most remarkable. Long Will, he would call me.

He was two years older, with a loose-limbed swagger and a larking exuberance. He'd get letters from home in a girl's looping hand, full of the latest news from the Metropolis — news now two or three months old, of course — which he'd call out while sprawling by the cook-fire of an evening, or leaning on a shovel while someone else dug a latrine pit. "A whale seen swimming in the Thames," he would announce, "as far upriver as Richmond." Or: "An entire estate at Hertfordshire changes hands at Old Crocky's gaming house — two hunnert acres, with great house and outbuildings, and a grotto in a garden complete with hermit." He gave us to understand that these letters were sent by a sweetheart who pined away for him in Bethnal Green, or possibly Shoreditch. Her name seemed variable as well, being sometimes Sal and sometimes Bess and occasionally Dorcas, thus raising the possibility that he had several different sweethearts all pining in separate districts. Personally I suspected the letters came from his sister, and thought him a fearful liar on the subject of sweethearts. I also thought what a fine thing it was to have a sister — or anyone else — who would care enough to write so often.

If the two of us were together, this performance might become a comic turn, such as you might see between songs at the Coal Hole back home.

"A mermaid has been offered for sale," Danny might announce, "at Billingsgate fish market."

"A mermaid?" I would exclaim. "But surely not!"

"Which on closer investigation revealed itself to be a species of seahorse."

"Oh! How disappointing for the fishmonger, Daniel, whose price was surely knocked down something cruel."

"But more disappointing still for the seahorse, Long Will."

"For the seahorse?"

"To have been so very nearly a mermaid."

Then we'd fall about in helpless hilarity, while old campaigners eyed us sourly and someone ended in chucking a clod of dirt. But we amused ourselves most wonderfully, and often would speculate about the times that lay ahead when we'd return home to London together. "The likes of us, Long Will," Danny would say, "we don't accept our future as it comes. We pluck it, like an apple from a tree."

*

On Thursday the world grew lighter again, a little. So I rose and went round to the room in Holborn to look in upon Miss Smollet. I found her quite solitary—the Badger had left town.

"Mr Starling," she exclaimed, seeming genuinely glad to see me—or leastways to see someone.

She had hardly gone out since the events at Fountain Court, or such was the impression I formed. She smiled gaily, but it was stretched and thin, and I had the notion she had not slept well. "Come in," she said. "Here, would you like to sit? Sit down, if you like." She cleared a tangle of clothing from a wooden chair, looked vaguely round for somewhere to put it, and added it to the tangle on the bed.

Birdsong floated from below. The room was above a bird-fancier's shop, which was strung like a Yuletide tree with birds in cages, hanging side-by-side from the rafters and lined up along the shelves. In daylight hours the whole house rang with them—and smelled, of course—and Annie Smollet in her attic perch might have been the topmost item on display.

"Look at me," she said suddenly, reaching a hand to her hair. "I must look a fright."

She did not. She was tousled and unpainted in a plain cotton dress, which inspired in me notions of shepherdesses, and sylvan glades. Not that a glade ever looked like the room in its present condition, though this was neither here nor there; clothes strewn with even more abandon than before, and the sour linen waft competing vigorously against the birdstink. Apparently the Badger had been the tidy one.

"She went to Chatham," Miss Smollet said.

The Badger had met a gentleman of means, and been offered a position. I didn't ask for details, though presumably the position was horizontal, with two or three rooms and an allowance to go with it—generous or otherwise, depending on the gentleman. It would continue 'til the gentleman grew to find her tedious, or else his wife smoked out the arrangement, at which point the Badger would be home again, such being the way these things normally ended.

"So here I been," Miss Smollet said. "All Alone."

She had a habit of speaking in Capital Letters, as if stepping from her own life and onto the stage, where Everything was Much More Dramatic. But she meant it too.

I'd brought another sleeping draught: my pretext for coming. "In case you still need it," I said, offering it up.

But she shook her head tightly, and said something odd. "I don't want to sleep here. Not in this room—not alone." Then she shuddered away a shadow that had fallen. "Take me out," she said suddenly. "Take me walking."

The day was soft with the promise of summer yet to come; by afternoon it would be genuinely warm. You could imagine a blue sky beyond the brown haze, and the breeze would surely have been fragrant with blossoms if it hadn't been wafting through London. Miss Smollet took my arm, and we set off amidst the hurly-burly. She wore a pale green dress and a shawl to match, and her cheeks were abloom with rouge.

I couldn't tell you exactly what we said, that morning. Mainly I recollect a sense of happiness. At one point she asked me to tell her about my adventures in the War, and I said this was not something I spoke of very much. When she asked why this should be, I pointed to a man on the corner juggling plates, and grew quite eager to watch. A while after that we came across a Punch and Judy man, a crowd clustering round, so I paid his boy a penny for each one of us, and angled us round to a better vantage.

"Who doesn't like a Punch and Judy show?" I asked Miss Smollet cheerfully.

In fact, I did know someone who didn't care for Punch. Mr Comrie took a jaundiced view, wanting to know what was so frolicsome about a big-nosed homicidal puppet who would cudgel his wife and baby to death, exclaiming: "That's the way to do it!" But Mr Comrie for all his virtues did not have much sense of humour.

Danny Littlejohn had actually worked for a Punch and Judy man — he'd been the boy who worked up the crowd and took the coins — and could talk about it at considerable length. Punch and Judy was actually a very moral play, he would explain, for it demonstrates to wives that they should try to live in peace with their husbands. That claim may be open to debate, but it is undeniable that the play proceeds with Mr Punch tricking Jack Ketch the hangman into hanging himself—which may not be moral exactly, but is Wery Ironical Indeed, and counts as the next closest thing. And of course the play ends with Mr Punch cudgelling the Devil to death, which is the morallest act ever performed by man, or puppet.

I knew I should not be thinking about my friend, here in the bright brawling clamour of spring sunshine, with gales of laughter rising up and Mr Punch laying energetically about him. It was the sort of reminiscence that could bring the Black Dog skulking back round the corner, so I looked to Miss Smollet instead, and that's when I saw the expression on her face, tight with visceral recollection.

I was an oaf. Worse than an oaf, I was a villain—cos this was exactly what she'd enjoy best, wasn't it? Scarcely a week after her experience at Fountain Court: a crowd hooting and braying as Mr Punch walloped his wife.

"Christ," I muttered, instantly ashamed.

"It's fine," Miss Smollet said. "It's quite good."

"Let's go."

"I think—all right. Yes."

She gripped my arm tightly as I steered us away, past a clutch of apprentices who whistled appreciatively at her passing and a legless old beggar who sat scowling in a wooden box with wheels. The crowd thinned a little as we angled onto one of the side-streets leading east, and Miss Smollet was almost vivacious again by the time we stopped to buy a bag of ginger nuts from a street-seller.

"Tell me more news," she said.

As we'd walked I'd been babbling of titbits I'd read about, or earwigged in coffee houses. Now I dredged up an anecdote about something Beau Brummell had said, so memorable that it has since gone out of my head completely. Then I worked up my nerve.

"Oh — and the most wonderful artefack was found near the London docks, by a young man walking."

I drew it out: a small silver locket on a chain. "It put me in mind of you," I said, with my best attempt at a casual air.

"The way it's been dented up, you mean?"

"No!" Though it was tarnished and battered worse than I remembered. "Look inside," I said.

Inside was a miniature portrait of Miss Annie Smollet herself.

It wasn't, of course. And now that I looked again, I saw that the resemblance wasn't as strong as I'd fancied. But she had fair hair too, this girl in the locket, and an openness in her smile: a look of fresh hope dawning that was the very pith and essence of Annie Smollet.

"You found this on the riverbank?"

"I did. Washed in with the tide."

A lie, though hardly the worst that was ever told since Satan came sidling slantways through the Garden. In fact I had spied it at a coster-stall on the Embankment, kept by a wicked old extortionist who demanded three shillings. Subsequently he turned his back to extort another customer, which was an error on his part.

"You are Very Sweet," said Miss Smollet, bending for me to slip it round her neck.

We had stopped at a corner of Newgate Street, not far from the foot of Snow Hill, down which a multitude would pour on Monday mornings when there were hangings — not that this was in my thoughts at the moment. There was a movement towards me then, and a scent of oranges. Lips brushed whisper-soft against my cheek, and I swear to the God who waits to damn me: Wm Starling could have dropped down dead right there and then, and in that instant counted his life well-lived. This may help to explain why I didn't hear clearly at first what she was saying to me, her voice gone suddenly quite low.

"He come to see me last night."

"What's that?"

"Outside my window. Bob Eldritch."

Of all the names she might have uttered, she'd come up with the very one. The one that could snap my head round and leave me staring, flummoxed.

"Miss Smollet — Bob Eldritch is dead."

She summoned a small, strained laugh. "'Course he is," she said. "I know that."

"So it was just a dream."

"I suppose."

The colour had crept up into her cheeks. She didn't meet my gaze.

"What did he do?" I found myself asking. "In the dream."

"He scratched to be let in," she said. "Scrabbling with his fingers at the glass, with such a look on his face—as if he'd break your heart, just looking. Then he opened his mouth, and screamed."

"Screamed? How do you mean?"

Miss Smollet summoned another small laugh.

"Have you ever heard a peacock?"

A Curious Incident in
Whitefriars Lane

The London Record
2nd May, 1816

Reports are circulating of several strange encounters with a Staring Man in the vicinity of St Mary-le-Bow Churchyard, all of them taking place in the hours of darkness. Most recently, a young woman was accosted by the man while returning to her lodgings after midnight. The woman, identifying herself as Summut Sal—"cos I'm known to take a glass of summut, sir, if a gen'lman should be offering"—shared her story with *The Record* at a public house in the district. In her own words:

"I was on my way from Never-You-Mind when 'ee comes up saying, 'Would I take 'im in?' I sez exackly what you'd imagine, which I won't repeat, but 'ee starts to follow and 'oo can say what would of 'appened except some mates of mine come by and that drove 'im off. What's that? Well, of course they saw 'im too; they ent blind. Eyes big as eggs, starting right out of 'is phizog—that's the first thing you noticed. A mate of mine, she sez, 'that's 'im, all right, that's the Boggle-Eyed Man.' She said there was another girl as seen him two nights earlier. 'Ee said to this other girl something very queer indeed. 'Ee said 'ee didn't have a nome to go to, though 'ee should of done. 'A nome as snug and quiet as could be,' 'ee said, 'with fine strong walls and a roof above that should last 'til the end of the world, except they stole it from 'im.'"

We would not normally have offered up this information for public consumption, being uncertain as to the reliability thereof. But here the tale grows stranger still, for we subsequently encountered a Sexton who had noticed the same man on an earlier occasion. The man was standing outside the gate, the Sexton said, gazing through the railings with great round eyes, as if longing for someone to let him in. Afterwards he recollected something singular about the man's appearance. It was pouring with rain, he said, and yet the man's hair was sticking straight up from his head, like quills upon a porcupine.

12

The item was buried on the back page, at the bottom of a column. I stumbled across it at a coffee house that I'd sometimes visit of a morning, while Mr Comrie waited for patients to manifest. I glanced through it once, not paying full attention. Then I read it again, more slowly.

I'd have read it a third time, had I not been jolted from my uneasy reverie by an animated discussion in the stall behind me. It seemed a Discovery had just this morning been made in the Death House at St Thomas's Hospital.

The Death House is where cadavers are kept, and dissected. As sister hospitals, St Thomas's and Guy's had always shared one between them.

Go on, then. Go down a creaking flight of stairs, and then proceed along a narrow corridor, hung with sconces. There is a heavy wooden door at the end. Brace yourself, and step through.

Imagine a room constructed especially for Old Bones, according to his own meticulous specifications, and where — of all the rooms in the world — he should be most completely at his ease. A long low cellar with a square lantern hanging from a central beam, and sunlight cringing in through narrow windows, set high up, at ground level. Sunlight itself is sullied here, and lingers wretched and reeking. There are specimens along one wall, and a fireplace opposite with a pot for boiling the bones — a great copper cauldron, such as trolls might gather round at some unspeakable feast — although these are not the elements you notice first. First you are assailed by the stench, which is staggering, even by London standards. A cock-tail of rot and pickling alcohol and human putrefaction that worms into the very pores of those who labour in this place and never quite leaves them, ever again, though they should spend a lifetime scrubbing with lye soap and steel bristles.

Next through watering twinklers you see the dead: cloven heads and ghastly grinning visages, stretched out on wooden tables. As many as a dozen, some mornings, with students and surgeons crowded round each one. They stand in pools of congealing blood, like crows around a fallen nestling, and as your gorge begins to rise in earnest you will notice limbs and bits strewn about the floor. Arms and legs and fingers, and morsels of skin and fat that will be discovered later on the bottom of boots, or in folds of clothing. There is something about the candles too, that gutter at the heads of the tables. They are squat and misshapen, these glims, and exude a sick-sweet musk that is not like any tallow you've ever nosed. It is not from a cow or a pig, you think, and the thought occurs — ye gods, yes you are, you are absolutely correct—they've gone and used the fat that came most convenient to hand.

And the sparrows. Somehow these seem most horrible of all. Excited little birds, flitting and brawling over human scraps, while rats the size of badgers gnaw at bones in the corners. Here's one bold fellow glaring red-eyed at a surgical student, who laughs and tosses him a bit of vertebra. Across the floor a severed hand seems to scuttle like a crab, until you realize that a small grey rat is dragging it by the thumb, and here you may lose whatever breakfast you had hazarded. I did, my first time in that place. Five years in field hospitals across the Peninsula, and Your Wery Umble seized a bucket and shot the cat.

The cadavers arrived surreptitiously, being for the most part delivered in sacks to the Death House Porter at a private entrance in the dead of night. The majority of these had been freshly exhumed, although Doomsday Men were always sharp-eyed for ways to avoid the intermediate stage in the resurrection process: to wit, the digging. I once knew a Resurrectionist who was strolling along the Borough High Street when a man took a convulsive fit and dropped down dead, twenty paces ahead of him. With wonderful presence of mind he rushed forward, crying aloud that this was his own dear brother. Sobbing and lamenting, he took possession of the body, availed himself of a donkey-cart, trundled the remains to St Thomas's and sold it to the surgeons, who had the poor fellow carved and dissected before his family had missed him for supper.

The cadaver that concerns us now was brought to the back

door in the darkness before dawn by two apprentices. The usual Porter had taken sick and gone home; the man who replaced him was new to the hospital, which explains how the corpse went unrecognized. Normally dissections commenced as soon as the sun rose, natural light being required for such close work, but several other cadavers had been delivered earlier. These were laid out already, with the consequence that this late arrival was left for several hours under a sack.

So it was afternoon before it was at last stretched naked upon a table. Students gathered round, as eager as those ghastly sparrows. The gaping wound in the throat caused a stir, though it was far from the first time that a fresh cadaver bearing marks of deadly violence had appeared on a dissecting table. The genuine excitement began a moment later, when one of the students—a lad named Keats—plucked away a rag that had been carelessly tossed over the face.

"God on a gibbet," he exclaimed. "It's Uncle Cheese!"

Keats was a friend of mine. He'd been apprenticed to a pothecary in Edmonton before commencing surgical studies at Guy's, which gave us an interest in common. I encountered him on that particular evening at the King's Head in Tooley Street, a regular haunt of the students, who were still buzzing with the afternoon's events.

"Half of them reckoned we should just proceed," he said.

This would have been the customary course of action—cut him up and then boil him down, all traces gone before anyone was the wiser. But there was the dilemma, cos half the students at the Borough Hospitals owed money to Uncle Cheese, including Keats himself. "One pound, three shillings and sixpence," he confessed wryly, "repayable at twenty per cent compounding. And how would that look, if anyone ever *did* catch wind?" So after some debate, the Porter was sent to notify the Magistrate, who arrived an hour later to claim the corpse and take down statements. The two apprentices were in consequence being sought on suspicion of murder.

"Though whether anyone's seeking them very hard, I wouldn't presume to say. This was Edward Cheshire, after all."

Keats chuckled drily, and coughed. Keats had an habitual cough, which he fretted about. He was an amiable bantam, a year or two my senior and scarcely taller than Your Wery Umble, which endeared him to me on sheer principle. He was a capable student who had shown some surgical skill, but he confided that he didn't like it much. Sure enough he was gone at the end of the term, and subsequent-wise was to scribble poetry of a strange dream-like intensity. I read a bit of it myself, and liked it in its way — though my own taste ran more to tales that galloped through a thunderstorm, with corpses piling up in the ditches on either side.

"Blanched almonds," I said to him, as I stood to go.

"What's that?"

"Your cough. Mix almonds with syrup of tolu, and a few drops of opium tincture. Two spoonsful, twice a day."

"Yes," Keats said. "Good idea."

His mother had died of consumption. You'd see him coughing in his handkerchief, then anxiously eyeing it for spots of blood.

*

It had made me uneasy, this news of the murder, though I couldn't exactly tell you why. I'd had occasional dealings with Uncle Cheese, on Mr Comrie's behalf—my employer was never eyeball-deep with the Resurrectionists, in the way that Atherton was, though you could hardly be a surgeon in London without crossing paths, and you'd hardly say I held a fondness for Ned Cheshire. But somehow there was a vague sense of connectedness; the sense of a pattern that was not entirely random, if only you could see it from the proper angle.

I was also being followed.

I knew it as soon as I left the King's Head. As I started along Tooley Street, there was someone behind me in the darkness. I looked round quickly. A knot of medical students lurched out of an ale-house across the road; light spilled after them for a suspended moment 'til the door swung shut again. On the next corner a sailor swayed against two nymphs, underneath an oil lamp. But six paces beyond the darkness closed round again, and the next lamp was no more than a candle-point in a void—which was the problem with a London night. A London night was as dark as a night in a forest, but it had more feral creatures in it. A man could get his throat cut for any of a hundred reasons, on any street in the Metropolis, without even being Uncle Cheese.

But the darkness can work in your favour, if you've a bit of the feral in yourself. Shadow-footing forwards, I turned right onto Hayes Street, just short of the Borough High Street, before veering abruptly right again into a narrow passage, where I waited. A moment passed, and then another. Then I heard them clear enough: the *tramp, tramp, tramp* of heavy boots. A thin shaft of light from a bull's-eye lantern slid past the mouth of the passageway, and a long grey form slid with it. I stepped out behind.

"Looking for me, then?"

He turned cat-quick, which I didn't much like at all—a man that size, so nimble on his stampers. Cos of course I was counting on myself to be much quicker, else I'd never have shown myself in the first place.

"You might have hallooed," I said to him. "Called out my name, if you'd wanted to talk. 'Stead of following after a fellow in the blackness of the night, which could give him wrong notions about your intent."

In the lantern's light his teeth showed long and yellow. I expect it was intended as a smile. "Friend Starling," he drawled. "The very man. We need to have a private word, we two."

"Then go ahead and have one."

I held my knife in my hand, having slipped it from inside my boot a moment earlier. A six-inch stiletto, scalpel-sharp, won in a game of hazard at a tavern in Spain. Odenkirk saw the glint and just smiled the more, as if to suggest that it might go very ill for Wm Starling if matters between us should come to pig-sticking. I suspected he was right.

Odenkirk had begun his days in a Workhouse: St Saviour's, in Newington Causeway. It was hard to credit—a man that size, suckled on Work'us gruel—but apparently it was true. This hadn't come from Flitty Deakins, neither; I'd made enquiries of my own. He'd managed to get himself apprenticed to an Irish butcher and spent several happy years at a slaughter yard in Smithfield, killing pigs, before moving on to less sanguineous work shifting cargo at the docks. It appeared he gravitated as well to a loose confederation of house-breakers and head-breakers—cracksmen and rampsmen, in the parlance of the trade—amongst whom he continued to find considerable scope for his old pig-sticking skills. He may indeed have found occasion to employ these upon his old master the butcher, who was discovered bleeding his life out in an alley behind a public house not long after young Odenkirk had given in his notice. The butcher was a terrible man for drinking, and prone to improving his apprentices with his fists. He'd been stuck, as fate would have it, like a pig.

By the time Atherton met him, Odenkirk was working as a bully at a night-house in Curzon Street. This was none of your reeking stews, but an establishment catering to gentlemen. It auctioned off twelve-year-old virgins for as much as fifty guineas—some of them being auctioned as virgins seven nights running. Next door was an even more exclusive establishment, where ancient creaking baronets who required correction might for a suitable sum present their shrivelled shanks to Mistress Riding-Crop for striping. At any rate, Odenkirk and Atherton had hit it off, or had at least each seen how the other might be useful.

Now here we were, just we two, alone in a London night. Hayes Street was otherwise dark as a shroud, and beyond us the river slid silent through the blackness. Above us was London Bridge, where hundreds clustered in shanties that choked the traffic, and hundreds more slept rough, clustered round fires in barrels.

"The Man Himself sent me to find you," he said. Meaning Atherton. "We're wondering if you've heard from the Deakins."

"Flitty Deakins? No."

"You're sure of this?"

"I just said it, didn't I?"

"Cos she's gone missing, you see. She's up and disappeared. And now we worry."

This was news to Your Wery Umble.

"Why would you think she'd come to me?"

"She done it before. Straight to friend Starling with a tale to tell."

"I ent seen her since that night."

He eyed me for a moment, weighing whether to believe it. Weighing Your Wery Umble too, perhaps, as a man might do who had the proper pig-sticking expertise. Seven stone and a half, he might have calculated—and somewhat less than that once hung by the hind legs to drain with all the other little piggies.

"Well," he said at length. "If you hear anything—where she is, p'raps, or where she's bound—you'll let us know."

"And why would I do that?"

"Cos poor Miss Deakins ent well. She sees wild sights, poor addled bitch, and is attacked by green-eyed Hindoos. God knows what might find her on the streets of London, unless her friends find her first. And of course we'd make it worth your trouble. Here."

His left hand was extended, a gold guinea glinting in the palm.

"A token of goodwill," he said.

"I don't want your money."

"'Course you do."

He exposed long yellow ivories again, to indicate that we were friends, despite occasional misunderstandings. Nothing but the very best of friends, united in Christian concern for Phyllida Deakins.

I took the coin. After all, why not? And if I ever caught wind of Miss Deakins's whereabouts, I would advise her to run as far and as fast as her trotters would take her, as if all the green-eyed Hindoos in creation were howling like djinns on her heels.

"You heard what happened to Uncle Cheese?" I said.

Odenkirk had. He shook his head, at the sadness of it. "Sorrowful news, friend Starling—and a caution to us all. Cos any one of us might be struck down, as poor Ned Cheshire was. Is that not a fact? Cruelly struck from out of nowhere, in the prime of life. Something for us all to think upon."

He leaned down closer, his champers as yellow and long and sharp as the teeth of the wolf in the tale.

"Lying in a ditch full of shit—eh, friend Starling? Down there with the poor dead moggies, and the dogs that bit. And if you hear from the Deakins, you'll be sure to tell us. You'll be very sure indeed—I know you will."

The skies opened up again as Odenkirk sloped off, and that smile of his followed me home. All the way to Cripplegate, hunched against the rain, flinching at every noise in the London night. At last I turned at the head of the street. There was a lamp on the corner, and light just ahead from the gin-shop.

And as I arrived, my heart stopped all over again. An apparition slid from the darkness to block my way: a young woman, soaked to the skin and shuddering with the chill, like a wandering ghost bereft of shelter.

"Miss Smollet!" I exclaimed.

The gin-shop was unprepossessing even by the standards of the district, *unprepossessing* being a word that you may take to mean small and dirty and redolent of ancient odours, the most prominent of these being juniper and vomit. There was a wooden counter with bottles behind, and a handful of tables and wooden stools. There were unadorned walls to lean against, and — and after a time — to slide down from, and a floor beneath to lie sprawled upon if necessary, though this was not encouraged by the proprietress. Missus Maggs preferred a better class of patron, meaning them as would leave on their own two trotters — or one trotter and a crutch, as might be, in the case of Tom Lobster returned from the Wars, or patients of Mr Comrie up the stairs. But a gin-shop was a gin-shop, and you took what staggered in.

Miss Smollet had been outside in the rain for hours. For Literally Hours, she said tearfully, although Missus Maggs would tell me the next day that it had been closer to twenty minutes. Miss Smollet had come into the gin-shop first, said Missus Maggs, but then sat without purchasing a single glass, since apparently she lacked the requisite jingle. This had caused Missus Maggs in due course to invite her to leave again; and another sort of proprietress — though not Missus

Maggs—might have wondered at the motives of such a young woman in coming penniless into a gin-shop in the first place. "Hattired in such a manner, Mister Starling, as no Modest Person would be, in a skirt that riz above the ankles, and wares right there up front, on display in the shop window. But I forms no judgements, which you well know, being as I am a woman as sees little and 'ears less, sitting upon my stool behind the counter, Mister Starling, minding of my kews, sir, and my peeze."

"I didn't know Where Else to Turn," Miss Smollet was saying now.

Sitting cold and drenched and wretched, with my own jacket wrapped around her shoulders. But at least we were inside again, and at a table nearest the fire, since Your Wery Umble possessed jingle where Miss Smollet did not. A golden guinea, in fact, courtesy of friend Odenkirk. She cupped her hands round a glass of hot punch, avoiding the slantways eye of Missus Maggs.

"What's wrong?" I asked her.

"Everything."

"Has something happened?"

"Yes!"

She drew a breath to steady herself, and slurped a mouthful of punch.

"Bob Eldritch," she said. "In a newspaper, this morning. Did you see it? So it ent just me. There's others has seen him too."

I started to remind her that the newspapers would print almost anything, and that some simple explanation surely lay behind it. But Miss Smollet was shivering again, with something that went much deeper than the chill. "You don't understand," she said. "He came again, a second time. He was at my window."

"When?"

"Tonight. Earlier — just after dark."

She swore it was no dream. She had been wide awake, sitting at the wooden box by the window that served as an *escritoire*, writing a letter to her friend the Badger. The candle had suddenly fluttered, she said, though the window and the door were both closed and no way for the wind to get in. Then there came a scratching sound that was not her quill against the paper, and when she looked up he was staring at her.

"He was outside the window — Right There — closer than I am to you! His hair standing up on end, and Great Staring Eyes, bulging out of his head. Oh, them Eyes — they were never like that in life, Mr Starling. Whatever could have happened to his eyes?"

Her distress was genuine. That was piercingly clear — never mind her tendency towards capitalization, nor her skills as an actress. Miss Smollet had been terrified.

And I confess that a certain sensation had begun creeping up Your Wery Umble's spine, as clammy and cold as a hand reaching up from a grave.

"Oh, Mr Starling — Will — what am I to do?"

Behind the counter, Missus Maggs while minding her peeze and kews had been leaning ever more precariously in our direction. She now leaned at forty-five degrees, like the mainmast on a crippled frigate. In another moment she would reach the tipping point, and crash to the deck in a tangle of sheets and rigging.

"I'll walk you home, Miss Smollet," I said.

"Home? Haven't you heard a word I just been saying?"

"I'll wait outside the house, and make sure no one comes. All night, if I have to."

I would have done it too. But her distress just grew keener than ever.

"Don't you see? That room's no good. I can't go back there — cos he knows where to find me!"

She sat huddled in such woebegone loveliness as would melt a heart of granite, let alone the poor organ of Your Wery Umble, which had commenced melting the second I saw Miss Smollet upon the stage three weeks previous, and had by the present moment achieved such a perfect state of liquefaction that it pooled about my soggy boots like rainwater. And of all the doors in London, she had come in her hour of distress to mine.

"What am I to do?" she said again, as helpless as a child.

"You will stay here, Miss Smollet," I said, decisively. "You will stay with me."

My crib was on the topmost floor, underneath the eaves. It was little more than a closet, with a pallet on the floor and a slantingdicular ceiling to thump your nob against, getting up, all of it smelling of mould and unwashed Will. It had been used as a storage room, and still was. Odds and ends of broken furniture were piled against the walls, and a threadbare rug rolled up, the way you'd roll up a rug with a body in it. There was not a cadaver so concealed at this particular moment — although there had been bodies here on other occasions. Mr Comrie never did dissections on the premises, but sometimes a Thing would arrive in the night, requiring to be stored 'til morning. I never minded them much — cadavers sleep quiet, though they're gassier than you might suppose. And of course they grow nose-ish after a day or two, especially in warm weather.

Still, it was my own room — the first I'd ever had. My books were stored on a shelf, all eight of them, including the adventures of Gil Blas, and *Tales of the Genii* and *Robinson Crusoe*. Sam Johnson's dictionary as well, Your Wery Umble having always been the tiniest bit of a scholard himself, in a haphazard way. In a battered trunk were my particular personal treasures. These included a barker that I'd had from a poor dead Lobster after the Battle of Albuera — a bone-handled pistol, exactly like one that might have been used by Claude Duvall the highwayman — and one half of a small brass locket that my mother had left with me at the Foundling Hospital. There was always a keepsake left with a foundling. My mother had the other half; we'd have matched them up if she'd ever come to take me back again.

Miss Smollet followed me up three flights of stairs, past Mr Comrie rumbling in slumber behind his own door. Stepping into my room, she stood wet and shivering.

"You must take off them things, Miss Smollet," I said. She'd catch her death, is what I meant. "We'll hang them up to dry."

"I'm very grateful to you," she said. "I'd be gratefuller if you'd turn round."

Behind my back, Miss Smollet's sodden garments whispered from her skin. And there stood a statue of Your Wery Umble with his glims squinched shut, scarce daring to breathe, like some blind acolyte outside the Holy of Holies itself—whatever that may be, for I confess I don't precisely know. But you'll take the reference nonetheless, and understand how I was feeling in that moment.

"Here," she said.

I took them as they were handed from behind, and bore them down the stairs to the surgery, where I poked a fire to life in the grate and hung the garments with reverence and awe. The shawl and the frock, draped over the backs of chairs, to scandalize Missus Maggs when she came in the morning to straighten. Then I fetched a rug back upstairs and found Miss Smollet sitting on the trunk, a candle guttering on the window ledge behind her. She was wrapped in a blanket, her wet hair hanging free about her shoulders, like a desolate mermaid on a rock.

"It weren't a dream," she said, somehow seeming forlorn and fierce both at once. "Tonight, and that other time. He was truly there, Will, at my window. Do you believe me?"

Her eyes were wide and searching, and I hesitated.

"I believe you saw something that gave you a terrible fright," I said. "But you're safe now. Not a soul in London knows you're here—not a single one, alive or dead—excepting my sole self. And I'll be on the landing until morning comes—right here, Miss Smollet, standing watch outside the door."

She smiled then, brave and tremulous. She might have been a heroine upon the stage — lorn and bereft and hunted by foes, but resolved to carry on. The waters of William's melted heart rose up above his knees.

"I hardly deserve such kindness, Will. You are Such a Good Friend to me."

"Right here, Miss Smollet," I repeated. "And I ent moving, neither."

You will imagine the welter of thoughts and feelings as I bowed myself out of my bedroom, and closed the door upon Miss Smollet, and sat myself cross-legged against it. Prepared to face down the Legions of Hell itself, should they come howling through the darkness up those stairs — but feeling at the same time more unsettled than I'd ever admit, and drawing some reassurance from the snores that rumbled through Mr Comrie's door below.

Cos of course I'd never told Miss Smollet about what Flitty Deakins had claimed to see — a corpse rising up in the stable loft at Crutched Friars, the night Bob Eldritch choked to death amongst the Wolves. But Miss Deakins saw green-eyed Hindoos as well — so I reminded myself, over and again. Flitty Deakins was addicted to laudanum, and no one could resurrect the dead, not even if they employed electrical means and swore that it was Science.

The light from Miss Smollet's candle showed in a thin line underneath the door. Twice she called out softly, anxious to know that I was still there at my post. I whispered back reassurance, and at length I heard her breathing grow regular and deep.

I drifted off to sleep myself, some while before dawn. Or so I must have done, cos I dreamed I glimpsed a shape at the foot of the stair, hunched and peering up at me. A white face and two bulging eyes like eggs, and hair standing straight on end.

I found myself lurching to my feet. But when I looked again there was nothing there.

13

That morning, I went to pay a call upon Isaac Bliss.

Isaac had been one of the smallest boys at the Foundling Hospital, and was thus one of the most beleaguered, on the universal principle that the weak must be baited and badgered, especially if they're crippled. I took the opposite position, and did so robustly, being one of the biggest. You'll arch an eyebrow, now, and regard Your Wery Umble askance, but I tell the truth. I got off to a rousing start in life, thanks no doubt to that vast blue-veined breast in Kent, and 'til the age of nine or ten was a strapping fellow. My problem was I petered out, and accomplished almost nothing at all thereafter, growth-wise.

A cynic might suggest that those early years shaped certain assumptions about myself, and left me with lifelong misconceptions about what I might accomplish, and how much I might aspire to, like one of those Northern terriers that won't stop strutting long enough to realize he stands shoulder-high to a rat. But I was for several glorious years a regular bruiser, and at Lamb's Conduit Fields I was able to blacken a few ogles and bash selected smellers in order to encourage a spirit of love and solicitude towards foundling-kind in general, and poor Isaac Bliss in particular. And indeed he was never "poor Isaac" at all, even at his most beleaguered, cos Isaac had a wonderful spirit, resilient past all reason.

I'd like to think he was fond of me in return, even as I lost my value in the smeller-bashing line. And in fact he lit right up with pleasure as he turned achingly from his work-bench in the cellar of Bowell the Undertaker, and saw me coming in.

"Will Starling!" he exclaimed. He'd been sitting on a three-legged stool, and now he creaked himself onto his feet. "It's grand to see you, Will—just grand."

"And you, young Isaac," I said. "You're looking well."

He held his smile. "Am I? Well, it's kind of you to say. Though I wonder, Will, if p'raps you're not quite right."

In truth, it hurt just to look at him. Isaac had declined quite shockingly from the last time I had been here, scarcely a month ago. His eyes had grown too big for his face, and his breath rattled audibly in his narrow chest. Worse yet, his skin had taken on that blue translucence that I knew too well from a hundred field hospitals. It's the look you see when Old Bones is standing just outside the door.

Old Bones never truly left Bowell's at all, of course, being present in every shadow. He was here in the stillness of the cellar, with its dancing dust-motes and its smell of fresh-cut wood and lingering putrefaction. But he'd never before stood quite so close to Isaac Bliss. Right there, looking over his shoulder, as Isaac bowed in his eternal question-mark, sanding a length of pine.

"'Ave you come on business, Will? Cos Mister Bowell's gone out."

"I ent here for him, young Isaac. I'm here to see a friend."

I don't know if he believed me, quite. Isaac was not a lad with friends who'd drop by to visit of a morning—or friends who'd drop by at all. But he beamed to hear it anyways.

"Well, that's grand, Will," he said, employing a favourite word. He creaked down onto the stool again, finding standing up a strain. "I seen another friend too, just t'other day. You recollect Janet Friendly, from Lamb's Conduit Fields?"

I recollected vividly. A long plain face with an ominous scowl and two large red hands, one of them frequently wrapped in a fist that was waving under Your Wery Umble's cork-snorter. Though I concede she often had just cause.

"How is she?"

"Oh, she's just grand. It seems she lives by St Clement Danes, with her Ma."

There was a surprise.

"Her Ma come back to fetch her?"

"She did, Will. Fetched her out, and took her home, not long after you left. They have a shop, the two of 'em together."

I beamed right back at that, though I couldn't help but feel a wistful pang. Cos that's what we'd all dreamt of, after all—each morning and each night, every foundling in the place.

"Janet's Ma," I said. "Well, ent that something."

"It is, Will. It's just the grandest thing."

But in fact I hadn't come just to visit. There was a question I needed to ask him—and I needed to ask it directly, before Mr Bowell should come down the stairs, or that viperous son.

"There was a funeral several days ago, on Monday. A man named Eldritch. You remember the one?"

Isaac blinked, and nodded. Yes, of course he did. "Mr Atherton brung the party in."

"Did you help prepare the body?"

"No, Mr Bowell done that himself."

"But it was here — the body. You're sure of that?"

Isaac gave a painful shrug, and looked perplexed. "I seen *a* body, Will. It was brung here under a blanket. Whether it was your Eldritch or no, I couldn't say. I never saw the man in life. And why would you need to know that, can I ask?"

He was about to grow perplexeder still, cos the question I needed to ask had been brooding in my mind since Annie Smollet had turned up in the night. Skulking on rat's paws somewhere deep, with all the other thoughts that are too shadowy and queer for the light of day. Now it had brought me here to the undertaker's cellar, where coffins stood against the walls and poor Isaac Bliss on a three-legged stool sat dying before my eyes.

"The body that come in, Isaac — this body that Bowell prepared himself. When the coffin left this place on the morning of the funeral . . . was the body inside it?"

Isaac blinked, and began to answer. Then he stopped, with a furrowed expression.

"It's an odd thing, Will," he said. "Odd that you should ask that partic'lar question."

"Why?"

Isaac's reply was to give me a great deal to ponder, in the days that followed. But the conversation had also suggested a solution to an immediate dilemma, one that waited for me outside on the street, pacing in muted agitation. Miss Smollet turned as I emerged from the Undertaker's.

"What did your friend say?" she asked.

I had shaken her awake in the first light of morning, before Mr Comrie had emerged snorting from his slumbers — and before Missus Maggs in the gin-shop downstairs had arisen to mind her kews and peeze. But that left the question of where poor Miss Smollet should go instead, for she couldn't bring herself to return to the house in Holborn.

"Your friend," she repeated anxiously. "What did he tell you?"

I decided to restrict myself to one small part of the answer. Leastways for the present, until I'd worked out what best to do next.

"He says," I replied, "that he knows someone who may have a room to let."

Janet Friendly's house stood amongst a cluster of ramshackle structures wedged along a down-at-heels patch of Milford Lane, south of St Clement Danes. There were street arabs staring, and washing on poles stuck out of windows, and on warm days the stench from the churchyard would waft its way across the Strand. The yard at St Clement Danes was known as the Green Ground; it was notoriously overcrowded, being also the graveyard for the workhouse in Portugal Street. And paupers will putrefy, especially when they're stacked four or five on top of one another, with a few inches of soil to cover the topmost. In summer the body bugs—mayflies, is what they were—buzzed like bumblebees.

Janet's house leaned forwards, its second storey looming partway across the narrow lane, as if intending belligerence to the house on the other side. The opposing structure leaned towards it with equivalent intent, and thus the two of them faced one another like two muskoxen bent on settling the issue of dominance over the herd. In this regard, Janet Friendly's house was much like Janet herself, and if Your Wery Umble were a betting man—which he was—he'd lay ten to one that hers would triumph, lunging suddenly with a mighty blow that would shiver the antagonist's timbers and reduce it to a pile of planks. I put this to her once on a subsequent visit, to see how she'd respond. She eyed me narrowly, as if deciding whether I was laughing at her, and would in consequence need clouting about the earhole—cos Janet Friendly wasn't, particularly. Friendly, I mean. The surname had been wishful thinking on the part of the Governors at the Foundling Hospital, or possibly just irony, after one look at the set of her infant jaw. But she had other qualities to compensate.

There was a sign in the window when Miss Smollet and I arrived, just as Isaac Bliss had speculated that there might be. A bit of cardboard and a charcoal scrawl: "Room to let." So we went in.

Sunlight slanted onto benches piled with old clothes and fabric. Standing amidst them were racks of outlandish outfits: jackets and doublets and capes and gowns, in rainbows of colour. Manikins stood like guests at a masquerade ball, and heads with wigs lined up in a row. It was all remarkably splendid, though of course it wasn't, not really — the wigs were horse-hair and the fabrics were coarse, and the ravishing dresses were patched and flimsy — but they still had their enchantment, for all that. There was a work-bench off to the side for mending and altering items that came in, and a low doorway led to a sitting room at the back.

At the counter was a customer, harbouring illusions about the price he might get for the bundle of old clothes he was offering. A large man, shrinking by the moment as his aspirations were cudgelled down to size by a horse-faced young woman of some twenty years; at length he slunk out with a meagre handful of coins, sadly diminished by the transaction. The young woman commenced sorting through the bundle he'd left, and turned an equine glower upon Miss Smollet and myself.

"H'lo," I said, the sight of her kindling a grin despite best efforts.

A vague recognition stirred in return, and she squinted Your Wery Umble into clearer perspective.

"Will Starling," she exclaimed. "Well, Christ on a biscuit."

I had always liked Janet Friendly, though God knew she could grind upon a man. We'd been good friends, in our way, at the Foundling Hospital — even on the days she was twisting my arm up bechuxt my shoulder blades for whatever transgression I had most lately committed. Usually it involved missing a chance to shut my peck-box.

"Will fucking Starling," she repeated.

"Janet." A woman's voice—Janet's mother's, presumably —emanated from the sitting room. "Language."

"Just look at you. Five years is it—six? And you never grew a fucking inch."

*

Mrs Sibthorpe, Janet's mother, had been upon the stage. I was to learn all of this in the days that followed my first visit—and I share it with you now, since Janet Friendly's story was quite heart-warming, in its wistful way, and perhaps we should take our warmth where we can find it, you and I, given where our own dark Tale is tending. Janet's mother had not been Mrs Sibthorpe in those days, but rather Lively Loo, who performed comic songs and dances at penny gaffs and free-and-easies—public houses, that is to say, where musical entertainment was on offer—in East London. In one of these she met Janet's father, who wasn't Mr Sibthorpe either, but a twinkling eye and a splendid set of sidewhiskers, last seen legging it down an alleyway in the first fresh promise of dawn. The actual Mr Sibthorpe had first seen her in a free-and-easy as well, a number of years after the child of Twinkling Eye had been left at Lamb's Conduit Fields. He was a quieter man entirely, Mr Sibthorpe; some might even say dull. "As riveting as a mackerel," as Mrs Sibthorpe was often to remind him, on days when the mantle of abandoned aspirations lay particularly heavy upon her shoulders. But he was a sober man, and a decent one, who ran a shop that sold theatrical costumes; he lived upstairs, and rented out rooms besides, to lodgers.

A few months after the marriage, he learned that his wife had had a child once, out of wedlock, and left it at the Foundling Hospital. As Mrs Sibthorpe wailed and rent her hair, he left the shop without another word, disappearing down the lane as a man with vastly superior sidewhiskers had done with such finality some years before. He was gone for several hours, walking the streets of the Metropolis, and returned with a settled expression and six words for his wife: "Perhaps you'd better fetch it home."

It turned out that Janet's mother had in the early days gone several times to Lamb's Conduit Fields, peering wistfully through the railings at the girls in their drab black uniforms, and wondering which one of them might be hers. One such afternoon she had glimpsed the child: a waif with golden hair and soulful eyes that would melt the heart of a granite gargoyle, let alone the heart of a mother who knew — instantly and beyond all doubt, by that mysterious instinct that binds the lioness to her cub — that this was the offspring of her very womb. So now with her husband's phlegmatic blessing, Mrs Sibthorpe hurried back all these years later to Lamb's Conduit Fields with her token in trembling hand, and presenting it to the Governors she was reunited at last with her own beloved child, which turned out to be Janet Friendly: fifteen and raw-boned and lank-brown-haired, with big hands and bigger feet and a chary short-sighted squint on her long phizog, three-quarters convinced that some trick was being played.

"And in fact it was," Janet would later say. "The trick was on her. Serves her right, for being such a maudlin twat. Ah, well—credit where it's due—she took me home anyways."

She did indeed. She showed Janet through the door of the shop in Milford Lane, and the rooms above where they lived. Mr Sibthorpe said "H'lo" to her, and after a day or two said something else. After a month he glanced to her one evening as they closed the shop and said it was a pleasant thing to have a daughter, which she took very kindly indeed, and would quite possibly have flung her arms about his neck right there and then if she had been of the arms-flinging inclination. Being the opposite sort, she mumbled that a father was no bad thing either, and left it at that. But they understood one another, and often of an evening they would go out walking. Sometimes they would walk up to Drury Lane, to see a play with the great clown Joseph Grimaldi, the finest Harlequin of the age. Or else they would just sit together by the fire in companionable silence, for Mr Sibthorpe was an older gentleman, much older than his wife, and was finding himself less vigorous than once he'd been. Thus they lived for several years, all three of them together, until one evening Mr Sibthorpe went an exceptionally long time without speaking, even by his own standards, and was discovered to be stone dead in his favourite chair. At the funeral, Janet found to her confusion that she was sobbing inconsolably. But she had a mother, and they still had the shop, and a little bit extra that Mr Sibthorpe had put by. So between them they did what you do, and carried on.

And now here was Janet on a morning in May, with Your

Wery Umble standing before her and Miss Smollet shrinking fetchingly at my side. I explained the situation, presenting a carefully abridged version: Miss Smollet was an actress, had been through some unspecified Tribulation not at all of her own making, and accordingly needed a room to lodge in. Janet listened, while Miss Smollet stood beside me looking enervated. A fine word, *enervated*, recently magpied by Your Wery Umble from Sam Johnson's dictionary, signifying one who is sadly wrung out by sleepless nights and uncanny encounters, but remains a vision of loveliness.

"Hum," grunted Janet when I'd finished.

"Is the room still to let, then?"

"Of course it is," exclaimed Mrs Sibthorpe, who had come in.

The room was on the second floor, overlooking the street. This was slightly worrisome, as it would put Miss Smollet directly at the point of impact should Janet's house decide at last to settle its issue with the building opposite. But the house was close enough to Cripplegate for Your Wery Umble to drop by when the mood took hold, such as mornings and evenings—and Janet Friendly was on hand, in case of emergency. Janet was no longer quite the amazon she'd been at Lamb's Conduit Fields, but on the whole I'd still back her against any boggle-eyed revenant in London.

"Yes," said Miss Smollet, looking in through the door. "Yes, I believe I could stay here."

"Of course you could," exclaimed Mrs Sibthorpe. Having been upon the stage herself, she was tickled to have an actress as a lodger.

"Four shillings a week," said Janet, who remained un-tickled.

"Three," said Mrs Sibthorpe.

"Mother, fucksake..."

"Language."

"Three shillings, then," Janet muttered, looking to Miss Smollet. "Payable in advance."

Miss Smollet hesitated, and looked to Your Wery Umble.

"I will see to the payments," I said, growing taller by the syllable.

Miss Smollet's eyes misted in gratitude. Janet's rolled.

"You are such a friend to me, Will Starling," said Miss Smollet.

Mr Starling was six-foot-four, and rising.

Afterwards Mrs Sibthorpe helped Miss Smollet settle, while Janet and I went back downstairs.

"Will fucking Starling," said Janet yet again. But this time I'd swear she was stifling a grin of actual fondness—though for Christ's sake don't tell her I made any such claim, lest there be clouting round the earhole in consequence. "What have you been up to, all these years?" So I told her a bit about this and that, and she told me a bit in return, and we even reminisced about the days at Lamb's Conduit Fields. It turned out Janet knew the whereabouts of two or three of the old foundlings, though several others were dead, and of course there was Isaac Bliss at the Undertaker's. We both grew a little sad at the thought of poor Isaac, and there was silence for a moment. Above us Mrs Sibthorpe's laughter tinkled.

"And you never heard from your own Ma?" asked Janet.

"Only that she's long dead."

Janet's long phizog softened. "I'm sorry to hear that, Will."

I gave a casual chuckle, as you do. "It's what happens in the end, when you're alive."

"And no other family at all?"

I changed the topic.

"You'll keep an eye peeled for her, will you?" Meaning Miss Smollet, whose voice came silvering down the stairs.

"Is someone after her, then?"

Janet eyed me shrewdly, clearly guessing more than I'd told her. But how was I to answer a question like that?

"Not in the way you prob'ly think," I said after a hesitation. "But she could do with another friend."

Janet gave a small dry chuckle.

"She ent for you, Will. I hope you know that."

"What?"

"Get your eejit heart broke."

I spluttered for a bit. "Miss Smollet and myself? I never said any such—"

"'Course you didn't. Not out loud. But it's the girl with the golden hair and the great dark eyes, all over again—from Lamb's Conduit Fields, remember? You fall for them headlong, Will. You always have, and it's always hopeless. And as soon as some gen'lman comes along—and one will, soon enough—someone standing on the sunny side of five foot, with a good deal more coin in his pocket—then she'll be off. I think you probably know it, but I'm telling you anyways, as an old friend. Assuming that's what we call ourselves."

I spluttered a bit more at that point, and suspect I may have been bright red in the phizog. Then I did what you normally do, when you feel an utter flat: invited Janet to mind her own business and left, trundling back towards Cripplegate. And reaching the bustle of Fleet Street, I passed by a broadsheet seller who was hawking for a penny the news: a woman had been taken up late last night for the murder of the money-lender, Edward Cheshire.

14

Meg had gone to see Jemmy the previous day, all the way to Woolwich Harbour. They told her to go away, but she paid them money and finally they brought him up from below, where they kept him in a cell with half a dozen others. He stood there gaunt and shackled, the stench of the cells coming off of him, his filthy clothes hanging slack from his wide shoulders. Blinking his eyes against the daylight, like a poor mangy bear that had stumbled out of a cave. He never said a word, but she knew he recognized her.

"You fool," she said, meaning how much she loved him. She had an idea he tried to summon a smile, the hangdog one he'd get when she berated him, bowing his shaggy head and shrugging feebly. She felt a stinging in her eyes. This would have been from the wind that had come up, a raw wind from off of the water, cos Meg Nancarrow never cried.

The marshes stretched out on one side, sodden and flat. On the other, the river reached towards the sea. A tall ship inched along the horizon, sails billowing, and the whole world lay beyond.

"I'll bring you home, Jemmy," Meg said. "I'll look after you, no matter what. Don't you fear."

"Time's up," said the Keeper.

"Fucksake," said Meg. "That ent been so much as a minute."

"You're lucky it was anythink at all."

Jemmy made a sound in the back of his throat as they took him away. A tiny sound, coming out of a man so large.

Meg made her way back to London, then. All the way back, arriving near midnight at the house near Fleet Ditch where she and Jemmy had their room, weary and aching at heart. They were waiting for her there, three Constables and a Magistrate from Bow Street. They came at her out of the darkness.

"Oho," said the Beak, as the Constables clamped hold. "We have you now, my girl. You are under arrest for murder, in the death of Edward Cheshire."

"What?" cried Meg. "The bastard's dead? I never!"

"Oho-ho," said the Beak.

He was a fat sleek man, shining in the lamplight with grease and self-satisfaction, and he knew very well what a vicious bitch he was dealing with. There was a dwelling not two streets away, known as the Old House in West Street, where unwitting victims — drunken sailors and the like — were lured by draggle-tails just like the one who stood before him now, struggling and spitting like a cat. They'd enter by the front door, those men, but they'd come out another way, through a trap-door that opened directly onto the Fleet, where they'd be discovered downstream in the morning half submerged in ooze.

"I never done it," Meg repeated. "I done lots in my life to answer for, but I never murdered Ned Cheshire!"

Gawkers were gathering despite the hour, drawn by the commotion. Candles in the windows opposite, and faces peering out.

The Beak took a rolled-up cloth from underneath his arm. "Then what," he said, unwrapping it, "is this?"

An ivory handled razor, stained with blood.

"That ent mine. I never seen it before. Who's saying that's mine?"

"We found it in that room of yours, my girl. Acting upon Information."

"Then someone put it there!"

The Magistrate chuckled.

"Oho."

*

Newgate squats like a vast brown toad at the very heart of London, just north of St Paul's Cathedral. The prison walls rise up, and up; great brick walls with no windows at all, to prevent any wretch within from getting out, and to block any ray of hope that might otherwise slip in, on the back of a shard of sunlight. It clutches the heart, just the sight of it. It brings to mind every transgression you ever committed, or might ever commit in future, inspiring a sudden mad urge to fall there upon your knees, crying: "Guilty! Guilty as sin itself!" It must clutch such an honest heart as Your Honour's, so you'll imagine what it always did to mine, cos God knows I walked a razor-thin line at the best of times, from which the slightest stumble could precipitate a man straight through the door which now stood before me: an iron door with its four sliding gratings for the Keeper to peer out of.

One of them slid open now, and an Eye peered down. I explained my errand to it, and after a moment there was the sound of iron bolts being drawn within. The door swung open with a grinding creak, to reveal that the Eye was paired with a second one, both of them sunk in the skull of the Keeper, who took the shilling I handed to him, and beckoned me inside. The door boomed shut again behind me, with an appalling finality. "This way," said the Keeper, and led me through more iron doors, with more iron bolts, down dank stone corridors where the stench was unbearable and the cries of woe were worse.

Meg was in the Female Quadrangle: a deeper circle of this Perdition. Three hundred women crammed into a space hardly big enough for fifty. Shrieking amazons, wailing mad-women, infants crawling through piles of shit — the Keepers were reluctant to go in there themselves. There was a lady try-ing to bring about reforms, a merchant banker's wife named Elizabeth Fry, who'd been petitioning the Governors to let her start up a Women's Curriculum. I thought: good luck to her.

We came at last to a door that led to the women's exercise yard. Leaving the worst of the stench and the din behind, we stepped out into a small cobbled enclosure with a desultory patch of sky far above. To one side was a sort of cage, with a roof and iron bars in front, for visitors to step into. Female prisoners would be brought to the other side.

"Gen'lman here already," the Keeper observed.

A man in a fine frock coat bent low beneath the roof of

the visiting cage. Across from him, behind the bars, Meg Nancarrow stood in shadow. There was something in the juxtaposition of the two — the arch of his posture, the belling of his coat like wings against her shrinking stillness — that made me think of a bird of prey, stooping for the kill. A tumble of golden hair, and I stopped in recognition.

Dionysus Atherton.

He was saying something to her, low and intense, and leaning still closer as he did. And upon her face was a spasm of naked fear.

He broke off quickly then, cos that's when he heard the Keeper stepping forward. He turned — saw the man — then saw me, not six paces away. He went still, and the handsome phizog turned to stone.

"Pleasure to see you too," I said.

He looked back to Meg, and this time I heard the words.

"I mean what I say, Miss Nancarrow. Hold fast to that. Even to the uttermost extremity."

And then he was on his way, shouldering past me without another glance. Across the courtyard and through a heavy iron door and gone, his footfalls swallowed in the din of Newgate. I let the door boom shut behind him before I turned back to Meg. She waited at the iron bars, with a Wardswoman keeping scowling vigil a few paces farther off.

"I'm very sorry," I said, "to find you here." Cos where else might a man begin?

"Bully for you."

The look of terror was gone, replaced by a wan defiance. And had it truly been terror in the first place, or something else entirely—some trick of the shadow? Standing there I was no longer sure. Her face was battered, a purple flower blooming round one eye. Clearly she'd fought them fiercely when they'd seized her.

"They're saying you cut his throat."

"I know what they're saying."

"Is it true?"

"And what would I tell you if it was?"

"Whatever you liked. It wouldn't go no further."

"How many times do I have to say it? No. I didn't. I never killed him. Thank you very much, and fuck you all."

That cold sardonic clarity; Meg was on the blue ruin. I nosed the sick-sweet waft of it through the bars, and was glad for her, cos Newgate was less horrible for those as had coins to jingle—as Meg must have done, when she come in. With coins you could purchase victuals fit for human consumption. They'd sell you a quiet place to lie down, if you had enough; and if not you could still secure sufficient daffy to take the edge off burning on the fiery lake. You could do halfways tolerable in Newgate Gaol, so long as your coin endured—right up 'til the moment they crapped you on the New Drop outside, with half of London howling. Money helped you very little then.

I gave her coins, through the bars. "From Mr Comrie."

She actually looked startled. "Why?"

"To help you through the next few days."

Mr Comrie had heard about Meg's arrest by the time I came stray-catting up the Cripplegate stairs towards noon, having installed Miss Smollet at Milford Lane. "Your friend get safely home?" he had asked with sour nonchalance, having learned — so I suppose — about Miss Smollet from Missus Maggs. But this was hardly uppermost in his mind, not with Meg Nancarrow taken up for murder. "You've heard?" he had demanded. "Bad business. Here," he added, handing me two guineas — I'd wager they were the only ones he had, or very near to it — and bidding me take them to her.

Now here she stood in shadow behind the bars.

"Tell him thank you," she muttered.

There were times when the anger would slip away, and you'd glimpse the girl there had been, once upon a time. The child who'd existed before the world got in the way, and wrecked all childish hope and aspiration.

"Half the surgeons in London, anxious for my welfare." The contempt crept back. "Such good, kind men."

"What did he say to you? Atherton."

She went still again, shrinking back into herself. As if the shadows had somehow deepened at the mere mention of the name.

"He said he would help me."

"*Help* you? Why?"

"What business is it of yours? It's nothing to you, what he said or didn't say."

Wrapping herself tightly once more in her mantle of defiance. Seething in shadow, where Will Starling was not going to reach her — nor anyone else.

A sudden clamour arose, beyond. Women howling, a fight

in the common room. Two of them pulling each other's hair out by the roots, while others urged them on. The excitement was setting off the lunaticks, who screeched in agitation.

"I will ask you for one kindness," she said then. "Get word to Jemmy, when it's done. After they've hung me."

"You never killed Uncle Cheese," I protested. "So they're not going to hang you."

But of course they were. That was plain from the outset, and it didn't matter whether she'd killed him or no. Hanging's just what they did to the Meg Nancarrows of this world — and I discovered all at once how much that grieved me. I am about to say that I liked her, though I don't suppose that *like* is the word I want. There was something about Meg much too dark and too wild for mere liking. But the thought of all that fine ferocity, convulsing itself down to a bundle of rags — I found I couldn't bear it.

The afternoon sun had slipped below the wall. The shadows grew deeper and Meg's face was in gathering darkness behind the bars.

"The trial's on Friday," she said. "That's what they're saying. So Monday morning's when they'll do it."

Sworn Testimony
of Linwood Buttons

Delivered at the Old Bailey Sessions House
10th May, 1816

Buttons, Your Honours. Linwood Buttons. Master Buttons, as I was known upon the stage. *Am* known, I might make so bold as to say, for I still appear from time to time, though not so often nowadays, and not before such men as Your Honours. Men of discernment, I mean by that, and refinement of the sensibilities, for Your Honours would hardly set foot in such pits as I am latterly reduced—what's that? Yes, of course, Your Honour—begging Your Honours' pardon—the night in question.

I seen them come out of the Three Jolly Cocks. A low tavern—Your Honours wouldn't condescend to spit—near the foot of Ludgate Hill. The two of them, the woman and the deceased. Or leastways, the man Cheshire, I should say, for he was not deceased as yet, but more as you might call predeceased, and walking. He come out first, the man Cheshire, and she followed a moment afterwards, as if with something on her mind to say to him. There ensues a terse exchange—I call it such, for such it was, Your Honours—warm words on either side, and voices rising. At the end of it they separated.

She goes off in one direction, and he continues in the other. Towards the north and east, sir, being the direction I was going in myself.

The theatre, Your Honours, since you ask. I was coming from the theatre, where I'd spent the evening. Drury Lane. Not on the stage myself, but in the gallery, looking down on Edmund Kean. The man himself — the lion of the London stage, oh yes — hurling himself about, to the rapture of the unwashed. And many of the washed as well, who should know better, for it's wrong, Your Honours — it's all wrong — not acting at all. Philip Kemble — *there* is acting. Decorum, sirs — the measured pace — the voice an instrument of grandeur. Acting is Noble. Such was the model I myself aspired to, in the salad days of my —

Quite, Your Honours. To the point.

The pre-deceased walks on. Yes, of course I recognized him. A pawnbroker. A money-lender. A few streets on he stops to warm himself at a fire, which two men had built at the corner.

What's that? Apprentices? No, hardly. Just two ragged men with no other place to go, such as any man might one day become, Your Honours, if Fortune wills it, and he finds himself cast off through no fault of his own, and out of fashion with the world before he's hardly possessed of whiskers to scrape from his chin. But this is not to the point — quite right — so I don't mention it. The pre-deceased walks on again, and for a time I lose sight of him. Then I turn into another street, tending towards Fleet Ditch. And suddenly there he is, a little distance ahead of me, standing by the mouth of an alleyway. What's that? Moonlight, Your Honours—I seen him by moonlight, for the rain had ceased and a shaft of moonlight had broken through. Just standing, but very still, as if he'd heard some sudden noise.

That's when she came out of the lane, behind him. Yes, Your Honours, the woman he'd been talking to before, outside the Three Jolly Cocks. The woman right there, in the prisoner's dock, who can cry out "No!" as loud as she likes, for she knows it's the truth. I seen her, though she never seen me, which is why I'm alive and standing here today. Like a Fury, Your Honours—that's how she come out. Like a Fury from an ancient tragedy. So sudden and swift that he never had time to turn, before she was on him. Clinging to his back, with a knife in her hand. I seen it flash in the moonlight—I seen her wrench back his head by the hair. And before I can make a single sound, poor Edward Cheshire isn't pre-deceased at all, but laying on the cobbles. His throat gaping open like a silent scream and his life's blood pouring out.

15

Master Buttons, on his hind legs on the witness stand, giving the performance of his life. He wore a new suit of clothes for the occasion, a fine frock coat and a fine white neckerchee, his thinning locks fresh combed and his complexion primed bright red by a sojourn in the King of Denmark across the road. Meg cried "You're a liar!" above the rising voices in the courtroom, but this was very grave. I saw it on the clocks of the jury: twelve good Londoners and true, assembled to hear the testimony and then get on with it, with dinnertime looming. I saw it on the beaks of the three Judges, looking down upon the rabble in the Old Bailey Sessions House. Tom Sheldrake saw it too.

Sheldrake in his wig, looking like nothing so much as a haggard cauliflower. Cos Tom Sheldrake had been retained as Counsel for the Defence—a great startlement to me, as I arrived to watch the proceedings, and squirmed my way into a space at the front of the gallery. It was packed, as is always the case with a capital trial. There's surprisingly few of these in London, now that the days of the Bloody Code are done and the Full Majesty of British Justice has left off hanging indigent thieves and ten-year-old pickpockets. I'd arrived just as the Under-Sheriffs were bringing Meg Nancarrow in. She wore a clean frock and a bonnet, and looked round the courtroom with such pale composure that a hush descended. A whispering began, cos here she was, and she was almost beautiful. She stood stone-still as the Prosecutor laid out the evidence: the bloody knife in her room, and a torn and bloodied dress. But she possessed such bleak dignity that the onlookers began to doubt what they were hearing—right up 'til Master Buttons took the stand.

Tom Sheldrake sank lower in his seat with every syllable the actor uttered, as if he'd disappear at last from view entirely, and end in seeping down between the floorboards. He looked no better than he had when I'd seen him two weeks previous, at Bob Eldritch's funeral. He looked as if he'd hardly slept—or washed—in all the days and nights since he'd flung himself headlong into the grave. He'd lurched in white with drinking—the Wreck of Tom, in search of a reef to founder upon—and proceeded to bungle so haplessly that I could have leapt down from the gallery to shake him.

Not that another barrister could have made much difference, I suppose. There's precious little that Defence Counsel can do at any criminal trial, which partly explains why trials are done so quick—under ten minutes, most of them, though capital trials can stretch out for an hour. But Defence can cross-examine, and this Tom did, rousing himself to fire random volleys of irrelevant questions at the Constables who had searched Meg's room, and the Ale-Draper—Alf, it was, Alfred Pertwee to give his full and proper name—who had earwigged her threatening Ned Cheshire at the Three Jolly Cocks.

MR SHELDRAKE: *"His 'weasand' slit? She warned him of his weasand being slit? Why, sir, should you employ that particular word?"*

ALF: *"Becos it was the word she used."*

MR SHELDRAKE *(angling tiger-like)*: *"But was it 'weasand'? Eh? Or was it another word entirely?"*

ALF: *"Another word like what?"*

MR SHELDRAKE *(terrifically)*: *"The witness will answer the question!"*

ALF *(baffled)*: *"Weasel?"*

Sheldrake couldn't call upon Meg herself, since the defendant is never permitted to testify. But Defence can summon character witnesses, and character is always of prime importance in the Eyes of the Law. Evidence is all well and good, but is the accused the *sort* of person who might commit the crime? So Sheldrake called upon Mr Comrie, who took the stand and glared stiffly across the courtroom, as if challenging the Majesty of British Justice to a prize-fight.

Aye, he knew the defendant. Had met her on several occasions, the first time when she had come to his rooms to seek his professional help for her husband, and subsequently in the Giltspur Street Compter.

Her character?

"The woman sat by him for a week. Never left his side. As if she could keep him alive through pure force of will—and God knows, I half believe she did. D'ye call that character? I do."

A murmur in the court. The Prosecuting Attorney rose with silken politeness to cross-examine. A physician, was Mr Comrie? No?

"A surgeon."

A *surgeon*. Ah. And he knew the accused in his professional capacity?

"What I said."

Though not in hers? For the court was given to understand that the accused was not unfamiliar with the pavement.

"Know nothing of that. And care less."

Quite so. And this man — the stricken husband — lying by death's door in the Giltspur Street Compter. Because...?

"Been attacked."

Good heavens. Where?

"A churchyard."

Why?

"Some question of a theft."

Of?

"A cadaver."

Gasps from the gallery. Mr Comrie stood his ground. The prosecutor blinked. Could the witness repeat that, please?

"A dead body."

Then the stricken husband was — what was he, exactly? — a *grave-robber*? And she sat by him for seven days — a soiled dove, with her body-snatching beau — as devoted as a latter-day Penelope.

"If you want to put it that way."

Which way?

"Sneering."

No further questions.

Then Master Buttons was called to the stand, in the fine new clothes that had come somehow into his possession. He performed. Finishing, he declined his head with perfect grace, like a tragedian in the moment of hush that precedes a storm of applause. He looked to Meg, as if she might herself clap hands and cry "Huzzah!"

"You have murdered me," she said.

The jurors turned in to one another, and after a moment or two they turned grimly out again: guilty. The chief Judge reached for the black cap, for of course the verdict was Death. Sentence to be executed on Monday morning. The body turned over to the anatomists, for dissection. God have Mercy.

Meg had stood 'til then in desperate composure, her hands white claws upon the rail. But now her face, already so pale, lost its last vestige of living warmth. She uttered a cry like a stricken bird, and crumpled.

Exclamations. Rising tumult.

In the gallery behind me, Dionysus Atherton sat still as a statue. He had been there since the trial commenced. More surprising still, it turned out subsequently that he had retained Sheldrake's services on Meg's behalf, and paid the bill. Now his face was grim and grey with the finality of it, but I'd swear there were other emotions as well, contending just beneath the surface of his calm. I'd swear there was agitation — and something else, that I could not understand at all: a flicker in those blue, blue eyes that was very close to triumph.

16

There had been some grisly business involving a dog the day before I had paid my very first visit to Crutched Friars. This had been the previous September, more than half a year prior to the events I have just been describing, and just a day or two after my own return to London from a journey I had taken to the Midlands in connection with my late mother. It is doleful, the tale of that particular journey, much concerned with breaking hearts and footsore foundlings trudging through unending rain, and I suppose I'll end in relating it to you some time, when we're both in the mood for leaky glims and sodden snotters. But first you need to know about the dog.

A mastiff, weighing fully seventeen stone. It had apparently been kept in the stable behind the house, where Atherton was wont to carry out his experimentations upon poor dumb creatures — cos of course they all did it, the surgeons and anatomists; they were all of them vivisectionists, of necessity. Mapping the frontier of the living organism; extending the boundaries of scientific knowledge, quarter-inch by bloody quarter-inch. Mr Comrie never had much taste for it after his student days at Edinburgh University, although he conceded the need. And any surgeon's neighbours grew bitterly familiar with the consequence: moggies disappearing into thin air, and Trusty the spaniel snuffling happily out into the morning light, never to return. But Atherton's mastiff was a deadly serious matter, having escaped and run amok — a creature of such size, maddened by whatever trials it had endured. It terrorized the street, attacking several horses and then leaping up to pull a driver from a carriage. The man must surely have been torn to shreds, had Atherton himself not arrived at the last instant with Odenkirk, who dispatched the beast with a shot from a musket. But even so there had been a lasting fuss, with the driver requiring payment before he would be mollified, and the owners of the injured horses as well, two of which had subsequently to be destroyed.

There had been something terribly wrong with the dog, beyond the obvious fact that it was mad; this was emphasized in the broadsheet reports that ensued. Several witnesses described a curious crick to its neck, and all of them dwelt at lurid length upon the eyes, which were of such a nature as forever to haunt the dreams — so it was claimed — of anyone who'd glimpsed them. There were subsequent reports that the mastiff was seen alive again, ranging through the London streets in the blackness of night in the company of Dionysus Atherton himself. But of course this was only to be expected. People will invent the most ridiculous tales, and the broadsheets will spread them about, and before you know it half the world is convinced they must be true.

In any event, the panic involving the mastiff had taken place on a Tuesday afternoon. I had arrived at Crutched Friars on the Wednesday evening, just at dark. In the course of my recent journey to the Midlands, I had discovered Atherton's name and where he lived. Now I knocked upon his door, refusing to go away until he came out to see me. When at last he showed himself, I told him who I was.

"You are a liar," he said.

But he knew it was the truth, just looking at me. I watched the recognition dawn.

"Christ," he said.

Night had fallen, and inside the house was ablaze with light. I heard laughter and voices behind him; he had guests. He wore a velvet jacket and a silk cravat, and his face was ruddy with wine.

"What do you want?" he demanded after a moment. The flat hint of Lancashire in his voice — just the barest residue, but it would creep out more distinctly with each bumper of claret. You can never quite hide where you come from, or who you've been. "Money — is that what you're after?"

"I don't want money."

"What, then?"

"So we are nothing to each other?" Hearing my own voice very small, and feeling my stomach knot with the realization: I had been a fool to come.

He produced a billfold, then, and took out a banknote. "Here," he said, and thrust it at me. Ten pounds.

"I don't want your money," I said again.

"Take it."

"My mother..."

"... Is dead these eighteen years. But of course you knew that. Didn't you?"

But I had not known, right up 'til that moment. Not for a certainty, although of course I'd suspected. I suppose the shock of it, the dead weight of finality, showed plainly in my face.

"Christ," he said again. "Well, so now you do know."

"How did she...?"

"What could it possibly matter now?"

Someone called from inside the house—a woman's voice, laughing and thickened with drink, asking to know what was keeping him.

"Nothing," he called over his shoulder. "Nobody."

He looked back to me.

"A fever," he said. "It was a fever that took her."

"Were you with her?"

"My sister was nothing to me when she died. As you are nothing to me now. Take what I offer you, and don't come here again."

I left him standing with the banknote in his hand, and went back to Cripplegate. We were already living there, Mr Comrie and I.

"Whaire've you been?" he called as I came up the stairs that night.

"Nowhere," I said. "It doesn't matter."

I stayed in my attic closet for three whole days, that time, just Wm Starling and his companion the Black Dog. When I emerged I discovered that life was going on, as life does. So I rejoined it.

Now here I stood outside his house at Crutched Friars once again, on the evening of the day of Meg Nancarrow's trial. His coach turned into the street just as the bell of St Andrew Undershaft was striking seven. A mild May evening, leaves rustling on the trees and the sun declining into the western horizon. Its last rays haloed Atherton as he stepped down. You might in that moment have fancied him Phoebus, alighting from his chariot.

I stepped out from beside the house, where I'd been waiting. The sun was behind me now; there was an instant before he made me out. Eyes slitting, hand rising to shield, then the souring of recognition.

"I saw you at the trial," I said. "You hired the lawyer."

Cos I'd made that discovery, asking about at the courtroom. One of the Clerks had told me.

Atherton shrugged, making no attempt to deny.

"Why?" I asked him.

"To defend her, obviously."

"That was a *defence*? She'd have done better with no one at all."

"Was I to know how badly he'd bungle?"

"The witness was bought. Master Buttons."

He had been about to shoulder past me, but this claim brought him up short. Meanwhile Odenkirk had emerged from the house behind us, and now stood slouching ominously on the step. "See this one off, Mr Atherton?" Atherton ignored him, training those blue eyes like pistols.

"You know this for a fact?" he demanded. "You make a serious allegation — and a woman's life is at stake. If you have evidence, state it now."

But of course I had no evidence. Nothing beyond the obvious, which all the world had seen — or as much of the world as had crammed into the courtroom while Buttons sent Meg to the gallows.

"You saw him," I said, "same as I did. He was an actor, performing — and wearing new clothes. A man who owes money to half the pawn-shops in London." Cos I knew a bit about Linwood Buttons, by now. I'd asked at the King of Denmark tavern across the road from the Old Bailey, where they knew him as a drunkard and a beggar. "Where would such a man come by a brand new set of togs, unless someone bought it for him?"

"Do you know where he is?"

I did not. Buttons had disappeared, immediately after delivering his damnable performance. Melted away into the million mingling souls of London.

"Do you know how to find him?" Atherton demanded.

But of course I didn't know that either.

"Well, then..." Atherton shrugged eloquently, and started to turn away again.

"What did you say to her?" I asked.

"Who?"

"Meg Nancarrow. When you went to see her in Newgate. What did you say to her?"

He regarded me as if I were some freakish Specimen upon his table: a stunted tatterdemalion Rainbow, presuming to hold one of London's Rising Men of Science to account. But he answered my question, as Odenkirk lounged lupine beyond.

"I said that I would help her, if I could."

"And what did you say when you went back there this afternoon?"

"What?"

"To Newgate. A few hours ago — not long after they brought her back from the trial. You went to see her again."

"You mean to say you have been *following* me?"

In fact it had been an accidental discovery. I'd gone back to Newgate to see Meg myself, less than an hour earlier, but they wouldn't let me in. She was being moved this evening, out of the Female Quadrangle and into one of the Death Cells on the other side. But someone had been to see her already, I had learned: Mr Dionysus Atherton, who at this moment seemed undecided whether to strike me down or laugh aloud.

He did the latter, barking out one mirthless syllable and shaking his head at my behaviour.

"I told her to steel her resolve. And that I would continue to do what I could for her."

"Which is?"

"At this point? There isn't much, Christ knows. I'll make a submission to the Judges."

There is no appeal of a court decision under the Majesty of British Justice, but the three Judges could indeed be approached. They would meet again on the Saturday following a capital conviction, to consider new information. They might in some cases be swayed, and make a recommendation to the

Home Secretary, who could commute a death sentence to transportation for life. Sometimes it happened.

"Why do you care in the first place?" I asked him then.

Cos that was the question that nagged me most of all. Why would a man like Atherton care?

"For a whore like Meg Nancarrow, you mean? I don't care—not personally. But I have an obligation to the family. Jemmy Cheese was acting in my employ on the night he was arrested. I need to preserve my reputation with the Doomsday fraternity at large. I'm a surgeon—I have to do business with them."

The twilight was deepening about us. A dray trundled along the street, against the vast rumble of London.

"And perhaps she reminds me of someone, long ago. Someone I happened to care about."

It was an extraordinary thing for him to say. I've wondered at it ever since—why he would say it at all, and to Wm Starling of all people. Some instinct in him to reach out, despite his loathing?

"Not in her look, so much. But there is something in her spirit, a defiance. My sister had it too."

He was looking past my shoulder as he spoke, into the distance. There was a boy in a green weskit on the corner of the street, with a monkey on a leather strap, begging. But I'm not sure Atherton even saw him; he was looking much farther away than that.

"You have her smile," he said then. "I don't suppose there's ever been anyone to tell you that. Your mother's smile."

Well.

In another tale entirely, this would be the moment for tears. Misty brimmings in two men's glims; sheepish swipings with jacket sleeves and gruff masculine murmurings, giving way to the clasping of hands and mutual embraces, with halting ejaculations about the damnable obstinacy of proud hearts and the brevity of life. As it was, we just looked at one another, across two paces and a chasm.

"Tell me something else," I said then, "Uncle."

I watched the word affect him. Stiffening the shoulders and ramrodding the spine: a word as welcome as a surgical probe up a sphincter. There was a small bleak relish in seeing that.

"What had you done," I asked him, "to the dog?"

"Dog? What dog?"

"The mastiff."

I am not even sure why I asked this now, all these long months later. But I did. Atherton stared down at Your Wery Umble. And then, for the second time in as many minutes, he laughed at me.

"What do you expect me to say? That I used the creature in some abominable experiment, motivated by unholy ambition and urged on by Beelzebub himself? Go ahead, then—believe what you want."

He turned on his heel and strode into the house.

The mastiff's eyes had been crimson—thus various witnesses had reported, or leastways so the broadsheets had claimed. Crimson and burning like coals. Subsequent reports had a tall man with golden hair appearing out of fogbanks in the night, with the beast slouching alongside. They were seen striding with fell purpose along Ratcliffe Highway, and on two separate occasions down Fleet Street.

I trust your judgement. You will take such reports for what they're worth.

The boy on the corner was ten years old, perhaps. I passed by him as I started away. He was Spanish, or else Italian; waifs and strays from the Continent had been washing up in London ever since Waterloo. A bottle-green weskit and a sweet olive face, and a small dejected monkey, displayed to passers-by for ha'pennies.

Odenkirk's eyes bored holes in my back all this while. He had remained outside the door after Atherton had gone inside.

"I wouldn't stay here," I said to the boy, on a sudden impulse.

He blinked. I wasn't sure whether he'd understood, so I sifted through my paltry Spanish word-hoard. Now he began to frown.

"Por qué?"

He might easily have been an orphan; many of them were. There were men who'd oversee a string of orphan beggars, taking half of the proceeds. The animals were rented by the day; monkeys were popular, as were white mice.

This was not a good street for him, I said, stringing my few words together. There was a man, outside that house—yes, that man there. He worked for another man, the one I'd just been speaking with. *Cirujano* was the Spanish word for surgeon. Dangerous was *peligroso*.

"D'you understand what I'm saying? You should go somewheres else. This ent a good place for you to be."

But when I looked back from the end of the road, he was still there.

I was already overdue at home that evening, in Cripplegate. But instead I hurried south and west, across Smithfield and then down to the bottom of Ludgate Hill, where I dropped a penny for the stone-blind beggar as he worked his customary pitch at the corner of Fleet Street. It was a busy corner even now, at the onset of night; traffic jostled and snarled. The blind beggar's name was Gibraltar Charley, as it happens. He played upon a little organ, and he had a dog that danced—a London mongrel shaved to look like a poodle. "Pray encourage him now, my tender-hearted Christians," Charley would call, sitting in his eternal darkness; "pray show encouragement to Tim, the Real Learned French Dog." A coin would clink to the cobbles, and Tim would dance on his hind legs. Tim was a trooper; if poodles were required, then Tim was equal to the task. Besides, this was not so bad, as a living. There were dogs in the sewers this moment, catching gigantic rats.

I continued past them, turning into Black Friars Lane and thence into the Three Jolly Cocks.

There were thirty-six men there drinking. I spoke to them—each one in turn—and discovered that six had been here the night of the murder, four of whom remembered that Meg had sat with a man whose round spectacles flashed in the firelight. Two of these had recognized him as the money-lender, Cheese. All of them knew Meg Nancarrow well enough; she had worked here, after all. Sharp words had been spoken; a threat had been uttered; oh yes, they had heard it too, just as Alf the Ale-Draper had said at the trial. Alf had been saying it ever since, behind the bar — all afternoon and well into the evening, since returning from the Old Bailey. Customers came in and stood him drinks, and clustered round to hear it all over again. Alf had been shaken to his very boots when he'd heard of the murder; he'd been shocked to the core — and yet, perhaps not quite so shocked at all, cos he'd always suspected what sort of a woman Meg was; he'd known it in his waters.

Grave murmurings. Alf Pertwee, bald and bloated, nodded sagely. In Alf's own considered opinion, hanging was too good for the likes of Meg Nancarrow. In bygone days they hadn't hung female felons at all — they'd burned the bitches at Smithfield.

But had he seen Master Buttons, that night?

Alf looked round for the source of the question. Looked down. Found with heavy-lidded ogles Your Wery Umble.

No, he had not. Was he certain? 'Course he was certain. He had seen the man Buttons before, but not that night. With Meg Nancarrow? No, he had never seen Master Buttons with Meg Nancarrow. Nor did he know where the man might be found.

"Then what about Dionysus Atherton?"

Cos a very dark feeling had started to gnaw. It was hardly a suspicion — it wasn't as tangible as that. Not even a question, really, that I could put into words.

"'Oo?" said Alf.

He had been at the trial, I told him. In the public gallery. A tall gentleman with golden hair, in fawn trousers and a sky-blue coat.

Alf frowned in recollection. "What about 'im?"

"Did you ever see him with Meg?"

"What, 'ere?"

"Or anywheres else."

Alf shook his head. No, he'd never laid eyes upon the gentleman. Why did I ask?

I didn't quite know how to answer that question. But something was very wrong, in all of this. Something was as wrong as it could be.

The belling of his coat as he'd stood across from her in Newgate, like the wings of a bird of prey. The arch of his posture, against her shrinking stillness.

"I mean what I say, Miss Nancarrow. Hold fast to that. Even to the uttermost extremity."

MORE HORRID SIGHTINGS

From a Broadsheet Account
11th May, 1816

New developments are reported in the phenomenon of the Boggle-Eyed Man, who first appeared some while ago in the vicinity of St Mary-le-Bow Churchyard, lamenting to passers-by that he had been denied his rightful lodging within the gates, and accordingly must linger homeless until the End of the World. It now grows evident that the Entity has begun to venture further afield into the Metropolis, either through some rising sense of desperation, or else in an increasing Boldness that can only bode ill for those who cross its path. It was sighted three nights ago near a churchyard in Whitechapel, standing like a phantom in the fog, and on the same night was glimpsed slipping down an alleyway near Haymarket. There is now a report, confirmed by several sources, of an uncanny encounter during daylight hours. A sweep, lowered by the ankles down a chimney in Gower Street, grew suddenly frantic. Deaf to encouragement from his master to be manful and cease his shrieking, the boy was at length pulled out, weeping most piteously and convulsing. After much exhortation and prodding, he was able to provide an account of his ordeal, and gave his interlocutors to understand that, halfway down the chimney, he had encountered the Boggle-Eyed Man, staring up at him from below.

There is a further incident reported of a female child, yesterday evening. Not long after nightfall, the child—six years old—passed by the vicinity of St Bartholomew the Great, Smithfield, bearing home to her father a meat pie and a pot of ale, purchased from a public house in Charterhouse Street. Hurrying past the churchyard, she heard a voice entreating her, and discerned a Figure standing in the darkness by the gate.

"Help me," said the Figure.

When the child asked who it was that spoke, the Figure in the darkness gave its name as "Bob" and solicited once again her immediate assistance. Caution contending with innocent Christian concern, the child stepped closer to ask what was the matter, to which "Bob" replied that he was lost and lorn, but might yet find his place if the child would but take his hand and lead him.

She might indeed have done so, being touched to her innocent heart, excepting that she saw just in time that "Bob" was possessed of two great bulging eyes, "with hair stood straight on end, most horrible," which revealed to her that this was no mere vagabond but the Boggle-Eyed Man himself, about whom she had been amply warned. Dropping the meat pie and the pot of ale, the child fled in terror, never stopping until she reached the haven of her home, where her father asked to know what had frightened her so, and "what the D—— had become of his supper."

"He has it, Papa," the child replied in high distress. "*He* has your supper—Boggle-Eyed Bob!"

17

Miss Smollet saw the report on the Saturday, just as I did. It was the name that bothered her most of all.

"He gave his name as *Bob*," she kept saying. Circling back to that one detail, each time I tried to object that a child's wild claims were hardly proof of anything, and neither was a broadsheet report. "But it's more than one report, and more than one child," she insisted. "People keep seeing him — I seen him twice. And the name! He called himself Bob, out of all the names in London."

That's when I finally told her what Isaac Bliss had said to me, two days earlier.

"He said it seemed strangely light — Bob Eldritch's coffin. When they took it out of the Undertaker's. He didn't help lift it himself, but he watched as two other men did. He said, 'They picked it up like it was practic'ly nothing at all. P'raps it was just that they was strong, and the man inside quite small — but it struck me as curious, Will, at the time.'"

And then I told her the rest of it, despite knowing full well where this must lead.

"Atherton tried to bring him back," I said.

We were outside the house in Holborn, just at twilight. I had accompanied Miss Smollet here to fetch a few belongings she wanted to have with her at her new lodgings with Janet Friendly in Milford Lane. The traffic rolled past into the gathering gloom, and the songbirds warbled faintly in the bird-fancier's shop.

"Bob Eldritch," I said. "The night he died. Atherton tried to revive him."

Miss Smollet didn't understand what I meant, not at first.

"I know that, Will. I was there."

"No, not at Fountain Court. An hour afterwards, in the stable behind Atherton's house."

She still didn't understand — not quite. But I watched the realization gather like a shadow across her face.

"There is a woman," I said. "A domestic. She drinks laudanum and tells wild tales. I could hardly believe her myself."

"What did she say?"

So I told her. There was a terrible silence from Miss Smollet when I finished.

"You're saying he — what — *Resurrected* him?"

"Or leastways made the attempt."

Behind us in the shop, the songbird chorus was dwindling as the voices fell silent one by one. Evidently the bird-fancier was draping the cages with the onset of night — or so I chose to presume. Here in the gathering darkness, with Miss Smollet's face greying with horror and the spectre of Bob Eldritch rising up between us, I could almost imagine a different scene instead: a scowling bird-fancier, grown sick to death of song, shuffling and muttering and throttling his lovelies each one in turn.

"You're right, Miss Smollet. It ent possible." I heard myself arguing against my own dark imaginings. "I know that, as a man of Science. A Surgeon's Assistant…"

But even as I spoke, I knew what I was going to do next. Cos I'd already made the preparations.

"Miss Smollet, I'm going to take you back to Milford Lane, where you'll be safe tonight. And I'm going to find out the answer to this, one way or the other."

"*How?*" she exclaimed, in rising distress.

But I believe she'd already begun to guess. After all, there was only one way to know for a fact whether Bob Eldritch had ever been buried.

"Will! Surely not—you wouldn't!"

But I would.

And I have wondered ever since, looking back: was this the night? The wild, black night when I stepped outside the sweet light of Reason, like a traveller leaving the last lamp-lit house on a forest road, and crossed once and for all into a Darkness so profound that I would never quite emerge from it again?

Or had that crossing come already? I have asked myself this question too. Perhaps the crossing had come a full year earlier, on the battlefield after Quatre Bras. And every step I had taken since had been nothing but one step deeper into Night.

The Fortune of War stands at the junction of Giltspur Street and Cock Lane, just across from St Bart's Hospital. The name had been chosen by an owner from the previous century, who retired from a naval career missing both legs and one arm — or so the story went. Myself, I could never quite see how a man might tend a bar while down to his last limb, but perhaps this is just Your Wery Umble being literal-minded.

The Fortune of War was much like any other low tavern in London, except for the little room in the back where on any given night there might be as many as a dozen corpses laid out — Things, to use the parlance of the trade; Stiff 'uns, in varying states of decomposition, each with a tag naming the man who brought it in — cos the Fortune of War was the favoured haunt of the Doomsday Men, north of the river. Several of them could at any time be found in the taproom, drinking. They wore rough jackets and slouch caps, and moleskins on digging nights. They had about them the air of wicked Sextons. From time to time one of the surgeons from St Bart's would hurry over to inspect the Things on display, as if they were so many codfish laid out on a plank, and if a price were agreed upon, a hospital Porter would slope over and lug the purchase to the Death House for dissection. If a Thing were beginning to putrefy, the owner might fail to find a buyer at St Bart's, in which case he would load it into a hamper and lug it round to another hospital, or to one of the private anatomy schools.

Just after midnight I pushed through the door, looking round through the fug of smoke 'til I spotted Little Hollis. There he was, as he'd promised to be when we'd reached our agreement earlier that evening: sitting with two or three others, and nodding as I caught his eye. Draining his jar, he made some excuse to his companions—you didn't discuss such Business as ours with them as were not partners in the enterprise—and then rose and high-arsed past me, out the door. I followed.

"Have you got the tools?" I asked him, as we stood together in darkness on Cock Lane.

He squinted upwards at the sliver of moon, a reek about him of old cellars and recent urine.

"'S been a change of plan," he said. "'S eighty-twenty, now. The proceeds."

"We agreed on fifty-fifty," I protested. "Equal terms."

"'S 'Ollis as supplies the himplements. 'S 'Ollis as contributes the hexpertise. So 's eighty per cent to 'Ollis—take or leave."

He eyed me slantingdicular, and spat. And he was bluffing, of course. Little Hollis had depended on Uncle Cheese to acquire information about corpses and make the arrangements with Sextons—and he had depended as well on poor Jemmy to protect him from rival gangs. The Resurrection trade was highly competitive, and a man in the way of being self-employed could find himself set upon most grievously. I guessed he hadn't been on a job since that dreadful night in St George-in-the-East churchyard, which explained why he'd been desperate enough to take up my offer in the first place.

But Your Wery Umble was hardly doing this for the jingle. Fifty-fifty or eighty-twenty, it made little difference to me — especially since I strongly suspected it would end up in nothing at all. But I let him believe I was mightily aggrieved, and made a feint at battling for sixty-forty before giving in and letting him have three quarters.

He allowed himself a grunt of sly satisfaction, before muttering that Your Wery Umble should be grateful for anything at all. "The likes of you, and the likes of 'Ollis. 'S a perfessional, is 'Ollis, a top perfessional, haccustomed to the likes of Jemmy Cheese, and Nedward Cheshire. 'S a terrible coming-down for the likes of 'Ollis. 'S a terrible loss he's suffered." He shook his head lugubriously. "And Meg Nancarrow too, on top of all the rest. 'S lost now too, is Meg. 'S no hope for the bitch."

"Do you believe she did it? Murdered Uncle Cheese?"

There was the barest hint of a pause.

"'S what they say, innit?"

"I think she's innocent."

"'S not for us to decide."

"Christ, I wish I knew what happened."

Cos on that night — as you'll recollect — I didn't *know*. Standing there in the darkness outside the Fortune of War, I had none of the pieces that I would subsequently jigsaw together; had no inkling, not as yet, of the visit that had been paid by Uncle Cheese to Crutched Friars, with Little Hollis waiting for him outside in the night, primed to dash for a Constable if Cheese should fail to emerge. Looking back upon it now — reliving that night outside the Fortune of War, all these months later—I can imagine a furtive look flickering across the sharp phizog of Little Hollis. I can picture the barest hunching of narrow shoulders.

But in that moment I saw nothing, preoccupied as I was with the ordeal that lay ahead. And then suddenly there was a scraping of boots against cobblestones, and Hollis flinched as a figure stepped out from the darkness behind us.

A slim form in a man's baggy jacket, far too large, and a cap such as low rough fellows wear, raising a bull's-eye lantern in one not-quite-steady hand.

"Let us Do This Deed," said Annie Smollet.

I had told her earlier that she was not coming with us. I had stated it in no uncertain terms, but Miss Smollet had paid no heed—she was coming, she insisted, and that was that. Now here she stood, in togs she had borrowed—or so I could only suppose—from a friend in the Wardrobe Room at one of the theatres, tucking a stray ringlet back under the cap and eyeing me with an air of desperate resolve.

Little Hollis peered in disbelief. "Aw, bugger me blind," he said.

"My Mind is Set," said Miss Smollet. "And when my Mind is Set, there is no budging it, not with Gunpowder nor Cannonballs."

I had the sense that she'd been rehearsing this all the while she'd been standing here, waiting for me to come back out of the tavern. And it was a rousing enough declamation, I suppose, in its way—assuming your notion of what we were about was drawn from the pages of a penny-blood.

"Lead," said Miss Smollet, "on."

Little Hollis looked back to me. "'S ninety-ten, now," he said bitterly.

St Mary-le-Bow lay half a mile to the south and east. We veered a little distance northwards first, stopping at a crib where Hollis had stashed his implements, and then we were on our way, Little Hollis high-arsing ahead of us and Miss Smollet keeping close to my side, talking in a low quick voice all the while.

"I know What Lies Ahead," she insisted, repeating it several times, as if saying it often enough would make it so. "And more than that, I know how the Job Is To Be Done."

It seems she'd been in a play once, with grave-robbing in it.

"I was the Girl who got Exhumed. It was a wonderful role, and highly dramatickal, for I'd been stabbed through the heart, and my wound commenced to bleed when the murderer looked upon my poor corpse. Fatal wounds will do this, Will, as everyone knows, to identify the guilty and bring justice from beyond the grave. This is a Medical Fact, documented by Learned Persons. And it was very thrilling. I rose up slowly, eyes wide with woe and holy vengeance, and lifted a trembling arm to point the villain out. It weren't a proper theatre, really — more like a penny gaff, stuffed with castaway apprentices baked on gin. But O! they gasped and cheered, Will, when I sat up, and I swear they would have done so anyways, even if my burial clothes was covering a bit more of me up top."

Of course she was Acting at this very moment, as if the three of us were players on a stage. But now we were skirting around St Paul's and slipping swiftly along Cheapside, and suddenly the stench was upon us with a shifting in the wind, and we stood at the rusted gate of St Mary-le-Bow churchyard. That's when it all at once became Very Real to Miss Smollet. She stopped dead with a tiny choking gasp, holding aloft the bull's-eye and clutching with her free hand at my jacket. And I confess that it was becoming suddenly Real to Your Wery Umble too.

It is one thing to conceive a Gothick Venture in your mind, or to sidle about a churchyard in the light of day, as I had done that afternoon, to remind myself of the exact location of the grave and to look for any telltale signs that Resurrectionists had already come. It is another thing entirely to creep through a rusty gate in the depths of night, with the shape of a church massing before you in the blackness and the stench of putrefaction rising all around, and to pick your way through jumbled stones and crosses, and slide wooden shovels from a burlap sack, and dig. Not even five long years of battlefield surgery can quite prepare you for that—and especially not when Bob Eldritch was here too, present in each creak of a lonely branch and each ghostly mutter of the wind.

"It's all right," I whispered to Miss Smollet. "The living ent here to spy us, and there's naught to fear from the dead."

But I swear I could feel bulging eyes upon me, with every slinking step I took. As we reached the grave, I took the bull's-eye from Miss Smollet, and trained the shaft of light.

"This is the one," I said.

A marker with Bob Eldritch's name, and a mound of earth. Little Hollis looked to me accusingly.

"'S already settling, the dirt. 'Ow long ago did you say this one was planted?"

I hadn't said, not exactly, when I'd enlisted Little Hollis in the plan. I'd let him believe that the burial was recent, since of course a cadaver loses all value once it's had too many days to putrefy. And I didn't answer him directly now, cos I just wanted to get this over with.

You've doubtless read scores of desperate penny-blood tales — haven't we all? — and seen any number of them enacted upon the stage. Corpses rising and ghosts wailing and devils appearing in belches of sulphur smoke. So I'll leave you to conjure the image for yourself: Miss Annie Smollet standing still as stone in the moonlight — cos there was moonlight now, I know there was; if there wasn't, there ought to have been — as Wm Starling and Little Hollis hunched and muttered and delved like moles. A shaft angling down, and then suddenly — finally — the jolt and the hollow thud as my shovel struck the coffin. I crouched breathless as Little Hollis slithered headfirst down into the earth. Strange, terrible noises — the creaking as he pried with the crowbar, as if Hell's rusty gate was opening beneath us. Then he was slithering out again, and handing me the rope.

But something was wrong. Something was entirely amiss — cos there was weight, dead weight, at the end of it. Hollis hauled, and I did likewise. The dead weight rose with my confusion, and at the end of an endless half-minute a shapeless lump was lying on the ground. The stench of putrefaction billowed as Little Hollis tugged open the shroud, and there lay the week-old remains of Bob Eldritch, blue and bloated in yellow lantern light.

Miss Smollet dropped the bull's-eye with a cry, and Little Hollis cursed.

"'S ruint!" he exclaimed bitterly. "Look at 'im—'s already rotten!"

And Your Wery Umble had been so certain that we would find—what, exactly? An empty coffin and proof beyond all doubt of some abomination against Nature, committed by Mr Dionysus Atherton? No, cos it could never have been as clear as that—and surely I must have known it, even in my moments of most purple supposition. Even an empty coffin might well have had a simple explanation: that Atherton had chosen to dissect his friend, and had staged a Christian burial for appearance's sake alone.

But *something*. I had convinced myself of that. Some evidence that Atherton was indeed the villain I had convicted him of being in my heart. And now I had nothing at all, save a newly dug hole and a reeking shroud full of bloated Bob. Little Hollis was beside himself with grievance, and left me to reinter the body by myself—cos what else was I to do with the thing?—with the aid of poor Miss Smollet, who ricocheted in her emotions from giddy relief to reeling confusion to throat-clutching horror at where we were and what business we were about. She was still in a state an hour later, as we found a public house by the docks that opened before the dawn, and I purchased two half-pints of blue ruin — one for each of us — no longer certain whose need for fortification was greatest.

As Miss Smollet drank hers down, the relief was for just a moment or two ascendant. She swept off her cap and shook loose her strawberry hair, to the startled appreciation of a table of watermen nearby. Eyes shining, she seized my hands in hers.

"We carried it off, Will Starling — didn't we? We Done the Desperate Deed. We dug him up, and there he was!"

She began to laugh, giddy with exhaustion and sudden wonderment.

"But I don't understand, Will. I don't understand it one bit. Cos we seen him lying there, blue on the ground — and yet I seen him scratching at my window too. Oh, it's the most comical thing you can imagine, becos my head is spinning with it, and I swear I will never sleep again, and — Will, what am I to do?"

She laughed as if she'd never stop, and abruptly burst into tears.

My own nob was spinning quite sufficiently on its own, and I wanted nothing more just then than to drag myself back to Cripplegate and sleep. But the new day had its own revelation in store, one that stunned me almost as much as the discovery of Bob Eldritch in his coffin.

Meg Nancarrow had made a full confession.

The Last Dying Confession
of Meg Nancarrow

As taken down by Under-Sheriffs

"I, Margaret Elizabeth Nancarrow, prostitute, of London, being under sentence of death at Newgate Prison and trembling in terror of the Judgement that awaits, do solemnly confess the following. That on the night of 1st May, 1816, I did meet at a low public house in Black Friars Lane with Edward Cheshire, known as Uncle Cheese, also of London. Harsh words was exchanged between us, and threats uttered, as heard by numerous witnesses, concerning a sum of money which I considered to be owing to me. Upon Edward Cheshire's departure from the public house, I followed after him as far as Holborn, where the dispute continued. After some minutes Edward Cheshire proposed that we put off the question until the following morning, when more sober heads might prevail, upon which he turned his back and started to walk away, in the belief that we two had agreed to part. Instead I flew upon him from out of the darkness, maddened by my greed and wrath; striking from behind I cut his throat with a blade that I had concealed upon my person, and afterwards flang the bleeding corpse into Fleet Ditch, as if its ooze might hide my crime from humankind and Heaven.

"I understand that there is no more hope for me on earth, and none neither in the Life to Come, unless I tell the Whole Truth, and never mind how Horrible it be. I declare furthermore that I acted entirely alone with no accomplices, and that the blood of this Foul Crime stains no other hand but mine. I pray that my Awful Fate will be an example to other women, who might be tempted onto the selfsame path: O Wretched Sisters, abjure your Wickedness, and Gin.

"My only comfort is in knowing that my husband, James Cheshire, known as Jemmy Cheese, will be sustained through the benevolent offices of Mr Dionysus Atherton, Surgeon, which support he has pledged through his goodness alone, and not for any merit that my poor husband or his dying Meg may possess.

"I do swear that every word in this statement is Heaven's Truth, having been copied down and read back to me aloud. And I pray that Our Lord, by whom one of the crucified thieves was saved, may yet find Mercy in His Heart for even such a sinner as the Murderess who kneels here weeping."

Signed: M Nancarrow

Witness: The Revd Dr H Cotton

Newgate, 12th May, 1816

18

There is a service for the condemned in the Newgate chapel, the day before the deed is done. The Condemned Pew is a black pen in the middle of the chapel, and the coffin is placed there beside the Guest of Honour to aid in disciplining the mind, cos who could say where idle thoughts might wander else, on this penultimate morning in the world. The Revd Dr Cotton the Prison Ordinary would preach a sermon upon the fires of everlasting torment that are ordained for those as die without a full confession of their sins and true repentance in their heart.

Meg on that Sunday morning was still refusing to confess, no matter how forcefully Dr Cotton implored, nor how hot the Fire was that he conjured up or how horrid the eternal suffocation. She sat through the sermon like a small fierce cornered animal and demanded afterwards to be taken back to the Press Rooms, where the condemned were allowed to spend their final days on earth. There were two of these, common wards with long tables and benches and narrow bunks and a fire at one end, separated from the rest of the gaol by the Press Yard: a flag-stoned courtyard, open to the sky, where in bygone times those prisoners who refused to enter a plea — wretches as hardened and obdurate as Meg Nancarrow — were stretched naked upon their backs and pressed to death with stones and iron weights. The Revd Dr Cotton began to despair of Meg's immortal soul, and perhaps also of the sum he might otherwise raise by selling the details of her Last Dying Confession to the broadsheets, as the Newgate Ordinary was widely suspected of doing.

Shortly before noon, Meg was informed by a Keeper that the three Judges had met the evening previous to review her sentence, and had issued their decision: no mercy. She turned ashen upon receiving this news, and trembled violently. Some while later she was reported pacing in agitation, and at one o'clock she cried out to see the Prison Ordinary, saying that she wished to make her peace at last. The Revd Dr Cotton arrived with all haste. Rumours of a Confession were soon leaking out, and by three o'clock the first of the broadsheets was on the street.

I saw her an hour later. At the furthest end of the Press Yard was a double grating with a gap between, where the condemned could receive a visitor — each of them on one side of the grating, with a Turnkey between them in the vacant space. They'd brought her out in shackles.

"Why would you make such a confession?" I asked her, bewildered.

"Cos I did it, Will, just like I said. Harsh words was exchanged, and threats uttered."

She was quoting the exact words I'd just read in the broadsheet that I'd purchased for two pennies from a hawker in Paternoster Square. The printed account was accompanied by a woodblock illustration of a woman in Olde Tyme Garb kneeling wretched at the headsman's block. This was possibly Anne Boleyn, broadsheet printers being notorious for reusing whatever illustration they might have to hand. Tomorrow morning those sheets would be fetching sixpence at the hanging—there would be updated accounts and ballad versions as well, with Meg's lamentations rendered in lurching rhymes.

"I flew upon him out of the darkness—that's what I did. I was driven by my greed and wrath." Her face was grey, but she spoke—she almost chanted—with a strange exalted defiance. "I cut his throat, and the blood stains no other hand..."

She broke off and stood trembling, but the look of defiance remained. It made me think of half-mad martyrs, going like bridegrooms to the stake. And was it true, what she was saying? Perhaps it was, after all—except somehow I could not believe it. Something was wrong, wrong, wrong, and had been from the very start.

"What can I do?" I said helplessly.

She seemed to falter just a little, then. A crack beginning to trace along the veneer.

"Go and see him," she said. "My poor Jemmy. Tell him what they done."

"I will. I'll go to Woolwich Harbour."

"No, not there. Not the Hulks. A hospital, here in London—he's being moved. A private hospital, to finish his sentence. I don't know which one. Atherton can tell you."

"Atherton?"

"It's been arranged."

"Wait—*Atherton* is doing this?"

"Tell Jemmy it's all right. Proper care—they'll look after him. No matter what becomes of me."

Her voice caught at that. The crack was spiderwebbing now; in another moment she must surely shatter like porcelain. I hardly heard what she said next, in the stumbling confusion of my own thoughts.

"D'you think they exist?" she was saying. Speaking so low it was almost a whisper. "The fires. The Devil, and Hell—d'you think it's real? Cos I do. Look around you—look at the world, and then tell me there ent the Devil. And maybe there's even God too—only not for the likes of us, Will Starling. For us it's just the other one—the Devil in Hell, and here in London, and the great fire burning right beneath our feet. But he swears to me it will never come to that. He says to me, 'Don't despair.' And he swears on his life that he'll look after my poor Jemmy."

Her eyes were locked on mine. Burning and great in her narrow white face, gazing out from shadow through the bars as if she stood shackled in Hell's anteroom already.

"You swear to me too, Will Starling. On your soul."

"I swear. I'll find where Jemmy is, but—"

"Swear something else. Swear you'll see that Atherton keeps his promise. And if he don't, then you kill him. Understand? You fucking kill him, Will Starling, if I can't do it myself."

*

Mr Comrie listened closely as I told him.

"She seems to think he could help her, even now. She seems convinced there's something he can do. 'And if he don't keep his word, then you kill him, *if I can't do it myself.*' That's what she said to me — exact words."

"The woman's half wild with terror, William. She might say almost anything."

"But she didn't say almost anything. She said *that.*"

He was holding the broadsheet report that I'd brought back with me from Newgate. He stared down at it for a moment — the confession, the last despairing dignity of poor Anne Boleyn in the woodblock illustration — then raised his eyes to regard me more keenly than ever.

"What precisely is your accusation?"

I hesitated.

We were in his surgery. He had actually seen two patients today — implements lay disordered on the table, along with a blood-caked length of bandage. Sawdust was strewn to cover the telltale blotches on the floor.

"Go on, then," he said. "What do you accuse the man of doing?"

And of course Your Wery Umble had no reply. I had nothing at all, nothing tangible, beyond the millstone weight I'd dragged home with me from Newgate — and a conviction hardening by the hour that everything in this dismal matter was amiss, and that Dionysus Atherton's shadow hung somehow over all of it.

Mr Comrie reached for the bottle. He was dishevelled with it already; another few drinks and he'd be oyster-eyed—but he'd lurch to competence if an emergency came pounding at the door. I'd seen him take off a leg when you'd swear he was too stewed to see. Done in two minutes and sewn up after, neat as nanny at her knitting.

"Is he guilty of arrogance?" he was saying. "Aye. Of pride and self-love and ambition, and worshipping at the shrine of his own golden self. Oh, he's guilty of those too—God's mighty swinging bollocks, he's guilty as sin itself. And the way he has treated you—I can never think of him the same way again, William, knowing how he's treated you. But a man can be guilty of all this—he can be guilty of all this and more—and still offer kindness to a poor condemned woman and her broken-headed fellow."

"I think she's innocent," I said. "And I think she's hiding something too. She *knows* something, Mr Comrie. But she's willing to take it to the grave."

He said nothing for a very long moment, and then looked round for a second glass. Seeing none, he reached for the mug used for holding quills. Dumped them out, wiped the mug with a bit of shirt tail, and poured a drink for me—brandy, or thereabouts. We couldn't afford to be particular, here at Cripplegate.

"She's bones already, William," he said at last. "So am I— so are you. We left bones on every field in Europe. The world is built on bones."

"So I should just let it go. Is that what you're saying?"

"That's one of the options."

"And the other?"

He took a swallow, and thumped down the glass.

"Get up off your arse, William. Go and do something about it, if you feel so bollocking sairtain. Instead of sitting here and making speeches."

And still I couldn't have told you—not on that Sunday night in May, twelve hours before the hanging was scheduled to take place—just why I was so convinced that something terrible was amiss. That some monstrous malignity was at work here, if only I could see it clear; some diabolical clockwork that was ticking Meg second by second out onto the Newgate scaffold. And perhaps the sense of clockwork itself came only later—the growing conviction that a hand and mind were both at work, shaping a pattern from events that still seemed random. Perhaps on that night I felt nothing more than a mighty sorrow, and so made it my mission to save poor Meg when no one else would try. Just as there had been no one else in all the world who would help my friend Danny Littlejohn, on the night when he lay weeping at the Gate.

So I went back to the Three Jolly Cocks. Alf the Ale-Draper was there, and a dozen men I'd asked already, along with a few others. But none of them had seen Meg Nancarrow on the night in question, nor Master Buttons. They'd been elsewhere, or left early, or come late; or they'd been too castaway on daffy to say what they'd seen in the first place.

They might all have been as blind as Gibraltar Charley, who had come in from his pitch down the road and now sat in his darkness at a table by the door, with Tim the Real Learned French Dog curled dozing on the sawdust at his feet.

"His name is Buttons," I said, to a trio of rough men near the fire.

They shook their heads. One of them had a ferret, which poked its head now from the neck of his shirt and then disappeared back within, to the great amusement of all.

"Fair hair," I persisted. "Wears it in ringlets."

"Oi! Leave off your pestering."

Alf the Ale-Draper, calling belligerently from behind the bar. Apparently he'd had sufficient of Your Wery Umble.

"I'm only asking—"

"And you've 'ad your answer, 'aven't you? Now clear off!"

It had gone nine o'clock; eleven hours remained to Meg. She would be in one of the Condemned Cells now. There were fifteen of these in Newgate, three levels of five, in a block built of stone three foot thick. You climbed up a stairway in the light of a charcoal stove. Nine foot by six foot, and nine foot high. A bench at one end; underneath it a rug, a Bible and a Prayer Book. A window, one foot square, and an iron candlestick fixed to the wall. The Condemned was allowed a candle 'til ten o'clock. On the last night, this might be extended.

"Master Buttons—aye, sure enough."

The voice came from the shadows as I reached the door.

"Henry the Fifth. 'Cwy God for Hawwy.'"

Gibraltar Charley stared vacantly into space, grinning slightly at the recollection. At his feet Tim opened one ogle, to assess the situation and smoke out if food might be involved.

"You *saw* him?" I asked in surprise.

"At Drury Lane. Years ago."

His hand reached out and fumbled upon the table for the tot of spiced rum. He drank, and smacked his lips.

"And then again t'other night. Just outside that door."

It took me a moment to credit what he was saying.

"The night the Nancarrow girl were here with Cheese," he said. "Always liked the girl. Never could abide the money-lender. And you ent hearing this from me."

"Wait. You're telling me what you saw *on Wednesday night*?"

He fumbled the mug back onto the table—as a blind man must. It is a hard thing to go through this world in darkness, although compensations exist. Blind men tended to do well as beggars, for instance. Some were said to make upwards of a guinea in a single day, which led the suspicious-minded to query just how blind such beggars might be.

"Buttons were speaking with another party," said Charley. "Intense conversation. Didn't hear much of it, but the other party said: 'We'll make it worth your while.'"

"And this other man...?"

"Didn't recognize him. Don't know the name."

"Describe him."

Charley's milky eyes slid sideways to meet mine.

"Long grey party. Like a wolf."

Master Buttons was known to frequent the Nag and Goose near St Paul's. So Gibraltar Charley had told me, and I arrived at a dead run. He wasn't there, and they hadn't seen him, leastways not tonight. But the Ale-Draper recommended me to a gambling hell by the north end of London Bridge, where they mentioned a gin-shop across the river, near St Saviour's. He was not there either, but someone had a notion that he lodged farther south, by Camberwell.

Finding the street, I commenced pounding upon doors. *Never mind what Odenkirk will do to you*, I would tell him; *concern yourself with the present moment, and this knife I have right here in my hand.* The third door yielded up the keeper of a lodging-house, who hadn't seen Buttons for nearly a month, but had an address for him. It was all the way out in Bethnal Green, where I arrived as the Watch was crying midnight.

Meg would hear the St Paul's bell as it counted out the hour. The Condemned were exhorted to spend their final night in prayer and tearful vigil, beseeching God to bring them to true repentance. Meg would not pray — or perhaps she would, after all. Perhaps as the hours stretched on she would drop to her knees and wring out her heart.

Master Buttons was not at the house in Bethnal Green. He'd decamped two weeks earlier, leaving behind a pair of old boots and a week's unpaid rent. The landlord had information that he might be in Whitechapel, in one of the netherskens around Mitre Square. If I found the villain I should send him word directly, and the landlord would apologize for having flung one of the boots at my nob, as he had done from a first-floor casement upon being awakened by my pounding.

Across the river again, to Whitechapel. But Master Buttons was not at any of the low lodging-houses around Mitre Square, nor along Aldgate High Street or Old Jewry neither, and I went to every pestilential one of them. The last landlord was cursing me as the bell sounded six o'clock. Dawn was a bruise in the eastern sky; London was stirring, and I had failed. Meg Nancarrow was lost.

The crowd would be arriving outside Newgate now. Thirty thousand would come out for a hanging, sometimes even more, streaming along Holborn and down Snow Hill. Meg would begin to hear them through the thick stone walls. A Keeper would arrive at six-thirty to offer her toast and coffee, and at seven-thirty she would be taken from her cell down to the Press Yard. There the Revd Dr Cotton would offer whatever rites she would accept and then turn her over to the Under-Sheriffs of London, who would strike off her shackles and bind her hands before escorting her in procession along Deadman's Walk, the passage that leads to Debtor's Door. It opens onto the scaffold, which would have been erected the day before. Mr Langley would be waiting there, and Dr Cotton would intone the Office of the Dead. Perhaps Meg's anger would see her through the ordeal. Christ, I hoped so.

I dragged myself soul-sick back to Cripplegate at last. As I reached the house, a crow-black tatter detached itself from a shadow. Someone had been waiting for me there.

"They murdered him, you know. The money-lender."

It was the voice that stopped me dead.

"They'd have murdered me too, and carved me up before the angels in Heaven had time to weep. But I was one step ahead of them."

A gaunt figure in a ragged cloak, and a pair of mad eyes staring.

"Miss Deakins!" I exclaimed.

"He knew, you see. That's why he had to die. The money-lender knew about the killings."

"What killings?"

"The *other* killings. I have it all noted down, Mr Starling. I have a Ledger—oh, yes indeed—I can find where the bodies are buried. And I can bring him to a Reckoning."

In the distance, St Paul's clock was sounding the three-quarter hour.

"Is this true?" I cried. "Or just laudanum and madness?"

"It is the Truth," said Flitty Deakins, "upon my last hope for my soul."

I turned then and began to run, as if my own life depended on it.

The Uttermost
Extremity of Justice

From a Broadsheet Account
13th May, 1816

An exclamation arose as St Paul's bell began to strike the hour. The atmosphere had been Festive unto that moment, as if the multitude were gathered for a holiday parade, with entire Families turned out together: lads upon fathers' shoulders, and wives with babes in arms, while vendors did brisk business selling comestibles and beverages. Others had their vantage from the rooftops and upper windows across the square, where space had been sold for upwards of ten guineas. Now thirty thousand necks craned, and sixty thousand eyes searched out Debtor's Door.

It opened and the cry went up: "Hats off!" The entire human mass—already pressed so close together as to seem one single organism—pressed closer still, and surged forward in hopes of glimpsing the Procession.

There they were, ascending the steps to the scaffold. Meg Nancarrow in the midst of it, the Fleet Ditch Fury, so small as to be all but overlooked, as if she were an Afterthought added to someone else's occasion. She wore a black dress, no doubt the finest garment her meagre lot in life had afforded

252

her, as if she were setting forth to attend a funeral. And of course she was; it was her own. A shout of excitement went up, and opprobrium.

She ascended the steps unaided, but reaching the scaffold she faltered, as if her legs would give way at her first sight of the Fatal Noose. It hung there waiting, with Hangman Langley standing gaunt and spare beside it, prepared to carry out his Awful Office. Hands reached to steady her. She continued on, to be positioned upon the drop. As she faced the multitude, those nearest were able to hear the Sheriff ask if she had final words. Her lips moved spasmodically at first, as if none would come. But at length she was heard to cry, in quavering defiance: "Do as you will. Cos that is all the Law there is, in this world or the Next. Remember that, if you should have cause to think of me again."

The white hood was placed upon her head, at which juncture a disturbance began at the back of the throng. A desperate shouting, which revealed itself as issuing from a Diminutive Youth. Crying that a dreadful Error was being made — that he had New Evidence which bore upon the matter — he plunged into the press of bodies, as if he would by some miracle win his way through to the scaffold and there put a halt to the proceedings. But he was swallowed in the multitude, like Jonah disappearing into the maw of Leviathan. Hangman Langley at a signal from the Sheriff released the drop.

There was a groan from the mob, a deep exhalation that came as if from underneath the earth itself, as if some vast block had shifted in the depths, and then a terrible roar arose from thirty thousand Londoners, here to witness Justice Done unto its Uttermost Extremity. The short drop had not broken the neck; the Fury was seen to contort most desperately. Cries of dismay, for the doleful aspects of the Confession had won considerable sympathy already, and this tide rose steadily as the struggle grew protracted. Many in the multitude exhorted the Hangman to go beneath the platform and speed her passage by pulling upon the ankles; the which he did not do, either through indecision, or else a conviction that such suffering was a Meet Reward for her crime, even though the crowd had quite turned against him by this juncture, and there were grounds to fear that Physical Violence might be offered upon his person.

At the very last, a new commotion broke out suddenly at the foot of the scaffold. It was impossible to see clearly what transpired, but subsequent enquiry would establish that the same Diminutive Youth, who had cried out at the commencement of the Proceedings, had by dint of some superhuman exertion wormed his way all through the press of humanity. He lunged forth now, shouting that a Monstrous Injustice was perpetrated, as if he would smite the Hangman and cut down the Murderess, even in her last shuddering instants. But he was set upon with stern vivacity by the Under-Sheriffs, who bore him down and beat him into sanguineous insensibility, even as all struggles of the Fleet Ditch Fury ceased forever in this Mortal Vale, and she passed on to give answer before the Highest Court of All.

Part Two

1

The Spanish boy has a name: Miguel. The monkey is Jack.
It is not a Spanish name — though this is neither here nor
there — because Jack is not a Spanish monkey. He was brought
back from some far-flung place by a sailor, who sold him for
a shilling to a man in a public house, who soon grew tired
of him. So Jack ended with another man who ran a string of
beggar children, and rented out animals to help them.

Miguel has returned to Crutched Friars this particular
evening, in his cap and bottle-green weskit, with Jack at the
end of a leather strap perched shivering on his shoulder. They
had attempted to beg at a busier corner near Trinity Square,
but were driven off with rocks by a sodger with no legs who
claimed that pitch for his own. Beggars are jealous of their
pitches, and Miguel has no one to stand up for him.

Both his parents are dead. He came to England some
months ago, with a man claiming to be his uncle, whom
he had met at the docks in Madrid. Here in London this
"uncle" had passed him on to the other man, who ran the
string of begging boys. There are any number of such boys in
the Metropolis, appearing for a time and then often enough
disappearing again, to another part of London, or somewheres

else. There is nobody to miss them when they do. Miguel sleeps nights at a doss-house full of runaways and orphans. Girls too. Sometimes there are eight or even ten of them in the same bed, all tangled together; you can't imagine what goes on in a bed like that. Or possibly you can.

It is not a busy place, this pitch of his in Crutched Friars. But people go by, and some of them are generous. The tall man with golden hair — the one who has been pointed out to Miguel as a *cirujano* — passes nearly every day, often in a coach but sometimes walking, especially now that the weather has grown fair, and he always gives a coin. Yesterday it was half a crown — a hand upon Miguel's shoulder with it, and a gentle word. Miguel didn't understand the word, which was in English, but the voice was unmistakably kind.

This particular day is a Friday. It is the day of Meg Nancarrow's sentencing, though of course Miguel knows nothing of that. It is getting on for evening. An hour ago, a young man had come out of the house where the *cirujano* lives — a diminutive youth with a dark triangle face. He spoke a few words of Spanish, urging Miguel to go away. But who is he to tell Miguel where to go? Miguel has had quite enough of this, of being told where he may go, and where he may not. He has the sweetest olive face, but a mule-stubborn look can creep across it.

Still, it is growing dark, and Miguel is deciding that he will go now, of his own choosing. Take Jack the monkey back to his owner, who will keep him for the night, and make his own way to the doss-house. But now someone else comes out of the house of the *cirujano*: the long grey man. He has a hard

258

face, but he is smiling. People very often smile when they come upon Miguel, with his monkey and that sweet olive smile of his own. He says English words, the man, and offers Miguel a bit of bread and cheese, which Miguel accepts gratefully and shares with Jack. The man gestures towards the house, still smiling, by which Miguel understands that there is more food in the house, and that he is being invited.

And why would he not follow, after all? The bread and cheese are very good, and he and Jack are hungry, and the long grey man is a nice man, once you begin to know him.

A Crossing-Sweeper works regularly on the next corner. He worked quite late, on that particular evening. When asked a number of days later, he will recall seeing Miguel go into the house—the boy in his cap and bottle-green weskit, with a monkey on his shoulder, escorted by Odenkirk. And does he recall seeing them come back out? He will frown in recollection, and shake his head. No, he does not recall seeing either come out, nor has he seen either one of them again.

"Why should you want to know?" he will ask Your Wery Umble, warily.

"It is in connection with an investigation," I will tell him.

"A inwestigation? Whose?"

"Mine."

2

If a man describes a battle to you, then he is a liar. Not one of the great battles, I mean—the genuine article, between two armies—and not if he took part in it himself. Oh, it's possible to piece together afterwards what must have taken place—comparing notes with other sodgers in the days and weeks to follow, magpieing shards and scraps of who-seen-what and fitting them into a pattern. But when you're right there in the middle then it's nothing but shouts and confusion, with a fog of musket-smoke hanging as thick as a London Partic'lar in the depths of November. There's wraith-shadows lurching out of it, and roars and screams, and all you know for a fact is you're still alive—though this can change in the next half-second, with the hum of a musket ball like a ghostly beetle—and all you can see quite clear is the friend dropping down right next to you.

You can see the field much clearer at night, after the battle's done. The haze of smoke has gone and it's just the darkness now, with a silvering perhaps from a moon and stars overhead. There are lights reflecting upwards from the ground as well, thousands of tiny points: the pinpricks of reflection from the buckles and breastplates and sabres and guns of all the men lying broken and dead. Moans and cries and the lamentations of horses. Here and there trudge stretcher-bearers, carrying one or two of those as might still be saved — but you don't usually bother, you know; there's no point in going out at night to bring more of them back, cos the field hospitals are full to bursting already, with the surgeons overwhelmed and the saws no sharper than butter-knives. So soon enough the field is left to those who fell, and the scavengers who'll come out with the darkness, scavengers human and otherwise. Quick, sharp movements on the periphery of sight: the hopping of ravens and the hunched stealth of larger shapes. The glint of a blade and a swallowed gasp as some poor sodger not quite gone is finished off.

The field at Quatre Bras was like that on the night of 16th June last year, when I went out to look for Danny Littlejohn. Marshal Ney had thrown half the French army at us here, while Napoleon led the remainder against the Prussians at Ligny — two days it was before Waterloo. There was a boy with no arms sitting in woeful contemplation who was not Danny Littlejohn, and scores bent higgledy who were not Danny neither, and hundreds more yet for me to sort through as I stumbled over limbs and called out his name. Corpses stretching on into the night, corpses strewn and maimed, on and on and on and on, as if an ocean wave of unimaginable size had dashed them onto an endless shore and then receded hissing.

A man begins to be a little mad, I think. Begins to think:

too many. Too many have died here, on this field and on this earth. The world has surely reached its limit, and so have I. I cannot stand the thought of one more death.

All of this was somehow mixed up in my thinking as I ran towards Newgate on the morning—one year later—when they hanged Meg Nancarrow.

I have bits and flashes of memory from that morning, though these are as partial and fragmented before the beating as afterwards. The sea of humanity stretching out as I pell-melled down the hill; the stick-figure of Meg on the far-off gallows platform, and her tiny white face before the hood went on. The suffocation of the press, and the desperation to fight through—limbs and elbows and "Oi, feck off!" The sudden sick impact as I felt myself slammed to the cobbles, and the blackness of an Under-Sheriff's boot looming to fill every inch of my vision.

I recollect arriving at Janet Friendly's house later, though not how I got there. I believe my conviction was that I must see Miss Smollet directly, and explain to her what had been done. I remember the look of shock on her poor face as I stood swaying in the doorway, and the phizogs of Janet and Mrs Sibthorpe too, cos it seemed that I was blood all over, with my coat ripped from my back and one of my boots—the fine Hessian boots of which I'd been so proud—missing entirely. "Couldn't stop 'em," I remember saying, over and over, hearing the words slurred like an old prize-fighter's, who has taken one too many grave-diggers to the nob. "Too many." They convinced me to lie down, though I kept wanting to get up again, despite the pain that was throbbing now in every inch, daggers of it stabbing with each movement. They must have sent to Cripplegate for Mr Comrie; I remember him arriving some while later, and exclaiming as he saw me.

"God's bollocks!"

"Been attacked," Janet was muttering. "That's all we can smoke out of him." Evidently I'd been murky about the details.

They managed to get me sitting on a stool while Mr Comrie probed my skull for fractures, and tried to ascertain whether my glims would point themselves in the same direction instead of wandering asunder like two drunkards reeling home. Janet stood glowering with a cloth and a basin of bloodied water—she'd been doing what she could to clean me up—while Miss Smollet and Mrs Sibthorpe hovered nearby in a flutter of distress.

I asked Mrs Sibthorpe what was the time, and she said past one o'clock. This was a considerable startlement: evidently Your Wery Umble had been staggering about London for hours, bloody as Banquo's Ghost, with scant recollection of any of it. But I was beginning to remember a few things clearer, and managed to explain to Mr Comrie. Arriving at the hanging and fighting through the crowd, desperate to tell them what I had discovered, and what a terrible mistake was being made. Finally reaching the scaffold, only to be battered down.

"They wouldn't listen," I told him. Weeping openly now, but no longer caring. "I fought them, but they were too many."

They were staring at me slack-jawed, Mr Comrie and the women. I expect they'd been thinking that I'd been set upon by villains in an alley — the usual explanation for such an appearance as Your Wery Umble had presented.

"Wait," said Janet. "Wait, now. The *Under-Sheriffs* at the fucking *hanging*?"

"Janet," said a small voice. "Language."

"Oh, Will," breathed Miss Smollet, whose glims — I do recollect this detail, despite the general confusion of the moment — were wide and shining.

And Mr Comrie was looking at me as he might through the bars at Bedlam Hospital, at a poor shitten lunatick chained naked to the wall.

"God's mighty swinging bollocks, William. *Why?*"

And it was imperative that they should know. All four of them, but Mr Comrie most of all. It was too late for Meg Nancarrow; she was dead — and more than dead, dissected. They'd have had her to one of the hospitals by half past nine, and laid out in the Death House five minutes after that. While Wm Starling had been reeling about London, raving about fearful injustices, Meg had been lying as naked as Eve while surgeons and students commenced to carve. Sparrows and rats and the guttering light of those reeking unspeakable candles.

But I couldn't think like this. I must be clear in my head, cos Mr Comrie must know.

"She never killed Cheese," I said.

"I know you believe that, William. I wanted to believe it too, but — "

"It was Atherton."

"What?"

"I have witnesses."

"William!"

Cos I was rising from the stool, and pushing away his restraining arm. My nob swam with it, and I almost fell again, but they had to know. I had to show them.

"Come with me!"

Then through the door, and into the blinding light of afternoon.

It has always amazed me, what men can do when the shock of injury is still upon them. I recollect a black-haired lieutenant at Vitoria who was carried into the field hospital with a shattered leg, and had it taken off above the knee. After we'd finished, he refused all assistance, saving only a tot of brandy, which he gulped down with a thick slurred mutter that losing limbs was thirsty work. Then he shook us off and heaved himself from the table to his feet—or to his foot, which is more to the point. And when I pointed him to the cart that was come to bear him off behind the lines, he hopped to it unassisted like a derelict crow. My last sight of him was sitting in the back of it, straight-backed and chalk-faced, rattling into the setting sun with an air both ruined and regal.

It was the same that day with Your Wery Umble—or so I suppose, looking back. My injuries were hardly as grave as an amputated trotter, though they were quite enough to lay me low for three full days afterwards, and leave me creaking subsequent like the image of my own great-grandfather. But as I staggered northwards onto Fleet Street and turned east, I scarcely felt the pain at all, so intent was I upon my destination. Mr Comrie bandy-legging beside me, and Janet Friendly and Miss Smollet hurrying after.

Where the Devil were we going? That's what Mr Comrie kept asking, and I told him: Flitty Deakins. Miss Deakins had come to me with the proof, and now the others should hear it from her very mouth.

"Atherton's sairvant?" Comrie was demanding. "The one addicted to laudanum?"

"This way."

"Whaire is she?"

A confusion come upon me then, and a dawning realization: I did not know.

"William?"

I had trailed to a stop, and now I looked to Mr Comrie, as if perhaps the answer might be written across his own furrowed phizog. But it wasn't there, or in the faces of Janet Friendly nor Annie Smollet neither, staring back at mine. I looked about me then, feeling myself begin to totter, but the answer was nowhere upon Fleet Street, nor on the faces of the houses looking down.

Miss Deakins had appeared to me out of the morning. I had turned away from her and run, all the way to Newgate. But where had she gone?

"She's here," I stammered.

"Whaire's *here*?"

"Somewhere in London. And she knows—she can tell you."

A look exchanged between them, then. Janet and Mr Comrie.

"Will," said Janet, carefully. "It's all right."

"It isn't! Atherton wanted her dead — and he's killed before."

"Will, you've taken a fearful knocking on the head."

"Wait!"

Cos it came to me then, in a flash of hope rekindling. Flitty Deakins wasn't the only one — there was a second witness who could corroborate my story.

"He seen Buttons on the night of the murder — the night Uncle Cheese was killed. Seen him with Odenkirk. Conspiring with Atherton's man!"

"No, listen to him," Miss Smollet was exclaiming, cos she saw Janet Friendly shaking her head. "I have a Belief in Will Starling."

I wanted to seize her hands in mine, and pour out my heart's gratitude. I wanted to wrap her in my arms. But first I must show them.

"He knows the truth," I cried. "Charley knows!"

Eastwards again, hurrying through the crowds. Pain throbbing cruelly now; the sunlight splitting through my nob, and I recollected my missing boot with the stab of each sharp stone. But we came to the bottom of Ludgate Hill at last, and there amidst the crowds and the clatter sat Gibraltar Charley with his hat upturned, while Tim danced dutifully on his two hind legs.

"Charley!" I heard the ragged elation in my voice. I'd brought them, and now they'd know, even if I should drop down dead with pure exhaustion. Cos in truth it was harder each moment to catch my breath, and Ludgate Hill was beginning to spin. "The man outside the Three Jolly Cocks—the man who was talking to Buttons that night—tell them!"

Charley lifted his milky eyes. "Pray encourage him now, my tender-hearted Christians. Pray show encouragement to Tim, the Real Learned French Dog."

"No, look—Charley, it's me. Will Starling. We spoke..."

But Charley's eyes looked blindly off towards the distant rooftops.

"A copper would give him joy, my tender-hearted Christians. A copper for Tim, the True Genuine Learned French Dog."

In my bewilderment I looked to Mr Comrie. I saw a great sadness in his face, and felt his hand take my arm.

"Come, William," he said quietly. "I'll take you home."

I believe I tried to pull away. But there was a rushing sound then and a darkness rising with it, which is the last thing I remember.

LETTER TO MR COMRIE
FROM MISS J FRIENDLY

15th May, 1816

Sir:

You said to me yesterday, when I come to visit Will: could I tell you anything obtaining to his state of mind, prior to the lamentable events of the day previous, which could of led to them? I recollect answering shortly, and saying that you might be better placed than I to offer such information, considering as I had not 'til t'other morning seen Will Starling once since leaving the Foundling Hospital six-odd years ago, whereas you been with him every day. I expect my mood was also affected by the sight of him, battered and swole as he was, and moaning senseless in his bed with fever. You ended in saying I might send you a note if I should think of anything, presuming of course that I knew how to write.

I'm sure this was very thoughtful in you, to consider that I might be an eejit.

Yes, Mister Comrie: I can write. This is me writing now. If you will come by the shop some evening, you may see me reading as well, and doing sums, and even counting up beyond one hundred.

But you also asked me something else, before I left. You asked: What was Will like, when he was a child? And there was something so very sad in you as you asked it, that last night I began to think you deserved a reply.

Let me start by saying this.

Will's father was a sea-captain — which possibly will surprise you to hear — though not of the philanthropical sort like Thomas Coram. He had been called from his bed in the chill of a December dawn, Will's father, and sailed from Southampton the following evening, leaving nothing for his unborn son but his blessing and a brass chronometer, the which had been given to him by his own father under circumstances remarkably similar, thirty years before. Thus Will revealed one day to a clutch of breathless foundlings, for Will could always tell a tale. He would say no more, leastways not at first, for Will was not at liberty — so he give us to understand, from certain cryptic looks and utterances — to divulge further details. But we naturally winkled them out.

He was a Privateer, Will's father, which did not make him a pirate but something altogether superior, for a Privateer sails under a Letter of Marque, signed by the King himself, authorizing him to plunder His Majesty's enemies. Will's father was doing so this very instant — so Will would confide to us in stolen moments in the corridor, or at the railings when we was outside taking air. He was attacking French merchantmen and sinking them as would not yield, all in the cause of confounding Bonaparte. He was sailing out of Gibraltar, in command of the French ship *Hercule*, which had been captured at Trafalgar and re-named the *Eleonora*.

It was a sloop, small but wonderful swift, with twenty-eight guns and two long-nines in the stern that Will's father in a whimsical way had named "Claude" and "Duvall," after the celebrated gentleman highwayman who once marauded upon Hampstead Heath with a barker in either daddle. Will's father was famous for his gallantry as well, though also for ferocity, which earned him the nickname of "Bloody Bill" Starling. If Will's father and Thomas Coram had met upon the bounding main, Will confided, Bloody Bill would most assuredly have sunk him.

"Bill — short for William," exclaims one of the smallest boys in the cluster on that particular day. "The same as you!" This being Isaac Bliss, who'd been listening with his twinklers round as dinner plates. Isaac wasn't near so badly bent in them days — no worse than a question mark.

"Aye," says Will, and swore us to secrecy. He'd of been nine or ten years old at the time.

"A remarkable coincidence, then," says I. "Considering as your name weren't Starling at all, nor William neither, 'til the Governors sat down to choose one for you, and one of them heard a bird sing outside the window. I wonder, if it had been a pigeon, would your Pa be Bloody Bill Squab instead?"

"Shut your cake-hole, Janet Friendly," says Will hotly, "cos you only shows how ignorant you are."

I told him to take his own advice, before someone earned himself a peg on the smeller — which someone duly did. But he bore it like a good 'un, and didn't peach, even when they whipped him for having blood on his jacket, claiming that his nose had bled on its own accord, out of pure contrariness.

So how much of the Tale of Bloody Bill was true? Well, I have my own opinion on that, Mister Comrie, as I do on many topics. But Will did possess a brass chronometer. He kept it wrapped in a bit of flannel, at the bottom of the little tin box he had for his personal treasures. He showed it to me once, so hushed and solemn you'd of thought he was unwrapping the pocket-watch of Moses himself, retrieved from Egyptian bulrushes. I've no idea where he got it from—and if I had to take a guess, I'd hazard that Will was no longer sure himself. He'd been claiming for so long that it come from his own father's hand, I suspect he'd come three quarters to believe it. And there actually was a ship named *Eleonora*, a 28-gun sloop. It was sunk the following year, by a 36-gun frigate off the Spanish Coast, with all hands aboard feared lost. There was an item in the shipping column of the newspapers. Will turned ashen when he learned of it, though afterwards he claimed to believe that some of the crew at least had escaped, and were even now scheming a triumphant return to England, with Bloody Bill to lead them.

So what am I telling you? I'm saying: Will Starling as a boy was far from a fool—the very opposite, in fact. He weren't exactly what you'd call a liar neither, leastways not in the customary way. But he'd make up tales in his head, and repeat them so often—to the rest of us, but most of all to himself—that he'd actually start to believe they might be true.

I believe he's begun telling himself another tale. A tale concerning a man called Dionysus Atherton, and I begin to suspect it's as dark a tale as you could ever dream.

I made a discovery this morning, Mister Comrie. La Smollet began to babble. That's the second reason I'm writing you this letter.

Were you aware that they dug up a body? The two of them—Will Starling and La Smollet, on Saturday night. A man called Aldridge, or Elditch—I didn't quite catch it, for La Smollet was in Full Flight—who'd been killed and then brought back to life.

Or some such.

God only knows.

If Will survives, I expect you'll want to ask him.

3

Sunlight trickled through the window, puddling round the bed where I lay propped against a bolster. Mr Comrie's own bed, as strait and hard as the Way to Salvation.

It was Wednesday afternoon. Apparently I'd been lying here, delirious and moaning, since Mr Comrie carried me back to Cripplegate on Monday. I'd been raving about Meg Nancarrow and Christ knows what else — Boggle-Eyed Bob and a bloated blue corpse, and a shrieking peacock with brilliant plumage who turned into Master Buttons on the stand, and a golden-haired Fiend who was not the Fiend at all but Dionysus Atherton. Miss Smollet had come by twice, I was to discover; once to deliver a sprig of flowers, which now wilted in a shaving-mug on the window sill, and once just to sit beside me. Janet Friendly came once as well, and Mr Comrie himself had kept vigil through the whole first night, fearing to let me fall asleep with an injured head.

He now sat beside me on a stool, spread-legged in his shirt, spooning broth into the invalid. As ungainly a nursemaid as ever clucked a tongue.

"God's mighty swinging danglers. Look at you."

He chuckled sourly. Mr Comrie was never a man to grow soggy at your pain.

"Half a dozen Under-Sheriffs. What were you thinking? Thrash them all, leap onto the scaffold and save the poor woman's life?"

I gave a small shrug, which brought on a spasm of agony. It began in my shoulders and neck and then worked itself down the entire length of me, such as it was. Mr Comrie waited while it passed.

"I went to Crutched Friars yesterday," he said then. "Asking after the Deakins woman."

That had my full attention, agony or no.

"The housekeeper told me the woman had disappeared. Gave me an address where she thought the Deakins woman might have gone—a doss-house north of Smithfield. So I went."

"And?"

"They recognized the description. Said she'd stayed for a night or two, last week. Then she moved on—said she was going to her people in Devonshire."

"No," I said. "That's not possible—cos I seen her, just outside, on Monday morning."

"Did you?"

"Yes!"

"Are you sairtain of that?"

Eyeing me keenly now.

"'Course I am."

But in the puddling Wednesday sunlight, was it possible that I had this all wrong? Perhaps Flitty Deakins had lied to me — or had never been here at Cripplegate at all. Perhaps she'd been some wisp of hallucination, produced by running myself ragged. Something I'd made up in my head, just as I'd made up that Gibraltar Charley was not quite blind at all, like half the other blind beggars in London.

"I ent completely mad," I said.

I confess the notion had crept into my own head, somewhere between the breaking of the fever and the first blessed light of dawn. Perhaps I had lost my way somehow, and would end as such poor wretches did, chained and wailing in Bedlam Hospital, for the entertainment of Sunday visitors. There was a notion to buoy the heart through the coal-black solitude of night.

I was waiting for Mr Comrie to give another sour chuckle, and wave the notion away. But he continued to gaze, keen and troubled.

"There's different kinds of madness, William. Hatred can be one of them."

"You can think what you want..."

"Digging up the Eldritch bugger's grave? God's bollocks!"

It burst out of him, more violent than he'd intended. Broth slopped over the lip of the bowl, and he set it down.

"There's no excusing what Atherton did. Not to Eldritch — I'm meaning what he did to *you*, William. Turning you from his door like that. Renouncing his obligation."

"He has no —"

"Aye, he damned well does. He has every obligation, William. He was my friend — he *is* my friend. But Christ I think the less of him, for the way he's treated you."

He remained flushed, but had succeeded in stamping the emotions back down into their hole, where they wouldn't humiliate us both by flapping about naked. Then he hitched the stool closer. We had never had this Talk before; it seemed we were about to have it now. He cleared his throat.

"I can understand how you'd hate him, William. The only kin you have, and he won't own you."

"I don't care."

"You're a liar."

Under other circumstances, I'd have turned my back. But I managed at least to avert my eyes, and stare past his shoulder.

His bedchamber was as Spartan as a barracks. The narrow bed, and a table with a basin and a pitcher. On one wall hung a bad watercolour of a Highland glen, and across from it was Sir Charles Bell's appalling scrotum. I fixed my squint upon it, as a vista well suited to my present state of mind.

Mr Comrie cleared his throat.

"He blames himself, in some wise—I expect that's what it is. For what happened to your Ma. I've a notion they'd been close. But he sided with the family when they cast her out. The disgrace of it, and all. Still—his own sister. And then she died. And then the sight of you, all these years later..."

"It's lucky he has you to excuse him."

"There's no excuse. But hatred can twist a man. That's what I'm wanting to say. A man can destroy himself, with hatred."

There was silence then. A hand upon my shoulder. Astonishingly gentle, for a man so ham-fisted with sensibilities.

"Meg's dead, William. So's your Ma, for the matter of that. Let them both rest."

I remained in bed for two more days with the pain, and for two days beyond with the Black Dog curled about me. At night the horse with half a head stalked through my dreams, with Danny Littlejohn on its back. But finally I got up.

Missus Maggs herself was observed to wince as I creaked myself down the stairs, and Mr Comrie asked where I was going. But I just kept on creaking, out the door and down the street, and all the way south to the foot of Ludgate Hill, where Tim the Learned French Dog danced and Gibraltar Charley played the organ. Just now he was playing an air that may have been an Irish reel, or possibly "Abide with Me"—blindness being his talent, more than virtuosity. Tim stopped for a moment as he saw me, as if he would exclaim: "You look a right piece of *merde*." Gibraltar Charley lifted milky eyes, sensing someone beside him.

"I've come alone," I said, "whether you can see that or not. I need to know the truth. Did Buttons meet with Atherton's man, that night?"

Amidst the din of London, the blind man sat in silence.

"If 'ee did, then it's too late for Meg," he said at length. "There's nothing for a blind man to say that could 'elp 'er now."

The milky eyes slid towards me.

"Christ," said Gibraltar Charley. "They done you up proper, didn't they?"

4

This is how it must have taken place:

It is well past midnight as she emerges from the boozing-ken. She has not gone many paces when she hears the coach coming up behind; rattle of hooves and creaking of wheels, slowing as it overtakes her. The blind slides down, and the smile of the gentleman within gleams out.

"It is very late for a young woman to be on the streets of London, all alone."

This is happening in March, I think. It must be March, or February—a month or two prior to the events I've been describing. I wasn't there and so I can't say precisely how it was. But such a great deal of time I've had lately to speculate and ponder—nothing at all but Time on my hands, and shackles. Time to sift through all the pieces I've scavenged, arranging them first in this way, and then in that, 'til slowly a pattern has emerged, and the shadow of a Truth has taken shape like a ghostly ship at sea.

And something very much like this must surely have happened.

There is certainly fog, on the night I am conceiving. Oh, we must have fog, for such a meeting—a true London

Partic'lar, slithering up from the Thames like the ominous creep of a cello. The murky glow of a bull's-eye lantern, and the gleam of Dionysus Atherton.

"You're Meg, aren't you? Meg Nancarrow."

She continues walking, up Ludgate Hill. The coach has slowed to match her pace.

"Do you know me, Meg?"

She stops, reluctantly. Peers warily into the darkness of the coach.

"You're him," she says, recognizing. "That surgeon."

"I am."

He had seen her once or twice before. He must have done, cos this would begin to make sense of it. Possibly he had met with Uncle Cheese on some previous occasion, at the Three Jolly Cocks. He had noticed her there, or someone had pointed her out. He had made enquiries.

A grave-robber's woman, and a whore. He likes rough trade. And there is something in this one — a feral essence — that stirs the blood.

He opens the door to her. "Get in."

She takes a step back instead."I heard of you," she says.

"What have you heard?"

"I heard of things you've done."

Or would she actually say this out loud? Possibly not — almost certainly not. She'd be too canny. But she'd step back nonetheless. He'd read the flicker across her face.

"Get in," he would repeat. "A night like this — the fog. It isn't safe."

The driver has stepped down from the box, and sidles round behind her. Meg discovers this as she starts to turn. A long grey man with a smile slashed across his face.

"The gen'lman," he says, "has extended a hinvitation."

But now there is someone else in the darkness too, looming very large in the haze of a lamp. One fist is beginning to clench, as is his face, with the suspicion that someone here may require some setting straight.

"H'lo, Meg," he says. "I come to walk you home."

"Jemmy," she says, relieved.

"These gen'lmen ent causing you no trouble, I hope?"

Meg lets the moment hang, just enough for the long grey man to mislike the odds, and for Atherton himself to draw reflexively back. The barest inch or two, but Meg has seen it. Her dark eyes take the measurement of him.

"No trouble," she says. "Nor no gen'lmen, neither."

Her smile renders Atherton risible, and puny.

"G'night," she says carelessly. She turns away then, one shoulder rounding as she clasps her shawl tighter, hunching at a keener slice of the cold. Jemmy awaits, putting one massive arm around her.

"A'right, Meg?" he says with a last suspicious scowl.

"A'right, Jem," she says to him, smiling in reply.

The swirling fog enfolds them, and they're gone.

As the surgeon watches after them, it would be possible to imagine an expression of pure malevolence. Fog will do that; it will distort.

*

Or possibly none of this happened at all. Perhaps this is nothing but vapours from an over-heated brainpan.

But I think it did, you know. It happened, or something very like it. That was the first time they ever came face to face—March, or February—and there, right there, he began to dwell upon her. He began to think what he would like to do to Meg Nancarrow—and what he would like to do with her after that.

Or else—and I have pondered this too, pacing forwards and back again, forwards and back—could it have been a different look entirely on his face? A stab of recollection so sudden and cruel that made him gasp aloud. A shock of similarity as Meg turned from him—the rounding of the shoulder, the hunching against the cold—exactly as another girl had turned, on a filthy night two decades previous. A night in November that had been—the most savage November night in all his life. Standing in his father's doorway, willing his heart to stone as she turned away from him and stumbled into the lash of the storm.

The spatter of footsteps and the tatter of a cloak, wrenched by the wind as she receded. And there had been an instant when he very nearly called to her—shouted her name against the night and plunged into the blackness to fetch her back. But then the moment was gone and so was she, swallowed by darkness as deep as ever claimed Eurydice.

5

Atherton actually kept his promise — kept it partways, at least. The vow he'd made to Meg at Newgate before the hanging. He'd called in a favour or leaned on some connection, and the upshot was that Jemmy Cheese had been moved out of the Prison Ship *Retribution* to serve out his sentence at a hospital. Except it wasn't a hospital, not quite: a private asylum. I learned this from Mr Comrie, who'd heard someone talking at Guy's.

A house in Camden Town, owned by a physician named Paxton who "boarded the mad," in the parlance of the trade — cos of course it was a trade, like any other. All the world was built on trade, and this was the Trade in Lunacy. There were dozens of such asylums, in London and across the land, and more of them springing up each year like toadstools. What is this world's true calling, after all, save the driving of its denizens mad? Your Wery Umble could say a very personal word or two in that regard, as you've begun to understand already — curled up days and nights with the Black Dog, stalked by lurid imaginings. But I'd made my own promise to Meg Nancarrow, and here I was on a fair day in May, hirpling northwards towards Camden Town and dreading with each step what awaited me there.

The private asylums varied wildly. I'd heard of a house in St Alban's where no more than six inmates were kept at a time, each of them paying five guineas a week, with a policy that discouraged physical restraint and even recommended kind words as a therapeutic strategy. At the other extreme were Pits of Hell—I'd been to one or two of those, attending Mr Comrie on chirurgical business. Here the Damned were bound in strait-waistcoats, and the strategies for cure were old and tried and true: immersion in ice-cold water, rapid spinning in the Revolving Chair, and of course blistering with cups and candles to draw out the infected Humours. Dr Paxton's asylum lay somewhere in between.

It was halfway down a row of houses, hunching dour and sullen between better-favoured structures like a middle child totting up grievances. A Keeper answered my knock, heard my errand, and bid me wait outside the door while he fetched the mad doctor.

"I've come to see Jemmy Cheese," I told Dr Paxton when at length he arrived.

A brisk man in early middle age, with a cool appraising stare. His eyes had widened despite himself at his first glimpse of Your Wery Umble—which I took as an achievement, in its way, considering the lunatick sights a mad doctor must ogle daily. My jaw had unswole back towards its normal size, but still I was all lumps and scrapes and blooms of purple souring into yellow.

"On what business?" he asked.

"My own."

"Then I'd advise you to tend to it," he said, beginning to close the door upon me. "And I shall tend to my business, and my patients.'"

"My uncle is Mr Dionysus Atherton."

I expected that might stop him, and it did.

"I am his sister's child. She died."

He wasn't sure whether to believe me—and who could blame him, after all? The golden glory that was Dionysus Atherton, and the battered scrap of Rainbow on his doorstep. But clearly enough he owed Atherton some favour, or was being paid good coin by him, or both; and besides, a man such as Atherton might very well have several bits of flotsam bobbing in his wake—encounters with actresses and dolly-mops, and servant girls from student days—one or two of whom he might drolly acknowledge as a "nephew." I watched this possibility cross Dr Paxton's phizog, bringing with it a small dry chuckle.

He glanced over his shoulder to the Keeper. "Show Mr...What is the name?"

"Starling." I did my best to shine the sunrise smile.

"Show Mr Starling downstairs," he said. "And my compliments to his 'uncle.'"

It was dim inside the house, with bars on the windows and bolts on the doors, and a general waft of decrepitude and faeces. But it could have been worse. There were fifteen or twenty kept here—so the Keeper said when I asked—most of them elderly. They were kept two and three to a room, like derelict linnets. An old woman somewhere squawked out monotonously, every ten seconds; another shuffled with infinitesimal steps, looking in her ragged nightdress so thin that she might have been two great eyes on a broomstick.

A door at the end with a heavy bar opened onto a stairway descending, and the Keeper gestured that I should precede him. "Mr Atherton's nephew will watch his step," he added. He was a twitchy man with the air of a stoat standing upright to take the temperature of the day. Just now he had taken on a smirking solicitude, having decided—so I gathered—to amuse himself by pretending Your Wery Umble was a gentleman.

The stairs led down into deepening gloom, and a heavy ursine musk. They were keeping Jemmy in the cellar.

He was alone, sitting cross-legged on a pile of straw, rocking slowly forwards and back again. I made him out by the soiled light filtering through one small window. It was barred, like all the others in this house, though it was scarcely big enough to admit a cat, let alone a man as large as Jemmy Cheese. Forwards and then back again, with a faint rattling at each commencement. They had him in a strait-waistcoat, the villains; he was chained as well, by an iron band round his neck to an iron ring bolted to the floor. There was a harsh metallic *chink* each time he leaned back, the chain pulling taut to stop him. I thought of a sad old lunatick bear, awaiting one final baiting.

"Alas," agreed the Keeper with his solicitous smirk, reading my own expression. "But it is for his own protection, sir, entirely, our guest being prone to Agitation."

Wallis was the name of this particular Keeper. So I would learn some days later, when it was cited in the newspaper accounts of what took place.

"H'lo, Jemmy," I said, and tried to smile. "It's Will. Remember me? I'm afraid I've come with very doleful news."

The dolefullest news I'd ever delivered—so it felt to me, standing in that cellar. This is quite a statement from a surgeon's assistant who'd told men every day for five long years that a leg was coming off, or that an arm was coming with it, or—dolefuller yet—that all remaining limbs were staying attached cos there was just no point in trying.

"It's your Meg," I told him. "It's worse than terrible, Jemmy —it's the worst thing there is—cos they've gone and hung her. They said she murdered your brother—did you know?" It came to me then, with an awful lurch, that he might not even realize that Brother Ned had been killed. "That's what they're claiming—but it's a lie, cos she never done it, Jemmy. She was innocent, but they hung her anyways."

He just kept rocking. Forwards and back again, forwards and back, rattle and *chink*. Christ, had he understood a single word I'd said? His face gaunt and slack and his eyes so dull that you'd swear there was no one behind them at all. I began to think it was better that way, lamentable as it was—better that Jemmy was gone far away, gone wherever men go when their heads are smashed in like eggshells, and would never need to live in this world again. But as he rocked backwards once again, there were tears streaming down his cheeks.

I could have wept then with him. I would have done, I think, in one more second. But that's when a small commotion broke out, above us. A bellow of protest, loud enough to filter down to the cellar. More bellowing, and a thin gibbering chorus rising up about it — one of the inmates was creating a to-do, and setting the others off. The thumple of hurried footsteps over our heads, and a shaft of light as the door opened up at the top of the stairs, and a voice — Dr Paxton's — calling impatiently for Mr Wallis to come up and assist.

Wallis hesitated, dithering between the need to dash and reluctance to leave a visitor alone.

"Mr Wallis! Directly!"

He shot a hasty look to me — "Just keep back from him," he commanded — and then a darker look to Jemmy. An instant's flash of unmistakable malice, like the glint of a serpent's tooth. "And you — remember the blistering, eh? Remember how much you enjoyed that experience."

Then he was gone. His boots thumped up the stairs, and Jemmy and I were alone.

I moved closer, as close as I could, and knelt down in the straw.

"Jemmy, listen to me. Just — please, listen."

He stopped rocking at last. The chain hung slack.

"I don't know how much you understand — or how much you could tell me, even if you did. But I need to find out, Jemmy. Did Atherton have a reason to want your brother dead? Was it something Ned knew — some secret?"

He didn't make a sound. But he didn't move, either. Poised between forwards and back again, head hanging low.

"What was it, Jemmy? What did your brother know, that was such a threat? And did Meg know it too?"

Cos that would explain everything, wouldn't it? Atherton's desire to see her dangling and dead. And the promise he made — to get Jemmy out of the Prison Ship — in return for Meg's confession. Yes, that would tie it up with a bow for Dionysus Atherton. Uncle Cheese in the grave and his secret with him, whatever that secret was. Meg Nancarrow now silenced forever as well — having confessed to the murder that Atherton committed, or leastways had Odenkirk commit on his behalf.

That must have been what happened. Kneeling on the cellar straw, in the ursine reek of poor Jemmy Cheese, I felt all but certain-sure. Right then Jemmy lifted his head and I swear I saw a flash — a flicker of something — *someone* — present behind those eyes. It was gone again in half a second and Jemmy began once more to rock: forwards and back again, forwards and back.

"I'm going to find them out," I said. "That's my promise to you, Jemmy. I'm going to prove what Atherton did, and I'm going to see him hang."

Jemmy understood, though he gave no sign. I knew, cos that flicker had been there.

And I'd seen something else as well. Each time that Jemmy rocked backwards — the *chink* of the chain pulling taut — he was wrenching at the iron ring bolted to the floor. And gaunt as he was, Jemmy Cheese was still strong. He was stronger than you could believe — and the bolt was coming loose. In due course it would surely give way, unless someone informed the Keeper.

I left Dr Paxton's house without saying a word.

Horrifying Assault Near Southwark Bridge

From a Broadsheet Account
21st May, 1816
A new and shocking depredation is reported in the matter of Boggle-Eyed Bob, concerning a Sailor who was attacked two nights ago walking eastwards along Bankside Street, near the Docks. Passing through a narrowing of the road, he was suddenly struck a Fearsome Blow from above, as by an Assailant dropping bodily upon him, from a ledge or rooftop. Precipitated to the ground, the Sailor was sensible of the stench of putrefaction before experiencing a Great Agony, as the Assailant sank its teeth into the flesh of his right shoulder. His cries brought men running from a nearby public house, to be confronted by an Appalling Tableau: an egg-eyed Creature crouched above the fallen Sailor, hair standing on end and mouth smeared with gore. The Creature snarled most horribly but fled at once, shambling hunched and herk-a-jerk into the night, at a swift and uncanny velocity.

6

The Wreck of Tom Sheldrake had chambers at the Inns of Court, just north of Fleet Street. There was an outer room where a Spavined Clerk worked at a table piled high with papers, the dust of ages rising and settling as he stirred. Beyond was Sheldrake's sanctum, an inner room with a desk and shelves of leather-bound books, and a Turkey rug and a window facing west, through which in happier days the afternoon sun would respectfully decline, irradiating the barrister with an amber light, as if he glowed from within with his own superiority. Today he sat shrunken, his eyes too large for his face. His wig lay strewn and lifeless in the corner, as if it had scuttled into the street at the unluckiest of moments and been run over by a carriage wheel.

"The fault was not mine," he said. Clutching it like a sailor to a life-rope. "I require you to understand this, Starling. I bear no blame for the death."

The Spavined Clerk had straightened as I'd come creaking through the door five minutes earlier. Eyebrows arched at the sight of me, like chalk-dusted caterpillars. But despite visible misgivings, he'd escorted me through to the Wreck.

"I ent here to accuse you," I said to Sheldrake now. "I ent here to talk about Bob Eldritch at all."

But the name itself was enough to set him off. His face folded in on itself.

"It was a jest," he said.

"I need to ask you about Meg Nancarrow."

"I was larking—that's all it was—everyone in the room knew that. Everyone except for Bob Eldritch, who got it all wrong, like the cork-brain he was, and died!"

Behind me, through the open doorway, dust rose slightly. The Spavined Clerk had lifted his head, gazing sorrowfully in at the Wreck of Tom, who lurched to his feet and began to pace distractedly, back and forth across the inner room. *Oh, yes*, said the Clerk's mournful eyes, as they briefly met mine. *Oh, indeed; it is thus, and has been so, and each day it is worse. Behold the Wreck as it Splinters.*

"What did he say, when he came to you?" I asked the Wreck of Tom.

He froze in mid-lurch. "*What?*"

"The surgeon," I said. "Mr Atherton. Why did he want you to defend Meg Nancarrow?"

He stared at me for another moment, as if certain I had asked him something else. At length he looked away. "That woman? God knows. Someone had to."

"But why *you*, Mr Sheldrake?"

Cos there was the question, wasn't it? Of all the barristers in London—clever and capable men, any number of them— why the Wreck of Sheldrake, drunk and bungling?

"What were his instructions?"

"His instructions?"

"When he hired you. What did he say?"

Sheldrake blinked, still half distracted by whatever it was that had clutched his thoughts a moment earlier.

"He believed the woman was guilty," he muttered.

"He told you that?"

"Guilty as Fallen Eve, poor bitch. But the forms must be observed. A fair trial, and then the hanging."

"And Meg—you met with her, to prepare the case. You must have done—yes? Before the trial, at Newgate."

"Of course."

"Did she say anything to you, Mr Sheldrake? About Atherton? Did she seem to possess any knowledge about him?"

"What are you talking about? What sort of knowledge?"

"That's what I'm asking. Anything at all—a hint—some secret she might have known..."

"Some secret?"

He blinked again, brow furrowing. "I seem to recollect..." And then broke off, visage darkening. "The Devil business is it of yours? What's this to you, or you to me?" He swelled into his old imperious self, or leastwise managed a wretched approximation. "The likes of you, coming here—presuming upon my time. Presuming upon privileged information."

"Meg was my friend."

"Some draggle-tail he'd had, and felt a fondness for. I have no idea what it was between them, and I wouldn't tell you even if I did."

And then he burst out again, abruptly. He gave a cry, as if in physical pain. "A human limb? Bob Eldritch, gnawing on someone's *arm*?"

There was a copy of the broadsheet amidst the clutter on his desk. He snatched it up and crumpled it, and flung it across the room.

"God's teeth!"

Christ knows I'd been unsettled myself, when I'd seen the broadsheet report first thing that morning — despite knowing what I did about the actual whereabouts of Bob Eldritch's corpse, bloated and rotting in his grave. Or leastways so I *thought* I knew, although a report like that can set certain doubts to squirming in the deep rat-haunted caverns of the brain. But Bob Eldritch was not my priority just now.

Sheldrake had lurched to retrieve the crumpled broadsheet. When he spoke again, it was hoarse and low. "Four nights ago. That's when he came to me."

"Atherton, you mean?"

He stood by the window, shoulders hunched. Uncrumpling and smoothing. A small despairing laugh.

"Fingers at the window. I thought it was dead leaves, blown by the wind. But oh, no —scritch-scratch— that hand."

And I realized. "You mean Bob *Eldritch*?"

"That face of his, staring in. Those eyes — and the hair, straight up. Oh, God help me. And every night since."

Despite myself, I felt a pricking at the back of my neck, as if my own hair were rising. And I found myself asking the question, dumbfounded: "What does he want?"

Sheldrake began to moan.

"He wants me to open the casement. He wants vengeance."

And of course I wanted vengeance of my own.

I could deny that, and present myself to Your Honour as naught but a selfless seeker after Truth. What would stop me, after all, since I'm the one who's telling you this tale? But let's have truth-telling between us, even if larger Truths are too much to hope for, in the roiling murk of this world's equivocations.

I wanted revenge on Dionysus Atherton. I desired it more bitterly by the moment, as I left Tom Sheldrake's chambers that afternoon and found my steps tending towards Crutched Friars, where I stood for more than an hour in the shadow of a tree across the street from my uncle's house, just watching. The curtains were drawn; no sign of life. No sign of life at all — though life there was indeed, as I know now. More life than I could have imagined, standing there on that Tuesday afternoon, eight days after Meg Nancarrow was hanged. When I look back now my blood runs cold, just to think of it: the life that was in that house.

But nothing moved within, or leastways nothing I could see. The street outside just trundled about its business as I watched from my place of shadow, a silent Changeling seething with dark imaginings. Trying to conjure the pictures in my mind: what he was doing this moment, and the next. What he had been doing all along.

And of course I wanted vengeance. A Revenger in a Tragedy of my own devising — I wanted it as dearly as ever did Vindice in the grand old gore-drenched play, carrying the skull of his beloved about with him, lest he should otherwise for an instant forget what villainy had been done to her, and to himself. I'd wanted it since the first moment I'd stood outside this house, just after my return from the Midlands half a year earlier, carrying my own discovery with me—about my Ma, and who she was, and what had happened. Lugging it like an old brown skull in a sack.

*

Miss Smollet was at Cripplegate when I returned. Sitting on the steps outside like my own better angel, in a summer dress and a straw bonnet with flowers, nibbling at a jam puff that she'd bought from a man with a basket, and feigning superb unawareness of several young men who'd stopped across the street to smugger in admiration. All of her attention was fixed upon a dollop of jam—red as a naked heart—that balanced precariously at the corner of her mouth and must be retrieved just in time by a delicate darting of the tongue.

She'd come to Cripplegate several times since my mill with the Under-Sheriffs, just to see how I fared. I was still creaking and limping, but at least my phiz was no longer such a bloom of jaundice and vermilion—I knew this from checking my reflection in a bit of glass, each time I heard her voice asking after me. I expect these visits were partly just an excuse to get out of her lodgings and avoid Janet Friendly. Still, she could have gone anywhere in London, and she chose to come here to see me.

And she came smiling, even though today she'd seen that broadsheet report about Boggle-Eyed Bob.

"He is Dead," she said, with fine conviction—so fine that I wondered how much rehearsal had been required. "We have seen him, Dead and Mouldering. So let them print what they want, Will Starling—becos We know the Truth."

That ability of hers to rally from any ordeal. Let the storm-wracked seas of life crash down in all their briny malevolence, and—lo—she'd come bobbing back to the surface like a cork. We were walking, now, her hand on my arm. She began to chatter on about this and that, and for the span of an hour or two an oppressive cloud lifted and I could almost forget about all the rest: about suppositions and black half-certainties that hovered and swooped like rooks, and Meg Nancarrow's white face upon the scaffold, and my own solemn vow to Jemmy Cheese as he rocked forwards and back again, forwards and back, the tears trickling down his cheeks.

Miss Smollet was selling flowers again, outside Drury Lane. Kean was appearing these days in *Bertram, or The Castle of St Aldobrand*, a gothick tragedy about the leader of a pirate band. Miss Smollet had seen it. It was very fine, she said, with much of what you'd most want in a play, such as crumbling ruins and a wicked monk and a hero tormented by midnight broodings. *Bertram* would close at the end of the month, when the major London theatres would go dark for the summer; Miss Smollet might then sell flowers outside the Theatre Royal Haymarket, which offered a summer season. But she had also spoken to a man who might offer her a place in a company touring the provinces—intelligence that was communicated in a sparkle of green-eyed hopefulness, and received in secret dismay by Your Wery Umble.

"The provinces," I exclaimed. "For the entire summer?"

"Oh, for longer than that. His circuit goes up into the

Midlands, and then all the way south again to Kent. I shall be tramping for Months, like a Gypsy."

"On foot, you mean? This company *walks*?"

She laughed. "'Course not—not literally. Nobody walks from Kent to the Midlands—leastways nobody who has any money, or any sense."

"I did that once. When we come back from the Continent, me and Mr Comrie, after Waterloo."

And somehow I found myself telling her the tale, of the search I'd made for my Ma. I'd never intended to say a word of it—and certainly not to Miss Smollet, my better angel—but it ended in spilling out. I suppose a skull in a sack just grows too heavy, in the end. You need to set it down.

We were sitting on a bench by this time, in a scrubby patch of green behind St Paul's. The great dome golden in the afternoon sun, and the ruffianly pigeons stalking past. "I was raised up in Kent," I began, "or leastways so you might say, after a fashion. That's where I'd been put out to nurse, after my Ma gave me up to the Foundling Hospital, so that's where I went last autumn to start my search. I had a notion someone there might recollect who she was."

And astonishingly enough, they did. I found a midwife who knew many of the women who'd taken in foundlings to nurse. And through a process of narrowing-down—what year I'd been born, and a hazy recollection that my nurse's name may have been Dolly—I arrived on the doorstep of Dolly's sister. Dolly had died just two months previous, I learned, which left me to feel surprisingly bereft, considering as I recollected almost nothing about her. But the sister led me to an old neighbour, who pointed me in turn to a man at a public house whose cousin had for years been in the transportation line, and made extra money by carting foundlings back with him from London. This cousin, when located, had a vague recollection of a dark-haired girl with a sweet sad triangle face, and a vague notion that she had mentioned hailing from somewhere in the Midlands, if only memory could dredge up a specific from the deep silt of two decades. After much furrowing of brow, and multiple drams of pale to prime the machinery, the name of a town came lurching from the depths.

"Lichfield, it was," I told Miss Smollet. "So I went there."

"And you walked?" Miss Smollet exclaimed.

In fact I'd taken mail coaches most of the way, paid for with coins liberated at public houses by means of three cups and a pea. But Miss Smollet's green eyes were shining, and walking suited the tale much better.

"Every step," I said gravely, "of the way."

"Oh, Will."

And she could see it now. It was clear in the moist distraction on her lovely phizog, she was picturing the scene. The solitary foundling, trudging through slanting rain along a rutted country lane at twilight—a lengthy twilight, lasting the best part of three weeks, and rain unrivalled since Noah built a boat—all the way to Lichfield.

"All the Weary Way," Miss Smollet repeated. She was very much taken by my tale. In fact, she seemed to consider being a foundling as highly romantickal, as I suppose you might if you'd never been one yourself.

"And you found them there, your family?"

"I found the house where they used to live."

My grandfather had been a cloth merchant, as it turned out. Dead now, as was his wife; none of the family remained. But there were people who remembered them, and knew the story—how my mother had gotten herself in the family way, and been turned out. Her father thundering vermilion wrath, and her brother—she'd only had the one, a beloved older brother, and no sisters—clenched beside him. And there *had* been rain on that particular night—so I was told, and I didn't doubt it for one second. A foul heart-sickening night in November, and a solitary figure hunching through it, clasping her shawl. She'd ended up in London after that. No one in Lichfield knew the particulars.

"And then?" Miss Smollet had begun to look worried, still hoping there might be a happy ending.

"She died, a year or two after I was born. A fever. I tracked her brother down, but he wouldn't tell me much about it. He didn't want to tell me much of anything."

"You found your uncle?" she exclaimed. "And he's here, in London?"

I felt the scowl closing over my phizog.

"We are nothing to each another."

"But—your uncle! Will, you need to go and see him."

I need to see him hang.

I didn't say this. Not out loud, with Miss Annie Smollet gazing raptly, imploring a happy resolution with her glims.

"It's late," I said.

And it was. Somehow it was evening already. I creaked myself to my feet.

"I'll see you home to Milford Lane."

"Milford Lane is no home to me," she protested. "And that is no ending to your tale!"

But it was all she would have from me. Cos it seemed there was something at least I could bring myself to deny Miss Annie Smollet, and that was one more syllable concerning my uncle. At length she resigned herself to this — or seemed to do, at least for the moment — and for a time we walked in silence.

But only for a time. Silence was not Miss Smollet's natural register, and soon enough she had set aside her exasperation, in the interest of waxing hopeful about the future.

"I'll be speaking to him again next week," she was saying as we crossed the Strand. "The man I told you about, who needs an actress for his tour."

And if the tour went well, Miss Smollet was continuing, she must surely find work on the London stage. Did I not think? And not just playing handmaidens at minor theatres, but genuine roles at Drury Lane and Covent Garden.

"And then, before I'm ancient and decrepit — p'raps when I'm five-and-thirty — I'll announce my retirement from the stage, and my engagement to be wed. He'll have a house on a fashionable street and five thousand a year, and he will be Quite Besotted." Then she caught herself, as if she'd seen a flinch — something game, but utterly gutted — in the Starling phizognomie. "But of course that wouldn't happen for Ages yet," she added quickly. "Not for Literally Years."

We had arrived outside Janet's shop. Candles glowed within, but the lane was still and quiet, the buildings muffling the night-time clatter from the Strand.

"Oh, Will," she said then, growing earnest. "You have become Such a Good Friend to me."

I searched for a smile to shine in return. Cos weren't those precisely the words I most wanted to hear? A friend.

"And I'll say something else, Will. I'll say: this must All Work Out for the Best—your uncle, and all of it—becos I have a Great Instinct for these things. I truly do. And I am Very, Very, Very Seldom Wrong."

As if green eyes and a lovely face could make it so, by sheer dint of earnest conviction. There was a movement towards me, and the scent of oranges. The whisper of lips against my cheek, and then I was standing alone in the moonlight.

When I arrived at last back at Cripplegate, Mr Comrie was in his surgery, halfway down a bottle. "The taverns?" he asked sourly. "Or a brothel?" Mr Comrie in moments of disapproval had a way of becoming one of his own Calvinist aunts.

But it seems he had a right to it, cos today my services had actually been missed. An operation had been arranged, which had slipped my mind completely—a cloth merchant in Chiswell Street who was greatly distressed by a bladder stone that had stoppered up his urine like a cork. The procedure would be performed at the man's house, as was standard practise in the case of patients possessing any means at all, and

Mr Comrie had set a time of two o'clock—intending all along to arrive in Chiswell Street at noon, this also being standard practise, in order to reduce the duration of mental suffering and also to thwart any attempt at escaping by patients whose nerve broke at the last. Having waited at Cripplegate nearly an hour for Your Wery Umble to present himself, Mr Comrie had given up and hurried to Chiswell Street with a brace of burly Assistants recruited from Guy's Hospital, arriving at quarter past one o'clock—just in time to apprehend his patient hirpling out the back door. As well the poor man might, since removal of a bladder stone involved trussing the patient precisely like a roasting chicken—drumsticks doubled back and arse most pitifully offered up—in order to cut into the bladder from underneath and then fish about with forceps. But alas a large stone would not pass on its own, and if left untreated the agony would just grow steadily worse until terminal rot set in—all of which Mr Comrie explained to the cloth merchant as they dragged him squalling back into his house and had the stone out in seventeen minutes, beginning to end.

This account I heard some weeks later. Tonight, I just muttered that I was sorry to have missed it, and started up the second set of stairs.

"Wait," growled Mr Comrie.

Apparently a note had been delivered in my absence. A slip of paper, tightly folded, and a message in an elegant spidering hand:

Mr Starling:

You seek information. I do not say that I possess it, nor am I certain I would divulge it, even if I did. I will say, however, that I am a man of regular habits. It is my habit to take my supper late, at ten o'clock. I take it at the Golden Lion in Temple Lane.

Cordially,

P. Nuttall

_7_

"You have seen him for yourself," said Mr Nuttall. "He is in a bad way, is poor Mr Sheldrake. It is very, very bad for my employer."

He shook his head in sorrow, side to side. The Dust of Ages filtered down like powder from a wig—which of course it was. Sheldrake's Spavined Clerk was one of the few men in London who continued to go out bewigged, here in the modern world of the year '16. He wore knee-breeches as well, and buckles on his shoes, like some latter-day Cnut taking his stand against the tide of Fashion—a tide that had long since immersed him and then gone out again, leaving Mr Nuttall stranded like a starfish on the shore.

"I am sorry for Mr Sheldrake," I lied. "But your note—you said you have information."

"I know what the note said, Young Starling. I wrote it. My note promised nothing."

There was a doggedness in the way he said it: stooped over his supper, eyeing me from behind the protective cover of tangled white eyebrows. Mr Nuttall picked up his knife and fork and resumed dissecting his cutlet.

Temple Lane lies just below Fleet Street. Mr Nuttall had

been here in the Golden Lion when I arrived, sitting on a small round stool at a small square table in one far corner, sipping his port and cutting his meat into fastidious bites, as if oblivious to the general din about him. The Golden Lion turned out to be a sporting tavern, frequented by the Fancy—the roughs and swells and dandies who follow horse-racing and pugilism, and anything else a man can wager his income on. The walls were festooned with paintings of great nags and millers: Cribb and Mendoza in fistic postures, and the Byerley Turk thundering down the stretch. At a table behind us a bibulous Sprig was delighting his fellows with a description of an Amazonian Mill he had witnessed at Wormwood Scrubs, where two women had recently battled for twenty minutes to settle a family issue. "Nanny Flowers showed herself most impetuous in the early rounds," he was saying, "but jibbed a bit in the twelfth, and went down for good from a half-arm dig in thirteen."

In the midst of it sat Tom Sheldrake's Spavined Clerk, with his port and his morsels of cutlet. It cast him in a startling new light, hinting at unimagined dimensions, and conjuring a sudden image of a Young Nuttall—lusty and un-spavined—swilling claret from a pint-pot and with sturdy gnashers wrenching gobbets from the drumstick of a goose.

I tried again. "Mr Nuttall, is there something you can tell me?"

"Tell me first, Young Starling: why do you ask?"

"I believe Meg Nancarrow was innocent. I believe

Dionysus Atherton killed the money-lender — or caused it to be done. I want to find out the truth."

"For what reason?"

"So that justice may be done."

"And you expect justice, Young Starling? From the Law?"

"Yes!"

Mr Nuttall blinked once, very slowly.

"No," I conceded, feeling myself flush. "No, I don't expect justice. But I want the world to know what the bastard's done."

"Why?"

"Why *what*?"

"Are you so determined to expose Mr Atherton?"

"Because I hate him."

Mr Nuttall's handkerchee was tucked into his collar, for a bib. Removing it, he dabbed carefully at the corners of his mouth, eyeing me all the while from behind those tangled white eyebrows, like a duck-hunter watching from a blind.

"Hatred," he said at length, "is always a potent motive. And a pure one, in its way. One knows where one stands, with hatred."

Behind us, a spirited dispute had broken out: whether Cribb could have beaten the great Broughton. Convictions were violently held on either side, as is invariably the case with mills that never took place, and especially when one of the principals was dead long before anyone present was born.

"I know nothing at all," said Mr Nuttall. "Nothing in the way of a Fact. But I do not care for Mr Dionysus Atherton. I do not like his airs, Young Starling, nor what he has done to my employer, for it is association with Mr Dionysus

Atherton that has broken—though I could not say precisely how—poor Mr Sheldrake. I hold him responsible; I blame him. And I have heard Rumours."

He leaned slowly towards me, lowering his voice. The eyes in their duck-blind fixed upon mine.

"Mark me carefully, Young Starling: I do not believe Mr Sheldrake ever knew of these. I believe Mr Sheldrake to be innocent in this—whatever else Mr Sheldrake may be. But Rumours will waft about the Inns of Court, and Clerks are often the first to hear them. These particular Rumours concern children."

"What children?"

"Orphans. Strays. Bits of flotsam that no one cares about, or misses. Waifs who enter the house of a certain surgeon, and are not seen again."

Behind us, a gentleman was asserting with table-pounding passion that Cribb would have fibbed Broughton's ears off, offering to prove his point by laying out the next man who contradicted it. There was a tightening band around my chest. I recollected the Spanish Boy outside Crutched Friars.

"What does he do to them?"

"I could not say."

"Who could?"

The Spavined Clerk leaned closer still. The eyes in their duck-blind took glittering aim.

"Think, Young Starling. Logick. If Edward Cheshire knew a secret—and his associate Meg Nancarrow knew it too—then who else might also have known?"

And I was a fool. Your Wery Umble was worse than a fool, for never having seen it 'til this instant. Cos there was the answer, right where it had always been: high-arsing through the graveyards of the Metropolis, with a sack slung over its narrow shoulders.

I reached the Fortune of War at a run. The door was still open, and the shapes of Wicked Sextons bulked here and there inside, amidst the garish glow from the oil lamps and the haze of tobacco smoke. Here in mid-May the Doomsday Trade had dwindled to a trickle — term had ended at the anatomy schools, and the warmth of the year caused cadavers to putrefy too quickly. But that was hardly cause for a man to give up drinking.

"I'm looking for Little Hollis," I told the Ale-Draper. Keeping my voice low, as you do in such a place, where there's no call for anyone else to know your business.

"Look round," the Ale-Draper grunted. "Do y'see the little fucker?"

"No."

"Then I'll wager the little fucker's elsewhere."

A sick-sour waft emanated from the room in the back where Things were stored — apparently the trickle of the Trade had not ceased entirely. Even on a good night, the Fortune of War could make you gag.

"Farting in his bed, would be my guess. That's where he was bound — or said he was — when he left."

"So he was here earlier tonight?"

"Sharp as a pin, this lad. Don't miss a trick."

I turned to leave.

"Popular man, our Hollis," the Ale-Draper added then, having evidently decided to wax garrulous now that sneers had run their course. "You're the second one to be asking after 'im tonight. That man of Atherton's was here earlier—Odenkirk."

Little Hollis had a crib somewhere east of Smithfield, or so I'd heard. I set off at a trot, though I wasn't at all sure I could find the place, not at this time of night.

As it turned out, I needn't have worried. I found him much closer to the Fortune of War—no more than a quarter-mile from the tavern, in a patch of weeds at the side of Long Lane. He lay flat on his back, staring up into the night, as many a man has found himself doing while wobbling homewards along that very stretch of road—or along any other road in London, or the world. A small knot of men clustered round him, including a doddering old Charley with a bull's-eye, amidst a general babble of consternation.

But Little Hollis wasn't lying on his back, as it had first appeared. In the lantern light he lay on his stomach, arms and legs splayed and arse elevated at the moon. And his eyes were staring in the same direction as his arse cos someone had turned his head right round on his narrow shoulders, as slick and clean as you'd twist the stem from a cherry.

8

Isaac Bliss is fading. He grows gaunt and elvish, with the pale translucence that is seen in the excessively old. He is becoming before your eyes his own great-grandfather, the man he will be at ninety. But of course Isaac will not live that long, or anything remotely close to it. He has lived a full life-span already—excepting only the last few grains in the glass—from birth to decrepitude. And here he is, not yet thirteen years old.

"Is the pain very bad?" the surgeon is asking him, gently.

"No," says Isaac. "Yes."

He is lying on a pile of old rags in the corner of Mr Bowell's workshop, where he has lain since yesterday morning, when he found himself too weak to rise. His breath comes in shallow rattles. The undertaker stands gravely looking on, and Young Thos his son and heir hovers atop the stairs, counterfeiting as best he can the sort of boy who would have gone every hour to sit by poor stricken Isaac, with a murmured solicitude and the offer of a cup of broth.

Mr Atherton kneels, stooping his golden head to listen to Isaac's lungs. There is concern on his kind face. "Are you well enough to ride in a coach, do you think?"

"If someone will carry me, sir."

"I cannot deceive you, Isaac. You are gravely ill."

"Yes, sir."

"But I believe I may help you still. I want to take you with me."

"To the 'ospital, sir?"

"To my house."

Naked fear flickers in Isaac's eyes. But the surgeon's own are blue with earnest reassurance, and his face is very kind.

"There is a bedroom that could be yours, Young Isaac. With a feather bed, and a fire, and a window overlooking the street. Will you allow me to take you?"

No one has ever asked Isaac that question—whether he will allow, or not—in all his long, brief life. In truth, Isaac is not completely sure he is being asked that question now, or whether his reply would make a difference. But the surgeon is so very grave and kind, and Isaac is weary beyond endurance.

"There," says the Undertaker, from the doorway. "What do you say to your benefactor, Bliss?"

"Thank you," whispers Isaac.

*

This had been some days earlier. A Sunday, in fact—the day before Meg Nancarrow's hanging, and a single day after I had visited Isaac myself. He had not seemed nearly so bad on the Saturday. But he'd declined quite shockingly that night, and on Sunday morning the surgeon was summoned.

I wasn't there myself, of course. But I am sure now that this scene took place—I can watch it unfolding in my mind—even though I had no inkling at the time. I weep to think that I had not the slightest inkling.

Look at them.

The surgeon lifts Isaac with infinite care, knowing how much pain this causes. Isaac weighs no more than a bundle of reeds; you can almost hear the rattle of dry bones as he is carried outside, and gentled into the carriage. Each jolt of the wheels causes fresh distress, but Mr Atherton has arranged cushions and a blanket to wrap him, and Isaac is able to sit up, at least a little, and look out at London passing. When they arrive at Crutched Friars, he finds that Mr Atherton is as good as his word.

He carries Isaac upstairs in his arms. The room is vast and lovely, with books in a bookcase and a thick Turkey rug upon the floor. There is a chair in the corner by the grate where Isaac might curl up, once he's feeling stronger. The bed itself is clean and canopied and impossibly soft, with pillows and bolsters. Isaac has never imagined lying in such a bed, all by himself. A boy could lie down in such luxury and never rise again.

"Now rest," says Atherton.

He has positioned Isaac to lie on his side, looking out of the window. It is the only way Isaac can settle, with his back grown so bowed that he nearly folds on top of himself. Outside is a tree, with birds singing. It is a jolly thing to see—and to hear, for the day is warm, a fine spring day, and the window has been opened—although it means that Isaac is unable to see the room behind him. He cannot see the bookcase or the door, or kind Mr Atherton standing there. This leaves him not quite easy in his mind.

"You see, Young Isaac?" the surgeon is saying. "There is no shelf in my house."

There is a room, though, behind a closed door partway along the entrance hall. Isaac had seen it as they came in.

"There's skeletings," says Isaac.

"The tiger—yes, of course—and the stoat." The one standing inside the door, the other on the stair-post. "I study anatomy. I have animal skeletons, as curiosities."

"Other ones too."

"Other skeletons?"

"Down the hallway."

The upstairs hallway, Isaac means. He had caught a glimpse, as they reached the top of the stairs. A small skeleton, articulated with wires, standing in a vestibule. Unmistakably human.

"A lad, it looked like," says Isaac.

Outside, the birds continue to sing with the sheer exuberance of being alive. In the room, there is the slightest of silences.

"Where'd he come from, Mr Atherton? That skeleting?"

"From a shop, Young Isaac. A dusty shop in the Gray's Inn Road, full of antique bits of this and that. The bones are very old—did you not notice? The skeleton is brown with age."

The surgeon's voice is warm with reassurance.

"Rest now, Isaac. There is nothing to fear. And I'll come back in just a very little while, to see you."

CURIOUS TALE OF
A FLEEING WOMAN

The London Record
22nd May, 1816

Readers are familiar with the "Boggle-Eyed Bob" sensation that lately gripped the Metropolis, and has been duly chronicled in these pages; though what this episode has revealed about the propensity of Ghouls to emanate from the churchyards of London, and what it has said instead about the capacity of Myth to seize the mass imagination with such force as to achieve the aspect of Actuality, we do not propose to judge, as lying outside our narrow sphere of competence. But yesterday evening we stumbled upon a new instance of the phenomenon, in the person of a Crossing-Sweeper who has been telling passers-by of a singular encounter with a mysterious Fleeing Woman.

The Sweeper, a ragged young party in an immense battered hat, who identified himself as "Nathaniel, Your Honour, Nathaniel Jugs, after my ears," has as his stand a crossing near St Helen's Church, Bishopsgate. This he sweeps clean for such coins as kind souls will give him, "at all hours, Your Honour, from cock-crow 'til the midnight bell, assuming you could 'ear a cock in this wicinity, which of course you can't, but you take my meaning in any case, as speaking in a figurative way." Last Thursday night he was startled from a standing slumber — "it being wery late, Your Honour, with scarcely no one on the street at all, and Nathaniel leaning on his broom" — by the spectre of a young woman, barefoot and wrapped in a cloak, running towards him. He could see clearly, he says, despite the darkness and a gathering fog, by the spill of light from a street lamp opposite.

He would have spoken, to ask if she required assistance, but at that moment a carriage clattered out of the night behind her, cutting off her avenue of flight, and a man leapt down to seize her. The woman uttered a croaking cry, and struggled mightily; but her assailant — or her keeper, for Nathaniel Jugs could not speculate which — overpowered her, and dragged her with him back into the coach, "kicking like a poor scragged wretch at the end of a Newgate neckerchee." The rattler tore off again at a terrific pace, "as if the Fiend himself was galloping in pursuit."

A small crowd had gathered about us, drawn by this singular oration. Encouraged by their interest, young Jugs now offered up the further detail: the Fleeing Woman's eyes had been red. "And not red with weeping, Your Honours; no, but red as blood." Just exactly, he continued, like the eyes of a gigantic mastiff that had run a mad a year ago — "Here along this wery street, Your Honours, the exact same corner we're standing on this minnit."

There were exclamations at this, and we felt each one of us a prickle of uncanny thrill, recollecting the episode to which young Nathaniel Jugs had so breathlessly alluded. It was in truth a delicious sensation, relishing as we do a lurid Tale that wraps itself in the cloak of Factuality. And now our Crossing-Sweeper was recounting how the Fleeing Woman had bitten the man on the wrist as he manhandled her — a long grey man, said young Jugs, like a wolf — and how he had responded with a backhand blow and a fearful oath, exclaiming as he wrenched open the carriage door: "He should of left you in H——, where you belong!"

9

My uncle once operated to repair an aortic aneurism. The patient was a Thames lighterman, a man of five-and-forty with a wife and four little ones at home, who had been brought to Guy's Hospital in desperate straits. Both his legs were cold and the cause was quite apparent: a pulsing and a swelling in the abdomen. The prognosis was bleak and certain-sure: no hope of survival past another few nights, at best — or worst, depending on how you see these things. The pain was terrible, with no means of relieving it.

So my uncle decided to cut. This caused a considerable stir at Guy's, the procedure having never been attempted on a living patient. Other arteries had been successfully tied, but not the aorta, the great vessel leading from the heart. And abdominal surgery of any kind was all but hopeless, corruption of the wound being certain. But my uncle said, very gravely: "This poor man is dead if I do not proceed. It is the only way." He stopped short of adding: "And the Truth, and the Light."

He spent that night in the Death House, practising on cadavers, and the following afternoon they carried the poor lighterman into the operating theatre. A packed audience of colleagues and students—as breathless a throng as ever watched Kean at Drury Lane—stood craning to see as he sliced the man open from groin to breastbone and reached inside. There was shrieking, of course—pain past all imagining—but block that from your mind. Marvel instead at the dexterity of the surgeon, locating the aorta blind, by feel alone.

He was suddenly still. He raised his head. "Gentlemen," he cried, "it is my honour to tell you that I have it in my grasp!"

Applause, and cries of "Bravo!" They were thrilled, each man in that room—excepting one, of course. The lighterman was wishing he could die upon the instant.

But he didn't. My uncle succeeded in tying off the aorta, and the lighterman was borne from the theatre alive, amidst loud hosannas for the surgeon. By the following morning, the patient's legs were growing warm, proof that the blood had found another path to circulate. But then they grew cold again; the lighterman became feverish, and at midnight he expired—as my uncle must surely have expected, from the second he reached for his scalpel. But the man was dying in any event, and he was after all just a lighterman. The following afternoon, it was my uncle's honour to announce to his adoring students that the operation itself must be considered a complete success, notwithstanding the death of the patient. "It is," he proclaimed, "a great day for Science."

I wasn't present that day, all of this having taken place some months before my return to London in the summer of the year '15. But it was subsequently described to me by several witnesses. And I mention it to you now, as something that crossed my mind as I made my way across London Bridge to Guy's Hospital, the same day I read the account of the Fleeing Woman in *The London Record*.

*

The corpses of four felons hanged for murder. These are owed by law each year to the College of Surgeons, four cadavers in all the year and not one more — the merest mouthful to the feast that must be annually offered upon the dissecting tables of London. But Meg's body was to have been one of them. This had been agreed, before the hanging. It would be cut down and carted direct to Surgeons' Hall, two hundred paces north of the prison. But it never arrived.

So I learned from Keats. I had come to Guy's on an errand from Mr Comrie, feeling unsettled in ways I could hardly begin to describe and possessing a whole new store of images to haunt my nights: Little Hollis on his stomach, staring upwards at the moon, and a mastiff with Meg Nancarrow's face and eyes as red as blood. It was the first time I had been to Guy's since the hanging, and I discovered that my abortive exploit was now the stuff of gleeful legend. Amongst the surgical students I was Mad Starling, who attempted to take Newgate Prison by force, as a Revolutionary Mob of One. Another Will Starling entirely — the Will Starling who had existed before all this business began — might have revelled. He might very well have strutted and winked, and touched one finger to the side of the cork-snorter when pinned down for an answer — "What the Devil, Starling, were you about?" — and flashed the dice in a smile that hinted at sly volumes. But I had no stomach for any of that now, and limped away with muttered evasions. In the course of this I fell in with Keats, and we took ourselves to a public house in the maze of streets west of St Saviour's, one little frequented by students.

Keats shifted uncomfortably on his stool, and debated the wisdom of oysters. It seemed he was uneasy in his bowels.

"The strain of operating," I suggested. Keats had apparently performed a minor procedure on his own that day, cutting a growth from the side of a man's face.

But no, he said, the carving had gone tolerably well; he had been surprised to find his nerve so steady. "I wasn't sure whether to be pleased with myself, or horrified." The bowel-wise unease had come on subsequently.

"Three pennyworth of isinglass, then," I told him, "dissolved in a gill of water. Highly efficacious for bowel complaint."

"If bowel complaint is what it is," he said, looking vaguely hunted, "and not cholera in the premonitory phase."

"Keats," I told him, "it ent cholera."

Keats was a good fellow, but a fretter about his health.

He grimaced, and changed the topic. It seemed he'd written a poem, which had been accepted for publication in *The Examiner*. He offered to recite it for me, and I said why not, feeling grateful at the prospect of distraction. Besides, I'm partial to a good poem, especially if it has a highwayman in it, or a cavalry charge, and a rhythm that gallops you along. This one turned out to be a sonnet, much concerned with solitude and trees, and I didn't listen much after the first few lines. When he'd finished, I assured him it was very fine indeed, just the sort of poem a fellow warmed to best, and he ended in asking me about the hanging. "Why had I done it?" he wanted to know, for naturally he was as curious as the others.

Cos I had known Meg Nancarrow, I said, and did not believe her guilty.

"She was a friend?"

"Yes. No. Not really. She didn't want friendship, leastwise not from the likes of me. But I wanted to help her."

"Enough to get yourself beaten half to death?"

I looked away, discovering I hardly knew where to begin. Or where to end, if once I started to tell Keats what was on my mind.

"The mastiff's eyes were red," I found myself saying.

Keats looked at me blankly. "Mastiff?"

"He did something to it—Atherton. Don't you remember? It was in the broadsheets, last autumn. Some terrible experiment—the mastiff ran mad and attacked two horses. Its eyes were red as blood."

Keats had begun to laugh, incredulous. Evidently his cholera was better.

"That nonsense in the newspaper this morning—is *that* what's bothering you?"

"Never mind," I muttered, wishing I'd never opened my gob.

"You're thinking that woman was—what—Meg Nancarrow? Risen from the tomb? *Surrexit Meg de sepulchro*?"

"'Course not."

"It's purest fiction, Starling."

"I know that, Keats! Go nurse your cholera and leave off."

He looked wounded at that, and after a moment I wished I hadn't said it. We both fell silent and sullen.

"If it *is* cholera," I said at length, "you should take calomel pills and castor oil. Keep to a diet of arrowroot and rice, with thin broth."

"It ain't cholera," Keats muttered.

But after another moment, he spoke again. And what he said surprised me very much.

"He came to the hospital today. Atherton."

Apparently Atherton had not been seen at Guy's for more than a week. But this morning there he was again, arriving in his customary manner—"as if there were banners streaming," said Keats—but even more so than usual. He dazzled down the corridors and left again soon after, without staying to deliver his anatomy lecture. The story spread that he was too busy, preparing some manner of anatomical presentation that he was to make two evenings hence, to all the leading men in London. It was rumoured to concern some great scientific discovery, arising from the dissection of Meg Nancarrow's body.

The thought of it was somehow grotesque. "Atherton?" I demanded. "*He* dissected her?"

"And I'm sure he did it beautifully. Mr Atherton is a poet, in his way. But his materials are flesh and blood, and that's what's so unsettling about the man—for the flesh is real, and the blood is someone else's." But seeing the look on my face, Keats began to laugh again. "A dissection, Starling—it wasn't a drawing and quartering. So you needn't look so horrified. But whether he did or no, it was never done at Surgeons' Hall—for the body never arrived."

"What do you mean, never arrived?"

"I heard that from one of the Porters."

I stared at him. "Then where did it go?"

"The Porter didn't know. But I heard someone say they thought it ended at Bowell's."

Mr Bowell's eyebrows operated upon the same mechanical principle as his smile, according to an ingenious arrangement of levers and pulleys. Just now they were being jerked upwards to express bemusement. The Nancarrow party? Here? No, indeed; no such party had been brought here on Monday last, nor upon any other occasion that Mr Bowell could recollect.

"They're saying otherwise, at Guy's."

The mechanism creaked again. Mr Bowell could not imagine why. "Nor why Mr Comrie's boy might suppose it to be any of his concern."

We were in the front parlour of his establishment, where Mr Bowell was wont to meet with his customers — the ones as still drew breath. It was a room where Old Bones might sit at his ease, with his skeletal trotters upon an ottoman and a nightcap on his head: a small, dim, narrow room, as if in token of the more permanent lodgings Mr Bowell had on offer, with oil lamps flickering and a rug upon the floor muting footsteps to a whisper. You felt you ought to whisper yourself, in such a room, lest those lying stiff and still just down the stairs be startled into wakefulness. I had hurried here straight from my meeting with Keats, arriving just as Mr Bowell was closing his shutters for the night.

"I should like to oblige you," he said, meaning the opposite. "But I never laid eyes upon the Nancarrow party—not in life, nor afterwards. You must consult the Surgeons, I think, or the Porters at the Schools of Anatomy. Or perhaps the Keepers at Newgate Prison—they might assist you—for many are buried right there, as you may know, under the stones of Dead Man's Walk; many of them as pass on within those walls, and thus go to their rest with no marker at all, and a seasoning of lime. But I cannot assist you; I have no knowledge. Good night."

But he was lying. I saw the uneasy flicker of it in his face, even as I saw the flicker of something else behind him. Thos Bowell the Younger was framed in shadow beyond the archway, watching. And if the undertaker had been touched by the cold hand of unease, then his son had manifestly been taken by it, and hoisted by the scruff by it, and shaken.

Young Thos was about to grow more uneasy still. Some small while later, he stepped out the back door to trundle his way to the jakes, only to be confronted by a dark youth with a triangle face who had been waiting for him there. "Christ Jesus!" squawked Young Thos, cos it is a mighty discombobulation to be thus waylaid in the darkness of the night, with your breeches already unbuttoned and nothing more upon your mind than a solitary sitting-down and a contemplative stink. But he answered what I asked, with the encouragement of an earnest offer to slice his danglers off him if he didn't. I had an impression he was eager to tell the tale—and he told it with a genuine relish.

Oh, yes, he said. Oh, yes indeed. The Nancarrow bitch were brought here in a cart, directly after the scragging at Newgate. The surgeon arrived with her, Atherton. A great flurry he was in, with orders snarled and directions shouted —"Do such-and-such, Young Thos," and "Look sharp, you young hound!"—and at first it seemed to Young Thos's rising consternation that the surgeon was bent upon trying to revive the corpse.

"But then he stopped. And such a look come over his phizog that it causes me to shake all over again, just recollecting."

Cos the surgeon had changed his mind, it seemed. He had decided to wait. To take Meg to another place, and revive her in another manner, now that it seemed certain she was dead.

My own consternation was now rising by the second. "You're saying there was doubt?" I exclaimed. "Meg may still have been alive?"

No, said Young Thos, with a look so unsettled it could not have been play-acting. That was what made it all more peculiar still. Cos Meg Nancarrow had been stone dead from the start.

"She were Dead from the second she come into the shop—take my word. I seen Dead every day of my life, bare nekkid on a table with its peck-box hanging open. I know what Dead looks like, and Meg Nancarrow were it."

I left with very much on my mind.

And never thought once to ask after Isaac Bliss.

THE SENSATIONAL END
OF BOGGLE-EYED BOB

From a Broadsheet Account
23rd May, 1816

All of London has raptly followed the career of Boggle-Eyed Bob, the night-stalking revenant that was first reported some weeks ago near St Mary-le-Bow Churchyard, importuning passers-by, before proceeding to horrid emanations and cannibalistic assaults upon the living. It now appears that this dreadful saga reached its terminus in the small hours of this past morning, when a trio of young gentlemen, late returning from a "spree" upon the town, were arrested by syllables of feminine distress, issuing from an alley near Haymarket. Investigating, they discovered a member of the Cyprian Tribe, being set upon by an assailant whose intent seemed at first to be violent conquest. But at that very moment a shaft of moonlight broke through the covering of cloud — as if it were no moon at all, but the Unblinking Eye of Providence — and in its silvery stare they perceived that the assailant was no mere mortal ruffian, but none other than Boggle-Eyed Bob, crouched over the struggling Drab like some monstrous toad.

The Creature fled at once, but the young gentlemen gave chase, emboldened by their superior number, and by the spirit of intrepidity which in such moments fills the heart of every true-born son of John Bull's Island, as it lately did upon the field of Waterloo. Others took up the hue and cry, drawn by their urgent calls for assistance, and soon a swelling throng pursued the Creature, bearing lanterns and makeshift weapons. The Creature ran with hideous speed, tending towards St Giles Rookery, in whose notorious labyrinths it seemed certain to escape pursuit. But Providence again reached out its Avenging Hand, directing the Creature into a close, where it turned with a shriek of unholy rage as the pursuers closed, and bore it down.

Reports remain confused and varied as to what next transpired. But it appears that, as the crowd belaboured the Creature with cudgels, a measure of some incendiary element, such as coal-oil, was dashed upon it, and was then ignited by means of a bull's-eye lantern, fiercely flung. As the Creature lay insensate, combustible material was cast on top, in the form of timber from a nearby tenement that had collapsed upon itself, as the wretched dwellings in that Foul Sink of London are known to do; and in the matter of a minute a great blaze had arisen, like unto the Fires of Smithfield that were kindled in bygone days for heretics and female felons.

What desperate thoughts passed through the mind of the Creature, if any thought remained, cannot be known. Perchance its final glimpse was of the Much Greater Fire that assuredly awaits. But certain it is that the earthly career of Boggle-Eyed Bob had ceased, and at the end of half an hour naught remained but ash and cinder, which now was dispersed into foul black rivulets as a torrential rain burst forth, as if Heaven itself would cleanse the Metropolis of all lingering pollution of Bob.

10

Miss Smollet received this news as you might expect: dramatickally. I'd gone to Milford Lane mid-morning, as soon as I'd read the broadsheet, to find that the tale had arrived before me.

"I did not wish for this," Miss Smollet said. She said it over and over, tugging distractedly with one hand at the other. But not as an actress would do upon the stage — much more as a very young woman might do, pacing backwards and forth in the lane outside the shop, with the sun on her hair and a clutching sense that she had somehow been the cause of something dreadful.

"I wanted to be left alone — that's all. I wanted him to Go Away. And we seen him in his coffin, didn't we? The two of us — you and me — with our Very Eyes. And d'you suppose — ? Oh, Will — oh, dear Christ — could it really of been him they killed last night? Or have they gone and murdered someone else?"

Janet Friendly had no doubts. We stood together by the counter as Mrs Sibthorpe coaxed Miss Smollet up the stairs to lie down.

"Three bucks on a ran-tan?" Janet snorted. "It could have

been anyone they killed. They stumble on someone in an alley, and suddenly there's a frenzy. God knows *your* eyes would bulge like eggs, Will, with half of London howling after you, and your hair would stand straight up too. I don't say I have sympathy for the bastard — he was attacking that girl, after all. But he was never Boggle-Eyed Fucking Bob."

And if Janet was cynical, Mr Comrie was purely disgusted.

"Was it Boggle-Eyed Bob? No, it wasnae Boggle-Eyed Bob. For thaire never was a bollocking Boggle-Eyed Bob to begin with."

He had grown particularly Scotch, always a sign of inner turbulence. I had returned to Cripplegate to find him in the surgery, hammering nails into the wall. Evidently he had decided to hang some new pictures.

"He was seen," I ventured. Cos by this point, I was no longer sure what I believed — about Boggle-Eyed Bob or about much else. Especially after the report of the Fleeing Woman, and the tale Young Thos had squawked out by the jakes last night, a combination that had kept me awake until the blessed light of dawn had begun to creep through the window of my attic room.

"Aye," muttered Mr Comrie. "Boggle-Eyed Bob was seen."

"By various parties."

"Outside churchyards, importuning little girls. In chimneys, making faces at sweeps."

"I thought I seen him once myself. Right here at Cripplegate — the night Miss Smollet slept in my room."

I had never told him this, and I hesitated before telling him now. He paused in his hammering, but did not turn round.

"Saw him whaire, precisely, William?"

"At the bottom of the stairs."

I pointed—a useless gesture, since Mr Comrie continued to look fixedly at the nail he'd been hammering, as if he could drive it the rest of the way through sheer intensity of Caledonian disgust. His voice was level and ominously calm.

"And saw *what*, precisely? If I might enquire."

"A figure," I said, beginning to flounder. "A shape."

"Describe it."

"Well—a sort of hunching."

"A 'hunching'?"

"A sort of a man's shape, hunching over."

"Such as children see in the nursery, William? When they've gone to bed with bogles on the brain?"

"Yes, I admit. I could have imagined..."

"Such as fools and old women see on dark nights, when witches ride about on broom-sticks?"

"But it's not just me. Half of London thinks—"

"And half of London is an ass! I expect much more of you."

He punctuated this with one last hammer blow, and picked up the first of the pictures: Sir Charles Bell's appalling scrotum, which apparently he had decided to hang here after all.

"There is Science, William—and there is Superstition. Reason, or Lunacy. One side, or the other—and if it's the other, then God help us all. This skulking about in the night —this digging up of graves—it will not sairve. Can you not see that? You're as much to me as any son could have been— and William, this is madness."

There was mottled anger in his face, and a genuine distress. I hadn't seen that distress since the road near Waterloo, when he'd arrived to find a horse with half a head and Your Wery Umble sobbing uncontrollably. I was about to see it again too — the very next night, at Guy's Hospital.

Cos in the morning, a note would arrive at the door. Mr Dionysus Atherton was to deliver a Lecture and Demonstration of Historic Moment. His old school friend's attendance was most strenuously urged, along with that of all the leading surgeons in London and luminaries of the Royal Society. A revelation was to fall amongst them like a thunderbolt; it was to scatter their assumptions like leaves.

This evening, old friend. Eight o'clock. Do not under any circumstance be late.

*

The operating theatre at Guy's is a cockpit, as you'll know if you've been in it — and God pity you if you have — with a raised gallery ringing the operating floor, on three sides. It was thronged with students and colleagues when Mr Comrie and I arrived, but also present were more of the Gods of Science than I'd expected. My uncle had invited them all, and they had come — though whether through scientific excitement, or a secret desire to see him fall, I don't presume to say. They'd never been sure what to make of him, all the titled grandees of the Royal Society. A brilliant man — oh, indubitably — and rising; but somehow Not Quite One Of Them. I saw Banks himself amidst the press — Sir Joseph Banks, the president of the Royal Society, who had begun his brilliant career as official botanist on Cook's voyages round the globe, and was now a weak-eyed man of sixty-odd, oppressed by gout and kidney stones. The surgeon John Abernethy was here, and his quondam student William Lawrence, standing upon opposite sides — as of course they must, in their mutual detestation. The Scientific Community was still very much a-twitter about the recent public lecture in which Lawrence had eviscerated his old mentor's views on a Life-Force in the blood.

Atherton entered from the back, through the passage by which Sufferers are brought into surgery on Wednesdays and Fridays at one o'clock. He wore a new frock coat for the occasion, and strode with a nervous exaltation. He hadn't slept last night, perhaps not in several days; that much seemed clear at once. But he swept in like Kemble playing Coriolanus, commanding the gaze of every man in the room — even those who had come rehearsing their sneers. The very molecules of the air were dancing about him.

"Gentlemen!" he cried. "I thank you for attending — and more than that, I congratulate you, because it is a momentous evening for every man here present. It is a momentous evening for every man who draws breath — and every woman too, and child. For what I am about to tell you will shake the Citadel of Mortality."

There were exclamations at that, and muted guffaws from the enemy camp, cos of course every Brilliant and Rising Man must have Enemies. Mr Comrie beside me gave a groan. "Listen to the man," he exclaimed. "What the Devil does he think he's about?" I stayed silent, watching in breathless fascination. I had a notion already where this night was tending.

"Gentlemen!" cried Atherton again. His eyes swept across the crowd once more, defying each one of us. The man could be splendid; I confess it. "We have heard much, of late, concerning the Spark of Life. What it may consist in — how it is extinguished. How it might even, in our fondest dreams, be rekindled. We have heard the matter debated, with deep learning and conviction, by two who are amongst us at this moment."

He meant Lawrence and Abernethy, of course. Lawrence, tall and supercilious, allowed himself a thin smile; Abernethy's pugnacious face darkened.

"I believe," my uncle continued, "that there is within us a Life-Force, as Mr Abernethy and others have asserted. I believe it is the principle of our existence, and may even be said in some sense to equate with what common men think of as a soul. But I do not propose to reopen the debate, tonight."

"Be thankful," said a dry voice, "for small mercies."

This was Lawrence. Some laughter, which my uncle affected not to hear.

"There was a woman hanged at Newgate, on Monday morning last," he said. "Her name was Meg Nancarrow."

The laughter died. An instant's silence, then the stirring of execration.

"God's bollocks," muttered Mr Comrie. "Oh, Atherton — you didn't."

But he had. That's exactly what he'd done. The conviction came upon me with a scrotum-tightening certainty.

"I have attended numerous hangings, gentlemen. Some of you have done so as well. It is Scientific interest that prompts us, a passion for studying the mechanism of Death. And I have often had cause to observe—as many of you have done also—that life may continue for some good while after all empirically discernible signs are extinguished."

He had begun to stride, back and forth, as he invariably did when he lectured.

"Meg Nancarrow dropped at three minutes past eight o'clock. At 8.27 all struggle ceased, and at 8.33 she was pronounced dead by the attending surgeons. I took possession of the body immediately upon its being cut down, having made prior arrangement to do so."

"What, bribed the Sheriff, you mean?" someone demanded, indignant. Banks.

"If you will. I had arranged as well for the body to be delivered to an undertaker's establishment nearby, where it arrived at six minutes past nine o'clock."

So Young Thos had told the truth, I realized—or leastways part of it. The body had gone first to Bowell's.

"And then, you—what?" Banks demanded. "You're not telling us you tried to revive the corpse?"

"No," said my uncle. "I did not. I decided to wait."

Uncertainty now. Mutterings of confusion.

My uncle's voice rose above them.

"As you will know, an attempt at revival was once made by John Hunter himself."

Hunter's famous bid to revive the Revd Dodd, hanged at Tyburn for forgery in the year '87. He'd had the corpse conveyed in secret, straight from Tyburn Tree to an undertaker's establishment.

335

"He failed, gentlemen. But he made the attempt—Hunter, the *fons et origo* of modern anatomical science. The father of scientific surgery, and Mentor to such luminaries as Mr Abernethy, whom I rejoice to see amongst us this evening. Hunter himself believed that a corpse might be resurrected, and he made the attempt."

"He did no such thing!" cried Abernethy. He had been standing in silence 'til now, his florid face growing redder by the moment. "John Hunter, sir, did not seek to resurrect a corpse. Our Lord did that. John Hunter sought to *revive* a man who might merely be unconscious."

"I concede the point, although it is a technical one."

"Technical?" sputtered Abernethy. "*Technical?* It is the difference between Science, sir, and Necromancy. It is the difference between legitimate endeavour, and Blasphemy!"

Voices rose again, some of them shouting Abernethy down. The students in the room were still with my uncle, in the main, as were many of the younger surgeons. And even those who deplored him were riveted to see where this would lead.

"I agree," retorted my uncle, "that Hunter's attempt was limited in scope and ambition. It was left to Signor Aldini to take the next long stride."

Aldini, the Italian, who had sought to resurrect corpses by means of electrical current.

"And Signor Aldini, sir, was advised that his experiments were grotesque," cried Abernethy. "Signor Aldini was denounced by all right-thinking men. Signor Aldini was invited to leave London, sir—and did!"

My uncle flushed at this, and for just an instant he seemed unnerved. He had surely expected opposition, but not such ferocity. He was Dionysus Atherton, after all; he strode golden and gleaming through life.

"Gentlemen! I stand here to tell you that Hunter was right, and Aldini also. Although they failed in their attempts, the theory was sound. The dead may be summoned back."

"God's bollocks, Atherton — what have you done?"

Mr Comrie's voice rose above the din. Atherton's eyes sought him out — found him, standing rigid amidst the throng. Found me as well, wedged in at Mr Comrie's side. A glow of triumph was on that handsome face. And then, as an awful hush descended, he told us.

"The body remained at the undertaker's for approximately half an hour, at the end of which I made my decision. Rather than attempt resuscitation directly, I would have it transported to my residence at Crutched Friars. There is a stable behind the house, and here the corpse was laid out upon a table at seven minutes past one o'clock — four hours and thirty-four minutes after death had been pronounced.

"As you well know, a pronouncement of clinical death may be far from definitive, even if the surgeon be both competent and sober. But I will say that the appearance of the body as it lay before me was wholly consistent with death by strangulation. There was no trace of heartbeat or respiration. The skin seemed very slightly cool to my touch, although I concede that this was a subjective judgement. The mark of the rope showed as a bruised indentation above the hyoid bone, angling upwards. The face was very pale, with the curious placidity that is often seen in victims of judicial hanging, despite the intense suffering that is involved. The tongue was black and protruding, and a frothy mucus flecked the corners of the mouth. The eyes were open and protuberant, and the hands had been clenched so tightly that the fingernails were driven into the palms. Bladder and rectum had both released.

"I swaddled the body in heated blankets to stimulate circulation, and at sixteen minutes past one o'clock, attempts at revival commenced. At first these involved initiatives to stimulate respiration by inflating the lungs with a bellows, followed by the administration of hartshorn and hot balsam. Subsequently galvanic stimulation was employed, by means of voltaic piles, with metal rods applied to the chest area. At the first such stimulation, the extremities juddered. Upon a second application, a groan issued from the subject. Upon a third application, the body lurched upwards at the waist, as if the victim sought to rise."

All air had been sucked from the operating theatre. Atherton stood motionless, now. He seemed to look at each one of us in turn.

"This proved indeed," he said, "to be the case. I caught her in my arms before she could fall back again. There was a discharge of black bile and blood from the mouth, after which a stertorous respiration resumed. The legs convulsed; the arms flailed; the eyes, shot red with blood, searched wildly, and found mine.

"You will imagine, gentlemen, my emotions in this moment. Holding her in my arms — a living woman whose death had been pronounced nearly five hours previous. Her lips twisted, trying to form words, which issued as a rasping sibilance, owing to the damage done by the rope to the vocal apparatus. I believed at the time that she was calling for water, which I provided. She dashed the cup from my hand, and I have wondered since if the syllable she had attempted was in fact 'woe,' this being a word she later described upon the wall of the room where I was forced to contain her, using faecal material scooped from a bucket that had been supplied to meet her most basic need.

"A period of distraction lasted for some days, on the final evening of which she briefly escaped custody. But after that she grew much calmer, and the following morning I went into her room to find her standing at the window, turning her face to the sunlight. She subsequently busied herself in cleaning the chamber, during the course of which activity I heard through the door a croaking rasp that I was joyful to interpret as her best attempt at singing. This afternoon she smiled with pleasure when I laid out the new gown I had purchased for her, after which she washed herself and combed her hair.

"Gentlemen." His voice was ringing now. "You, of all men — as fellow surgeons, as Men of Science — will understand the immensity of what has been achieved. At the very least, this is to challenge the accepted definition of clinical death. At best I have upended all previous assumptions as to what may be possible to modern Scientific Medicine, in the matter of human longevity."

He let the silence hang. A low strangled murmuring began, rising with each instant.

"Odenkirk!" cried my uncle. "Mr Odenkirk — lead her forth!"

The murmurs had become a tumult. Every eye turned with Atherton to the entrance at the back. I was dimly conscious of Mr Comrie clutching my left shoulder — a shoulder that had been kicked with particular industry by the Under-Sheriffs — but I scarcely felt it, riveted with all the rest upon the open doorway, through which at any instant Meg Nancarrow must issue, like Eurydice redeemed.

And no one came.

"Odenkirk!" my uncle cried again.

From out of the din, the first harsh caws of laughter.

Then Odenkirk appeared, sloping hurriedly. But he was alone. Something had gone wrong. I saw it in his urgent expression, speaking into Atherton's ear.

"Good God," exclaimed some wag, "he's resurrected her as a *man*!"

A bellow of derision; the giddy merriment that comes on a flood of relief. Catcalls and jeers. They were on him now with a vengeance, all of those who had come in secret hope that he would fail; and with each moment the others were turning as well. I stood feeling the ground give way, as if I had been some imp of infinitesimal consequence on the very fringe of the battle on Heaven's Field, watching the vertiginous instant at which Lucifer, Bearer of Light, began to totter, gazing down with disbelieving eyes into the Chaos that swirled below.

Atherton stood stricken. He exclaimed something to Odenkirk in muted fury. Then he caught himself and turned, making one last attempt to command the moment.

"Gentlemen!" he cried. He had turned quite pale. "Gentlemen, it falls to me to inform you that a woman resurrected from death itself, with such consequence to her mental state as remains to be fully determined, has broken from close custody and now is somewhere loose in London!"

11

Jemmy Cheese hears her calling to him. Not an actual voice; it is not that, exactly. Just a sudden conviction, so intense as to sweep away all the other wisps of thought that drift and mutter at the edges of his waking dreams, that she is calling.

This is the way he would describe it — if indeed he could describe it to you at all, which he cannot. Jemmy Cheese has not had words since they cudgelled him down in the churchyard at St George-in-the-East. He sits rocking slowly in the straw on the dank cellar floor of Dr Paxton's house in Camden Town, as he has since they first brought him here. Chain and strait-waistcoat; sad old lunatick bruin. Forwards and back again, forwards and back; rattle of the chain as it sags, and the sharp metallic *chink* as it pulls taut. His neck is one great suppurating sore inside the iron band; the stench in the cellar is so thick that you can practically see it hovering, like mist on the Woolwich marshes where the Prison Hulk *Retribution* lies at anchor many miles to the south and east.

But thoughts come to him. Not as they did once; but they come, fluttering for a moment before slipping back into the darkness, like bats. Thoughts and images: a patch of night sky through the small barred window, which seems to become a different glimpse through a different window, into a room where his Meg once lay curled beside him. A fluttering and a confusion; the sudden conviction that something has gone terribly wrong, if he could only grasp what it is, and think how to set it straight. That strange dark boy who came: *They've took her, Jemmy — it's worse than bad.* It makes him moan with a desolate anxiety; he shakes his shaggy head from side to side and rocks harder, forwards and back again, rattle and *CHINK*.

Darkness through the window, and the wan white face of the moon. Thoughts fluttering, maddening, here and then gone. If only his hands were free, he might seize one of them as it bat-winged past. He strains his arms within the strait-waistcoat, and feels the shift. He has lost weight since coming to this cellar — two stone, at the least. There is more room inside the waistcoat than they've realized. And Jemmy Cheese is still fearfully strong.

The ghost white moon in the window. An overpowering sense that she is calling.

"Jemmy."

The ghost white moon.

A small white face. A white face in the window, and blood-red eyes looking in.

"*Jemmy.*"

Some while later the cellar door is unbarred. Light spills down and the Keeper trudges into it. Mr Wallis, conducting his midnight rounds.

"Fucking stench," he mutters. "Fucking animal. Fucking make you sick and—oi."

He breaks off, peering. Lifts his bull's-eye for a better look. Jemmy Cheese lies slumped, as still as death. His eyes in the lantern-light are blank and staring.

"Oi," says Mr Wallis, moving closer. "Are you alive, you stinking pile?"

Jemmy Cheese is indeed alive. More than that, he is in full possession of a Thought. He caught it by the wing as it darted past, and now he has it in his grasp. It is a simple thought, but very powerful, and it is not going to get away from him now.

"Oi," says the Keeper once more, giving a nudge with his boot. When that provokes no response, he delivers a rousing kick.

Jemmy stirs. There is a metallic rattle: the chain. Mr Wallis notices—half an instant too late—that the bolt has pulled loose from the floor.

12

By the following morning, half of London had heard about Atherton's calamitous presentation. The taverns and coffee houses were abuzz, and the newspapers were off and running. There had been a mordantly witty drawing in one of them, a surgeon dressed up as one of Lazarus's sisters, with a harried expression and a sign that read: "Lost—One Risen Sibling." By Sunday the first sermons against blasphemous practices would be thundered, and by Monday the tone of the newspaper drawings would change. One would depict a surgeon who was unmistakably my uncle, levitating a corpse right out of a coffin with an expression of unholy triumph, while in the shadows two desiccated devils, like bats, clutched one another in horror. "He will empty H—— itself!" cried the first. But a third and wiser devil smirked. "Not so," he said. "He will increase our number in the end—by ONE!"

And of course the Scientific world was consumed by the overwhelming question: what had Atherton actually *done*?

Mr Comrie believed that my uncle had done what he claimed: acquired the body, and revived it. "But mind—I said *revive*." Scowling over a glass of pale at the Black Swan.

"I do not say *resurrect*. For the dead do not rise up and walk, William—not this side of bollocking Golgotha."

This was two nights following the debacle. The Swan was busy, and bursting with vitality. Three apprentices at the next table tried gamely to impress a pair of shop girls, and a lugubrious baritone in the corner was bawling out "Life Let Us Cherish," which seemed on the whole appropriate.

"So she was cut down alive?" I said.

"'Course she was," he snapped. "And it's not as if that's never happened before."

"Half-Hanged Smith," I said.

"Exactly."

Half-Hanged Smith was a man named John Smith, scragged for house-breaking in the last century, in the days when you rode the Wooden Mare at Tyburn. Cut down after twenty minutes, Smith proceeded to choke and twitch, and came sputtering back to life right there beneath the gallows. He was duly reprieved and went on to live another twenty years, during which time he was convicted twice more for house-breaking. Smith was not a man who learned easily from his mistakes.

"But Smith was revived at once," I pointed out. "Atherton left Meg for nearly five hours."

"Or so he claimed."

"You think he was lying?"

He eyed me with immense Scotch understatement.

No one had seen my uncle since that night, when he had fled from Guy's with Odenkirk. He had posted a reward— that much was known—one hundred guineas for information concerning the present whereabouts of Meg Nancarrow, payable upon her apprehension. He was said to be ranging through the city each night, seeking her out in all the sinks of London. But she was nowhere to be found. There were reports, but these were too wild to be believed. Meg sighted on a ghostly ship upon the Irish Sea, which disappeared into a bank of no earthly fog; Meg appearing in a spout of fire and galloping across Hampstead Heath upon a coal-black horse.

"Lying about the five hours? Aye. Unless I'm wrong, and he was lying about all of it." Mr Comrie scowled down into his glass. Despite everything, he retained his old fondness for my uncle. "All of it, start to finish, and he never had the body in the first place. But why would a man do that? Any man, and Atherton most of all? To make himself a laughing-stock—ruin his reputation. And for what? It makes no sense to me, William."

There was something that made even less sense than that. A question had been tugging relentlessly, like the small dark demon of doubt at my sleeve. If Atherton had wanted Meg dead, then why would he try to revive her at all? If Uncle Cheese had been murdered to keep him silent—if Little Hollis had been topped for the exact same reason—then why in the name of God and the Devil would Atherton bring Meg back to life?

In the old days, I could have shared this with Mr Comrie. But a shadow had fallen between us of late, and I left feeling more alone than I'd done since the night my friend Danny Littlejohn had died, and haunted besides by a spectre near as unsettling as the horse with half a head: the gnawing fear

347

that I had somehow got it all wrong, and misunderstood everything that Atherton had done—and why he had done it—and where it would lead.

But in the morning came two revelations, and suddenly everything had changed.

The first was the news that Jemmy Cheese had escaped from Dr Paxton's asylum. It seemed he had somehow wrapped his chain round a Keeper's neck; snapping it like a twig, he had barged up the cellar stairs and then out into the night before anyone could stop him. And hard on its heels came a second piece of news—news I'd been seething for ever since Meg's trial.

Master Buttons had been found.

I'd had eyes watching out for him, all over London.

It sounds considerably grander than it was, put like that. You may conceive an image of Your Wery Umble at the centre of a web, his ogles hooded and his cogitations deep, dispatching agents across the length and breadth of the Metropolis. In fact I'd slipped coins to a few of the street arabs who loitered about Smithfield and Cripplegate, with a promise of more if they brought me information.

And one of them did. Barnaby, his name was. Ten years old or thereabouts, with a hatchet face and a sly knowing air—the sort of lad who would make a success of himself one day if someone didn't hang him first, which seemed on the whole more likely. He was waiting for me as I came out the door of the gin-shop.

"Seen 'im," Barnaby announced. "Buttons."

Barnaby never quite looked straight at you. He had a habit of squinting towards the horizon instead, as if something much more interesting was off in that direction.

"You're certain it was him?" I demanded.

"Said so, dint I?"

"Where is he?"

Barnaby grew absorbed in studying the clouds that were forming high above the dome of St Paul's. I fished out sixpence.

"A shilling, this is worth," he said.

"I'll give you another tanner, if the information turns out correct."

"Prime fucking intelligence, this is."

"First you tell me where he is."

"Fuck you very much," muttered Barnaby. But he told me. "Got a crib just south of Piccadilly, this Buttons. Near Haymarket."

It turned out to be a lodging-house in a lane off of Norris Street, where a ragged old man with a prophet's beard lay in a spreading puddle, and three younger men played pitch-penny against a wall. Yes, said the Landlord who answered my knock; Master Buttons lodged here, though he was out at present.

I kept my voice calm. "D'you know where he might be found?"

The Landlord hawked and spat, in the direction of the derelict prophet. "Try Fishmonger's Hall."

I knew the place: a gambling hell not far away in King Street, just west of St James's Square. It doubtless had a proper name, but everyone just called it the Fishmonger's, on account of its being run by William Crockford. A rising man, was Crocky, who grew up in a fish shop next to Temple Bar, and made his start in low hells out by Billingsgate. He'd migrated steadily westward as his wealth grew, and undoubtedly aspired one day to a club in Mayfair, where the likes of Beau Brummell gamed, and entire estates were won and lost between dining and dawn. Just now he was in between the two extremes, catering to a middling class of blackguard.

The club in King Street was rough enough, with bitter complaints from the neighbours, concerning bellows and fights and cries of "Help!" and "Murder!" in the night. But it was still too respectable for the likes of Your Wery Umble. God knows, it was too respectable for the likes of the Fishmonger, who remained what he had always been: a short wide shark of a Cockney, with dropped aitches and fawning politeness to his betters, and the keenest mathematical mind in London. But here I had my stroke of good fortune — or so it seemed at the time. As I arrived, the bully at the outer door was preoccupied with a drunken half-pay lieutenant who was convinced that he'd been cheated, and needed thus to be escorted out quicksticks before words unduly rash could be uttered, and challenges issued, and two chalk-faced punters with barkers drawn should find themselves standing across ten paces of Hampstead Heath in the mists of a bleak chill dawn, instead of being where such gentlemen belonged instead — safely inside, losing money to the Fishmonger. And before the frogmarch had been concluded, I was through the door and in.

The club was one large room, with a threadbare carpet upon the floor and candelabra hanging over the crowded tables, all of it reeking of smoke and sweat. There was Crockford, greasy and obsequious, gliding sharp-eyed through the press. Merchants and half-pay officers, a few flash-talking ruffians and the seedier species of professional sharpers, and of course their favoured prey: town toddlers, sprigs and second sons who lacked the wit to see how easily they were taken in.

And there in the midst, playing at hazard, was Master Linwood Buttons. A sheen of desperation was upon him.

He didn't belong here, any more than did Your Wery Umble. He should have been haunting the copper and silver hells near Covent Garden, where you could gamble with half-crowns and shillings. But it seemed he'd risen in the world since I'd seen him last: on his hind legs at the Old Bailey, dispatching Meg Nancarrow to the gallows. He wore a double weskit now, as the dandies do, with a long white scarf wrapped round his neck. It was fastened with a gold pin, and somehow he'd come into the requisite guineas to hazard here in King Street — though he surely would not have them for much longer. Crocky was at this moment gliding into the vicinity, as sharks will do when blood is in the water.

"Five, now — I call five!" Master Buttons's voice rose above the general din. "Five is a certainty, gentlemen!" He dashed the dice onto the felt. Two fours came up.

"Oh, bad luck, Squire," murmured the Fishmonger at Buttons's elbow, the very image of carnivorous sympathy.

"Foul fortune hindeed, but no matter—*nil desperandum*, Squire, as the hemperors of Rome was wont to say—cos why there's never fortune so foul as it may not change."

"Eight, then—here's my eight!" cried Buttons, cursing bitterly when six came up.

I watched him, still and silent as a spider. Confront him now? No, surely not. Wait for him—follow him outside, shadow-footing to some private place. With luck his blunt might hold out 'til nightfall, which would make my shadow-footing so much easier. I found myself actually hoping he would win, just a little, to prolong his stay at the table.

"Eight!" cried Master Buttons, rolling again. "This time eight is guaranteed!"

And would you credit it? The God who watches over knaves and villains was smiling upon us both. A five showed, and a three, and Buttons crowed in triumph.

I watched from my shadows for another while, then withdrew back out the door and waited on the street. Then I waited some more—four hours, by my watch, as the sun declined and the night came on.

Eleven o'clock, and the night was alive with din. Carriages a-clatter, and shouts from a chop-house at the corner. Nearby New Street would be bustling, and Haymarket beyond would be a second Gomorrah, with gin-shops crammed and Nymphs of the Pavement laughing like crows. An argument erupted across the road—two Cyprians, considerably the worse for drink. They proceeded to shrieks and hair-pulling, and that's when Master Buttons stumbled out of Fishmonger's Hall, behind me.

"She lifts us up upon her wheel, the goddess Fortune. And then she dashes us down again, the bitch!"

His voice rose into the upper reaches of tragedy. He was addressing the warring Cyprians, I think, but mainly he was shouting at the universe. He tottered in the spill from a gas lamp, pale with drink and dejection. His gold pin was missing, and his white scarf trailed down into the mire. The Cyprians paused in their hair-pulling, advising him to go fuck himself, which he took as an example of exactly how things are in this cess-pit of a world. Then he was off again, unsteady but moving briskly nonetheless.

I touched the knife in my pocket, and spidered after. He crossed the square and staggered towards New Street. Here he stopped and stood swaying, as if baffled by the traffic; then abruptly he lurched into the midst of it, defying it to run him down like a dog. I darted after, and was very nearly run down myself by a rattler in full career. Reaching the other side I discovered that I had lost him.

But no — there he was again, illuminated by the glow from a gin-shop. Sloping into a passageway that would lead towards Norris Street, to the north and east.

I broke into a run.

The passageway was narrow, no more than three feet wide, and black. I heard him before I caught a glimpse: a sporadic splish-splashing upon cobblestones, and thin wretched blubbering to go with it. Master Buttons was weeping as he pissed.

My glims adjusted and I made him out. Standing in a silvering of moonlight not three feet in front of me, phiz to the wall, bracing himself against it with one hand while the other directed the dragon. His head bowed in such abjection that even a spider might feel the tiniest pang.

"How much did it cost them, to buy you?"

He gave a cry of startlement and lurched round, midway through his business.

He he had no idea who I was. But he surely saw the knife in my hand.

A sharp intake of breath. "What do you want? Leave me be!"

His breeches were unbuttoned, the one-eyed lad still free and flopping. A decent size but shrivelling by the second.

"Thievery, is it? Money, you want? Well, you're too late—I lost every penny!"

"Odenkirk," I said.

That stopped him.

"Atherton's man. I'm supposing they needed an actor, so they hired one. One who owed Cheese money into the bargain, and was only too pleased to see him dead. Am I close?"

His mouth opened once, and closed. He tried again. "I don't know what you're talking about."

"I think you do. And I think you'll tell me."

Leastways that had been my plan: to terrify the truth right out of him. I'd know what Odenkirk had said to him that night outside the Three Jolly Cocks, and I'd know why Buttons had lied at the trial. And by the time he'd finished

354

squeaking it out, I'd have testimony that my uncle had ordered the killing of Uncle Cheese, and the fitting up of Meg Nancarrow for the crime. It would remain the barest fraction of the whole—but I would have made a start.

But Master Buttons turned out to have more spirit than I would ever have suspected. He licked his lips, and I saw him weigh his choices. Turn and try to flee? Or caterwaul for help?

"Tell me, or I swear I'll slit your throat."

He lunged instead.

He was banking on his superior size, I expect. He'd gambled that he could seize the knife and wrench it away—and he might very well have done it, cos he was quicker than I'd expected. But this was not his night, from start to finish. His breeches were still unbuttoned. They drooped about his hips, and now they snagged him. He lurched forwards and down with a frantic curse, grabbing at my wrist as he did.

I wrenched back, but the blade had been turned upwards in the struggle. Or so I could only suppose, piecing it all together afterwards. In the moment it was nothing but confusion, and struggling, and a queer wet gagging sound.

He was suddenly haloed in yellow light. A strange and remarkable effect, produced by the arrival of a lantern in the mouth of the passageway behind us—though this didn't occur to me, just at first. At first, I just stood there gaping. Master Buttons was on his knees before me, face upturned, as if savouring one last triumphant moment upon the stage. His mouth moved but no words came out. A gurgling rattle and a gushing of blood, like water pumped from a faucet. Then slowly, almost elegant, he slumped sideways against the wall and subsided onto the cobbles. The handle of my knife protruded from his throat.

And there stood Your Wery Umble, with Buttons's life's blood bubbling about his boots, and an exclamation — "Christ!" — behind him. I turned into the yellow glare. The bull's-eye was clutched by an elderly Watchman. He had a staff in his other hand, and a look of holy horror on his face.

"Ho!" cried the Charley. "Help! Murder!"

Tragic Passing of an Infant Prodigy

The London Record
28th May, 1816

With sorrow we must relate to our readers, and especially to those whose memories extend to theatrical activities in the closing years of the century past, that a once-bright light in the Firmament of Thespis has been extinguished forever. In the small hours of Tuesday morning, "Master Buttons" was discovered, slain, in an alleyway near Haymarket. "Out, out," as the Bard has inimitably summed the quintessence of the human condition, "brief candle."

Born to theatrical parents, the star that was Linwood Buttons ascended to its apogee during the brief vogue of the Infant Prodigy a quarter-century ago, appearing upon the London stage in numerous incandescent performances, some of which may still be called to mind. A cherubic stripling with a piping treble voice, he was much lauded for the melodic cadence of his delivery, and for the ingenious "points" of his performance—those crucial flourishes by which each Player may be measured against the great pantheon of the Lions of Tragedy which extends from Burbage through Garrick to Kemble and Kean. When, in blackface, he essayed the Moor, his voice swooped thrillingly into its lowest register upon the fatal utterance, "O blood!"; whilst as the Melancholy Dane he shuddered convulsively in all his limbs upon first seeing the skull of Yorick, before fluting, in such manner as perfectly to express the futility of all mortal aspiration, the plangent bi-syllable: "Alas!"

In latter years he appeared less frequently "to strut and fret his hour upon the stage," and in due course passed from the recollection of that notorious admirer of each succeeding bauble of novelty, the Public. From time to time Rumour hinted at a quondam Prodigy, much fallen in the estimate of Fortune, who had been glimpsed at a gaming table near Covent Garden, or in some low tavern in the Seven Dials, cap upturned before him, declaiming Bardic pearls before the swinishly besotted. And now the fall from Fortune is complete. A gentle Child of Thespis has been struck down by an assassin's hand, in that Sink of London widely known as H—— Corner; from which Infernal Depth we pray that he may be lifted up, and "flights of angels sing him to his rest." We pray fervently as well that Justice may "with Tarquin's ravishing stride" tread down his murderer.

We are able to report that the assailant is identified, and that the hunt is well advanced. Our sources at Bow Street relate that the villain is known to have sought the Poor Player at his lodging earlier that same day, and subsequently located him at a gaming house in King Street. Evidently he stalked Master Buttons as the latter left this establishment, setting upon his victim from behind and striking him down "unshriven, with his sins upon his head." Eluding pursuit the felon fled, but subsequent enquiry at the gaming club established his identity, for he had been recognized there; one of the patrons had recently sought out the services of a surgeon by whom the wretch was employed.

His name is Starling. He is described as a youth of diminutive stature, a known thief and blackguard who scavenged the battlefields of Europe during the late war against Corporal Bonaparte. Latterly he has served to assist a surgeon in Cripplegate, in the course of which occupation he has had cause closely to collaborate with the unholy gentlemen of the Resurrection Trade. No doubt he has gone to ground in some rat-hole of the Metropolis. But the Arm of British Justice is long. We are confident that it will reach out, and seize the murderer of Linwood Buttons, and haul him wriggling into sunlight.

13

And there you are. You're haring through the streets of London, and it did not happen. It could not possibly have happened—but it did. And the crunching underfoot is the shards of all you ever hoped for, as the realization comes: *This is you, done. The one life you're ever going to have, and you've just slung it aside.*

East and south across the Strand, towards the river. Cripplegate was too far. I needed to change these clothes; I needed to think.

Janet Friendly.

The house was dark. I scrambled for a pebble, beneath her window. A second and a third, 'til finally a candle glowed. The scrape of the casement opening, and a long dour face beneath a nightcap, glowering down through the mists of sleep.

"Will? The fuck—?"

"Just let me in. Please."

A minute later the door was opened. "I should of thrown a boot," she muttered, as I slipped past. The shop was ghostly in the light of Janet's candle; mounds of clothing lay like silent sleepers, or the dead. "Swear to God, I should of emptied a chamber pot. I should—"

The words died as she saw me more clearly.

"Jesus Christ," she said. "You're hurt."

"No."

"You're covered in blood."

"Not mine."

"Oh, Will. Oh, Christ on a biscuit. What have you done?"

I told her and she sat down — whump — on a wooden chair. It took a considerable deal to poleaxe Janet Friendly, but Your Wery Umble had just succeeded.

"I never meant it," I said, dismally.

"They'll hang you anyways."

And of course they would. I'd plead my innocence of heart, lighting the courtroom with the most abject smile that ever foundling wore, and the black cap would come out inside half an hour. They'd have me onto the scaffold the very next Monday morning, and there'd be no Jack Ketch with his own neck in a noose and Mr Punch tooting huzzah; but only Wm Starling, kicking his heels for the edification of all assembled, with his last dying confession available for a penny, blaming it all on Avarice, and Want of a Father's Correction in Boyhood.

Janet took a breath, and stood. "Right. You need to get out of London. Now. Tonight. Take off your clothes."

"What?"

"Look at you. Like fucking Macbeth, emerging from Duncan's bedchamber. And don't let's stand upon maidenly modesty, like virgins on our wedding night. Off! Chrissake, no one cares."

I pulled off my jacket and shirt and let them drop, as Janet sifted swiftly through the piles of clothing and slung a pair of breeches at me.

"Do you have money?"

I had blunt squirrelled away in my room at Cripplegate —but how long would it be 'til the Law was there? It depended how long it took them to retrace Buttons's steps to Fishmonger's Hall, where one question must surely lead to the next.

"Never mind," said Janet, reaching for a tin beneath the counter. "I have some—and yes you can fucking well accept it, so shut your cake-hole. Now go! You might of been followed."

She saw my gaze go longingly to the narrow stairs that led to the rooms above. Where Mrs Sibthorpe was still asleep, and Annie Smollet.

"There's an idea," snapped Janet. "We'll wake La Smollet, and have a scene. We'll have *Romeo and Juliet*, right here at Milford Lane. Exactly what we need—more drama."

She was right, of course. Not that it helped.

"I'll explain to her," she muttered, softening just a little.

"Tell her I never set out to kill anyone."

And it was starting to sink in, the finality. Master Buttons, slumping sideways with my knife outthrust from his throat. And he wasn't rolling over, neither, and rising to take his bow, as huzzahs rained down from the gallery. He just lay as he had fallen, gazing up at me with Danny Littlejohn's disbelieving eyes, their last light dying into bottomless reproach.

"I'll tell her, Will. I'll get word to Comrie too."

"Tell her—"

I didn't finish the thought, on account of its constricting in my throat.

"Tell La Smollet that you love her, Will? Why, of course. I could clasp her lily hand as I did it, if you like. I could blubber up the contents of my overflowing heart, and weep whole buckets, you fucking eejit. Now go, before someone finds you here! Get yourself out of London — get yourself out of England. Send word to us when you're safe."

Next second all the oxygen left the world, cos Janet had taken me in a hug so fierce that it nearly stove my shoulders together. It nearly set my hair afire as well, since she hadn't set down the candle first. But she stepped back before permanent damage was done, and for the barest of moments there was something stricken in her phizog, and a glimmer in her eyes that could nigh on be mistaken for tears.

"I should of emptied the chamber pot," she said.

14

A light rain is falling as Alf the Ale-Draper padlocks the door of the public house behind him, and commences on his waddling way along Black Friars Lane. It is very late, past two o'clock, and the dark street is otherwise deserted. After pausing to piss he continues, weaving just a little; for what publican would be sober at such an hour? He belches, and begins to warble an air. He has a high reedy voice, does Alf, quite comical in a man so large.

> *"On the green banks of Shannon when Shelah was nigh*
> *No blithe Irish lad was so happy as I.*
> *No harp like my own could so cheerily play*
> *And where ever I went was my poor dog Tray."*

It is a sad air, this one; it does not end well for the dog. But Alf himself is in a contented mood, a man at peace with the universe. The public house has taken on a new girl, whom Alf had just an hour earlier, on the flagstones in the cellar. Just as he has all the girls who come to work at the Three Jolly Cocks—as he'd on various occasions had the Nancarrow bitch, the one who went and got herself scragged. He has a notion he may have been rough with the girl tonight, as sometimes happens, Alf being a large man with exuberant appetites. Still, they deserve what they get, being nothing but filth. They're unfit for wiping boots upon, as he is often reminded by his mother, with whom he lives. His mother is a Christian woman, very nearly a saint.

"Poor dog! He was faithful and kind to be sure,
And he constantly loved me, although I was poor…"

The rain is falling more heavily now. Through the darkness, Alf discerns two shapes ahead of him: one massive, the second much smaller. They appear to be waiting for someone.

"When the sour-looking folks sent me heartless away,
I had always a friend in my poor dog Tray."

They don't move, whoever they are, remaining just outside the penumbra of light from a street-lamp. Alf squints, rhinoceros-eyed; he does not see well at the best of times, and should have brought his lantern. The first is an immense man, he discerns after a moment, with ragged clothes hanging loose, as if he had once been larger still. Alf has the vague notion that he might recognize the man, if he could see more clearly. With him is a woman, slender and dark-haired, her face muffled in a cloak.

Alf slows a little as he reaches them, but continues singing.

"But he died at my feet on a cold winter day,
And I played a sad lament for my poor—"

He breaks off with a grunt. He has stumbled, one of his size-fifteens catching against a cobblestone. The immense man puts out an arm to brace him, which is considerate, Alf thinks. The arm goes around him; so does the other.

"Set him straight," he hears the woman say. Her voice is a strange, low rasp.

Alf makes a sound like: "Woof." It is unrelated to the song, having more to do with the fact that the man has taken him in a bear hug, so powerful that it squeezes the breath from his lungs.

"That's the way," says the woman, in her rasping voice.

Alf would dispute this, if he could find the requisite wind. It is not the way at all, he would say, no matter how kindly the hug is intended. He would further explain that he needs to be going now, for his mother lies awake if he is late returning home, and frets herself.

"Argh," he says instead.

The man picks him up, right off the ground, which might cause Alf under other circumstances to exclaim in admiration, considering that he weighs twenty stone and this man has just hoisted him like an empty barrel. The arms continue to tighten.

Alf's mouth goes very wide. This is in part because his ribs are cracking, but also because he has had a considerable shock. The hood of the woman's cloak has fallen back, and in disbelief he has recognized her: a narrow face, pale and gallows-grim, with two eyes burning at him red as blood.

"Set him straight, Jemmy," he hears her say. "Set this fucker very straight indeed."

*

Alf will be discovered some while before dawn, when an early rising Crossing-Sweeper espies through the gloom what he takes at first to be a dead horse, lying at the side of Pilgrim Street. Identification will follow, and the newspaper reports will speculate that the victim must have been struck down accidentally by a heavy dray, or cart, and run clear over by the wheels, so cleanly had the back been broken.

15

It is no hard thing to disappear in London. A million souls to mingle with, and tens of thousands of rooms in attics and cellars across the Metropolis, where a penny would buy you a bundle of straw and three pennies an actual bed—with four or five others in it, of course, not counting the vermin, but still—under any name you might care to invent. Even if you had the ill-fortune to be recognized, there were a thousand lanes down which a sharp lad might slip, and if all else failed and the hounds had your scent, there was always the rookeries. The tangled slums of Jacob's Island and the Old Mint, or the Holy Land itself: the vast appalling rookery of St Giles, where an entire regiment might go to ground.

I stayed for a night at a lodging-house in Aldgate, then moved on to another along the Ratcliffe Highway. I told myself that I was just gathering my thoughts, and deciding where best to flee. But as two nights stretched into three, and I shifted to another ken farther east, I had to admit the possibility that I wasn't leaving London at all. On the fourth morning, I woke up in a nethersken down by the Docks, wedged on a pallet in the sleeping room between an old man in an ancient shooting jacket with wooden buttons, and a younger one with whom I had shared a tot of gin in the kitchen the night before. My new friend wore a brown shirt that had once been check, and a pair of ladies' boots with the toes cut out. He had been a partner in a counting house, he said; an educated man, and now here he was, fallen all the way to this. "But once a man falls far enough," he said with a sort of lugubrious satisfaction, smacking his lips and eyeing me bleakly, "he might as well finish the job. Eh? He might as well go the whole hog. And here we are, boyo. The pig in its entirety, bristles and all."

Clambering out from between them, I skirted past the kitchen, where some of the lodgers were already gathering. There was a yard outside with coster-carts scattered round, and several lumps of rags, still a-slumber. I washed myself as best I could at the stand-pipe, and then reached a decision.

It seemed that I was not leaving London at all. I made my way towards Smithfield instead, where I found young Barnaby watching a cock fight. The combatants were disputing against the wall of a slaughter yard, hemmed in by a ragamuffin crowd. Barnaby clocked my approach with one slantways eye, as if he were a species of rooster himself.

"Been 'earing about you," he said cryptically.

"I need to send a message."

"Sent one to that actor, didn't you? Fuck me. I 'eard — oi!" He broke off to shout encouragement to the smaller of the combatants, a scrawny bantam which made up in poultricidal fervour what it lacked in stature. "Now peck 'is 'ead off!"

"A message," I repeated. "I'll pay you sixpence."

"Sixpence now, and sixpence after."

"Twelve pennies, for a message?"

He cock-eyed me again.

"Danger pay. You're a desperado, you. Worth my neck to be seen with yez, and—oi! Yes! Now fecking finish 'im!"

I'd have sent young Barnaby to Mr Comrie, except they'd be keeping an eye for certain on Cripplegate. So I sent him to Milford Lane instead. He was back an hour later, extending a grimy palm. "She'll be at the place you said. Eight o'clock tonight."

I arrived at the churchyard just as the clock was striking the hour. Darkness had fallen and a chill wind had arisen, agitating the trees. A knot of vagrants idled by the east wall, passing a jar and casting glances in my direction, as I waited ten minutes and then another quarter-hour. Still there was no sign of Janet, which began to make me uneasy.

I was repenting as well my choice of a meeting place. St Sepulchre's, I had said—of all the churchyards in London—directly across the street from Newgate Prison, squatting mute and malevolent in the night. I found myself staring towards Debtor's Door itself, outside which Meg Nancarrow had kicked and choked just two weeks previous—and where Your Wery Umble would take his own last bow on a Monday morning yet to be specified, if the Majesty of British Justice had its way.

At half past the hour, I was beginning to wonder if young Barnaby had simply pocketed my twelve pence and lied. But that's when a familiar figure came hurrying at last along the street outside the railings, and turned in at the gate.

"You fucking eejit," Janet hissed by way of greeting, and cast a worried look over her shoulder. "I think I may of been followed."

A prospect to make the blood run just that little bit colder. I looked swiftly round.

"Have you lost them?"

"I ent sure. I done my best. Jesus, Will. Christ on a biscuit. I expect you been reading about yourself?"

Yes, I'd read all the newspapers at a coffee-stall. And this afternoon I had paid a penny for a broadsheet account of the murder, in which I learned that I had done it to avenge the death of the Fleet Ditch Fury, with whom I had some sinister connection.

"There'll be ballads soon," I said, essaying negligence. "By next week there'll be a play."

"They've been to the shop. A Magistrate, and two Constables. First thing yesterday morning."

News to make the blood run colder still. But it was something I should have been expecting—if they'd been to Cripplegate, then they'd assuredly have spoken to Missus Maggs, who'd have smoked out my connection with Janet and Milford Lane. Missus Maggs had doubtless smoked out a great deal about me, whilst minding her kews and peeze.

"What did you tell them?" I demanded, forcing calm.

"What would you think? I said I hadn't seen you."

"Did they believe you?"

"Christ knows. What matters is, they know who your friends are — they know where to look. And they're looking everywhere."

We had retreated deeper into the darkness by the church wall. A snatch of rough laughter from the vagrants, and as the wind shifted a waft from the burial ground on the other side.

"Will, what the Devil are you still doing here, in London?" Then, presuming to read the answer on my clock: "Aw, Christ — don't tell me. Don't even say it. La Smollet?"

She was right, or partly so. The thought of never seeing my Annie at all, for months or even years — that was bleak. So was the thought of leaving London itself: the Metropolis no more than a smudge on the horizon through the window of a mail coach, and then the green of England receding, along with every friend I had in this world, and Your Wery Umble greener still, hanging over the railing of a ship.

But above it all, I had to know.

"I need to find Meg Nancarrow," I said. "I have to know what he did. To her — and to the others."

"Who — Atherton?"

"Yes."

"What others?"

"That's what I need to find out."

"Fuck 'im, Will. Fuck all of it. It's none of your concern!"

"But it is. That's where you're so wrong. It is all of it my concern."

"You must be mad," said Janet.

She was right about that too, I think. Looking back, I suspect I was indeed halfways mad, that night in St Sepulchre's churchyard. We go through times in our lives when we're none of us quite sane. The sight of a man's blood pooling about your boots — there's a sight that will leave you feeling cold and sick and horribly unmoored, as I'm very sure you do not know yourself, and I congratulate you on your innocence. It sent Lady Macbeth running Bedlam-mad, that feeling, and she was forged of stronger steel than William Starling.

Besides, Lady Mac had just one murder on her soul, and my killing of Master Buttons was all mixed up in so much else. In the hanging of Meg, and the whispered words of Nuttall the Spavined Clerk, and the gnawing conviction that Dionysus Atherton had committed such deeds as banish us beyond the warmth and the light of the great communal fire that we cluster round together, all of us who are human in this world. My uncle: bone of my bone, and blood of my blood. And all of it reflected back in the dying light in Danny Littlejohn's eyes.

Yes, I believe I may well have been mad, that night in St Sepulchre's churchyard.

"No more of this," Janet was saying. "You have to leave *now*. And here — I been to Cripplegate — the Scotchman gave me these."

She'd pulled a handful of coins out of her pocket. Five gold guineas.

"His life's fucking savings, I expect. Or else he sold some tools. There's prob'ly some poor bastard on his table right this minute, about to have his leg cut off with the wrong-sized saw, and all so Will Starling could pay for passage to the Continent. And here he is, still in London, the eejit!" She forced the coins into my hand. "No, just take the money. He wanted you to have it, so it's yours. Take it—*go*. Before someone else comes looking for you, Will, cos next time they may find you!"

And there was something about the way she'd said it. Something that struck my ear askew, and made me wonder if the Constables hadn't been the only ones to come knocking at Janet's door.

"Someone else?"

"Never mind," she said instantly.

"Janet?"

She turned away, pulling her shawl more tightly round her shoulders. "Just—it don't matter. It's nothing you need to know."

"Tell me."

"There was a man," she said at last. Grudging the words, as if each one of them must be extracted like a molar. "Come to the shop this afternoon, looking for you. Not one of the Constables—he was nothing to do with them. But he'd found out, somehow, that we knew you. Someone told him to come to us."

"What man?"

"He said his name was Sheldrake. He said he had a message. 'Tell Starling, she wants to see him.' That's all he'd say. 'Tell Starling, he is summoned.'"

She.

All of London, stopping with that syllable.

"But forget about him, Will." Janet was pleading now. "Forget about all of it—just go. Send us word when you're safe. Cos God knows you're not safe here—not in London, and especially not in this churchyard, if there really was someone following me. Just—*please*."

I'd never seen that look on her face before. She gave me another of her rib-splintering embraces, and then she was gone, hurrying away into the darkness of London.

And I saw then that Janet's intuition had been correct. She had indeed been followed, all the way from Milford Lane. Someone was standing in the gloom, just inside the churchyard gate.

"Oh, Will," said Annie Smollet.

She wore a dark green cloak, borrowed from the shop. Snatched in desperate haste, no doubt, as she hurried after Janet out the door, and it was purest coincidence that its coloration suited her so perfectly.

"Janet wouldn't say where she was going, Will. But I knew. I just knew she was going to meet you. So I followed."

And Christ knows I was glad she did. Gladder than anything I could ever recall, standing there in St Sepulchre's churchyard with a sweet slow ache of joy.

"I was so afraid I wouldn't see you again," I said.

"Can I be so very much worth seeing? I don't think so, Will. I think I ent worth seeing so very much at all, not when it's Worth Your Life."

"I might, Miss Smollet, beg to differ."

I actually said that. And I've a notion I accompanied it with a little bow, as another man might have done — such as Claude Duvall the highwayman, perhaps. In a corner of my mind I winced, imagining how Janet might have eyed me if she'd been here at the present moment, and hearing in the night wind a whisper of her judgement: *Oh, you twat.* But Janet was a quarter-mile distant by now, hurrying south and west towards Milford Lane, and here in the darkness of St Sepulchre's churchyard it was just Wm Starling and Miss Annie Smollet.

She wore the hood of the cloak up, obscuring her face, as if she'd forgotten that she wasn't a fugitive herself. But her eyes gazing out from the folds were bright with genuine emotion.

"Tomorrow morning," she said. "You'll go away from London. I want you to promise me. If not for your own sake, then for your friends'. For my sake, Will. I want your Solemnest Oath."

And to this day, I am not sure what I would have said in reply, had we been allowed the span of just five more seconds. I might very well have melted in those green eyes, and relented, and done what the secret part of me already longed to do: climb down from the lonely steeple of my avenging zeal—Christ knows the wind cuts like a sabre when you're up so high, and so very much alone—climb down to safety, and scurry like a sleekit for the tall, tall grass. But that's when two bull's-eyes winked at the churchyard gate, and two Watchmen peered in.

They weren't looking for Your Wery Umble, in particular. Just a pair of Charleys making their rounds. But Miss Smollet gripped my arm.

"We can't be standing here," she whispered. "You need to be in Hiding."

I did not dispute the point. Her grip tightened.

"I know a place you can stay tonight. Come with me, Will—quickly."

"I can't go to Milford Lane."

"Not there. Holborn."

The bird-fancier's shop was dark when we arrived, the windows shuttered and the birds silent within, asleep in the scores of cages. It seemed the Badger had recently moved back into the room upstairs, having parted with her gentleman. "It Broke her Poor Heart, Will," Annie had told me as we hurried along Holborn. He turned out to be a fraud, this gentleman, his two thousand a year pure ephemera, and two other Badgers on the go into the bargain. But through a stroke of good fortune, the Badger would not be using the room on this particular night. Apparently she had already scooped up the shattered fragments of her poor heart and gone off for a few days with a new gentleman, which Annie considered very plucky in her, and evidence of a Shining Spirit.

Annie still had a key of her own. She led me up two narrow flights of stairs, feeling our way in the dark. Arriving upon the topmost landing, she fumbled with her key in the lock, and then fumbled within for a match and a candle, and then finally the room glowed into existence, as if she'd conjured it herself. It was much as I had seen it last, strewn with clothes—evidently the Badger and her Shining Spirit had left in haste. Annie opened the window to dispel the must, admitting the waft from the privy in back and the rumble of Holborn Street beyond.

"Are you hungry?" she asked. "Wait here."

She came back in twenty minutes with some bread and cheese and a meat pie, fetched from a public house, along with a pot of strong ale. We made a picnic of it sitting on the bed, and once we'd finished she brushed crumbs from her lap and raised her eyes to search my face, composing herself into gravity.

"Now," she said, "you must tell me everything that has happened, from the Very Beginning right up to This Moment."

"How much has Janet—?"

"Janet don't tell me much of anything, Will, on the grounds that she considers me a twat. No, you don't need to deny it, cos it's the Truth—that is Exackly what Janet considers—and the Truth is what we must live with. And I say nothing against Janet Friendly, neither, except she can be a towering twat herself."

So I told her. Leastways told her more or less, leaving out some of the more lurid details, and those elements as risked provoking Miss Smollet into such flights of capitalization that she might never return to me again, but rise in ascending spirals like an escaping songbird, through the window and into the night sky beyond, where somewhere far above the choke of London the stars must shine in a sweet clear sky just exactly as they had shone on the first night of Creation.

But I told her of my certainty that Atherton had fitted Meg up for the murder of Uncle Cheese—though why he should revive her afterwards remained a mystery that tormented and perplexed. I hinted at dark Rumours of other killings as well, for motives that remained unclear, describing my clandestine conference with Mr Nuttall the Spavined Clerk. I spoke of Flitty Deakins and the Wreck of Sheldrake and Jemmy Cheese; and last of all I told of my midnight encounter with Master Buttons, when I drew my knife to frighten him and it all went horribly wrong.

When at last I finished, the candle had burned halfway down. Somehow two hours had passed. Miss Smollet sat saucer-eyed, like a child transfixed.

"Oh, Will."

I had bungled the ending of the other tale I'd told her—the tale of my journey to the Midlands. But apparently I had gotten this one right.

"There is one thing I still cannot understand," she said. "Why hate him so much?"

I began to say that I didn't hate Master Buttons—not as you can hate an enemy, cos I never knew the man. I hated what he'd done, that was all.

She shook her head. "Not him—the surgeon. Why do you hate Dionysus Atherton?"

There was confusion in those green eyes, but a kind of penetration too. Miss Annie Smollet was never a fool, no matter what Janet Friendly thought.

So I told her the simplest part of the truth.

"The man is my uncle," I said.

Her eyes saucered again, more spectacularly than ever. "Your *uncle*? The one you told me of? Who won't even admit you exist?"

I was regretting the confession already, and braced myself for escalation into opera. But Miss Smollet surprised me. She just shook her head slowly, side to side, in bitter wonderment.

"What he done to me, Will—that was bad enough. To sit there laughing, that night with the Wolves, when he should of been protecting me instead. But *this…*"

She shook her head again. "There are Villains in this world, Will. There are Contemptible Hounds—and then there is Mr Dionysus Atherton. And one of these days, p'raps, I shall Say So To His Face."

"Just stay away from him," I said quickly. An unsettling thought—what Annie Smollet might be capable of doing in a moment of Dramatic Impulse. "I have no actual proof—not yet. But I believe that he is dangerous."

"Oh, yes," she exclaimed. "If just one quarter of what you suspect is true—one thirty-second of one twelfth, Will—then Mr Dionysus Atherton is the most Perilous man in London!"

She had risen and moved to the window, where she stood in an actorly way. But when she turned back, both feet remained rooted in the world. "And now you'll forget all about him," she said firmly. "No, listen to me, Will Starling—cos you'll do what I say. You'll put that Villain from your mind, and you'll go away tomorrow. You'll go away, and stay away, 'til you've Cleared Your Name."

Leastways I'd thought we had both feet in the world. Evidently one of them had lifted, just a little, and was tending in the direction of Drury Lane. She had already decided how this story would play itself out.

"You will clear your name, Will, and then Come Back."

Cos of course that's what would happen, if we were upon the stage. A Young Hero might very well expect to be in such a plight as currently faced Wm Starling, by the climax of Act One — indeed, it would not be much of a play if he weren't. And matters would no doubt seem graver still by the end of Act Two, with our hero shackled in Durance Vile, awaiting execution in the morning. But Act Three could be relied upon to produce an Unexpected Witness and a Stunning Revelation, which would almost certainly concern the Hero's ancestry, and never mind being the bastard nephew of a surgeon. He would be revealed as the heir to a title and a vast estate, shipwrecked at birth and given up for lost, now miraculously restored to the bosom of his *et cetera*.

There is a danger in going too often to the theatre. And Janet Friendly had been right about my Annie, to a point. She did not necessarily see life as it was — she saw potential roles for herself to play, and she was working herself up into one of them this moment: poised by the window in the tiny room in Holborn, illuminated by a single candle, treading on a discarded item of Badger wrapping. She was working up The Girl Who Would Wait, However Long It Took — which of course had more to do with the splendour of the role than with her actual feelings for Wm Starling. I know that for a certainty, looking back; I suspect I knew it on that evening too.

Yet there was something lovely, underneath. Annie Smollet might not go deep, but the shallows were genuinely sweet. I actually knew a good deal about her by now—more than I'm sure she realized. Things she'd hinted at, or tossed off without thinking. The only child of a pretty, fading mother; a succession of rooms and a succession of stepfathers, some of them less kind than others. One of them, at least, who would loom in a doorway in the night, reeking of brandy. A child, once trusting, shrinking back—and here she was at one-and-twenty. Open-hearted and lovely—never you mind the teeth—and against all odds, still prodigiously gifted with Hope.

"You will sail to France," she was saying. "You will make your way to Paris, Will, and take a room there. And you will write to me—letters, Will, that I will Cherish Always. You will describe your life in Paris in these letters, and I will keep them tied with a ribbon."

She spoke with such shining conviction that I could see it. Here in the little room in Holborn, I could almost for a space of time believe it.

"It will be a garret room, Will—a stone room, very cold in winter, and I fear there will be rats. But Will, it will be *Paris*. And you will become a pothecary. This comes to me, Will —I see it just as clearly as I see your own dear face. You're so clever about potions, and will win renown as a healer."

Returning from the window, she sat beside me on the bed.

"I will think of you Very Often," she vowed.

We were sitting quite close now, a foot apart. My hand, on the blanket between us, brushed hers. Her face in the candlelight was half turned away.

"Perhaps you will think of me too," said Miss Smollet.

A wisp of her hair had worked loose, and hung over her forehead; I took the liberty of brushing it away. There was colour in her cheek, and her lips were slightly parted.

"I expect it would be all right, you know," she said. "If you wanted to very much."

I'd been with girls before. I mention this now, in case it crosses your mind to wonder. Various of them, and no more than half requiring payment — cos how could a young man be alive in London, and not? A city with vitality burbling right up through the loins, with bosoms burgeoning and rakes a-roister everywhere you looked. But never like that night in Holborn.

Arching over me in the candlelight, her breasts swaying as she leaned. The first cascading moment, and a look on her face of pure beatitude. Somewhere in the midst of it all, someone whispered: "I love you." She laughed happily to hear it, low in her throat. "He says it right out loud," she said. Then folding herself down over me, her hair tumbling across my face and her breasts pressing, soft and firm.

Afterwards we lay curled beneath the blanket. "You'll take the mail-coach in the morning," she said, "to Plymouth. Then you'll set sail on the very first tide."

At length I slept a little, even though you don't want to sleep on the best night of your life — cos that's what it was, you know. The joyfullest night I ever had, before or since. The joyfullest I ever will have too, this side of Judgement —considering as I'm down to the very last few, and none of them looking better than graveyard-grim. I knew it too, that nothing could ever be better than this night, even as I was living it.

When I woke up, she was sitting at the window. The candle had gone out long since, but I could make out the shape of her in the first hint of dawn. Wrapped in a blanket, her hair hanging round her shoulders.

"Annie?"

"Your uncle." Her voice was rich with indignation. "And to think I ever imagined having Feelings for that man!"

"Come back into bed."

She did, and after a time I must have drifted into sleep again with Annie in my arms, cos in the darkness there was someone else in the room. On the *escritoire* by the window sat my friend Danny Littlejohn, legs dangling.

"Have you told her the truth, Long Will?" he said, looking down on the two of us together. "Go ahead—tell her what you done. And then watch her hike her skirts and run from you, boyo, just as fast as them slim white trotters will flash."

He winked then, and grinned, in that sly larking way of his.

"Family tendencies—that's what it is. Taking after that uncle of yours."

When I woke again it was mid-morning. Sunlight flooding through the window, and birdsong rising from below.

I was alone in the room. My Annie was gone.

16

That very night Dionysus Atherton burst into a night-house in the Seven Dials with Odenkirk sloping at his heels, acting upon information that Meg Nancarrow was within. But the woman turned out to be a castaway Irish draggle-tail, her glims no more shot with blood than any other nymph's might be who was reeking and bloated with blue ruin. Shoving her away from him, Atherton flung a fistful of coins at the other whores, crying: "There are a hundred guineas more—mark me!—one hundred gold guineas for information that leads me to her!"

Leaving the night-house he went to a low tavern by the river, where he sat brooding with a bottle of pale until the light of dawn crept upon him. He had the look of a Crusoe, shipwrecked into obsession.

*

In the light of the same morning a woman sits by the fountain in Trafalgar Square. The square is already teeming, despite the early hour, with crowds and street-hawkers and mendicants. An old man sells wooden toy rattles, and beyond him a shabby black sailor walks with an actual scale model of Lord Nelson's ship *Victory* on top of his head, which seems with each loose-limbed step to dip and then rise again upon a turbulent sea of shoulders and hats.

The woman by the fountain wears a drab grey dress and a shawl pulled over her head like a cowl. She sits hunched with weariness, as if she were a Pilgrim on a journey grown far too onerous already. A man is with her, a great shambling man in rags, who has fetched food and drink — a meat pie from a stall, and a bowl of saloop — but no, she says, she thinks she is not hungry today. Her voice is like something dragged behind a cart.

She tilts her head to smile up at him, but as the shawl falls back she winces against the sunlight.

"Too bright," she whispers.

Her neck is cricked a little to one side, like the stem of a flower that has been bent. The great shambling man draws her closer, in order that his bulk may block the glare.

At that exact moment another woman is crossing Trafalgar Square, towards them. This fact is asserted in certain strange Epistles that were shortly to appear, published in the Correspondence columns of newspapers, to the growing astonishment of the Metropolis. Flitty Deakins had been to a pothecary's shop in a lane behind St Martin's Street, from which she is now returning with a small brown bottle. Hurrying past the fountain, she sees the woman in grey lift her head, two eyes like red coals burning out from the folds of the shawl.

Miss Deakins has seen the face of Belial, leering in at her through the window of her chamber. But the face of Belial is as nothing at all, to this. Miss Deakins recoils with a cry, cos she once saw this face in life, when the woman came to Crutched Friars in the company of Doomsday Men. And now here is the face again in death — oh, surely it is Death itself, staring out of those terrible red eyes? — cos Meg Nancarrow was hanged outside Newgate two weeks ago.

Miss Deakins gives another cry, of terror and wonderment commingled, and drops in holy dread upon her knees.

*

This is where the tale grows wild. We will need dark nights and thunderstorms as we proceed; howling winds, and hearts afire with unspeakable yearnings. But upon my oath and upon my soul: what I am telling you is true. Even when I am left clutching after the facts, like poor Jemmy Cheese flailing blindly as Thoughts in darkness bat-wing past, I am sure beyond all certainty that the Tale itself is true, in the way that tales both great and tattered may point towards a distant Truth that the light of a thousand facts cannot illuminate — and never mind the frailty of the teller.

Besides, what reason would I have to lie? What could I hope to gain, in my position?

It is late on a Saturday night as I write these words, the 16th of November. Today dawned blustery and raw, and the night is bitter, even here cocooned in stone walls three feet thick. There will be a service for the Condemned tomorrow in Newgate Chapel, and the coffin for company, to aid in banishing trivial thoughts and fostering a spirit of true contrition. Appeals are still in process, though I have no reason to hope, Time being measured now in quarter-inches of the candle stub and the muffled tolling of St Paul's bell.

It concentrates the mind most wonderfully—so Sam Johnson famously said—when a man knows he is to be hanged in a fortnight. From this I conclude that even the great Sam Johnson could be a twat. In my own experience, the prospect does very little to concentrate the mind, and does much instead to panic it into wild chaotic flight, like a school of minnows beneath the long black sliding shadow of a pike. It brings on night-terrors that extend right through the light of day and on into a worse night still, as a fortnight shrivels to a week and the last remaining hours drop one by one like dying petals.

But there are blessings that remain to me, and I must count them. I have gloves and paper and ink that has not yet frozen. I am wearing two coats at this very minute, and a blanket round my shoulders for good measure, and there is no icicle at all at the end of my nose, leastways not yet. And I have a task. I write as swiftly as I can, and have asked my friends to see this narrative through if I am unable to finish. They are good friends—God knows, they are better than I deserve—and have given their word.

Yes, I'm afraid it has become that sort of tale.

Onward.

The Wreck of Tom Sheldrake had not yet sunk, but the icy waters were rising. He would appear from time to time at his chambers, but with each manifestation he grew thinner and less substantial. This I was able to ascertain through young Barnaby's nosing and prying, since naturally I could no longer risk going to the Inns of Court myself, or even trying again to contact his Spavined Clerk.

Hollow-eyed and unshaven, the Wreck would drift into the outer chamber where Mr Nuttall still laboured at his desk, the pile of papers — now sadly dwindled — at either elbow. With a rictus of greeting, Sheldrake would flinch into his inner room, where he would be heard pacing and muttering. Sometimes he gave out a spectral wail, as if he were become the ghost of his own still-living self, here to haunt Tom Sheldrake down into the grave. Then suddenly he would burst out again, looking wildly round and demanding to know if anyone had come looking for him. Once he had a razor in his hand, and a thin ruby line beading his throat. This alarmed Mr Nuttall considerably; no shaver misses his chin by several inches, however much he is distracted.

He had tried then to ask after Sheldrake's health, but it was no use; the Wreck retreated into his chamber, slamming the door. There came dolorous mussitations and the telltale sounds of furniture scraping, from which the Clerk deduced that the entrance was being barricaded. This caused him much disquiet, as he had seen such a change before: an aged relation, his mother, who had grown convinced that the neighbours were massing in secret for an assault upon the house. The family had in the end been forced to lock her in an attic, from which she had periodically escaped, with high determination and shouts of wrath, to do battle.

Abruptly Sheldrake disappeared. For several days he was not seen at all, and Mr Nuttall began to entertain dire visions: Sheldrake hanging pear-shaped from a rafter, or bobbing blue and ghastly to the surface of the Thames. Then just as suddenly he was back. It was evening, just at twilight, and the Clerk—down to the last three papers in his pile—looked up to see his employer in the doorway. Tom Sheldrake was paste-white and reeking of gin, and so wasted by lack of eating that he seemed scarcely more than sticks and twine. But he wore a new frock coat with a bright canary weskit, and a gay sprig of flowers in his lapel.

"Mr Sheldrake," exclaimed Mr Nuttall. "Has something happened?"

"*Happened*?" Tom exclaimed. "Everything has happened, Nuttall—life, death. All of London is happening, at this instant. The world is happening—look out the window! We are spinning at this minute, sir, upon our axis. We are hurtling through Infinity. And you ask, has something *happened*?"

"I meant, are you quite well?"

"I am very well indeed," said the Wreck of Tom.

This seemed unlikely to be true, and Mr Nuttall hesitated. "I was about to close up for the night, sir," he said. "Would you have me stay instead?"

"I would have you do as you will," said Sheldrake. He leaned in closer as he said it, as if imparting words of great significance. "Do you understand what I'm saying to you? I am saying, *do as you will*."

His breath was as foul as a three-day corpse; his eyes glittered with desperate animation.

Thus he appeared as he returned to his home that night. He had rooms near King's Cross, where he lived alone, with a cat called Roger for company. I almost liked that in him, when I found it out. It is more difficult to despise a man with a cat called Roger.

This was on a Tuesday, 4th June. I had remained inside the room at Holborn for two whole days after awakening to find Annie Smollet gone. The first I spent in anxious expectation, thinking at each minute to hear her footsteps tripping up the stairs. But she didn't come, not that day nor the next, which I spent curled alone upon the bed with the Black Dog pacing on the landing and birdsong and birdstink rising from below. Finally I roused myself, and leaving a woebegone note slipped lorn and lightheaded down the stairs — two days it had been, with nothing to eat — into the mutter and snarl of Holborn. With the darkness, I was waiting outside Sheldrake's lodgings.

He came along the Gray's Inn Road, his bull's-eye bobbing him into view. As he passed, I stepped swiftly in behind him.

"You sent word you wanted to see me, Mr Sheldrake?"

He turned with a gasp, and I let him see my knife.

"Just so's you know, Mr Sheldrake — if this is a trick or a trap, I'll kill you. Nothing personal — not a threat — just a solemn promise. Play me false and you are a dead man."

He gave a laugh at that, a high queer sound of strangled mirth. "Dead, sir? Whatever can you mean by *dead*? I think you must be more specific, sir, for death" — a finger to the side of his nose, and a ghastly wink — "death is not entirely what it was. Indeed, I think you may be behind the times."

His eyes had grown to unnerving size as his phiz had hollowed around them, just as Barnaby had reported. Cadaver-gusts of breath. But a fine new weskit as well, and a sprig of flowers — I thought of descriptions I had read, of condemned men in the olden days being trundled to Tyburn Tree on a cart, bung-eyed with drinking but determined to exit game, making desperate merriment with the crowds along the way.

"Is she alive?" I demanded.

"She, sir?"

"Meg Nancarrow."

"Ah. Then that depends, sir. That very much depends."

"On?"

"On what you mean, sir, by *alive*."

I raised my knife, touching the tip to his throat. His apple bobbed.

"You went looking for me, Mr Sheldrake. You said I'd been *summoned*. If you know where she is, then tell me now."

He offered the rictus of a rakish smile, essaying the gay sad dog of old.

"Indeed, sir. Come, sir. Sheldrake's just the fellow. Follow Tom."

We crossed the Gray's Inn Road and continued, heading west. I was still half thinking this must be a trap, and that round each corner a clutch of Constables would be waiting, cudgels in hand. But there was no one, except the usual night-walkers of London.

"It wasn't murder," I said, matching his shambling pace. "The actor—Buttons. They're saying I murdered him, but it wasn't that."

I don't know why it seemed so important that he understand this. But I might have saved my breath.

"No murder done." A ghastly wink. "Quite right. No blood upon my good friend Starling's hands—no stain upon those soft white daddles."

"I said it was never *deliberate*."

"And why those hands should be unstained—of all the hands in London, sir, drenched in gore up to the elbows—why these alone should be so pure, remains a mystery. But there you have it. There it is. Starling's hands are white."

He touched his finger once more to the side of his nose, raising the bull's-eye with the other hand as he did so. His face was a jack-o-lantern in the glare.

Sheldrake quickened his pace now, angling west and south, until we crossed Kingsway and reached Great Russell Street.

"Where are we going?" I demanded.

But I'd guessed the answer already.

The Holy Land—St Giles Rookery. A vast squalid labyrinth, stretching out from Great Russell Street in the north, to the church of St Giles to the south. St Giles-in-the-Fields—cos there had been green fields here once, and trees, instead of bricks and filth. Tonight fires flickered here and there in the tangle of courts and narrow stinking streets, with human creatures crouching round them. Derelict buildings jumbling together, leaning drunkenly shoulder to shoulder like old reprobates conspiring. Streams of filth down the middle of the lanes, in place of the brooks that trickled in that long ago unfallen time, with lumps of excrement instead of smooth wet stones. And now I had no further fear of Constables. No Officer of the Law would set foot here, not by night — nor even by daylight, without a dozen more to back him, armed with muskets. And even if they did, what could they hope to accomplish? Anyone familiar with these narrow streets could disappear in half a minute; and if you truly knew the Holy Land, you didn't need to use the streets at all. You'd know of doorways connecting one building to the next, and passageways leading from cellar to cellar. You could disappear into darkness and never come back out into the light of day — by your own choice, or by someone else's. You could rot in one of those cellars until you were nothing but bones and fungus, and no one who knew you would ever be the wiser.

The Wreck of Sheldrake tacked onward, hurrying down one alleyway and turning into another, forging through the murk and stench while unseen eyes peered from the darkness and shadows in the night retracted into holes upon our passing. We stopped at last in a slanting doorway, somewhere in the dark heart of the maze. A sliver of yellow moon peered down askance, then slid behind the clouds again. I had tried as best I could to keep track of all our twists and doublings back, bracing myself against the prospect that I might have to extricate myself at speed from this dreadful labyrinth. And Christ only knows what Minotaur awaited.

Sheldrake's mood had changed. "Lily-white hands," he

said, looking bitterly down at me. "Of all the daddles in London."

"Is this where she stays?"

"I did not ask to see these things," he burst out suddenly, "or know them!" On his face was the same look of anguish as on that afternoon in St Mary-le-Bow churchyard, when he'd flung himself into Bob Eldritch's open grave. "Did I ask Meg Nancarrow to hang? No. Did I ask Bob Eldritch to choke himself to death? No, sir—never in life! I say again, sir; I did not. I did not wish it—I was not consulted!"

Then he lurched through the doorway and into the blackness within. I followed.

Stench, and uncanny stillness, and the certainty that eyes were watching: this was my first impression, and it was overwhelming. There might be three floors and two dozen separate rooms in such a dwelling, each room housing six—or ten—or twenty. From time to time a teetering building would give a terminal lurch and then collapse right there on top of itself, with Ragged Souls scrambling like ants to escape out the windows. There must be dozens in the house with us now, but in that moment you didn't hear a single one of them. In the glancing light of Sheldrake's lantern, I glimpsed for an instant a twisted boy peering down from a half-landing above us, with a parent—or some larger Imp—behind him. Then they were gone, and I followed Sheldrake onto some rickety stairs leading down into deeper darkness.

There was no railing, and often enough there was no step either, the boards having long since rotted through, or else been ripped up for firewood. Houses in the Holy Land were all consumed by fire in the end, but this mainly happened piece by piece. The winters here were the worst in London, with January knifing through broken windows patched with paper and rags. Twice I missed my step and nearly fell headlong, until we reached a level passageway. It was dank and strait, with puddles of water—I prefer to think it was water—gathering underfoot. Rats scuttled in the blackness behind us, and the Wreck of Sheldrake sloped on. There was a branching passageway, and another doorway.

Sheldrake stopped.

"Through there," he said, pointing. "Down."

I waited for him to lead the way. But Sheldrake was shying back now, like a horse that has balked with white rolling eyes at a gate and will not be driven one foot farther, not if you were to beat him 'til he bled.

"No," he said. "Not Tom." His voice had broken, with his nerve. "I've done what was demanded of me. No more. She wants to see *you*."

He bolted, taking his light.

More steps led down, at my feet—but the blackness below was not quite complete. A faint garish glow seeped upwards from the depths. I took one very deep breath indeed, and started down into the void. Six impossible steps descending to a half-landing, and the seep of light grew more discernible with each one, as if it would rise like Stygian waters to my ankles, and then my knees. A turn to the left at the landing, and then six more steps, down into a space that surely squatted just atop Signor Dante's First Circle. Or beneath it.

A cellar room, stinking of smoke and human creatures, with a ceiling so low that even Your Wery Umble could scarce stand upright. A table with candles burning, and three or four ragged forms crouched round it, at a meal. White faces stared up at me, and then a tatter of black shifted out of the shadows in the furthest corner of the room. An ancient woman, as angular and sharp as Atropos the Third Sister snipping thread.

Except she wasn't old at all. I saw that now, as my eyes began to adjust to the stinging gloom. Her face was pinched but scarcely lined, and her own eyes were bright with laudanum and zeal.

"Mr Starling is here. A friend is come. We rejoice," said Flitty Deakins.

She had been staying until very recently at a Servants' Lurk—a low lodging-house inhabited by domestic servants who had lost their place. There were such dosses throughout London, full of wretches who had been dismissed for thievery and bad character, and who now devoted their waking hours to plotting robberies—and worse—in retribution. This particular Lurk was near Charing Cross; Miss Deakins had returned there after I had left her on the morning of the hanging.

This much I would piece together afterwards. But in that first moment, as you'll understand, Miss Phyllida Deakins's domestic arrangements were not foremost in my mind.

"Where is she?" I cried. "Is she alive? Can I see her?"

Miss Deakins cocked her head. "I don't know, Mr Starling. Can you?"

I looked round urgenttly. But it was just Miss Deakins and I in this reeking cellar, and the ragged shapes round the table, and not one of them was Meg Nancarrow.

"I fear I am being mischievous with our friend," said Flitty, addressing herself to the others. "Poor Mr Starling." Her face had crinkled itself into amusement. "I fear I have always been mischievous. My father would say this, Mr Starling. 'Phyllida is my own dear darling girl,' he would say, 'but I fear there is mischief in her.' My father was a man of the cloth, a clergyman in Devon. Did you know that?"

"I want to see Meg."

"I was the youngest, Mr Starling, and the apple of his eye. I would walk with him across the fields to visit his parishioners, and I was a good girl, good as gold. They would all tell you so; they were unanimous in this opinion. 'But I fear my Phyllida is mischievous,' my father would say, 'and I pray this will not bring her to a Reckoning.' This was a great preoccupation of my father's, Mr Starling — the Reckoning that awaits each one of us, at the appointed hour."

"*I want to see Meg!*"

It came out of me as a shout, shatteringly loud in the cellar room. Miss Deakins flinched back a little, her mad eyes squinting like a cat's recoiling in distaste.

I turned at the sound of creaking on the stairs. More ragged shapes had come down behind me — two or three of them, blocking the way. It occurred to me then that I couldn't get out, unless they should allow it. I expect the same thought occurred to Flitty Deakins; she smiled just a little.

"Who are these people?" I asked her.

"Friends," she said.

"Of yours?"

"Of hers. We're all friends of hers. That's why we're here."

"Is Meg alive?" I asked again.

"Unlike the children who went into the surgeon's stable at Crutched Friars."

"You know this for a fact?"

"I saw them go in. I have no doubt what was done."

And here she stood: the eye-witness I had been seeking. Black tatters and poppy-bright glims.

"Experimentation, Mr Starling. Taking them to the brink of death, and beyond. Seeing how far they could go, and still come back. Animals first, and then children. Beggars and waifs, whom no one would miss. An old man went in once, and a girl — some dolly-mop who'd been fished from the Thames. She'd flung herself in, I believe, for some such reason as dolly-mops have when they do these things. Odenkirk had her over his shoulder — she'd drowned herself, but she wasn't quite dead. I saw that, because she opened her eyes — right at the very end, before the stable door closed behind them."

She had grown so thin that I wondered if she was eating still at all, or whether all her sustenance now was opium and milk. And in dwindling she had somehow hardened, as if some alchemical process had begun, distilling her down to the purest essence of herself. She was more Flitty Deakins than she had ever been before—and more purely, profoundly mad.

That's when the first true doubt began to lodge.

"I was to be next, Mr Starling. They'd have done for me next, if I hadn't escaped. My father's own dear darling girl, on that table of theirs..."

"I need to see her, Miss Deakins. I need to see Meg Nancarrow."

The ravings trailed into silence. The hooding of mad eyes.

"You need proof that she's alive. Is that what you're saying?"

"I'm saying I want to see her."

"And she wants to see you too, Mr Starling—that's why we brought you here. She's grateful for what you tried to do, and she hopes you might do more. But first we need proof from you."

"Proof of what?"

"Proof that you are with us, Mr Starling. To the uttermost extremity."

An Epistle
to the Londoners

As printed in The London Record
5th June, 1816

There was a terrible surging in her head, she said to me, as if her vital essence were being forced upwards by the weight of her body against the rope. Her skull was swollen to grotesque size and must surely burst, like the belly of a lamb with bloat. This went on, she said, unbearably. At last there was an explosion of light, and in that awful radiance she saw the angel.

"But this was no Nursery-Angel," she said to me, "for children. Nor like unto the two bright angels, Phyllida, that once were in your care."

No, this was a great and terrible Being, taller than trees. In its hand was a flaming sword, and in its visage she glimpsed an overwhelming Truth.

"What Truth was revealed to you?" I asked.

The Great Question that was never put to Lazarus. He rose up and walked — so the Gospels say — but Lazarus never spoke a word of where he had been, or what he had seen. Nothing to cause his sisters hope, or horror; no word to oppress his friends with mortal trembling, or to gladden their poor hearts with joy.

She replied: "I saw that we are free."

We were standing on the rooftop as she spoke. There is a rooftop where she will stand with her Jemmy in the grey of twilight, the setting sun behind them and their shadows stretching out across London.

"We are free," said Meg Nancarrow, "and may do as we will. And O!—there will come such a Reckoning."

17

I had picked up a copy of the newspaper at a street stall near Covent Garden, not long after dawn. The Epistle was printed at the bottom of a page, where it had already been discovered by a group of dishevelled Corinthians lurching home from a spree. One of them declaimed aloud while his friends clustered about him in hooting incredulity.

There are moments in life when you blunder in front of a window, or a glass. And you stop to see the most risible creature peering back at you, in some hideous weskit that he has mistaken for the very pineapple of fashion, a kingsman slung round his neck like the banner of his pretentions, with an expression of adolescent constipation that is clearly intended as Deep Sagacity. You blink — you may even for an instant begin to laugh — until the realization dawns: *this is a reflection, and it is mine.* You've draped yourself in Rainbow togs and swaddled yourself in fervent convictions, but in that reflection there you stand: exposed in the knobbly white nakedness of your own absurdity.

The Epistle of Flitty Deakins was my looking-glass that morning. The anxious chitter of voices started up again, somewhere deep in the rat-holes of the mind. The rats had begun to skitter as I stood in that cellar the night before, listening to her raving about dead children and poor doomed dolly-mops. Even in that ghastly cellar, I knew what I was hearing: a tale told by a madwoman. And here in the light of a London dawn, could a sane man continue to believe it?

Far better men than Your Wery Umble have lost their faith in God, and been left quite shattered. I think, looking back, that I had plunged into my own crisis of faith that morning in Covent Garden. A different manner of crisis, but no less devastating.

I'd begun to question my certainties about the Devil. And without the Devil, then how are we to proceed? Where are we to point, and blame? There is no one and nothing left to loathe, except the reflection staring back.

Last night had not gone well, even after I'd climbed back out of that cellar and stumbled my way free of the Holy Land, back to the nethersken by the Docks where I'd stayed before going to Holborn with my Annie. Arriving at the head of the street, I stopped myself just in time as I glimpsed two forms in the darkness on the corner nearest the house, revealed in hints and flashes by the light of their lanterns. A red-haired man in a scarlet weskit, and a smaller and darker companion, impersonating as best they could two fellows merely out to take the air on a rain-drizzling night down by the London Docks, and finding this stinking corner to their liking.

Bow Street Runners.

I didn't recognize this particular pair, but I was familiar with the species—Special Constables hired by Bow Street Magistrates' Court, to run down malefactors. Someone at the nethersken had recognized me, and sold me.

I shrank back into the night before being spotted, but it had been a near-run thing, and now the hounds were clearly closing in. I slunk all night through an oily rain, arriving in Covent Garden as the market was stirring to life. That's where I picked up the newspaper, and read the Epistle. Afterwards I slunk some more, and then I went to Milford Lane.

The rain had stopped an hour or two before, the cobbles still slippery as the morning sun rose above the houses. A shopkeeper was outside taking down his shutters, and a boy threw a knotted rag for a flop-eared puppy while the city rumbled to life beyond.

Janet came out the door of her shop, stopping dead as she saw me and then looking round in dread, as if half-expecting Constables to loom along the rooftops. "You can't be here," she hissed, seizing my arm and dragging me to a more sheltered spot in the mouth of an alley. "They come again last evening—Bow Street Runners. Asking after you, up and down the lane. Will, they're watching this place."

The man at his shutters was looking our way—the way you do, idly wondering if something is the matter, when voices are urgent and phizogs tight. The little boy had glanced over too, partway through retrieving the knotted rag.

"Is she here?" I asked.

"La Smollet, you mean? No. I ent seen her, nor heard from her neither, since the night I met you at St Sepulchre's."

Here was news that brought fresh desolation — and an ever-deepening unease.

"D'you know where she might go?" I asked.

"No."

"Would you tell me if you did?"

"Yes! Will, I swear to you — she left three nights ago, and she ent come back. I can't abide the giddy twat, but I wouldn't lie to a friend."

"D'you think she's all right?"

"The fuck should I know how she is?"

But she saw the expression in my face. Softening, she touched my arm.

"Will, I'd lay good odds that she's fine — I'd wager the shop on it. And cos why? Cos coming out all right is what La Smollet does. Whatever happens, her sort will end on their feet. At the end of the world, it'll be the rats left standing — and Annie Smollet. And I say this in tolerance, if not exactly love."

A cart had lurched into the lane, here to collect night-soil. Another door or two had opened; more glims were sidelonging our way. The little boy and his puppy stared with the slack-jawed idiot interest that runs in both species.

"If she comes — if you hear from her — tell her I'm leaving."

I meant it this time.

"Say goodbye for me. Can you do that?"

"Yes, I can do that, you fucking eejit."

It came upon me, then: this was really the last time I'd ever see Janet Friendly. That long scowling face and those red hands balled into fists. I discovered the thought made me remarkably sad.

The puppy had commenced barking at us, dancing back and forth.

"Will, *go*."

And I went. I turned and hurried from Milford Lane, after a last shoulder-snotting clutch against Janet, and a last despairing gaze towards Annie's window.

But I couldn't leave London — not quite yet. Not 'til I had paid one final call.

18

They would go out riding in the fields together, my uncle and his sister — so one of the Lichfield neighbours had recollected. My uncle had a spirited chestnut gelding, sixteen hands at the shoulders; she would ride behind on a fat white pony.

One afternoon she took a fall. She had been six or seven years old at the time, the neighbour recollected; her brother had been nine or ten. She had tried to follow when he jumped his horse over a fallen log, cos she would follow him in anything. But the pony had stumbled and pitched her headlong; she lay horribly, like a discarded doll.

Dionysus had carried her home in his arms, gasping through the wood in horror that he had killed her. But she came round after a time, and was laid out on a settee when the waddling red physician arrived. She wailed when he touched her twisted ankle, and her brother rose in impetuous rage — Dionysus, nine or ten years old, driving the physician from the house and announcing that he would care for Emily himself. This he did, swaddling the ankle with a blanket she'd had since infancy and sitting up with her the whole first night. She was on her feet three days later, and by the end of a week was hobbling gamely along the lane with her brother's arm for support. A wisp of a girl in a white muslin dress, and her brother beside her: tall and golden and shining with solicitude.

On the November night that would follow ten years later, when she was driven weeping from the house, her brother would stand as white as marble, and as hard.

The rounding of her shoulder as she turned. The spatter of footsteps receding and the tatter of a wind-wrenched cloak, ghosting into insubstantiality.

She had haunted him ever since.

*

By mid-morning the heat was rising. It would be the first truly warm day of the year, a foretaste of August days to come, when the sun would bake through the brown haze and London would ripen with the stench of itself. Offal and livestock and rotting vegetables; on such days the backstreets might just as well be open sewers, and churchyards could gag you at a hundred paces. There'd been hotter days in the Peninsula, of course — any number of them. I can recollect marches through hundred-degree heat and humidity, and sweltering field hospitals where sweat ran in rivers down Mr Comrie's face and you expected that limbs must commence to rot before the bone had been sawed halfways through. I have no doubt that Hell will be hotter yet, when I get there. Still, for sheer stinking wretchedness, you have to admire a summer's day in London.

Bloody Bill Starling might dispute that—Bloody Bill my pirate father, with tales of whose exploits I had regaled the wide-eyed foundlings at Lamb's Conduit Fields. Bloody Bill had after all sailed round the Horn of Africa, and straight along the Equator, for weeks. *Now that was heat*, he would surely have said, had he been here present at this moment. Heat was drifting becalmed for two months in the middle of the South China Sea, as Bill had done in the Year '03, with the barrels bone-dry and tongues swollen black. Heat was the Black Hole of Calcutta, of which Bill might on some subsequent day tell a tale that would congeal the blood. But Bill would not be weighing in just at the moment—nor indeed at any other moment I could think of—cos of course Bloody Bill Starling did not exist.

Janet Friendly had taxed me with that, in our days at the Foundling Hospital.

"You pure made the fucker up," she accused me one afternoon by the railings. "But you just can't admit it, can you? And you know why?"

"No, I don't—but I expect I will in two more seconds," I flung back, "cos I expect Miss Janet Know-All is about to tell me."

"You can't admit it, you eejit, becos you've started to fucking believe it. You've told it so often, you've forgotten you made it up in the first place."

I cursed her roundly for that, earning myself a drubbing in return, after which I went off in the highest of dudgeons, vowing I would never speak to Janet Friendly again—and didn't, for nearly a month. But the worst of it was, she was right. I'd invented Bloody Bill. I'd cobbled him together from bits and scraps, and then I'd told his tale so eagerly and so often that it came to seem not just plausible, but real.

Leaving Milford Lane, I made my way east through the winding lanes along the river. Gradually I found myself tending up Ludgate Hill and past St Paul's Cathedral, where I bought a cake from a coster-stall and forced down three mouthfuls before tossing it aside. The pigeons were upon it instantly, like Death House sparrows upon a choice bit of finger—or like Bow Street Runners upon a fugitive. Then I found that I was moving farther east, slipping into the jostle along Cheapside and then tending southwards again, crossing Gracechurch Street and veering onto Fenchurch Street.

And just as All Hallows' clock began to strike ten o'clock, I arrived at my uncle's door in Crutched Friars. The housekeeper came to answer my knock.

"Ohhhhhh," gasped Missus Tolliver. Her eyes flew wide.

She'd seen me before, of course. She knew who I was. And she'd read the newspapers.

"I need to see him," I said.

"Ooooooh."

This latter vowel may have been a question: *Who?* But I think it was mainly the quavering astonishment of a house-keeper who discovers a ragged murderer on her doorstep, at ten o'clock of a morning in June. I forced past her, into the house.

The entrance hall seemed smaller when you saw it in the light of day. A paltry thing when compared against the hall that Atherton imagined for himself in Mayfair, once he stood alongside Mr Astley Cooper as the leading surgeon in London. His entrance hall in Mayfair would be airy and wide, with oil paintings upon the walls and a marble staircase sweeping upwards. There would be an entire wing for his Specimens, and a drawing room done in the Egyptian style, which remained very fashionable this season — had been so ever since Napoleon's campaign upon the Nile — and a vast dining room where Atherton would host Lords and Baronets, men with grouse moors in Yorkshire and five thousand a year, and all the foremost men of Science and the Arts. Lord Byron himself would no doubt attend, if ever he returned from the Continent. Edmund Kean would yearn to come, but would not be invited.

Here at Crutched Friars, the stairs lay directly ahead, a narrow corridor leading past them. There were two closed doors; a third at the end was half open.

"Stop!" cried Missus Tolliver.

It was a modest library: two bookcases, an armchair and a fire, with a second door — closed — leading through to the rear of the house. Atherton had been sitting at a cluttered desk in the corner, scribbling at some papers. Now he turned at the commotion, and rose.

Missus Tolliver huffed up behind me. "'Ee barged in, Mr Atherton! I couldn't stop 'im!"

"Tell her to leave us," I said. "Tell her don't go running to fetch Odenkirk — or the Law."

"It's all right, Missus Tolliver," he said. "Go upstairs. My nephew is welcome here."

Missus Tolliver's mouth rounded into another O. "Your *nephew*, Mr Atherton?"

"That is what I said."

The first time he'd ever acknowledged me. Missus Tolliver flabbergasted several more vowels, then withdrew in confusion, leaving us alone.

The curtains were drawn against the morning sun; my uncle stood in shadow. "There's a price upon your head," he said. "Did you know?"

In fact I'd discovered it just this morning, noted in the newspapers. Fifty guineas, placed upon my nob the night previous by no less a personage than Edmund Kean. Apparently Kean when just a lad had once seen Master Buttons on the stage, and now felt a great sense of grief, arising from his generous spirit. It seemed Kean often felt generous towards his rivals, especially once they'd been reduced to shit-arsed ruination — or better yet, murdered dead in alleyways — so he'd raised a subscription and posted a reward, which would doubtless win him considerable approval. With luck it might also attract larger audiences to his *Bertram*.

"So you're a murderer," said my uncle.

"They're saying worse of you."

"We have something in common, it seems."

"We have nothing in common."

"What do you want?"

He looked dreadful: haggard and unshaven, his shirt hanging open to the navel. I guessed the rumours had been very close to the truth — he had been searching through the sinks of the Metropolis ever since Meg's disappearance,

413

ranging down dark passageways and wrenching through doors. He had the look of a man who has not slept in many nights, and begins to think he may never sleep again.

"I want to hear it from your mouth," I said. "What you did."

"I told them that night at Guy's Hospital. You were present."

"I want the truth."

"The Truth." There was wormwood in his voice. "As little a thing as that."

There was a decanter of brandy on a table in the corner, and a tumbler. His hands were unsteady as he reached and poured, and swallowed half at a gulp. "The truth is, I saw an opportunity."

"To be rid of a woman who could put your head in a noose?"

"No," he said. "To confound them."

"And that is all?"

He actually barked a laugh.

"*All?* To resurrect a woman, hanged before half of London —and you say, 'that is *all*?' We have differing perspectives, you and I."

The drink seemed to settle him, a little. He drained the rest of the tumbler.

"I saw a chance to make my name," he said. "And to save an innocent woman."

"You knew her to be innocent?"

"So I believed. So I decided, at any rate."

"So you bribed the Sheriff and brought her here, and left her lying for five hours. To make very sure she was dead."

"Did I?"

"That's what you told them at Guy's."

414

"Well," he said. "Perhaps I exaggerated."

A haggard half-smile, sly and sheepish at once. The smirk of a boy caught out in some clever transgression.

"I am just a bit of a showman, nephew. You've noted that? Perhaps I can never quite resist. So perhaps it was a little less time that passed."

What *had* he been like, as a boy? The queer thought came suddenly, catching me off my guard. The tall golden youth who could smile like this—just exactly like this, rueful but winning—and disarm each one of them at every turn. The cleverest boy in all of Lichfield.

"And what did you expect they'd do," I demanded, "when you trotted Meg out? That night at Guy's—if she hadn't escaped. What did you actually expect?"

"I expected them to *see*. All those narrow eyes, and narrow minds…"

"And what about the Law? They'd have took her and hung her all over again."

He dismissed this impatiently. "They'd have done no such thing."

"Why the Devil not?"

"Because I would not have stood for it."

"She was—*is*—a convicted murderess. She signed a confession."

"And I had sworn to protect her. I had given her my Word."

"Listen to yourself," I cried, incredulous. "Can you actually believe—?"

"Christ! Can no one understand what I've done? Five hours —two hours—what does it matter? The woman was dead—I gave her life. I did that, Will. *I did it*. I called to a woman on the farthest shore, and she came back to me!"

It burst out in genuine passion: grievance and rage and —above all else—confusion. All his hopes and golden prospects, dashed to flinders. Here he stood in the rubble, bewildered and desperately injured, and it came creeping upon me then, the vertiginous realization: I could learn to pity him. Worse than that—oh, ten times worse—I could begin to *understand* him.

The boy who was always first, from the day he was born. The first to propose some daring exploit, and the first to prove he could carry it off. The foremost boy in every room, with a charm that burgeoned before him like the bow-surge of a frigate. You'd forgive him almost anything, a boy like that—his small transgressions winked at, and the large ones overwhelmed by the swell of his passage. Capsized like skiffs that blunder across a tall ship's course; left broken and scattered and bobbing in its wake. A father whose buttons burst with pride, and a dark little sister who worshipped him. It must shape a man, to begin his life that way. It must free him, in ways he can hardly guess. And limit him.

His back was to me again. He poured another drink and threw it back.

"I need to find her, Will," he said. Using my Christian name, for the second time. "I only wanted to help her, and now I must find her again. I have posted a reward."

"I know that. A hundred guineas."

"Is that why you're here—for the money?"

"I don't know where she is. But I've seen Flitty Deakins."

He looked round quickly, not quite comprehending.

"She claims she's seen Meg," I told him. "That letter, in the newspaper..."

And he realized.

"Those ravings? That's Phyllida Deakins?"

Cos of course he'd read the Epistle, the same as half of London had by now. This morning's newspaper was amongst the pages strewn across the desk top.

"The deranged, drug-addled bitch."

"Yes," I said. "Poor Miss Deakins."

That gaze — impossibly blue — held mine. There was an uncanny depth in those eyes, a fathomless quality like the sky itself, or the sea, as if you could search forever without finding the bottom. I had the unsettling sense of being searched in return, as if my phizog was a code that could be deciphered, and after a moment Atherton's own face altered.

"You're right, of course," he said. "Poor Miss Deakins. We must keep that in mind."

There was something that Keats had said about him once, a curious observation. "It's as if he doesn't *know*," Keats had said. "Watch him, sometimes — the way he watches others. As if he isn't sure how he should respond, until he sees the proper sentiment in someone else's face. Then he can mirror it back to you. As if he's — I hardly know how to frame it — a child in all his feelings, just learning to toddle his first steps. Such remarkable development of the intellect, and yet so stunted in the heart."

"Poor Miss Deakins," Atherton repeated now, shaking his head. "Some buck ruined her — that was the story, when

Odenkirk sought it out. Down in Devonshire, where she'd been hired as a governess. It was another servant, I suppose —or one of the sons of the house. A child was conceived, and of course Miss Deakins was turned out. God knows what happened to the child, though I think we can guess. Born in a ditch by the side of the road, and left there. Her own family disowned her."

"Just like my mother's family."

He flinched, and stood quite still.

"Who was my father?" I asked him then.

"She would never say."

"Not even to you?"

"I turned my back on her, along with the rest."

And it cost him something to say that—to admit the truth, and to me of all people. I watched his face harrow at the memory, and I knew it had cost him dearly.

"Have you ever seen an image?" he asked.

"Of my mother? No. How could I?"

He gestured.

"On the desk."

Amidst the shamble of papers, there were other objects. A round polished stone and a cat's skull for a paperweight; an old scalpel used for sharpening quills, and an overturned inkpot, bleeding its last onto green blotting-paper. Nooks with correspondence tucked in, and in one of them an oval cameo. The portrait of a dark-haired girl of sixteen or seventeen years—younger than I was myself, as I stood gazing down at her. Dark hair and dark eyes, and an elfin loveliness. My own face smiling back at me, but transformed into something beautiful.

"You see it, of course," said my uncle. "The resemblance."

The room was beginning to swelter now, with the rising heat of the day outside. The heavy green curtains were open just a crack; a yellow line of sunlight stole through them, bisecting the Turkey rug upon the floor. The cameo was cool as ivory in my palm.

"She'd have come for you, Will. If she'd lived, she'd have fetched you out of the Foundling Hospital, as soon as she was able. She'd have cherished you, and giving you up would have riven her heart. I knew my sister, better than anyone in this world, and that is what she would have done."

More silence, then. The sound of two men breathing.

"I could have helped her," he said. "If only I'd found her in time. Even a day or two, before the fever had taken such hold. I had no training then, not in those days. But even so I would not have let the fever take her. I am convinced of that."

He spoke with such dogged conviction that I swear I could see the great Truth taking form. A citadel that he had built up in the telling, stone by stone, mortar and pestle, each day since my mother had slipped away from him forever.

"I'd have saved her—as I saved Meg Nancarrow. I gave back Meg Nancarrow's life, however much she hates me for it now."

"You need to get out of London," I said then. "They're planning to kill you."

And I found myself telling him all of it—what little I knew.

"There's a band of them, in the Holy Land. Flitty Deakins is one. The others are just—I don't truly know what they are." A handful of outcasts, paupers and ragged outlaws, some of them surely as mad as Flitty herself. But they were dangerous. And if Flitty Deakins could be believed, there were more of them every day. "They say they're following Meg Nancarrow, though they won't say where she is. And Christ only knows how far they might go."

"Why are you telling me this?"

"So you can save yourself."

My uncle remained in shadow. It cut him past bearing, to hear how bitterly he was hated. But I believe—I am almost certain—there was wonderment on his face.

"You have done me a kindness," he said. "More than I have ever done for you."

And there we stood, just two men: an uncle and a nephew, separated by a chasm, but bound together by so much else. Bound by all the ties of blood, and aching.

I see myself in this face as well.

There was the thought that came on the moment, unnerving me with its intensity.

I have always seen myself.

"I won't say let bygones be bygones," my uncle said. "I won't insult you like that. But I wish we were not enemies, Will. I wish that of all things."

He extended his hand. God help me, I reached out to take it.

And the side door creaked wide. It opened onto a vestibule, which led in turn to a hallway beyond. Someone was standing, slender and tousled with slumber. A tumble of strawberry hair upon the shoulders of a thin white nightdress. She blinked through the dissipating mists, and then stopped short as she saw Your Wery Umble. Stopped dead in the act of stretching, like a kitten in a patch of sunlight.

"Will," exclaimed Annie Smollet.

19

Garrick had a trick he would perform in parlours. David Garrick, Sam Johnson's great friend, and the foremost actor of his age. This was many years ago, of course — I never saw Garrick myself, nor Sam Johnson neither.

I first came into possession of Sam's dictionary shortly after the Battle of Salamanca in July of the year '12 — a dog-eared copy, much thumbed and stained, given to me by a sweet-faced Geordie sapper with a scholarly inclination, who lay dying by horrid half-inches from a stomach wound. I have it with me at this moment, lying open at my elbow as I sit here at my lucubration — from the Latin *lucubratio*, "study by candlelight; nocturnal study; anything composed by night" — my thanks to you, Sam. I would thumb through the pages in spare moments, scavenging bright bits to try out in speech, and thus gaining a regiment-wide reputation as a curious hybrid, half waif and half parrot. I gained as well the whimsical feeling that Sam and I were old chums and travelling companions, and imagine my wide eyes when I learned that I was — just like Sam himself — from Lichfield, or leastways my forebears were, on one side. When I was there I asked after the house where he had been born, but they looked at me oddly and shrugged.

And listen to me now—rambling like a sad old pantaloon, with time so short and so much still unsaid. You could almost imagine me ravaged with woe, subsiding into tearful reminiscence. You could picture me shackled and despairing, rocking myself forwards and back again, forwards and back.

Garrick. That trick of his.

He would hold himself just out of view behind a doorway. Stepping quickly into the opening he would project some attitude or emotion—joy, love, fear. Then he would disappear from view on the other side of the door, and in an instant reappear, this time projecting another emotion entirely. And not just projecting, but *becoming* it. Back and forth he would go, in and out of the open doorway, all human emotion embodied in quicksilver sequence. Love, jealousy, rage. Back and forth—twenty-five times, thirty, in less than a minute—despair, elation, torpor, resolution. A master of his technique, was old Garrick.

But acting is more than technique. It is feelings too— and Garrick had something intriguing to say about that. A player in the white heat of the moment may be amazed, he said, by the intensity of his own emotion, how the surge of it could come on all of a sudden—and no mere make-believe of feeling, either, but the genuine article. True emotion, kindled by the joy of playing, lifting him like a kite.

Looking back, I've come to think that this is what happened with Annie Smollet. She'd cast herself in a role, that evening she followed Janet Friendly to St Sepulchre's church-yard and found Your Wery Umble standing there. And as she played her part, a great gust of Feelings began to blow. This bore her aloft and swept her down Holborn Street to the room above the bird-fancier's shop, and it never subsided 'til dawn came peeping through the window, bringing the light of Reality with it. Then finally she did what all kites must, and came fluttering softly down. And who can blame a kite for being a kite?

As I say, I came round to this way of thinking long after-wards. I wasn't so philosophical on that morning at my uncle's house, when Annie came through the vestibule door and stammered to see Your Wery Umble. I would like to relate that I drew myself to the uttermost extension of my height, delivering a cool observation that buckled Miss Smollet with shame, and left my uncle riven with the icy knowledge that he had earned a Dreadful Enmity. But I'm afraid this would stretch the truth.

I stood stuttering in distress. I babbled something inco-herent to Annie, and shouted something else at my uncle. Then I turned and fled the house.

I went to an ale-house after that, then to another, and a third, where I maundered for a time and then erupted into bitter denunciations of Mr Dionysus Atherton — calling him traitor and hound — until the other patrons wearied of this and one young fellow loudly invited me to take my mewling elsewhere. He was a butcher's boy, I think — I'd been stumbling in the general direction of Smithfield. I challenged him, as any young man of spirit would do, provided that he were sufficiently drunk and broken-hearted, and an imbecile into the bargain; and I have no doubt that I would have fibbed him senseless, except that a fist came thundering like a coach and four and the world went suddenly sideways in a clatter of tables and stools. I sat in the lane outside for a time after that, staunching the claret that dripped from my nose, and drooped like an expiring tulip.

In due course I was no longer alone. A pair of battered boots stood before me, above which two shins disappeared into breeches too short. These were tied at the waist with a length of twine, and my gaze travelled up a filthy weskit to a familiar hatchet face.

"Bugger me," said young Barnaby, looking elsewhere, "if it ent the fugitive."

It didn't occur to me to be surprised to see him. It had a certain logic, after all, this district being Barnaby's customary haunt. On another afternoon, when Your Wery Umble was more sober and less despairing, it might indeed have seemed just that tiniest bit unlikely — that Barnaby would be the one to come across me, of all the street arabs in Smithfield. It might have crossed my mind to wonder whether Barnaby had in fact been keeping an eye open for Wm Starling, for reasons best known to himself. But not today.

"I need you to deliver a message," I said.

There was a house in Crutched Friars, I told him — a surgeon lived there, named Atherton. A young woman was with him, Miss Smollet.

"Tell her I need to see her. Tonight." Eight o'clock, I said, and named a church, St Alban's in the City Road. "Can you do that?"

Barnaby held out his palm.

"Tell her she must come alone," I said.

I arrived at St Alban's as the bell was striking eight. The church was empty, except for a pair of old women in black, bowed in prayer like penitential rooks, and a Sexton pottering at the back. It smelled of must and piety, as churches do, with a sick-sweet residue from the churchyard beyond. The last rays of twilight slanted through stained glass, and in the dimness dust-motes danced in rainbows.

I hadn't been inside a church for more than a year; not since Danny Littlejohn died. Not that Your Wery Umble had been a great habitué of churches to begin with. I'd been to my share of them on the Peninsula, but they had been converted to field hospitals by the time I got there, with mutilated men for a congregation, and surgeons red with gore standing in for priests. You could say I served five years at that altar, if you were inclined to see it that way, handing up the scalpel and bonesaw in place of the wafer and wine. But I couldn't say it breeds in a boy a spirit of True Religiosity, that sort of a church. The conviction that a Merciful God is gazing down with all His Saints assembled, and that there will one day very soon be archangelic singing in place of shrieks and moans, and that the stench of blood and shit and rot will be lost in the hyacinth waft of the Fields of Heaven. And what happened to Danny left me less convinced than ever that there was any place for Wm Starling in any House of Redemption in all this great wide weeping world.

Still, I'd asked Miss Smollet to meet me in a church tonight. So who knows? Perhaps I had inchoate notions that meeting in a church might yet invoke some crucial Blessing; that Miss Smollet stepping through the door might see the configuration—Wm Starling standing in the nave in an attitude of Patient Suffering, lit by candles and dimly irradiated by the last glow of the dying sun through stained glass—and begin to discern the depth of her folly. And I would say that I did not blame her, not for anything at all; that I had no claim upon her, nor the slightest justification for believing that she had ever been mine in the first place, not even for the span of a single night. I was going to tell her all of this, but in such a way that she would perceive what a Noble Heart stood here Crack'd, and understand in a sudden dazzle of remorse that she had Erred most calamitously, cos she *did* love Wm Starling, and had loved him to distraction all along.

Eight-thirty, and Miss Smollet had not come.

A dying bluebottle beat its head against the stained-glass window beside me. In the glass was an image of St Peter, robed and haloed. You could tell it was Peter by the golden key he held—the key with which he opens Heaven's Gate, as I've no doubt he will on the morning Your Honours arrive.

Eight-forty-five. The penitential rooks had left, as had the Sexton, after lighting candles here and there about the church. I'd done my best to clean myself up before coming, brushing my coat and washing my face at a stand-pipe in the road. I was fragrant as a courting beau, allowing for the residual waft of gin. The drunkenness was ebbing now, and the sick nob-splitter that follows was taking hold.

The clock struck nine, and what had I been thinking? I looked towards the window, and I swear that St Peter himself in stained glass avoided my eye, as a plain gruff fisherman must do when the truth is too awkward to acknowledge.

I am Fond of you, Will. That was the word she would use, if ever she came. *We've been Friends to one another, and I'm so very sorry if you somehow misunderstood . . .*

But she wasn't coming. I knew that now, though I waited for another hour and more, as the last light died behind St Peter and the church was dark in the gutter of candlelight. I left just after ten-thirty.

And now here I stood again, across the street from the house at Crutched Friars.

The night had gone quiet, or at least as quiet as a London night can be. Traffic on the streets beyond, and the mournful baying of a hound, rising and falling nearby. From the stable, perhaps, behind my uncle's house. Dim light glowed behind two or three of the windows; through one of them, a window on the second floor, I suddenly saw — or imagined — a shadow behind the curtains, as of someone passing.

Was she still there?

The window had been left open, against the heat of the day. The curtain stirred with the whisper of a breeze, and in that tiny movement I could almost believe myself certain. Fingers reaching to twitch back the edge of the fabric; a slim form in a white nightdress, and a tumble of strawberry ringlets.

But was she there? And was she alone? Or was she in his arms?

It is the worst rack that ever was devised, and we twist ourselves upon it most exquisitely. You'll know this only too well if you've ever stood outside a lover's house in the blackness, gazing up at a lighted window. And of course you have — admit it. We've all been that dark and malignant imp, if only in our thoughts; banished from the wedding feast and peering from the ring of outer darkness, with suffocating heart and gangrenous imaginings. You'd climb to the window — you truly would, if only in your thoughts. You'd find a trellis, or lizard your way right up the wall, if only to confirm the Very Worst and force yourself to watch it.

And if she was still there, was she somehow in danger?

The most gangrenous imagining of all, and I kept circling back to it. I had all but resolved to pound at the door — to burst through and confront whatever awaited inside, be it Hell itself, or Odenkirk. But in that agony of indecision, I realized something else: I was no longer standing alone. There were shadows behind me — two dark substantialities in the greater darkness of the night. Two silent shapes, one hulking and grim, and the second a wisp beside him.

The red-haired Bow Street Runner and his smaller, darker colleague — that was my first conviction, and it stopped my heart. But it wasn't the Law at all.

"So it *is* you. The surgeon's boy — haunting the darkness," said Meg Nancarrow.

Her dark hair loose and tangled; a shawl clutched round her shoulders. She shivered as the breeze came up, despite the warmth of the night. Jemmy's arm was around her; he drew her close.

"You done what you could for me, Will Starling," she said. "You have my gratitude for that."

Her voice a ragged whisper, and her eyes were pools of blood—exactly as they'd said. The blood vessels had burst, with strangulation. I'd seen the phenomenon before, though never so shockingly. Her neck was cricked to one side, and one corner of her mouth quirked down, the way you see sometimes in those who have suffered convulsive seizures.

"It's true, then," I said, finding my voice. "You're alive."

Cos it's something to stop up the syllables in your throat, believe me. Standing in filtering starlight, with a woman they'd hanged 'til she was dead three weeks ago last Monday.

The shadow of a thin, ironic smile. She reached out her hand.

"Go ahead and touch me. I'm not a ghost."

Bones as frail as a sparrow's. Her face was pinched and grey, as in someone whose pain is constant.

"Is it very bad?" I said to her.

"Don't matter."

Liquid rattled in her breathing, which I liked least of all. It made me suppose that the heart had been overtaxed. Some permanent damage sustained, during the ordeal.

"If I could suggest—a compound of succotrine aloes. Any pothecary will have it. A wine glass full, taken every other morning…"

I trailed away. A remedy against Decline of Life; I had sometimes seen it work to some effect. But my magpied knowledge of potions seemed suddenly laughable.

Jemmy held her closer. It was the first time I had seen him since that day in Dr Paxton's cellar. His eyes were remote, but there was someone behind them, gazing as if from some distant mountaintop.

"It's good she has you," I said to him.

"Yes," said Meg. "I'd be lost."

I think he smiled at that. He made a movement with his mouth. I'd seen this in field hospitals — men who'd suffered traumatick injury to the brain. Some of them would recover, more or less, over time. Some would erupt into sudden rages, out of nothing. I'd never seen one the size of Jemmy Cheese, standing by his Meg.

"What did you see?" I asked her then.

How could I not ask it, after all? A woman who had crossed the River, and come back again — if that's what had truly happened. Except she hadn't come all the way. The current had taken hold before she could reach the shore, and was trying to draw her down.

"When I was dead, you mean?"

A sound like pebbles sliding. Meg had laughed, bleak and brief.

"I saw Atherton's face," she said, "staring."

"Nothing else?"

"I don't claim there's nothing. How would I know that, after all? Just, I never seen it."

A warm wind continued to rise. Meg shivered again.

"You should go to someone for help," I said.

"A doctor, you mean? Or a *surgeon*?" That sound again, of pebbles.

431

I heard myself blurting: "What did he do to you?"

"I couldn't rightly say. It was dark, and then it wasn't. You prob'ly know better yourself—consorting as you do with surgeons. But you're right to ask. What *did* he do to me, and why? I have a right to know."

The liquid of her breathing, and the night wind prowling in the trees. The mournful hound, wherever it was, had fallen silent. She gazed fixedly across at his house.

"Are you going to kill him?" I asked.

"First I need to be certain."

A face in a tangle of wild dark hair, and two eyes as red as blood.

"Miss Deakins would have done it long since. Just judge him, and kill. But that's what they done to me, Will Starling —and I'm better than they are. Whatever else I am, I'm better than them. And I will have the truth before I decide."

*

Odenkirk emerged from the house just at dawn. The time in all the day when the air is soft and London itself smells almost fresh, and a man may yawn and scratch his danglers and feel that there is Hope still stirring in the world, and Promise stretching out before him. The darkness was half-leavened into grey, and he saw me standing in it. Standing alone across the road, staring back at him.

I watched him subside into stillness: glims narrowing to slits, danglers abandoned half-scratched.

"Friend Starling," he said, and sidled closer. "Is there something brings you here?"

"I been waiting for you," I said.

Birds had begun to sing in the eaves along the street. At the end of it a solitary cart rattled through the gloom. Odenkirk sidled two long steps, and then two more. He stood now in the middle of the road, six swift strides and a murderous clutch away. And here we were, just we two: Little Red-Cap and the Wolf.

Little Red-Cap gets eaten. That's the true original ending of the tale—leastways the tale as I heard it at my blue-veined breast in Kent. There'd been another version since, written by two German brothers. I'd heard this from a Prussian cavalry officer in a field hospital, who discoursed upon children's fables while he lay rotting slowly upwards from the left stump. In the telling of the German brothers, he'd said, the wolf ends up dead instead—which was preposterous, it seemed to me. Cos who'd give odds on Little Red-Cap, up against a wolf?

"I am a Gypsy," I said, "come to tell your fortune."

"My fortune?"

"You are a dead man."

I saw then the look that ten thousand pigs had seen, in their final instant upon this earth. Ten thousand pigs and Uncle Cheese, and Little Hollis last of all. I turned and ran for my life.

Odenkirk lunged in pursuit. Down the road, his long strides devouring the distance between us. Oh, he was horribly swift, and in half a moment more he would have me in those hands. Then we were round a corner and into the alley that lay beyond, and Odenkirk slid to a stop as he saw them waiting in ambush: a dozen dark shapes with cudgels, and stone walls rising up on either side.

"You see?" I said. "A dead man."

Odenkirk swore a mighty oath, as villains do upon the stage — or in secluded alleys, near Crutched Friars. He snatched out a cosh he kept concealed, preparing to lay about him, right and left; breaking the heads of every man present, and saving the brainpan of Wm Starling for the last. I expect he might have done it too. Odenkirk was a terrible man.

But not half so terrible as Jemmy Cheese, who rose now in the gloom behind him, like the spectre of Reckoning itself.

20

There was another boy I especially recollect, the night I went out to look for Danny Littlejohn. A raw recruit, this other lad had been, one of the wave who took the shilling after Corporal Bonaparte returned from exile in March of '15, and the whole bloody lunacy started up again. A stone-cutter's son from somewhere in the North, with a red coat two sizes too small and great raw stone-cutter's hands. A spent ball had come trundling along the ground towards him, moving scarcely faster than a man might jog. Without thinking—without knowing—he stuck out one large foot to stop it, the way you'd stop a child's ball bouncing away from a game. It did for him, of course. Spun him sideways and left him to sit in blinking stupefaction, with the leg so bent it was practically torn off. The femoral artery was shredded in the process, and so naturally he bled to death sitting there. He was still half-sitting when I came across him long hours later, with shoulders slumped and head hung low and the whitest phizog on all that chalk-faced field.

Danny Littlejohn was no raw recruit, having fought for more than a year all along the Peninsula. But he'd left in the spring of '14, and that's what somehow made it ten times worse. Set sail on a troop-ship and gone home, with a "Ta-ra, Will—look for me in London when you're done." But then he'd turned around and signed back up. I never understood completely why, and Danny never quite exactly said. I think it hadn't gone as he'd hoped, back home; I've a notion there was not much work, and bad company instead—some matter of thieving, and the long arm of British Justice reaching out. However it was, he came back, and Quatre Bras was the very first action he saw, this second time.

A line had been buckled by French lancers, and was pulling back—so I was told by an old Infantryman who saw Danny fall. "He was just there, beside me," the Infantryman gasped, "and then he weren't." He knew the two of us were particular friends; he'd watched us singing a comical song just the day before, and chuckled gruffly along. It was in a field hospital just at nightfall when he told me this, the old Infantryman having subsequently fallen himself, a ball shattering his shoulder.

As darkness closed I went out to find Danny—just up and left, with men still on tables with legs half hewn and Mr Comrie behind me bellowing for light. I searched all that long dark night, picking through the legions of the dying and the dead, who lay strewn across the battlefield like leaves. But I was going to find my friend, even if I had to sift every fallen leaf in all Creation, and at last—at the end of a thousand others—there he was, still alive, sitting on a hillock against an overturned cart.

"Long Will," he said. "Bugger me, you took your time."

Against all odds he wore that crooked grin, the grin that was purest Danny. His head lolled a little as he sat and his two hands were folded across his belly, just exactly as if I'd found him at his post-prandial ease, belching somnolent satisfaction at his supper.

"Long Will, I b'lieve I may require a surgeon. P'raps you should fetch your friend Mr Comrie. D'you think?

I knelt. "Let me see, Dan."

"I'm afraid I been a bit of a fool," he said, "to end up in this manner."

He tried to laugh a little, but the pain rose up to choke it. His hands clenched upon his belly, as if by dint of careful effort he could hold his guts inside. But they kept slithering out, shiny and coiled, to spite him.

"Oh, Christ, Long Will. Go fetch a surgeon."

But no surgeon on earth could help Danny now, cos you couldn't cut into the abdominal cavity. Corruption was certain if you tried, a worse death than if you'd done nothing at all. And Danny's death would be bad enough as it was — I'd seen that at once, with a certainty that hollowed me inside. Danny's death would be worse than bad, and such deaths could take days.

I held his head and gave him a mouthful of water. He sputtered it down.

"Go now, Long Will — hurry. But first give me something for the pain. You're so clever with the potions, and I don't believe I can stand this anymore."

"I've nothing, Danny."

"Yes you do. I know it."

437

He wept then and cursed me for keeping it all for myself.

"Judas himself would share a potion with his friend," he said. "Judas who's burning in Hell this second. I wouldn't let you suffer so, you bastard. I couldn't bear it."

"Nor can I, Danny," I said. "I can't bear it neither."

I took his nose between my thumb and forefinger, and covered his mouth with my palm.

"I'm so sorry, Dan," I said.

He struggled, of course, though every movement brought fresh agony. He jerked and juddered like a man on a rope at Newgate. His eyes huge and horrified found mine, and I have wondered ever since what he saw in those final moments, as his lungs screamed out and the blood vessels burst: the leer of Old Bones himself, or just his poor friend Will?

Or perhaps did he see — and this was the worst thought of all, and one that only intruded long afterwards — did he see at the last a hard cold glint such as others in their dying had glimpsed in my uncle's eyes? Those who had drowned in the bottomless blue gaze of Dionysus Atherton.

*

They carried Odenkirk back into the Holy Land between them: feet dragging, head lolling, like a man fished out of the Thames. And who would look twice at that, in the glimmering of dawn? Just another merry London buck who'd outdone himself on the ran-tan, and was being taken home by his friends. They slapped him back to consciousness in the cellar, and then commenced to beat him all over again. It was Flitty Deakins who did this, Flitty and some of the others. When

Meg came down the stairs, she was very angry. "We ent animals," she said to them. "We are not wolves." They stopped then, Flitty and the others, falling silent and shame-faced and then shuffling back as Meg came amongst them, followed by Jemmy. I was watching from the shadows as she knelt by Odenkirk, like a mother comforting her great bleeding boy, and asked him for the truth.

He had no fight left in him, and babbled it out through broken yellow teeth. Yes, he said, he'd killed Edward Cheshire, murdered him on my uncle's instructions. He'd helped in the killing of others as well, orphans and strays and derelicts used in medical experiments, just as Flitty had been claiming all along.

Meg was cradling his head now, in her lap. Odenkirk gazed up into her face, imploring her to understand.

"Ned Cheshire knew," he said. "That's why he had to die."

"He'd heard rumours, that's all," said Meg, looking bitter and very tired. "There was rumours about, of Doomsday Men being asked for corpses not quite dead. Rumours is not the same as knowing."

"But Atherton feared that you knew," said Odenkirk. "And then someone called in the Law, when the money-lender's body was recognized. Uncle Cheese, on the Death House table. So a murderer was needed, somebody to take the blame. Someone else had to hang, Miss Meg—and he decided that would be you."

Their voices were low. A great intimacy had begun, between them. She brushed a matted clump of hair from his forehead, and her fingers came away blood-red.

439

"Then why didn't he leave me dead?" she asked. "I was dead, if that's what he wanted. But then he brought me back again."

"Becos he could."

"That's all?"

"A woman hung before all of London? He could never resist a chance like that, to show what he could do. And so he went ahead and done it."

"And afterwards. At the end of all of that, he thought I'd—what—*thank* him?

"He thought you'd love him."

Another voice had said this, from the shadows. My own voice, constricted by a coiling certainty.

They stared towards me, Meg and all the others.

"There was a young woman who died," I said to her. "Choosing you out—then deciding to raise you up—it was all tangled up with making amends, somehow. With making amends to his sister. That's where it all begins."

Meg blinked once, very slowly.

"Beginnings is all very fine," she said. "But what matters is making an end."

Odenkirk had commenced to blubber softly.

"Oh, Miss Meg, he's a dreadful man. A most terrible man, is Dionysus Atherton. He drug me down, but I swear I'm not like him."

"I believe you. Hush."

"And I can help you now. I know where bodies is dug, at Crutched Friars—I know every one, cos I dug them myself. I can show you."

"I believe you've done enough," she said.

"Oh, Miss Meg, I done such deeds. Such horrid deeds I done. Can you forgive me?"

Her left hand supporting his shaggy head, lifting it closer. Those eyes as red as blood, and a soft smile on her haggard face; it hardened.

"No," she said.

His own eyes grew very wide, at that, and his feet began to judder. Meg with her right hand had slipped a knife beneath his ribs and pushed it quick and clean into his heart. Odenkirk gave a last soft exhalation, as of an infant drifting off towards slumber, and was gone.

LETTER FROM
MR DIONYSUS ATHERTON

6th June, 1816

Comrie—

You will forgive the scrawl. I fear we are past the point of penmanship.

By the time this reaches you, I will be gone. The street arab who delivers it may solicit a reply, but don't bother. His name is Barnaby, and he will be trying to extort payment for a note he knows damned well he can't deliver, as I am leaving London directly. I may go abroad, at least until the present to-do passes. Fleeing in the night, with my reputation in tatters and the Fleet Ditch Fury—so I am reliably informed—shrieking for my blood. Such a turn of events, old friend. Such a shock to your quondam school chum—discovering himself less than universally loved. You must imagine him scribbling in heartsick disillusion. Picture a teardrop sparkling in his eye.

But hear this, Comrie. You must understand: the tales they are spreading are lies. I am a healer and a man of Science. I have done nothing that you have not done, or attempted, or leastways wished you dared—you, old friend, and every other surgeon in London. If I am guilty, then so are you. So are all the others. Not one of you has the right to judge.

'You must hear something else, as well: I would have done my duty to the boy. I could have — *would* have — opened my house to him, and my arms, but he would never allow it. He hated me from the very start, old friend — hated me long before he first laid eyes. He looked at me and saw Belial leering back. And what chance did your old school chum ever have, against the Devil?

The War destroyed him, I think; and I think you know that too. War destroyed Will Starling, and you took him there. Perhaps you can make your peace with that knowledge. I hope so, for your sake.

Be well, old friend.

Yours,

Atherton

21

The assault upon Crutched Friars commenced just after nightfall, as was reported in the newspapers. Much of their information came from the one misfortunate servant who was inside when it happened, and who still had the swooning vapours twelve hours later: Missus Tolliver, the housekeeper. She'd gone to bed early with a headache, and was awakened by the sound of a hob-nailed boot kicking down the front door. When asked how she could tell the boot was hob-nailed, Missus Tolliver replied that *you* should have your door kicked in at all hours of the night, and then talk to her about footwear. Hurrying out onto the landing, she discovered that the house had been overrun by shrieking banshees. No, she had not previously seen a banshee, but she knew very well what they shrieked like.

Here Missus Tolliver's account grows patchy, owing to the fact that she flung herself headfirst into a closet with her arms up over her head, on the reliable principle that horrors are best confronted back to front, arse upwards. But accounts from neighbours suggest that some dozen persons entered the house, of rough attire and desperate demeanour, carrying lanterns and cudgels. Leading them was a lumbering slack-faced giant.

They rampaged through the premises, overturning beds and wrenching hangings from the walls, shouting for the surgeon to reveal himself. Others began ripping up floorboards, in search of the Evidence that Odenkirk had sworn was here. When Atherton did not offer himself up, nor mouldering corpses neither, they commenced to smash whatever they might reach, starting with the ghastly room stacked with Specimen jars, the contents of which could be seen the following morning, strewn like blown-up bits on a battlefield. Howling from the house, they kicked open the door of the stable in the back, setting free the creatures within. These turned out not to be Bengal tigers and two-headed apes, as popular rumour had always supposed, but just the usual candidates for anatomical study: rodents and rabbits and moggies and mangy dogs. They were a wretched lot for the most part, skin and bones, but overjoyed to be at liberty, and some of them had considerable spirit left. One elderly German boar-hound took it upon himself to guard the property, as a Prussian gentleman would do, and rising to the occasion bit the first Constable who arrived to investigate.

Storming back into the house, the attackers laid hands on Missus Tolliver and dragged her caterwauling down the stairs, where she was hauled to her knees and found herself facing a female creature all in black, so thin and gaunt that she might have been made of sticks bound together.

"Where is he hiding?" the creature demanded. Two great glazed eyes were blazing.

Missus Tolliver near to died, recognizing who it was.

"Flitty!" she exclaimed. "Miss Deakins—don't you know me? We are friends!"

"We are not," said Flitty Deakins. "And I ask you again: where is Dionysus Atherton?"

"Gone!" cried poor Missus Tolliver. "Gone, Miss Deakins —fled this house. Left half an hour ago, with a few possessions thrown together."

"Gone where?"

"He would not say! Oh, Miss Deakins, as you are a Christian, let me be!"

Flitty Deakins would have done no such thing; Missus Tolliver saw this writ like Judgement on that face. Flitty Deakins would have cut her throat and had her liver afterwards, sliced paper-thin like the famous ham they served at Vauxhall Pleasure Gardens—so thin, they swore, you could read a newspaper through it.

It was commotion from the street that saved her life. A crowd had gathered despite the hour, and a shout went up that the Constables were on their way. The attackers milled in a moment's confusion, then fled out the back door, taking Flitty Deakins with them. She was shrieking for vengeance with each receding step, said Missus Tolliver, who by now had fallen face down again and resumed the proper posture for such moments: arms over the head, haunches to the moon.

I read the accounts in the newspapers myself, days afterwards. Read them at my leisure, having very considerable time on my hands thereafter—nearly six months of it, as events would transpire, in Newgate. But on the evening in question, the evening we stormed Crutched Friars, I was very much preoccupied. While the rest of them had been rampaging after my uncle, I had rushed through the house in desperate search of Miss Smollet instead. Lunging into rooms and shouting out her name, fearing at each turning that I'd find my Annie murdered, or much worse. But she wasn't in the house, nor in the stable neither, cos I searched there next, by the light of a bull's-eye snatched from a fellow marauder. I cast round for a shovel—a pickaxe—something to dig with—the wild fear clutching that she might already be buried. Here beneath the floor, or outside in the garden—mouldering with all the others that Odenkirk had sworn he'd concealed, though we hadn't begun to root them out, not yet.

I found something else instead. In a corner of the stable was a rough wooden door, and a room behind it smelling of mould and rot, with shitten straw strewn across the floor. There was a lantern hanging on a hook, and a work-bench in the corner, on which a skeleton had been most carefully laid out. The bones were brown with boiling, and awaited articulation with wire.

A boy's skeleton, with little twisted legs, and a spine bowed like a barrel hoop.

I howled.

*

I found Barnaby at an ale-house in Smithfield, in the midst of a rabble clustered round a rat-catching ring.

"Tell me where he went!" I cried.

"Where 'oo went?" said Barnaby, slantways.

But he knew very well, cos the sly little bastard had left Crutched Friars earlier that evening with a message to deliver—I'd learned that from Missus Tolliver, before fleeing Crutched Friars myself. The others had scattered, Jemmy and the rest; I'd no idea where they'd gone.

"Atherton!" I cried. "Where is he? *Say it!*"

Presumably he saw pure murder in my face, cos he didn't even ask for money first.

"'Ee's staying at a coaching inn tonight. Leaving London by mail coach first thing tomorrow."

"You know the name of the inn?"

"I b'lieve I 'eard it mentioned."

"Is she with him?"

"The girl?"

"Yes, the girl! Did she go with him, when he left Crutched Friars?"

"She did," said Barnaby. "Most dramatickal she was," he added. "Like a hactress on the stage."

Behind us in the ratting ring, a one-eared terrier named Titus was doing mighty execution upon the vermin, to roars of approval. He'd killed a dozen already, breaking their necks with a lunge and a toss; the corpses lay strewn about him, and the remainder huddled together in a corner. There is doubtless a legend burgeoning this instant, in dark holes where rodents gather: One-Eared Titus Ratsbane, who comes for vermin children who disobey.

"Tell me the name of the coaching inn," I said.

"The White 'Art," said Barnaby. "In Islington."

And looking back, I scarcely know that boy — the Wm Starling who left the ale-house and set off alone towards Islington, with all the deadly resolve of Titus Ratsbane himself. I can watch him in my mind; I look down on him in fearful wonderment.

I found the White Hart by pounding on doors. A tidy gabled building in a rutted yard, with stables to one side for the post-horses, and lamplight glowing dimly within. A candle-point winked into existence at my repeated hammering, and the door was opened at last by a squinting Innkeeper.

"Full," he grunted, peering out. "Got no room."

"Atherton," I said.

"Atherton? Got none of them. No Athertons — no room. Good night."

My foot stopped the door.

"Tall man," I said. "Yellow hair." Cos of course he'd be using another name. "A young woman with him."

This rang a bell for the Innkeeper, and a shilling provoked recollection. A man of that description might possibly be in the taproom.

A low room with benches and heavy wooden tables. A gaping hearth at one end, above which a boar's head glared glassy loathing. Atherton sat by a mullioned window, writing by candlelight. He sat alone, the other guests having long since retired.

He startled to see me in the doorway, bleak as death.

"I've come from Crutched Friars, uncle. I saw Isaac's bones. My friend Isaac Bliss."

Just the two of us, in the guttering light of the single candle. Paintings of hounds and hunters on the walls, and portraits of famous highwaymen staring insolently from the shadows, barkers primed. I had a pistol of my own, purchased at a pawn-shop in Temple Bar with one of Mr Comrie's guineas. Atherton had begun to rise; now he froze.

"Will, what the Devil are you doing? Put it down."

"Experiments on the living, uncle. Finding the point of death, and trying to bring them back. Yes? And how long did it take my friend Isaac to die?"

"Isaac was dead when he came to my house."

"You're a liar. Odenkirk confessed it all, before Meg killed him. A rehearsal for reviving Meg—is that what Isaac was to you? Was he *practice*, uncle? And how hard did he die?"

"Odenkirk is dead?"

"I don't care about Odenkirk!"

But evidently Atherton did. He hadn't known about the killing, and it shook him.

"Christ Jesus," he said.

He was haunted now, and hunted. And I seemed to glimpse someone else gazing back at me, someone strange and familiar all at once, in the shadows and lineaments of that stricken face.

"No," he said. "No, Will—you won't kill me."

I cocked the hammer.

"You'd murder your own father?"

The world stopped then, and everything in it.

The ghostly lines of my own face, tracing themselves through his, like the shadow of a palimpsest emerging. And I have known this, haven't I? In some dark instinctual part of me, in some foetid hole where rodents writhe, I have known it from the start.

And it seems to me that I can watch him now — look down from my Newgate eyrie upon Will Starling, the one who went to the White Hart Inn that night. Watch him blink his glims in stunned incomprehension, and take one tottering half-step back, like a prize-fighter who has taken a good old English peg to the liver from Tom Cribb himself. Cos it takes an instant to be felt, a blow that terrible. It freezes a man first, leaves him paralyzed and gasping, before the agony rises on white-capped waves of nausea and the bottom falls out of the universe. I can hear myself stammer a furious denial, even as the certainty takes hold.

It is the truth. Yes, of course it is. He is monstrous — and I am his — and I have known this all along. I am tainted with him, and everything that is in him. The world is foul with the both of us.

Candlelight flickered over Atherton's face, and shadow. A reflex of purest guilt — something furtive and unutterably ashamed. And then the beginnings — oh, God damn him — of a smile. A small defiant creeping smirk, both loathsome and self-loathing. The cleverest boy in Lichfield, and a small dark sister sobbing.

I fired.

Atherton lurched backwards, clutching at his shoulder. Hit, but not killed. I snatched then for my knife, as a woman's voice cried out in Capital Letters.

"Help—O, Help!—O, Villainy!"

Annie Smollet had come down the stairs. I glimpsed her, framed in an attitude of operatic horror, as through the chaos I was aware of something else: the thunder of footsteps without, and something the size of a bullock bursting through the door. It would reveal itself to be a red-haired Bow Street Runner, with a smaller darker colleague on his heels. They had come in fearful haste, so I would afterwards learn, acting upon intelligence that the fugitive Starling would be here. In the moment I knew only shouts and blows and a fearful weight crushing down upon me, and another glimpse of Annie Smollet as she rushed to support the wounded Atherton.

And outside the door, someone capered all this while. The urchin Barnaby, madcap in his triumph.

"Pay up!" he was crying. "Pay up, you fuckers—fifty guineas on 'is nob, and every one of them is mine!"

A FURTHER EPISTLE
TO THE LONDONERS

As Printed in The London Record
11*th June,* 1816

He thinks to himself: *I have outrun the Reckoning.* He is deluded. A Reckoning waits like a green-eyed man in a turban, its teeth filed to pencil-points. It will come at him out of the darkness, shrieking like fifty gibbons. And it will come upon others of his kind, for he is worst, but not unique. London is lousy with such men; it wriggles and it crawls.

I say to you: such men are an abomination.

Suffer them not to live.

22

It was Flitty in those last wild days, driving them on to disaster. I can't say that for a certainty, cos I wasn't there present in the flesh. I was locked up instead in Newgate Prison, where I'd been dragged straight from Islington by my two friends the Bow Street Runners, and now awaited trial for the murder of Master Buttons. But it only stands to reason.

Flitty had been Bedlam-mad from the start, and in Meg she'd found a pole-star for her delusion. That's how it was, I think, more or less—cos who can say for a certainty what takes place in any mind, least of all the mind of one as deranged as poor Phyllida Deakins, with grief and laudanum and self-loathing. She'd invented in the Risen Meg someone who could grant her absolution—I'm convinced that was the nub of it. Someone to tell her: "Be free henceforward, and do exactly as you will." Meg herself never had a plan, beyond settling scores with those as had wronged her worst; it was never more than personal with Meg. But Flitty's rage was of the more exalted kind, that species of Holy Rage that howls out against sinners and sinning, and kindles great purifying bonfires.

So now Flitty Deakins had taken up the torch — and they were bound to follow someone, the rabble that had gathered round Meg in St Giles Rookery. Half-mad paupers and muttering vagrants — petty criminals with towering grievances — all that tag, rag, and bobtail of the lunatick and lost, drawn by a licence to smash and a mob to do it with. And as Meg began to dwindle and fail, it was Flitty who exhorted them onward.

It began with a surgeon from St Bart's, set upon and drubbed half to death in Smithfield. Another surgeon was chased down the Borough High Street in broad light of day, and then came attacks upon private schools of anatomy, three in a single night. Two in Southwark, and a third in St James Street: doors kicked in, a Porter maimed, the premises set ablaze. The fire in St James Street spread to houses on either side — good London burghers, fleeing in their nightshirts — and that's what did it. Attacks on surgeons might be winked at; they might even be enjoyed, if the surgeon were sufficiently soprano as he shrieked himself down the High Street. And one maimed Porter more or less does not signify very much, in the vast clockwork of the universe. But the destruction of property — the burning of homes in a respectable district of London, where values were substantial, and rising — that was different. That was Anarchy.

Two dozen Constables led the way into the Holy Land, backed by Infantry. They marched left-right with bayonets fixed, as the denizens scuttled and stones and bottles rained down. They had with them an informer who knew the Rookery maze, and knew moreover which house Meg's people were hiding in. When they failed to come out at the first shout, two volleys were fired, tearing through rotted walls and the bits of rag that were stuffed in the windows. Their Captain ordered the charge, and they kicked through the front door, where Jemmy Cheese awaited.

Meg had been hit in the second volley — so it appears, from all reports. She was down, and Jemmy was stooping to lift her as the Lobsters thundered in. With a roar he rose at them. Seizing the first man, he broke him — just like that. Cracked his spine and slung him aside, then turned upon the others, fists like cannonballs. Cos this was not that long-ago night in the churchyard, where Jemmy had gone down meek and guilty. This was Meg lying crumpled in a widening pool of red, and Jemmy was going to kill the whole British Army.

He might have done it too. He would surely have killed another several, since they could only come at him one by one, through the single doorway. Others were blazing through the windows now, musket-fire like muslin fabric ripping, pop-pop-pop. There was a ball in his shoulder, and another in his thigh, which only made him rage more fiercely.

Except now the building was on fire.

It could have been an accident — a candle knocked over in the confusion. A blue tongue licking the edge of a tattered curtain, and then — before anyone had time to think — a surge of flame and a belch of smoke and dry rotted wood going up with a whoosh. But I think Flitty Deakins set the fire deliberately. No one knows this for a fact, and no one ever will, not with poor Flitty as she is now, chained to a wall in Bedlam

Hospital and spitting out curses on Dionysus Atherton. But I'm sure of it, based on what she was seen to do as the flames rose up, and what she was heard to moan as they dragged her out of the wreckage afterwards, charred and raving like a witch only half burnt at Smithfield. I'd practically stake my life—assuming that I had a life worth staking.

Flitty had seen Meg fall, looking down from a landing. She'd seen Jemmy rush to her, and heard the shouted orders from outside, so she snatched up a coal-oil lamp and dashed it against a pile of rags in the corner. She snatched up another and set fire to a room on the second floor, splashing the oil like a priestess gone wild as ragged shapes scrambled out the door. They saw her then from below, the Sodgers and Constables in the street—saw her leaning out of the window above them, with smoke billowing about her and the crackle and shimmer of flames rising, shrieking at them like the lunatick she was and calling upon Michael Archangelus to swoop down with his sword. But there was method in it too, cos she'd sown confusion. She'd caused a distraction and bought time for the others—for Meg and Jemmy, most of all.

Jemmy had picked Meg up in his arms—"cradling her like a injured kitten," one of the Lobsters would say afterwards. Several of them saw this, though the house was already filling with smoke, and two or three of them glimpsed him lunging up the stairs. But they were forced back by the heat and smoke, and stumbled choking into the street, where there was shouting and milling and bellows for buckets of water. That was the fear, all of a sudden—those tinderbox houses all jumbled together. A fire could rip through the Holy Land

and rage out right across London. And that's when Jemmy was seen on the roof, with the smoke rising about him and Meg still cradled in his arms. A shout went up, and one of the Lobsters fired off a shot, which took Jemmy clean in the throat and killed him.

The Lobster was afterwards certain of that. A man named Davies, a coal miner's son from Carmarthen. He had bad feelings, he said, about killing a man in such a manner—shooting him down on a rooftop, and not on a battlefield. But he was sure that the ball brought Jemmy down; he saw Jemmy stagger, and topple. There was another man who later claimed something different—that Jemmy had not gone down at all, but had stumbled and then recovered. Through the smoke, he claimed, he had seen Jemmy leaping onto the next rooftop, still clutching Meg in his arms. If this was true, then Jemmy might very well have leapt to a farther rooftop still, so close were all the buildings together, and clambered in through a window to hide somewhere 'til darkness fell.

But of course that's not what happened. Jemmy was shot down by Infantryman Davies, and died on that rooftop with Meg in his arms, even if their bodies could not be identified the next day when Constables dug through the rubble. There was nothing so surprising in that, considering the intensity of the blaze, though naturally the most fanciful rumours were soon spreading. Someone claimed to have seen two figures rising straight up into the haze of the London sky, which opened to swallow them. There were sightings afterwards in Glasgow and Liverpool, and a curious story about a farmer's wife in Essex who found two vagrants: a hulking man who never spoke and a strange dark-haired woman with blood-shot eyes, hiding in a shepherd's hut. They were both considerably injured, though alive, and the farmer's wife offered to fetch them a bit of food. When she returned, the hut was empty. They were gone.

23

That same night, there is someone else in Tom Sheldrake's bedchamber. He knows it the instant he gasps himself awake, bolting upright.

"Roger?" he whispers, hoping against hope.

It is not the cat.

In filtering moonlight the curtain shivers. The window has been opened. Clutching the bedsheets tightly to his throat, Tom Sheldrake discerns the pungent waft of wood smoke. A dark shape smoulders at the foot of the bed.

"Roger!"

This time it is not a question. It is a desperate cry to his feline companion, who might yet against all odds come screeching through the chamber door, fang and claw and fury, to the defence of his best friend in life.

No such luck. Roger is at this moment in the parlour, balled and quivering under a sofa.

Tom Sheldrake sits rigid.

The shape at the foot of the bed is a man, burned almost beyond recognition. Charred black, his white eyes bulging like eggs.

"A candied plum," he says, bitterly.

"Bob!" cries Sheldrake. "Poor Bob—dear Bob—my friend!"

And so it has come at last. Through the fog of panic and last evening's brandy fumes, Sheldrake understands that the Reckoning has arrived. It sits on a wooden chair, reeking like a smoke-house and sparking at the extremities. Bob's left foot sputters back into flame; with a muttered curse he stamps it out.

"A candied plum," he repeats.

"An accident!"

"Down my gullet."

Tom Sheldrake moans.

"Dear Bob—*dead* Bob. Oh, tell me how it is, to be dead?"

"It is grand, Tom," says Bob, still stamping. "We gather in moonlit churchyards, and marvel that we waited so long to die."

"Do you truly?" cries Sheldrake, clutching at this straw.

Bob boggle-eyes him sidelong with infinite contempt, and Tom shrivels.

"Oh, Bob," he says, and moans again. "I am hateful, old friend. I am foul."

"Yes," Bob agrees. "You are."

"But tell me there is some hope of redemption. Say there is always hope, old friend. As long as we live, there is always hope, and some sliver of light in the Darkness beyond."

Bob Eldritch does not reply. There is the faintest hiss of dissipating smoke as his left foot is finally extinguished. He straightens.

Something icy is clutching round Sheldrake's heart. "Bob?" he whispers. "Old friend? What do you propose to do?"

The chair scrapes as Bob rises. There is the sense of a greater shadow rising with him, as deep and voracious as the Past itself. Tom Sheldrake would shriek, if he could.

When he regains his senses, the chamber is crepuscular with dawn. No trace of Bob Eldritch, save a lingering waft of woodsmoke. But there is something on the seat of the chair.

A length of rope, coiling like a serpent.

24

Annie Smollet came one afternoon to visit me in Newgate. This was in early August, some while before the trial took place, there having been delays. I wasn't sure she'd come at all, considering the way things had ended between us — but here she was. She had broken with Atherton, by this point. "I Hate Him," she assured me, in fine flashing spirit. "I hated him from the beginning, Will. Except I forgot for a few weeks, on account of my Tender Heart."

As far as I could ever determine, she had gone to Crutched Friars on that fateful day in June with half-formed intentions of berating Atherton for his treatment of his nephew, with an eye to brokering a tearful reconciliation between the surgeon and Your Wery Umble Narrator, which would have been a fine accomplishment indeed and worthy of celebration upon the stage. But Dionysus Atherton was a devilish handsome man — she'd thought so from that very first night, when she'd floated on his arm into the Coal Hole — and furthermore a man who might still be seen as Rising, despite recent backslidings of a lamentable nature. And one thing — as things do — led to another.

Now she was back in London again, living once more above the bird-fancier's shop with the Badger, who had endured a run of rum luck with gentlemen. Annie herself had met a man who might offer a leading role in a play, about which she was Exceedingly Hopeful. I couldn't help but feel happy for her, after a fashion.

She was also the one who told me the sad tale of how Tom Sheldrake had come to the end of his earthly career. She had learned about it from Mrs Sibthorpe, who as it turned out knew poor Sheldrake's housekeeper, who had found him hanging from a rafter in his bedchamber, stone dead with his eyes staring horridly. There was a note in his weskit pocket, imploring forgiveness from the family of Bob Eldritch and requesting someone to look after his cat. It was all Most Doleful Indeed, but Annie drew comfort from knowing that the poor gentleman was now At Peace. She drew even greater comfort from thinking that Bob Eldritch had Found Peace Also — as most clearly he must have done, since there had been no further sightings of him anywhere in London, which was a Great Relief to All Concerned.

She described all of this to me through the double grille in the Press Yard. Your Wery Umble stood shackled on the wrong side, the din of Newgate howling at his back. My Annie was more lovely than ever, in a blue summer frock and bonnet. Like an emissary from a magic realm that lay far beyond the prison walls, which cast long shadows even in mid-afternoon.

My Annie, I just wrote. Well, she had been, hadn't she? She had indeed been mine, leastways for a sweet infinitesimal blink of Eternity. I have lately tallied up my nights in this world and have determined that Your Wery Umble will have existed for 7,387 of them in total, once all is said and done — counting the present night, right now, as I'm scribbling these words. The present night, and the last of them. And Miss Annie Smollet was entirely mine for one. So: 0.0135 per cent My Annie, rounded off.

"And I believe something else as well," she was saying to me, earnestly. "I believe that at the last there is a White Light shining, and into this White Light we are Gathered. Becos that is how it happens, Will, for the likes of poor Mr Sheldrake and for Bob Eldritch and for all of us — for me and for you and for every soul now living. I believe it, Will, becos it is True. And you must Hold Fast to that Truth, no matter what Lies Ahead in the Days to Come."

She spoke with wonderful conviction — though you can never be really sure, with an actress. And she stretched her hand out most yearningly through the bars, before letting it fall tragically short, which was a most affecting thing for her to have done.

"Such larks we had, didn't we, Will? Such lovely larks, the two of us."

My Annie left soon afterwards, in a glimmer of brave tears, promising she would come again.

She didn't.

The deep bell of St Paul's has just struck three. Five hours remain — but I am almost done telling you this tale. My candle stub has two inches left, and will last until light filters in. I have ink enough, and paper.

On we go.

The trial when it came was a foregone conclusion. Mr Comrie had somehow retained an excellent barrister, a man with a measured stride and a voice like a church organ, which played entire arpeggios on my behalf — but there was never any point. The black cap was out before you knew it, and there was Your Wery Umble, condemned.

Mr Comrie has come nearly every day since to visit, and Janet Friendly too. There have been long delays, due to wrangling and appeals for mercy, but the two of them have never flagged. Often they've come together, Janet holding his arm as they cross the Press Yard. Taller than he is, with her red face ruddier than ever now that November is here — as ungainly a pair as ever warmed a cockle. I said so yesterday, which caused Mr Comrie to grow quite pink, and inspired Janet to offer me such a clout, if I would oblige her by stepping closer to the bars, that my teeth would rattle like peas in a metal bucket. But when they left she took his arm again.

This afternoon, when they left for the final time, she was blubbering openly. Gobbets of snot and great gulping sobs, which was very hard to bear. Mr Comrie lingered. I gave the pages I had already written to the Keeper, who stood in the space between the two grilles that separated us. He eyed them suspiciously, but passed them on; I don't think Mr Comrie had been expecting quite so many.

"There'll be more," I told him. "I'll finish tonight. The Ordinary says he'll give them to you."

He nodded.

"I'm setting it down," I said. "All of it, from the beginning. I want it to be known, what he did."

Mr Comrie nodded again, his mouth clamped clam-shell tight. He was blinking furiously; the cold wind was in his face, which evidently made his eyes water, and caused him to mistrust his voice.

My own voice was set on betraying me now, and came out queer and breaking. "Mr Comrie? I don't know if I can do this, tomorrow morning."

"Yes, you can," he said huskily. "I'll be thaire. Look at me, as long as you can. We'll see this through, the two of us, together."

*

The Revd Dr Cotton came to see me afterwards. A florid man in late middle age, much concerned for the state of my soul. He asked was I prepared now to confess, and I told him yes I was. He murmured lugubrious relief to hear it, and quickly set out paper and quill, urging me to speak my confession aloud while he transcribed.

"I killed Danny Littlejohn," I said.

He stopped in his scratching. "Who?"

"My best friend. He was fuller of life than anyone I ever

knew, and I took it away. I thought I was doing it for the best, but Christ only knows if that's true, and Danny died hating me — that's what matters, and surely I deserve whatever is to come. That is my Last Dying Confession, before God. Get what you can for it, from the broadsheets."

*

My father came to see me last of all.

He'd returned to London after the fire, there being no danger now to keep him away, though Flitty Deakins was still shrieking her threats. She was — she remains — chained to a wall in Bedlam Hospital, vowing to emanate from that dreadful tomb and bring Judgement upon Dionysus Atherton. She will rise, she says, at the hour he least expects, and at this hour such a Reckoning will come as will make the devils themselves cry out in consternation. But my father was hardly disconcerted by poor Flitty. He had returned to his work at Guy's Hospital, and was hinting that he would soon publish the true account of his experiment. He was still more infamous than celebrated — but then infamy is accounted no mean achievement, in this Age of ours. Infamy has a cachet of its own. And there exists no actual proof that would convict him — cos who would believe Flitty Deakins? Or William Starling, either?

He came to Newgate just at twilight. The last rays of the sun were dying, and a gnawing cold had settled.

"I regret to see it come to this," he said. "I would not have wished it."

He had been drinking, but was himself again: such was my first impression, looking through the double grille. He stood slouched, hands in pockets, looking about him like a man who had a thousand better places to be, and would proceed to one of them directly. He had that gleam about him, as of old.

"Will you come tomorrow morning?" I asked.

"No."

"No timepiece?"

"Do not be grotesque."

"No last blessing upon your departing child?"

"This was not my doing. You brought this upon yourself."

"It was *all* your doing."

Silence between us, and the scrape of dried leaves across paving stones. The wind was rising; a storm was coming on. The Turnkey stood nearby, hunched against it.

When you saw my father more closely, you realized: there had been a change, after all. He seemed coarser, and somehow diminished, as if you'd surprised an actor backstage after the performance, and saw that the splendid costume was tawdry and cheap, and the actor himself beneath the paint much older than you'd supposed. The blue eyes would not quite settle and there was a hint of scarlet spiderwebbing on his cheeks.

I felt a terrible weariness, and a desperation.

"Tell me the truth," I said. "I just want to hear you admit it."

"Meg Nancarrow was dead, beyond all doubt. She was dead, and I brought her back. I succeeded. That is the truth—whether anyone else will believe it, or no."

"No. The truth about the others."

"Others?"

"The others you killed. Say it out loud. A last request from a dying son."

The sky behind him was darkening into black. His face was dark as well as he leaned in closer to the bars, and his voice was low and hard.

"Edward Cheshire is dead. So is Meg, and Little Hollis, and Odenkirk. There are no witnesses — no blood-drenched hands — no bodies. So I cannot guess what 'others' you might mean."

The shadow of a thin cold smile. He straightened, as if to leave.

"Father."

The word hung between us like a corpse from a gibbet.

"At least say you lied about that one thing," I said.

He stood in silence for a considerable moment. The cold wind continued to rise.

"You are your mother's child," he said at last, "entirely. I see her in you — she is there in every lineament and gesture. I see nothing of myself at all."

The final words he ever spoke to me. I watched as he moved away, into the gathering night. Despite everything, I felt a lifting, then.

I called out to him, one last time.

"Atherton."

He stopped, but did not look back.

"Tell them I smiled."

Epilogue

London, 1841

Comrie here.

A quarter-century has passed since the events described above. I am an old man now, or nearly so, though my Janet would doubtless put it differently. She would assure you that I was an old man to begin with, at least in my thinking of myself, and have finally acquired the aches and the rheums and the white hairs to suit. I have occasional pains as well, in my chest and arm, and scant breath remaining after walking up a flight of stairs. This exasperates the grandson, who does not stop running until he drops in a heap, and I confess to finding it an exasperation myself. As a surgeon, I also understand what it means.

Let me be clear: I do not complain. But it has seemed to me that I should begin to tie up loose ends, at the end of a long and untidy career, and one of these has been to put in order the pile of papers that William left me. I'd promised him I would do so, but somehow I kept setting it aside for another day. You know how it is; life intervenes, and there hasn't seemed an urgency 'til now. You know how that is too. Time seems all but limitless, until it isn't.

But I've done it, finally — as you'll know already, having read this far. It remains for me to add the last few pages.

I will be brief. I was never a man for the syllables, as William has told you, and besides I am tired. It is late, past ten o'clock, and I am writing these words by lamplight in my surgery, at our house in Tavistock Street. An entire house these days, with a son and his burgeoning brood living with us. It has turned out so much better than I would ever have expected, on the whole. My Janet professes herself astounded. And having promised brevity, here I am: wittering.

The proof emerged in 1822, six years after William was hanged. That's when a Doomsday Man named Semmens came to his own lamentable end. It seems he and a partner, a man called Pilchard, had been pursuing the logic which dictates that corpses are most easily acquired while still upright and whistling. Semmens would befriend them at a public house, and invite them back to his lodging for continued conviviality, during which proceedings Pilchard would come up behind and smother them with a pillow. The corpses could then be sold to anatomists who didn't look too closely into cause of death. By this I mean half the anatomists in London.

Semmens had taken a certain urchin to a Surgeon early in 1816. This came out in the Confession he gave the night before they hanged him. He'd been shrilly proclaiming his innocence 'til this point, but now he broke down and began babbling out every dirty deed he'd done since the day when as a villainous tyke he first threw stones at the cat.

The urchin had expired from cold and privation, or so Semmens supposed when he came across the body lying slumped against a churchyard wall. And so he did what any Doomsday Man would do: loaded it into a sack and lugged it straight to a Surgeon he knew of, in Crutched Friars. His knock on the side door was answered by the Surgeon's Man, who led him round back to the stable and demanded to be shown the Thing, upon which Semmens dumped it from the sack and they both realized: a flutter of respiration remained.

"Leave him," said the Surgeon.

He had come in silently behind them, and now his voice made Semmens jump.

"Ent dead, though," said Semmens. "Look—he's still alive."

"He'll be useful to me, that way," replied the Surgeon. "I can use a lad, not quite dead."

"Ent my affair," Semmens said then. "But what do you propose to do?"

"I propose," said the Surgeon, "to pay you four pounds, and send you on your way. And you won't mention that you were ever here tonight."

And Semmens never said a word, until his Last Dying Confession in Newgate Prison. The confession caused a considerable stir, convincing a Magistrate to dig up the grounds behind the house at Crutched Friars, and then tear up the floor of the stable, where they found the remains of a dozen corpses buried, and odds and ends of personal effects. Amongst these was the mouldy scrap of a bottle-green weskit such as once had been worn by a Spanish Boy, and a leather collar on a thin leather lead, such as might go round the neck of a monkey.

So it was true, beyond all doubt. The truth was all along as poor William had insisted.

*

They hanged William on a filthy November morning. Lashing rain, and wind howling from the north. God's bollocks, I thought, they'll be stringing him sideways. He'll flutter like a flag. Janet came with me, though I urged her to stay away.

"You'll need me," she said.

"I don't want you to see this."

"Fuck what you don't want."

Atherton wasn't there. Nor was Annie Smollet.

You may be interested to learn that Miss Smollet subsequently landed on her feet. By that Christmas she was on the stage, playing the leading role in *The Double Death of Lady Lazarus; or, Meg, the Fleet Ditch Fury*. The script was a ridiculous thing, tied together with twine, with an ending in which the Fury sailed to the New World and opened an ale-house in Boston with her silent hulking beau, which was one of the enduring Rumours. But it ran for 173 performances, and Annie Smollet was a great success. She went on to enjoy a lengthy career, finally retiring to marry a chinless imbecile with a title and three thousand a year. So there you are: a happy ending.

William would want you to hear that. He never bore a grudge towards Miss Smollet. And he went to the scaffold as game as they come, shuddering as he reached the top step, but that was the cold cutting through him. Wind whipped the

Hangman's coat, and poor William wore nothing more than a shirt. But he held his head high as they positioned him, and found our faces gazing up at him from the very front of the crowd. Saw his friends at the last, just before the white hood went on. And God bless him, he actually smiled.

Janet cried out as he dropped. The customary six inches, was all — not nearly enough to break the neck of such a wisp of a lad. I had expected that, of course. I knew the neck would never break.

Atherton was at the churchyard three days later, when we put the coffin in the ground. Muted and lugubrious in black.

"By God, that you would dare to show your face," I said.

Janet would have clouted him then and there. She balled her fists and turned bright red.

"I have lost a son," he said, with the air of a man much wounded.

I very nearly clouted him myself. Instead I told him of the papers I was editing. William's account of what had happened, step by step.

His expression grew dark. "Take care what you publish, Comrie. Take very great care indeed."

"Oh, I shall. I'll be meticulous and thorough."

"I warn you again, for old friendship's sake. I will ruin you."

But it never came to ruination — not on either side. Because that same afternoon, Flitty Deakins died in Bedlam Hospital, which led to a singular consequence.

Pneumonia took her. Her lungs had never recovered from the fire, and the end came quickly. It came kindly too, as pneumonia does, which was a blessing—assuming you feel she deserved any manner of blessing. Poor mad Phyllida, chained to a shit-smeared wall and raving of a Reckoning to come.

Atherton acquired the corpse. It was easily done, there being no friends to care about a funeral; just slip four pounds to the Porter. If I had to suppose, I'd say it simply amused him—Flitty Deakins, with her horror of dissection, stretched naked beneath his scalpel in the Death House. Rats and sparrows brawling for bits as her Nemesis carved her up.

Except there had been delays. The corpse had been stowed for a time in a cellar at Bedlam Hospital—not long, just two or three days. But that's long enough for putrefaction to set in, and the anatomist must of course take special care, with a putrid corpse.

Atherton did not. Perhaps it was just careless showman-ship—a cavalier swipe of the scalpel. Perhaps stiffness in the shoulder as well, scar tissue from the wound William had given him. But I think it was more than that. He hadn't been the same since William's arrest, and in the week since the hanging he had not been sober at all. He'd been unsteady on his feet at the funeral; he'd passed a hand over his face, and I noted then how it shook. "That is no hand," I thought at the time, "for a surgeon to possess. He will need to pull himself together."

However it was, he nicked his finger during the dissection. The merest nick—a flake of jagged bone. Flitty Deakins

476

gaped up at him, her mouth stretched wide in a rictus. In the reeking gloom of the Death House, by the guttering light of candles fashioned from human fat, it could very nearly be taken for unholy glee.

The headache began within the hour, and that's when he knew.

"You mad, pathetic bitch," he said. "You have murdered me."

It is a dismal way to die. By noon, the pain in his head was intense, and as night fell delirium set in; he moaned and thrashed and cried out most piteously to be left alone, evidently believing that devils were gathering in the corners of the room. They were twisted and desiccated, he seemed to think, like bats. His organs began to haemorrhage, the blood unable to clot. An hour before dawn it was over, and the most gifted man I have ever known was dead.

*

William's struggles had ceased at the end of twenty minutes, his body hanging limp. At 8.21, death was pronounced by the attending surgeon, a man named Inverarity. A good man; I'd known him at school. I had been to his house, in fact, a day or two previous. He lived very near Newgate, behind St Bart's Hospital. At twenty-three minutes past the hour, the body was cut down.

It was the crowd that had thwarted John Hunter those decades previous, in his bid to save the poor Revd Dodd. There was the irony of it. A mighty throng had come out to witness Dodd's hanging, so great was public sympathy for him. A hundred thousand clogged the streets around

Tyburn, blocking the passage of the cart. Hunter had made arrangements with a nearby undertaker—a table was prepared, the equipment laid out—but they couldn't get Dodd's body through for nearly two hours. Otherwise, Hunter might have carried it off. The greatest Scientific Surgeon of his age—if anyone had the skill, it was Hunter. His plan was to warm the body in front of a fire and then to inflate the lungs while administering stimulants: hartshorn and hot balsam, forced up through the rectum. After this, electrical shocks were to be administered from a Leyden Jar, which could have been useful if the heart had arrested, though not strictly necessary, assuming that the body had been cut down soon enough, before death was absolute. Owing to a premature pronouncement by the attending surgeon, through error or prior agreement. I had myself revived a drowned girl, nearly twenty minutes after respiration had ceased. And if you could revive after twenty minutes, then why not thirty, or even more? It helps if the body is very cold.

There were no more than five thousand gathered for William's hanging, owing to the filthy weather. They filled only half the square, and directly afterwards they dispersed. When a knot of them impeded the cart, Janet lowered her head and charged, roaring like a bull and battering right through. *By God*, I might have exclaimed to myself, if I'd not had so much else upon my mind. *By the Lord and his mighty swinging bollocks, that was magnificently done.*

*

If Hunter had succeeded, he would presumably have spirited the Revd Dodd out of London — out of England entirely, if possible. Dodd might conceivably have settled in a town in France. Married an actress, even, if he was the sort of man who fell in love with actresses. And who knows? Perhaps he was. I know very little about poor Dodd. He might have corresponded regularly with old friends from London, who were reassured to know that he was well and contented, with an Apothecary's shop behind the high street where we might imagine him at this moment: perched upon a stool, measuring and mixing, grown pot-bellied in middle age. All this might indeed have been possible, had the great man succeeded.

But of course John Hunter failed.

THE END.

Acknowledgements

The early years of the nineteenth century were fraught with controversy over scientific explorations into the essence of life itself — much like the early years of a certain other century that springs to mind. Particularly contentious were attempts to resurrect the dead; and in the summer of 1816, the year in which the fictional events of *Will Starling* take place, Mary Shelley sat down at a villa in Switzerland to tell ghost stories with a group of friends and conceived the idea for *Frankenstein; or, The Modern Prometheus*. Her novel galvanized into existence an entire genre, and my own tale unfolds in the long shadow that Victor Frankenstein and his Creature continue to cast.

Although *Will Starling* is a work of fiction, it rests on a foundation of research, and I owe a debt of gratitude to sources too numerous and varied to be listed here in full. A marvellous overview of science in the Romantic Era is to be found in Richard Holmes's *The Age of Wonder*. To those interested in the history of medicine and surgery, I heartily recommend Wendy Moore's biography of John Hunter, *The Knife Man*. Also splendid is *Digging Up the Dead*, Druin Burch's biography of the Regency surgeon Astley Cooper. A treasure trove of information about early surgeons and surgical practice, it includes a harrowing account of an operation to repair an aortic aneurism in 1817, which suggested the dark anecdote that Will tells about Dionysus Atherton's fictional attempt to do the same. Will's knowledge of potions and remedies, including his advice to John Keats concerning cholera in its premonitory phase, owes much to the 1835 edition of *Every Man His Own Doctor*. Readers are strongly cautioned not to try these remedies at home. If you suspect you have cholera in the premonitory phase, please consult a physician.

The craft of surgery made great sanguinary leaps on Peninsular battlefields, and I learned much from Robert Richardson's biography of Dominique Jean Larrey, *Larrey, Surgeon to Napoleon's Imperial Guard*. There are many memorable eyewitness accounts of Napoleonic warfare; *Soldiers at War*, edited by Jon E. Lewis, includes that of Captain Alexander Cavilie Mercer, an artilleryman who fought at Waterloo and saw there a horse that remained upright and alive despite having had the bottom portion of its head swept away by a cannonball. The image haunted my dreams, and proceeded to haunt the dreams of my Umble Narrator.

Sarah Wise, in *The Italian Boy: Murder and Grave-Robbery in 1830s London*, offers a comprehensive study of the Resurrection trade, focusing in particular on the infamous "London Burkers" murder case. *The Diary of a Resurrectionist 1811-1812*, available in a facsimile edition, is the actual diary of an anonymous grave-robber. *Victorian CSI*, by William A. Guy, David Ferrier, and William R. Smith, opens a fascinating window onto early Victorian forensic medical knowledge, including a physiological analysis of death by judicial hanging. As for what came after death — or at least what Regency anatomists actually attempted — I am indebted to Andy Dougan's highly readable *Raising the Dead: The Men Who Created Frankenstein*. Other valuable companions included Donald A. Low's *The Regency Underworld*, Kellow Chesney's *The Victorian Underworld*, Judith Flanders's *The Invention of Murder: How the Victorians Revelled in Death and Detection and Created Modern Crime*, Kelly Grovier's *The Gaol: the Story of Newgate, London's Most Notorious Prison*, and Catharine Arnold's *Necropolis: London and Its Dead*. Although Henry Mayhew commenced his monumental chronicling of the London underclass some years after the fictional events of *Will Starling*, his influence is felt throughout.

Peter Ackroyd is the author of many wonderful books, and his *London: The Biography* is extraordinary. All inaccuracies are of course entirely my own.

While all of the primary characters in *Will Starling* are fictional, there are cameo appearances by historical figures. Edmund Kean was the greatest actor of the era, and Raymund FitzSimons conjures a vivid portrait in his biography *Edmund Kean: Fire from Heaven*. The young John Keats was indeed a surgical student at Guy's Hospital in 1816; John Abernethy and his quondam pupil William Lawrence were leading surgeons and bitter rivals; and Isaac Bliss's name appears on a list of foundlings at Coram's Hospital, though he is otherwise lost to history. The pioneering surgeon John Hunter is repeatedly referenced in the novel, and his astonishing collection of anatomical specimens — which provided the inspiration for Atherton's Collection Room — may be seen at the Royal Hunterian Museum in London. Oh, and the Real Learned French Dog Tim actually danced for coins in 1816, though he went by the name of Bob instead.

I am forever grateful for the encouragement of Chris Labonte and Scott McIntyre. I owe a deep debt of thanks to those who read and suggested improvements to the manuscript as it evolved, including Susin Nielsen, Amy Weir, and Jude Weir. Mary Sandys provided much indispensable advice on matters historical and linguistic; her close attention led to many improvements, as did Peter Norman's perceptive copy-edit. My editor, Bethany Gibson, was unfailingly wise and wonderful. Heartfelt gratitude as well to Susanne Alexander and the rest of the team at Goose Lane, and to Chip Fleischer·and Roland Pease at Steerforth. And heartfelt thanks to my friends at Transatlantic, including David Bennett, Barbara Miller, and Stephanie Sinclair, and especially Samantha Haywood, agent *extraordinaire* and notable keeper of promises.

Throughout the lengthy process of researching and writing the novel, I was wistfully aware of the shade of Dr. O.A. Weir — the first surgeon I ever knew — smiling over my shoulder. Dad, I just wish you'd had the chance to read it.